CULLEN T. MADRID

Across the Stars

The Gay Space Opera

First published by Cullen T. Madrid 2022

Copyright © 2022 by Cullen T. Madrid

All rights reserved. No part of this publication may be reproduced, stored or transmitted in any form or by any means, electronic, mechanical, photocopying, recording, scanning, or otherwise without written permission from the publisher. It is illegal to copy this book, post it to a website, or distribute it by any other means without permission.

This novel is entirely a work of fiction. The names, characters and incidents portrayed in it are the work of the author's imagination. Any resemblance to actual persons, living or dead, events or localities is entirely coincidental.

Cullen T. Madrid asserts the moral right to be identified as the author of this work.

Cullen T. Madrid has no responsibility for the persistence or accuracy of URLs for external or third-party Internet Websites referred to in this publication and does not guarantee that any content on such Websites is, or will remain, accurate or appropriate.

Designations used by companies to distinguish their products are often claimed as trademarks. All brand names and product names used in this book and on its cover are trade names, service marks, trademarks and registered trademarks of their respective owners. The publishers and the book are not associated with any product or vendor mentioned in this book. None of the companies referenced within the book have endorsed the book.

Library of Congress Control Number: 2022921940

First Edition Published: 2022

Second Edition Published: 2025

Second edition

ISBN: 978-1-7362401-5-1

This book was professionally typeset on Reedsy.
Find out more at reedsy.com

Foreword

(A bespectacled old man, with a pristine white beard, confidently climbs the stairs to the podium. His black tuxedo blends in with the shadows, creating the silhouette of an awards statue. The conductor then raises his palms and silently commands the attention of the orchestra. He then gracefully sweeps his arms through the air and the music begins.)

The Cosmic Syndicate is crumbling. Several planet systems are declaring their independence and joining the rival Axis Republic. Disagreements abound and tensions keep rising; a civil war is all but certain.

Adding to the chaos, a prominent social influencer and activist, who is also the son of an influential Syndicate senator, has been abducted. Each side denies responsibility and blames each other.

Desperate for a resolution that will avoid kick-starting the conflict, the Syndicate's secret police have dispatched their best agent to find the missing son, and douse the ever-rising flame of war...

CHAPTER 1

The large diplomatic barge lumbered through the space-time tunnel of jumpspace. The stars and other cosmic matter flew across the viewports in long, stretched blurs. It traveled as fast as its aged engines would allow. Time was of the essence.

Between the seams of this reality and other dimensions, there existed this "in-between" where the various particles of space-time could be manipulated by starships to travel faster than the speed of light, thereby traversing the vast Madridium Galaxy in a matter of days, rather than years. Several jumpspace lanes existed throughout the realm, and most were well-maintained and well-traveled.

This particular lane was neither. Every so often the barge, christened *The Peacekeeper*, would encounter turbulence and violently shudder. To the flight team on the bridge and the rest of the crew, such shudders were nothing too abnormal and merely the regular happenings of an experienced ship making her thousandth journey across the stars.

To *The Peacekeeper's* lone passenger, who actually *was* the peacekeeper, the ship's shudders were representative of anything *but* a normal ride through space. Nervous already because he never really liked space travel, the random and violent lurches made Specter Mycroft Zajonc nauseous. This in turn made him angry, which exacerbated his already underlying fury and irritation that was constantly simmering. It didn't take much to get him angry these days, and now he was especially on edge.

The ship's bouncing made Mycroft's dressing difficult. On multiple occasions he misbuttoned his undercover protective vest, and quite a few times he dropped his unsheathed throwing knives and almost cut himself. Those close calls only exacerbated his irritation.

The Peacekeeper bounced again, and Mycroft dropped his undercover utility belt and was thrown to the floor of his cramped cabin. Furious, he searched for his scattered effects, and while doing so his mind drifted back to one of the few recurring thoughts in his head.

"Why for fuck's sake is the ship shuddering? What's there in fucking space for us to bounce on?" he asked the pilot at the beginning of their journey, 18 hours ago. Mycroft was just as anxious then as he was now.

The captain had the nerve to chuckle. "Rest assured, sir, there's nothing to worry about. Just some routine turbulence."

The Specter's eyes nearly leapt out of their sockets. Mycroft had danced with death for many years without thinking twice, and on more than a few occasions almost didn't survive. But this "turbulence" was too much for the aged veteran. "In *space*? How can there be this much turbulence *in space*?"

This time, the captain hesitated answering for a few seconds. "Well, sir...*The Peacekeeper* is going on ninety years old, and while she does creak a bit in hyper speeds she is still a good ship."

Mycroft could not conjure the words to respond, and just terminated the video call. He'd been brooding in his room ever since, only to stop when he was informed they were nearing their approach. He hoped the ritualistic routine of dressing would help calm his nerves.

Back in the present, he looked at his reflection in the mirror. Salt and pepper hair, slicked back unnaturally with heavy product, covered a stern, heavy-jawed face. Sad, sunken, and exhausted eyes stared back at him, just barely hiding the cold, blooded Specter lurking behind them. His muscled body was tucked under a crisp white

CHAPTER 1

bodysuit, and covered with light protective armor, designed to be worn underneath clothing. Cleverly tucked within the armor were several small throwing knives, a pair of larger bowie knives and bayonets, and two pairs of small, self-defense pistols.

The Specter's preferred weapons were knives, partly because they were so prevalent in the galaxy and hard to track, and because they were easy to conceal and bring into "secure" environments. The pistols were meant as a last resort in times of trouble, and as a decoy, to give the ruse that all of the Specter's weapons have been found.

Mycroft removed one of his bowie knives and slid his thumb over it. Another calming ritual that he could not explain but always put him in the right mindset. The ship shuddered again, and he nicked his finger.

This was why he liked flying alone, in his little one-person interceptor, he mused. He had always hated space travel, but at least his personal ship made traveling slightly more tolerable. For one thing, the damn thing was made in this decade and it didn't fucking shudder as though it was about to fall apart!

When he discovered he would be traveling "pedestrian style", as it is referred to in the trade, Mycroft lobbied his superiors very hard to fly by himself. But as usual the Specter Chiefs overrode his wish and stuck him in this death trap. They claimed it was because he could be guaranteed safe passage in a Syndicate diplomat ship, for even across the Line of Control–the hard border between the Syndicate and the Axis–no one dared fire at a diplomatic ship—that would start the war immediately.

Even when Mycroft retorted that slipping into places secretly and undetected was the core of what Specters did, he was shot down. He knew it was pointless to protest, and no matter what he was told, Mycroft believed the Specter Chiefs simply enjoyed seeing him work harder. Ever since he joined the Specters, he's always gotten the roughest missions with the least amount of useful and necessary tools. He was always prohibited from using his own materials because they would "give him away." His work was always made that much harder... just because.

Riding in this barge, Mycroft mused, made his presence stick out like a sore thumb, which would all but draw a target on his back...and put in doubt his return home.

Mycroft once again had trouble with the buttons on his dress jacket. This time not due to the ship but because the damn garment was so complicated. The jeweled buttons matched the others scattered about his torso, and formed an intricate and asymmetrical pattern. The desired effect was to make Mycroft look like a high-powered politician in a highly publicized setting. It cost more than his annual salary, and not only was he uncomfortable in it—he'd always rather be in his battle armor—he thought it was plain ugly.

The ship lurched again as he was putting on a heavy fur cape, and he dropped it to the floor. In regaining his balance, he stepped onto the cape and left a shoe print in a highly visible spot. Mycroft's irritation expanded into anger, and his train of thought once again drifted.

He was the entertainment for the Specter Corps, the one everyone told stories about and *wanted* to hear stories about. The one his colleagues bragged about, and compared themselves to. That didn't necessarily bother Mycroft so much because, he concluded, that was simply the luck of the draw. He was a good agent and hard worker, and he knew how to handle the attention well. After all he was by no means a celebrity, but the attention nevertheless made him uncomfortable.

But what truly pissed him off was when he was *intentionally* placed into one of those situations, solely so he can be the subject of a story. Not only did everyone forget the fact that he was the poor fucker doing the quick thinking and making the narrow escape in the story, but they assumed this shit was *fun*, which could not be farther from the truth.

CHAPTER 1

Mycroft brushed off the cape as best he could and successfully put it on before another bout of turbulence struck. Altogether, the complete outfit was stunning, and Mycroft had to admit that he did look rather attractive in it. But he struggled to move within the confines of the stiff, heavy fabric.

"When I signed up for this, no one ever said that I had to play dress-up."

The brilliant white suit covered in soft blue jewels and the startling red cape reminded him of the picture of the kidnapped kid the media was plastering all over. No doubt the similarity in both colors and style was an intentional coincidence. For one thing, it reminded Mycroft why he was playing dress-up in the first place, and of the fact that he refused to take mandatory leave in order to do so. That small realization made him grow even angrier.

"I could be sleeping right now," his deep voice murmured. "At least I'd be fuckin lying still."

And crying my eyes out in between episodes of contemplating suicide, he silently finished in his head. As much as he didn't want to admit it, Mycroft was better off in this death trap. It served as the perfect distraction from his depressing home life.

"Gee, Mikey, that's really healthy."

Unfortunately, his assignment was not any less hopeless: finding a kidnapped celebrity.

The son of a prominent Syndicate senator, Ulysses Pircilla was an influential voice in the populace's ear, mainly based upon his comments and views of the galaxy's current cessation effort. Ulysses' message of reunifying under a new government structure and dismantling the Cosmic Syndicate struck a chord with a population that have felt more and more left out by those in power, however his provocative and confrontational style has only enflamed the divisions of an already polarized populace, and made him few friends. The number of names and groups that wanted Ulysses "out of the picture" was growing as fast as the number of planets seceding the Cosmic Syndicate, with each having their own definition of the phrase.

Everything came to a head 48 hours ago when an as yet still unidentified person, or persons, staged a bombing at one of Ulysses' rallies. After the dust settled and the survivors were accounted for, nothing was found of the senator's son except for a note, stating Ulysses was "taken to a safe place where he would remain alive...for now."

The Senate unleashed all of its resources to find Ulysses. The kidnapping of a senator's son was so important that even the secret police, the Specters, were dispatched. Now Mycroft was charged with finding out who took Ulysses, where he was, and how long he would remain alive.

The number of named groups who could have done this was in the hundreds, and identifying which had the strongest motive was all but impossible. Hell, it could have been some of Ulysses' own followers, Mycroft thought, who were disappointed that their messiah didn't listen to them and share his influence in politics...

In a way, Mycroft concluded, the little shit had it coming. Ulysses' father, Senator Pircilla, was the swing vote in the declaration of war against the Axis Systems, and in many ways the fate of the whole galaxy rested in the family's lap. Ulysses naturally couldn't control himself and had to stir the pot, rather than lay low and let the grown-ups handle everything. With tensions as high as they were, *something* was bound to push the pendulum in either direction. And now that poor teenager was the keystone to everything.

The ship shuddered again. A pain sprung up Mycroft's spine and landed at the base of his head, developing quickly into a migraine. Mycroft meandered to the sink and splashed cold water on his face, to calm himself and to erase the lingering thought in his head; He hoped

CHAPTER 1

he wasn't too late.

This triggered the onset of a painful memory, too fresh to stay buried within Mycroft's mind. His eyes burned with tears and every muscle in his body shook. He swore he wouldn't think about this anymore, especially during the mission, and he definitely wouldn't allow himself to cry. He had spent too much time thinking about it already.

Mycroft's mind tried to block out the images playing before him. Fragmented stills of a body convulsing on the floor, struggling to reach to the comm on the wall. The pictures shifted to Mycroft entering an apartment with a bag of fresh medication, and suddenly rushing to the dead body splayed before him.

"If only I was earlier," he repeated in a low voice.

Two lonely tears cascaded down Mycroft's face. Rage and sadness flowed through him, steeling his fragile countenance and restoring his resolve. The Specter could slowly feel his control return. But rather than get lost in his emotions, Mycroft relished this little moment of sadness.

But then his irritation returned when he realized he was once again, unwillingly, proving correct the concerns of the Specter Chiefs; that the death of his husband was interfering with his abilities.

Mycroft had done a great job managing his grief initially, utilizing the emotional management techniques each Specter is taught to essentially block out everything for any desired length of time. This was not necessarily the healthiest technique according to the agency's grieving counselors, but that was his best skill, and the only way he felt comfortable to deal with things. Specters were taught to compartmentalize, and block out every other memory that isn't necessary or germane to the task at hand, and this was how he was conditioned to live his life.

However, Mycroft soon started to slip, forgetting certain objectives, and misunderstanding simple procedures. His mistakes quickly caught the attention of his superiors, who ordered a full psychological evaluation. The corps' psychologists were concerned that Mycroft's immense success in blocking memories was unhealthy, citing a concerning example where the Specter forgot the manner in which his husband died. Mycroft reasoned this only showed the effectiveness of his skill, stating, "After all, you all don't call me the best for nothing."

Ultimately the Specter was placed on administrative leave until he "got back to one hundred percent." But when the news of the senator's son's abduction broke, Mycroft was requested to return to active duty by a small group of his superiors. So much for taking time to heal, he mused.

But it still took a hearing in front of the full assembly of Specter Chiefs to get Mycroft cleared for the mission.

"Only you would argue against leave time, Mycroft," his superior and mentor, Silas, said at the conclusion of the hearing. "I don't know if that shows dedication or stupidity."

The memory caused Mycroft to chuckle. The Specter Chiefs especially wanted him for this mission because "crossing the Line of Control into Axis Space was not for the 'inexperienced.'"

Looking into the mirror above the sink, Mycroft couldn't determine if that was a compliment or an insult. He did look older than his actual age—40—but that was mostly attributed to the trauma he experienced those three short weeks ago.

It was amazing how much life can happen in such a short time...

Suddenly a strange feeling overcame Mycroft, as though all his organs catapulted to the bottom of his body, resembling a fast elevator suddenly coming to a halt.

A melodious chime played over the intercom, accompanied by the soothing, yet authoritative, voice of the ship's captain. "Sir, we've exited jumpspace and are making our final approach to the Line of Control."

CHAPTER 1

"I'll be on the bridge right away," the Specter responded.

Mycroft gave himself the final once over, making sure all of his weapons were secured and hidden well enough beneath his outfit. He was hardly ever undercover, and he was always amazed that all his weapons could be gracefully concealed within an everyday outfit. He was, though, well aware that this lightweight body armor was no match to the protection offered by his usual suit, but hopefully he wouldn't need to take advantage of it.

The element he always put on last was the pride of his–and *every* Specter's–arsenal, an ethellite sword. It was a six-foot beam of pure energy emitted from a small, handheld hilt, capable of cutting through most organic and manmade material. Made from a small cell of the Ethellite Star, the brightest point of the galaxy, the sword could be used in combat for a full 60 minutes before burning through the heating element and needing replacement. The sword was the Specter's preferred weapon mainly because it could be hidden practically anywhere, and could be used and concealed within a matter of seconds. Most citizens of the galaxy didn't know what an ethellite sword even was, making the chance of encountering an untrained user practically impossible.

Concealing his sword in the hidden compartment in his bootleg, Mycroft took one last look at himself in the mirror. Right now there was no doubt in his mind that he was the best dressed Specter in the galaxy, despite the fact that he was also one of the galaxy's deadliest killing machines.

The Specter Corps were the enforcers behind the enforcers, charged with keeping the Cosmic Syndicate in line and avoiding war at any means necessary. Supposedly the Syndicate's secret police, a majority of the galaxy's citizens do in fact know of their existence, and the running joke is that without the Specters, the Primarch and the Senate would be the most powerless things in the Syndicate.

Mycroft would go so far as to add to the punchline: and without the Specters the galaxy *wouldn't* be at the brink of war.

Really, the true genesis of the cessation movement came after the Senate formally acknowledged the Specter's existence five years ago, and how a few members of the Syndicate were using them to spy on fellow members. Within that short time, the Axis Systems was formed and split from the Syndicate, quickly amassing an armada rivaling the strength of the Home Fleet. Since then the chaos has only gotten worse...

As he left, Mycroft gave one final look at his cabin. At least these ships had more room than his little spit fighter, he thought. *Sometimes the Specter Chiefs had a point.*

When he arrived on the bridge, Mycroft could sense the tension in the air. A look at all the faces determinedly performing their duties showed only the utmost professionalism, and not an ounce of their true emotions. Everyone was smiling under a strong veneer of sheer focus.

The viewport before them was filled with the blackness of empty space. The calm, motionless picture was ironic, considering everyone was looking at the Line of Control, the hard border between the Axis of Republic Systems and the Cosmic Syndicate.

"And I was expecting a welcoming party," the captain uttered. A few of the crew chuckled, adding in their own disappointments at the lack of visible excitement.

Mycroft just smiled as he leaned against the deck railing. "Now, now Captain. You can't really expect the entire Line of Control to look like the images in the media? After all, you are a military pilot."

The captain scoffed. "But you don't think every picture in the media is all wrong. They're usually half right." A wry smile curled onto her face.

"With even *that* half being less than partially true," Mycroft retorted.

CHAPTER 1

Soon the whole group was chuckling, momentarily forgetting the solemnity of their mission.

Then, the voice of the computer calmly announced, "Approaching the LOC in ten, nine, eight..."

"Here goes nothing," the captain said, bracing herself. "We're all about to make history folks."

"Albeit not a very good one," Mycroft muttered under his breath.

"Three, two, one. We are officially in Axis Space," the computer announced.

"Congratulations, Specter. This is the first military ship in Axis Space," the captain looked at Mycroft, wearing a small expression of pride. Mycroft responded only with raised eyebrows.

Filling the viewport before them was a bright orange globe orbiting a gigantic sun. The planet Chaffee; a largely desolate world, split in half eons ago by a mysterious cosmic event. The remnants were rich in resources and mined by the few settlements still present on the surface. The majority of Chaffee's residents, however, resided in the massive orbital ring surrounding the planet's equator.

Once an industrial powerhouse to the Syndicate, the planet Chaffee currently served as the capital of the Axis of Republic Systems, and was the beginning of the Line of Control. The planet's leader, Count Lucilous, also served as the de facto leader of the Axis and had a reputation for being an interesting character.

While no one wanted to directly admit it, the Specters believed that Lucilous was responsible for Ulysses' kidnapping, or at least possessed relevant information. Mycroft's objective was to "request" that the Count provide any aid he could in this matter, as its resolution will be mutually beneficial to both the Syndicate and the Axis.

Secretly though, Mycroft believed pursuing Lucilous was pointless, because even if the count was involved in the abduction, he would ensure that he doesn't personally possess any details to share. But what did that matter, all the Specter was doing was following orders.

Mycroft studied the viewport intently. He was more surprised by what he didn't see. "Considering this is the new military capital of the galaxy, I'm surprised there aren't any carriers or battle cruisers protecting the capital."

"What the Axis does have is all scattered throughout the rest of the LOC," the captain responded. "And since they know a diplomat is coming, they probably don't want to give off the impression of fortification."

"In complete opposition to the Syndicate," Mycroft mused, as he remembered the Syndicate's capitol station, the *Imperatrix*, always traveled with a military escort, even in peacetime. "Clever."

The Peacekeeper traveled closer to the planet Chaffee. The orange globe increasingly engulfed the whole viewport. Soon, those on the bridge could clearly make out the swarming dots of the various ships landing and taking off from the orbital ring. The ship continued traveling unimpeded.

As the multiple sensors within the bridge indicated *The Peacekeeper* was officially entering the orbital ring's tracking zone, Mycroft grew uneasy. He paced the length of the bridge's observation deck, craning his neck to see every angle out of the massive viewport.

"Things are too quiet. Captain, do you detect a patrol escort?"

"No, Specter Mycroft," she replied, looking over a technician's shoulder. "The stars are clear. There's no reading of any patrol ship within range. Perhaps they don't view us as a serious threat and are giving us the royal welcome?"

"That's highly unlikely," the Specter replied, grinding his teeth. "They're waiting for us to make the first move, and they just want us to *think* they don't mind us being here."

"Still though, if they're trying to be everything the Syndicate is not..." the captain let that hang for a second, but then realized what she was saying. "On second thought, welcoming isn't quite the word I'd use."

The Specter smiled. "See? This is what you call the *appearance* of being a good neighbor."

The captain spat on the floor. "That's all I have to say to that!"

Mycroft feigned a look of disappointment. "Now, now. We must do our part as well. After all, we don't want this whole performance to fail because we can't hold up our end of the deal. Hail the station and ask for permission to board."

The captain looked sideways at the now stoic Specter, genuinely surprised. "*Ask* for permission? Why? They haven't bothered to hail us! Besides, aren't we the expected ones?"

"Again," Mycroft reiterated, "we are making like nice neighbors. Now, please *try* being nice! It's only for a few hours."

With a heavy sigh, the captain slowly strolled to the comm station and summoned Chaffee planetary control. She used her nicest tone she could muster. "With all due respect, the representative from the Cosmic Syndicate is requesting permission to land in Axis territory." She made a point to give Mycroft a beaming, fake smile, which was returned with a thumbs up.

The chime of an incoming transmission announced itself almost immediately. Suddenly a stern face filled the middle of the viewport. Her uniform was buttoned so high it looked suffocating, and if the woman pursed her lips any more she would kiss the screen.

"I am the undersecretary to the prime minister, Count Lucilous. On behalf of him and the entire parliament, we welcome you to the Axis of Republic Systems. You are cleared to land at bay thirteen, where you will be escorted to the prime minister's personal office."

"We look forward to it," the captain responded after a long, awkward silence.

The undersecretary blinked a few times. She only responded with a

"Hmm" before signing off.

"How hospitable," was Mycroft's response. "She gave us the honor of speaking face to face."

The captain was less than amused. "I wasn't entirely expecting to be on camera. The bitch wanted me to say 'thank you.'" She spat again in disgust.

Scratching his chin, Mycroft contemplated. "She wanted to see as much as she could find out about us before we landed. No doubt she expected the representative to be on the screen with you. Too bad she was disappointed."

"Yes, it was too bad," the captain smirked. "You know you really should dress that way more often."

The Specter gave the captain a stern look for a few moments, before it gradually transitioned into a smile. "You know I can have you court-martialed for that."

The captain's smirk disappeared, and she cleared her throat. "In all seriousness, I don't like this." she replied. "You're going in alone, straight into the heart of the enemy, and they are already casing you out."

Mycroft clasped his hands behind his back and curtly nodded. "Thank you very much for your concern, Captain. I am touched, however this is exactly what we Specters do, and I think I can handle myself just fine, thank you."

She was unsatisfied. "Still, no one has ever infiltrated the heart of the Syndicate's arch rival on the eve of a civil war. Even for an old military brat like me, this is a tough motherfucker! You need backup, or at least a partner."

Mycroft could not agree more with anything the captain just mentioned, however this was the hand that he had to play cards with. "Oh? And who is going to come with me on such short notice? You?"

The captain brandished her small pistol in a quick and flowing move

CHAPTER 1

in less than a second. "I can keep up with the young ones," she winked. The Specter only smiled, and calmly placed his hands on her shoulders. "Captain, words cannot describe how right you are. But once you safely land this ship in docking bay thirteen, you will have done your part. Now I must do mine. It is not yet the time where we must pull double duty, but when the time comes you will be the first on my list."

Despite its advanced age, *The Peacekeeper* gingerly flew through the veil of speeding industrial ships and came to a gentle rest in the docking bay. Immediately, a generous cadre of Axis officials assembled to greet the incoming representative.

Standing at the front of the line, and the first to shake Mycroft's hand, was the undersecretary from earlier, who looked exactly the same as on the view screen. "Greetings. On behalf of the prime minister, welcome to the Axis of Republic Systems."

"The pleasure is with me," Mycroft replied as he shook hands and casually studied the officials behind the undersecretary. While some looked like genuine politicians—he recognized a few from their days in the Syndicate—others were obvious military and security personnel in disguise. Even from his brief glance, the Specter noticed he was being studied, and closely.

"Please, allow me to present a select few officials from the Axial Congress, the Constabulary, and our Interstellar Corps," the undersecretary said. "The prime minister regrets that he could not meet you in person."

A likely story, the Specter thought. "No apologies necessary, I completely understand." Not that any were offered. "Running a... *syndicate* is no doubt an all-consuming effort. I feel welcomed enough by all the officials here." Mycroft politely clasped his hands together. He knew how to be subtly rude too.

The undersecretary clearly got the hint. After looking Mycroft up and down, she curtly replied, "If you will follow me please." Without waiting she turned on her heel and sped away.

Along the journey from the hangar, Mycroft discreetly observed as much as he could, using his trained eyes to swallow large swaths of detail in swift glances. No matter where he looked, whether it was a storage closet or a mechanical room, the place was swarming with heavily-armed security personnel. One even guarded the bloody lavatory!

The amazing part was how out in the open all of this was, without any attempt made to hide or disguise anything at all. On the one hand it felt like Mycroft, as a representative of the Syndicate, was being baited; after all he couldn't get the captain's comment about the Axis being the Syndicate's complete opposite out of his mind. But on the other hand, Mycroft thought that this was a sign of the Axis' intense paranoia. Was the prime minister preparing for the ever-encroaching war...or was this new government not working out quite as the separatists had hoped?

The bustling undersecretary entered a non-descript conference room, devoid of windows or anything decorative. It contained a dozen flimsy, uncomfortable chairs that surrounded a heavily used table. Everything in the room was the same color, a drab, office-tone beige.

Not exactly the trappings one would put an honored representative, the Specter mused. My, my, he thought, reflecting back on his earlier comments, these people are sensitive.

"Please wait here," the young woman said. "We're afraid we cannot offer more suitable quarters for your stature, as this is primarily an industrial facility and is not yet equipped for formal state visits."

Mycroft made a show of looking disappointed and hid his arms beneath his cape. "And am I to understand that the count has his own quarters on-station? Certainly they don't resemble this?"

The undersecretary stiffened and crossed her arms behind her back.

CHAPTER 1

"Correct, the prime minister does have quarters on the orbital ring, but only he is allowed there, as only he is the prime minister!" She gave the Specter a stern look.

I get it kid, titles are important here, the Specter thought. "Very well. I shall make do." So much for the hospitality. Actually, these accommodations were more along the lines of what he was used to, anyway.

Her face remained the same, stoic expression. "A servant will be around in a few moments to provide you some refreshments. I cannot speak as to how long the prime minister will be... you understand."

"Of course." Mycroft curtly bowed his head.

The undersecretary left the Specter alone. Beneath Mycroft's feet, the steady pulse of the giant mechanical ecosystem rumbled gently, an ever-growing threat to the galaxy.

The Specter was surprised at how open the Axis had been so far in showing how legitimate they wanted to be, while simultaneously not being shy at how new they were at being their own governors. The pomp and circumstance at the landing bay with those "officials" was sheer performance, but the apology about the lack of stately quarters seemed genuine. Perhaps the Axis was truly trying to be a legitimate counter to the Syndicate? But then the obvious security oversight everywhere was a sign that no one really trusted anyone. And the fact that the count didn't allow anyone to refer to him as anything other than "Prime Minister," and the fact that the Axis' first state visitor was not treated to the count's personal amenities, only reinforced why these people were the prime suspects in Ulysses' abduction. So much effort was being made to appear as though this was nothing more than an industrial settlement, yet that was obviously farther from the truth.

A servant arrived and delivered a platter of refreshments; various finger foods and a steaming carafe of liquid. Mycroft inquired what the treats were, but the servant merely looked deeply in his eyes before bowing and exiting the room. Mindful that he was being watched, Mycroft gingerly reached for a small canape and discreetly sniffed it.

"Don't worry, it's not poisonous. I assure you. Even though that little shit definitely has thought about it" a voice thundered from the far corner of the room.

Startled, Mycroft jumped and threw the canape at the wall and reached for his boot, before he realized who was speaking.

A section of the wall slid away to reveal another corridor, and in the opening stood the stately figure of Count Lucilous, the prime minister of the Axis of Republic Systems. He was dressed just as formally as Mycroft, in a simple yet elegant black unisuit with a light jacket, embroidered on the breast with the family crest in silvery blue. The lining of the jacket was the same color as the embroidery, and it shone through with each of the count's slightest movements. He carried a wooden walking stick, topped with a brilliant, fist-sized jewel that twinkled by itself, on its own and from any angle. A bushy mop of light hair topped a slender, artificially dark-skinned face.

The count appeared to float into the room. "Perseus has wanted me dead ever since I declined to publicly express support for the poor Senator's son's kidnapping. He never really liked him. Frankly, I don't think anyone has. But," the count twirled his fingers as he selected a canape, "I can't help being nice sometimes." His greasy lips twisted into a wicked smile as he bit the canape violently in half.

Mycroft could barely hide his disdain. Before him stood the nexus of a majority of the galaxy's problems, and a truly evil man. "I'm sure Senator Pircilla appreciates your politeness and concern for his son's welfare, Count."

"Certainly, for only such a thing as a kidnapping can bring the two unstoppable forces to a screeching halt," the count sneered. "Let alone force us to come together in pursuit of a common goal. Unfortunately,

CHAPTER 1

it's not the one everyone wants."

"Ah, but hopefully this will be the first among many future collaborations," Mycroft replied. He selected an appetizer and ate it and was surprised at how good it tasted – or how hungry he was.

The count swallowed another canape and licked his lips, responding only with a disinterested "Hmm mmm."

Mycroft wondered if that pesky undersecretary rubbed off on her boss, or if she was copying him because the count pursed his lips in the same way. Already within these few moments the Specter was ready to punch in that smug face. His thoughts momentarily drifted. All he had to do was ignite his sword and strike the man down, and the galaxy's problems would be solved in less than five seconds.

But unfortunately they would not, as the Syndicate's military leaders aptly reminded everyone, *constantly*. Earlier in the cessation effort, the Specter Corps petitioned the Senate to grant the authority to assassinate Count Lucilous, leaving the independent systems within the Axis to negotiate separately with the Syndicate. But that was deemed an impossible scenario, as it was becoming increasingly obvious that Lucilous was the only thing keeping the Axis from its own infighting, and the galaxy's new titan was truly not as strong as it portrayed itself. The Senate declared that negotiating with the count was the only way any part of the Axis would peacefully return to the Syndicate. Mycroft was one of the only senior Specters to mostly agree with the decision.

But, with the continued mismanagement that has come to be expected from the Senate, Mycroft was in the unfortunate position of being the galaxy's last hope for peace.

The count suddenly realized something, and stopped perusing the platter. "Pardon me, I haven't introduced myself. I am Count Lucilous, prime minister of the Axis of Republic Systems and leader of the planet Chaffee. Continues is a list of all sorts of companies I'm in charge of but we'll skip the formalities." He stiffly held out his hand, not too far away from his torso.

Mycroft shook the proffered hand, standing out of his chair to make up for the difference. "I am Zajonc, Administrative Officer of the Department of Treasury's Bureau of Senate Assets. The Primarch personally sent me."

"Ambassador," Lucilous' deep voice thundered. "Such a pleasure to have you in our beautiful star system. I trust your journey was a pleasant one." He pulled Mycroft into a close hug and gave the man a few hearty pats on the back.

The Specter was surprised the count's hands were so clammy. A sign of nerves, perhaps? "I can never complain about an uneventful journey. I appreciate the hospitality, Count." The real intention of the hug was to confirm whether each other was armed. Mycroft found the usual "concealed" pistol, but nothing more.

The two released each other. "We do wish we had more formal accommodations for our first guest of state, but alas some details have to be sacrificed for the time being. Just like the formality of current titles. Please, sit and get comfortable." Lucilous gestured to a chair and offered the tray of food to the man. "Take the canapes, they're the chef's specialty."

Mycroft obliged, taking a few moments to read the man before him while the full facade was in effect. This was the first time the Specter had encountered Lucilous outside of formal public occasions, and he didn't have any previous behavior to compare too. But Mycroft could tell that the count seemed pleased or excited about something, and it certainly wasn't the Axis' first state visitor.

The closer the Specter observed his adversary, the more clearly he could see a smile on the attractive face, and it was quite sinister.

"Pardon me for asking, but are you amused by something?" Mycroft figured it was better to just go and take the plunge than to wait for the

CHAPTER 1

right time.

The count's face widened into a full smile, showing perfectly capped teeth. "Yes. Two things, actually. On the one hand, it is amusing that the almighty Cosmic Syndicate needs to reach out to the rival *it created* to solve its problems. And I'm amused that a veteran Specter such as yourself is still making the effort to put on the ruse. Did you expect me to keep pretending that I didn't know better? Or do you really think you're convincing as a member of the Department of Treasury?"

On the exterior, Mycroft showed confusion, bordering on offense. How dare the count see through his ruse and accuse him of being something he didn't say he was. Conversely, it was only a matter of time before the man figured it out. After all, in these times, why wouldn't the Syndicate unleash every tool at its disposal?

But internally, Mycroft was battling a flood of intense shock. While the existence of the Specters was technically public knowledge, it was not common knowledge who the actual Specters were. Only the Specter Corps' knew, and it was still official policy to deny the agency's existence. It was just safer for everyone that way.

The count's smile grew even wider, as he noticed the shift in Mycroft's countenance. "Don't be a victim of shock, dear boy. The Axis can smell a Specter. It's the only way we can survive as a people."

Mycroft couldn't tell if he was more pissed that he let his emotions slip for even a fraction of a second, or that he had made the same comment to the Specter Chiefs before embarking on this journey. It was annoying that his superiors continued to ignore the advice he gave based on his decades of experience and training, and even more so that those decades of experience were falling victim to his personal trauma. He fucking hated proving the chiefs right.

Mycroft then offered an innocent smile. "I hate to disrespect you, Count, especially in your own arena, but I'm afraid you are incorrect. I am not a Specter, as much as I am flattered by the compliment. I am merely a veteran from the Syndicate Commandos, which I hear the myth of the Specters is based off of."

"Myth of the Specter? My dear man, you are in need of studying history. The Specter are no more a myth than the lack of effectiveness of the Syndicate's Primarch." The count took a moment to cross his legs, relishing in having the upper hand. "After all, it was the revelation of the existence of the Specter Corps that led to the creation of the Axis."

"Ah yes," Mycroft used the count's arrogance against him. "But do you really think that the Specters actually exist, or were they created solely as a scapegoat to blame for the creation of the Axis. After all, someone has to be responsible besides those in charge."

Mycroft smiled and took a canape from the tray, relishing the flavor and the count's look of disgust.

"I don't appreciate being taken for a fool, Ambassador," was all the count could muster himself to say. "You and I both know you aren't being totally honest with me."

Taking the opportunity to think while he was clearing his mouth, Mycroft wanted to respond with, "And you are with me?" but refrained. Instead, he proffered. "Correct. I wasn't entirely sure how the information would be received, which is why I initially kept it to myself.

"I am not a member of the Treasury Department, you are indeed correct. In fact I'm with the Reunification Office. We didn't want to publicize this at all, as the media would have a field day with the image of the Syndicate speaking to the Axis first."

This small victory did little to assuage the count's attitude. "No, we wouldn't want that, now would we? Heaven forbid the aggressors be seen as what they truly are. You know, this is a prime example of why the Axis was created in the first place; to counteract the constant lying!"

CHAPTER 1

All the Specter offered was a raise of his arms. "We are all humans, and imperfect by design."

The count offered a small sinister grin. "That's the most accurate thing you've uttered since we've met. Now, pray tell, what possible assistance could I offer the Cosmic Syndicate?" He slowly sipped from the beverage flagon accompanying the snack tray.

Mycroft actually wanted to continue the verbal fencing, for he quite enjoyed politely outfoxing this pretentious piece of shit. But alas, he had to play his cards close to his chest, and chose to proceed with only the facts, leaving out his charged emotions as much as possible. "Certainly you are aware of the kidnapping of Senator Pircilla's son, Ulysses?"

The smile floating on the count's face slowly disappeared. "The galaxy's favorite provocateur? The great speaker of change, who really is nothing more than a spoiled rotten rich celebrity, desperately clinging onto Daddy's coattails? To tell you the truth I've been quite enjoying not hearing his whining for the last few hours.

"Unfortunately, that's been replaced with constant coverage of his... absence. It's virtually the only story the media is covering besides the Great Separation. Please note that I speak for the entire Axis Republic in offering my sincerest regards to the senator and his family. I do not have any children, and can only imagine the pain they are going through." The count wore a seriously concerned look on his face.

"I'll be sure to forward your regards." Beneath the table, the Specter clenched his fists so tight that his knuckles cracked.

The count finished his drink and definitively slammed it on the table. "And no doubt, you're here to interrogate me and see if I know anything, for you Syndicate and Specters are convinced that we Axis are personally responsible and only want to unleash a full-fledged war. First of all, I want you to know that I am not offended, even though I have every right to be. Ever since our creation, the Axis has been nothing but the bastard child of the galaxy, constantly getting blamed for intentionally disturbing the peace. We have known nothing but persecution and attack, but we certainly are not going to settle for being attacked on our own soil!"

Mycroft was now the one to be surprised. He didn't expect things to escalate so quickly. "Count, I cannot speak–"

"Secondly!" Lucilous declared, "And I want you to pay extra, strict attention. I have not, nor would ever, personally direct any member of our security forces or government to kidnap a rival politician's family member. No matter who they were. I can assure you that none of our private citizens have been ordered to carry out such a task as well. And if it is discovered that an Axis member indeed committed this heinous act, I can personally promise you that they will be punished to the fullest extent of our laws. The Axis does not tolerate disobedience of any kind."

"Count, no member of the Syndicate has accused the Axis of being responsible. We are–"

"Officially," the count spat.

"At all!" Mycroft spat back. "We are merely here to verify what we already believe to be true. No one believes, nor has insinuated, that you are personally responsible, Count."

A satisfied look covered the face across the table.

Mycroft had to tread carefully. "Our intelligence agencies know that you are too smart to have any path lead back to any government official, especially you. And it would be too easy to create a shell company and go about things that way."

The count loaded his mouth with another canape. "Personally, I think it was one of the criminal syndicates that only want to stir the pot and get attention. With all the attention on the war effort, the Black Pyres, the Varholak Clan, or even the Stein/Ways are all feeling a bit left out. They probably only want some bluechips and will let the poor kid go unharmed. Certainly the Specters don't need help from the Axis to do that!"

"Interesting. Aren't those groups allied closely with the Axis? Do you have information regarding their actions you'd like to share with us? The Varholak Clan actually contacted the senator and offered to find the kid for a hefty fee, and the Black Pyres are all too busy with the illegal weapons trade."

Lucilous proffered a forced smile. "Well, certainly those aren't the only criminal syndicates in this grand galaxy. The Specters cannot assume that we Axis are responsible for everything. I know that goes against the narrative, but you, Ambassador, have to at least see the facts!" The count was getting more impatient and not hiding it very well. He could tell he was getting painted into a corner, and he didn't like that at all.

Mycroft remained as calm as he could, a perfect counter to the count's growing rage. "I must ask, dear sir, when are you going to accept the fact that the Specters do not exist?"

The count slammed his fist on the table, his rage more apparent. "Oh for fuck's sake give it a rest! You and I both know who you are and where you came from, so let's save some time and just cut the bloody act! After all, isn't time of the essence to save your precious provocateur?"

Mycroft remained silent and stared intently into the count's eyes for a few moments. "No matter what I say you won't believe me. If I confirm your suspicions and say that I am a Specter, you'll only continue to doubt every word I say. If I continue to press the truth, you will still continue to doubt every word I say."

"Now you know the life of an Axis!" the count screamed. "No matter what we say or what we do, we're damned to eternity, as was so aptly stated by your precious Neo-Fates Council. Fuck, even the Universe has deemed us worthless."

Lucilous violently rose to his feet and paced around the room, his hands flailing in his trademark fashion. "This is one of the reasons we formed the Axis. No matter what we tried, the deck was always stacked against us. The Cosmic Syndicate wanted total control. Too many secrets were kept from the people and the Senate doled out too many lies. Instead of treating its citizens like the sensible, intelligent people they are, the Syndicate treats you like a retarded child that is completely incapable. The plebeians are not worthy of knowing the truth, and everything must be hidden. Even those few answers that are given are incomplete and as incomprehensible as a riddle.

"Here at the Axis, citizens are free to make their own choices and live their own lives. The Axis believes in trust, and only by practicing trust can we achieve greatness. Just look, within a few short years we have grown from a burgeoning political voting bloc to the Syndicate's main competition. The two of us, right now, are standing in proof that the Axis way is the effective way." He paused, put his hand on his heart and recited in a patriotic tone. "*'Unity through freedom, freedom through choice'*. These words form the foundation for our way of life. The same theory of governing the Syndicate has forgotten."

The count made his way to a wall panel. He pulled a hidden lever and a full minibar slid out from the wall in front of him. He commenced mixing two cocktails, while he continued his tirade.

"Perhaps this senator's son did not get kidnapped but ran away? After all, with all the crises facing the galaxy at the same time, he probably couldn't hack it and just booked. No doubt, being the son of the tie-breaking vote on the War Declaration Act was stressful, as were the increasing threats from his adversaries. You forget, dear Ambassador, that Ulysses was not an angel with pristine wings."

It took everything Mycroft had to not lunge across the room and impale the count with his sword. That lying piece of shit had no sense of humanity at all, and he was fucking disgusting. The way the man

CHAPTER 1

easily transitioned from tyrannical autocrat to a guy shooting the shit at the bar was both fascinating and terrifying. The longer Mycroft spent with him, the more he wanted to kill the count. But alas, that would be counterproductive.

"*Was?*" Mycroft queried. "You think Ulysses is dead?"

The count expertly poured the mixture into two glasses. He licked his lips with a loud smack. "Have you ever known the criminal syndicates to keep their word? Just because they say they'll keep the kid alive does not mean they will. A criminal can never be trusted."

Mycroft nodded when the glass slid over to him. "But one thing every smart criminal never fucks with is money. When they tie a price to a service, they'll make sure they'll get that price for the service."

"Ah, how right you are. But that's assuming we're dealing with a smart criminal." The count winked and raised his glass. "Cheers," and drained it all with one gulp.

Mycroft's glass remained untouched. "It takes a smart criminal to stage an attack and sweep Ulysses off the way that they did."

The count poured the remainder of the tumbler in his glass and took a seat across from Mycroft, far on the other side of the table. "You're asking me to think like a criminal? Surely you can't be serious."

The Specter lifted his glass to his mouth. "I'm asking you to share any suspicions you may have. At this point, and I truly hate to admit this, we're almost at our wits end."

A husky, deep laugh emanated from the count. Clearly, he took pleasure in seeing another's displeasure. "That's apparent in many ways, my friend. In many ways." He took another slow sip from his drink.

Mycroft sipped from his the smooth, strong liquor basking his senses lightly. He hated to admit it, but he told the count, "This is very nice."

"Thank you, it's the official Axis cocktail! I have yet to meet anyone who didn't like it. And thank you also for lying to me, Ambassador. You presented yourself as requesting my assistance, not copying my own notes for yourself." Lucilous feigned a look of offense. "The next thing you're going to ask me is to tell you where I've been for the last few days."

This was why the count gave him a drink, Mycroft mused, to throw him off guard. Even under the fog of his cocktail, Mycroft still had a firm grasp on the situation. His hand inched closer to one of his concealed weapons, for he sensed things were about to turn ugly. He honestly was surprised at how well things were going so far, but it was just a matter of time. On top of possessing a terrible temper, Lucilous was known to be a formidable fighter, and now was the time when Mycroft needed to be on the top of his guard.

The Specter tried to keep his expression calm. "I don't know what you mean, Count. I've been completely honest with you since the beginning of our interaction. I am not requesting to copy your notes or to see any of your secret files. You know better than that. Again, I'm merely seeking from you as much assistance and information as I can regarding the whereabouts of Ulysses Pircilla. I assure you that you are not at all a suspect. We just want to close out any open and loose ends."

It was the count's turn to stare at Mycroft for a few moments. "Tie up any loose ends?" He was not amused. "You really do want to know about my fucking whereabouts. You piece of shit! You come in here disguised as mutual assistance when this is a goddamn interrogation!?" Lucilous gave a sinister smile and downed the rest of his drink, "You are a clever son of a bitch!"

Mycroft grinned, and finished the rest of his drink. He knew that the count truly didn't see this coming. The man was right, he was clever. And a bit inebriated, since he was tooting his own horn.

He crossed his arms in his lap, and wore a smug smile. "Don't try to force out the story, just let your thoughts flow out nice and easily."

Count Lucilous clenched his jaws so tightly his muscles rippled. He clenched his fists too, squeezing so hard he shattered the glass he held. His arm muscles pulsated with anger, his strength just begging to be unleashed. The man's eyes grew a deep shade of red. The graceful and elegant politician turned into a rabid animal. Even Mycroft was growing afraid of this creature across from him.

Suddenly, just as quickly as he transformed, the count returned to his former docile self. He grabbed a napkin from the minibar and wiped his hands and mouth. He cleared his throat politely while he deliberately cracked his knuckles. He then slowly rested them, palm up, on his lap. Clearly this was an anger management coping technique.

Lucilous asked in his most polite voice. "Might I inquire, just who does the Cosmic Syndicate think I am that I can convince a group of criminals to attempt a suicide mission in kidnapping a senator's son, and a celebrity within his own right? I'm just curious as to how powerful you all think I am?"

It was Mycroft's turn to laugh heartily. "Oh please, no one is saying any such thing. Where shall I begin? You're the prime minister of a galactic republic, as well as an influential industrialist in your own right."

"That doesn't answer my question," he responded coolly.

"Oh don't you give me that bullshit! People look up to you, Prime Minister, and count on you to give them direction. You yourself declared in one of your numerous speeches that you will 'reluctantly be the light that guides the cosmos to the new frontier'. Face the facts; we both know how influential you are, and just what your soft power is capable of."

Lucilous was annoyed, yet couldn't help but show just how much he appreciated being quoted. "You're making me sound like a god!"

All the Specter could do was raise his eyebrows. "What, you don't think so? At least to your cult of personality, that's what you are!"

The count was angry once again, his brows furrowed and his eyes returned to their crimson shade. "See, there you go spouting that Syndicate nonsense propaganda. Just because I'm the prime minister does not mean I'm the bloody *leader* of the Axis! Hopefully you'll understand this, but I have a purely ceremonial role. According to our constitution, I preside over the congress, but I have no control nor influence over it."

"On the contrary I do understand. And while that may be so, there is no denying that you are, indeed, the power behind the throne. The puppet you installed as the governing state councilor makes absolutely zero moves without your approval, and has no ideas that don't originate from your own head. You are the Axis of Republic Systems, and without you the whole collective will split with infighting. You are truly no different than the Syndicate, I hate to tell you."

The count broke out into a hearty laugh. "My, my, my, you are flattering me! If I had even a fraction of the power you've just described, then trust me, the cosmos would be a much better place."

"I find that hard to believe," the Specter replied. "Everyone who says that is only looking through their own point of view."

"Now, now, you've hurt my feelings," the count lightly touched his chest. "You know if the Senate would have listened to me and just gave me a chance to negotiate, we wouldn't be in this predicament to begin with."

"Oh, negotiate? You gave the ultimatum to meet your demands or be cut off from Chaffee's industries. And even back then, you claimed to just be the lowly senator abiding by your planet leader's choices. I thought you didn't have any power or influence whatsoever? Since when did that change?"

The Count was about to answer when a steady, high pitched beeping

CHAPTER 1

erupted from his wrist unit. With the skill of an experienced statesman, the man's temper disappeared in a breath and he activated the message.

The voice of the undersecretary erupted into the room. "Prime Minister, your attention is needed immediately in the southern processing center." The voice sounded quite afraid, as though it was quite the urgent matter indeed.

The count didn't betray any emotion, remaining calm and stoic. "I'll be right there." He disconnected the transmission and flashed an artificially polite smile to Mycroft. "I apologize for having to cut this...chat... short, Ambassador, but I have an urgent matter to attend to that cannot wait."

"Oh, but I *can* sir," Mycroft replied swiftly, flashing his most diplomatic smile. "I totally understand your need to attend to other business, but you have yet to answer my question, as we so quickly got off topic. Since we have quite a few other points to cover, I'll wait until you are available for further conversation." He held his smile for an uncomfortably long time, driving home his point.

The count was visibly irritated by Mycroft's insistence. "I don't know how severe this issue might be. Or how long it will require my attention." His tone was rather pointed, and he was careful to enunciate every word. "As far as I am concerned, we have nothing further to discuss."

Mycroft smiled. He knew he held the upper hand, which undoubtedly made the count uncomfortable. "But by all means we do. I'll wait. I'm anxious to get these answers so we can fully clear your name from our investigations. We wouldn't want the Axis to continue living under this... *specter* of anxiety. You don't have to find accommodations for me, I'll rest on my ship."

The Specter rose to follow Lucilous out of the conference room, but the count placed two firm hands on his shoulders and politely, yet gently, pushed him back into his seat. "Nonsense! You are my guest, and deserve only the finest accommodations we can offer. Please wait here, and one of my servants will escort you to my personal quarters. We would not dream of having you wait an interminable amount of time in this corporate squalor. Again, welcome to the Axis Republic."

The count bowed curtly and quickly left the room. Mycroft looked at his wrist unit. They had been in there for 30 minutes and didn't discuss anything productive.

But Mycroft still considered the encounter a victory. The count's unbreakable confidence and veneer of control was not as strong as he'd expected, and Mycroft saw right through it. What caught his attention was what the count did not say. He did not equivocally denounce any such involvement, nor did he outright say that he would not orchestrate something. And the fact that the count was continuously hung up about speaking to a Specter was meant as a distraction. Yet Mycroft could tell the count was scared of him for some reason, and it was clear that something was being hidden.

Mycroft was willing to believe that Lucilous had no direct, or even indirect, involvement in the kidnapping, but he was not ready to give up the fact that the count knew something about it. Just because Lucilous didn't have his fingers in the bowl didn't mean he wasn't going to get a piece of the pie. It was odd that the count listed the criminal gangs that were already cleared by the Syndicate's authorities. And it was odd that Lucilous possessed details that weren't released to the media. No doubt the Axis had spies everywhere, but Mycroft was not going to believe that that was a coincidence.

And he was interested to see what exactly this issue was that took away the count's attention.

The Specter took out his communication unit and contacted the ship to inform them he would be taking an extended stay.

CHAPTER 2

Lucilous stormed down the hall, anger seeping out of every pore in his body. He clenched his jaw so tightly it cracked in multiple places. He stomped his walking stick so hard that it made a few dents in the metal floor. The various guards and workers in the hall gave the fuming count a wide berth.

"How in the fuck did I let Mycroft get the upper hand," Lucilous kept asking himself. "After all, he was only a stupid secret policeman, who was truly incapable of investigating anything. How did that shit pull a double cross like that, masking a negotiation as an interrogation?" The count had been interviewed thousands of times and knew when he was being given gotcha questions, but this was somehow different.

The liquor was mixing with the count's anger and clouding the man's judgment, forcing him to second guess himself.

"That piece of shit was a Specter, no matter what he said. Reunification officers don't dress that fancy. But then again, he could have been an affluent man like himself, and bought his way to the top. After all," the count contemplated, "not everyone can have brains and money like yours truly.

"Why did I have to go on grandstanding? Fuck, that's what made me start bragging, and him start poking fucking holes in everything. If all I did was stick to the script..." Well it didn't matter since he was *miraculously* called away to an emergency. He couldn't have planned it better himself.

But why did that bastard insist on staying, Lucilous kept wondering. He should have just killed him then and there.

Lucilous paused his stride for just long enough to slam his fist into the wall, leaving a sizable crater. The leather of his glove was hardly scuffed, and his knuckle was uninjured, yet his rage was insatiable. The few passerby who noticed his outburst paused for a few moments, but dared not say anything for fear of being the next one in place of the wall.

He took a few moments to breathe and collect himself. Even using all of his anger management techniques didn't make too much progress. All he wanted to do was kill that sonofabitch so he could go back to focusing on his current projects, which were more important than this silly little civil war. His 100% focus was required.

His life depended on it.

But as his teacher instructed, *"We only get to use what is at our current disposal, and through that we create greatness."*

After a few moments, Lucilous continued down the hall. Stomping past the lowly workers who took the trouble of saluting him without as much as a glance.

He had no choice but to deal with the specter later, and he was a bit thankful because, frankly, he didn't quite know how he was going to do it.

Lucilous arrived at the processing bay, a giant freight hangar with various industrial equipment. Crates of varying sizes were neatly stacked, creating a maze within the large enclosure. The smell of engine lubricant and various industrial chemicals filled the air. A smattering of technicians gathered around a small, opened shipping container. One technician held a clipboard while another held a pressure syringe. They all wore worried looks on their faces. Joining them were guards who held their weapons ready to fire.

CHAPTER 2

The targets were a half-dozen rough looking thugs, each wielding their own jury-rigged weapons. Each wore a different style of armor, ranging from full-heavy assault to just barely covering the vital areas. The only unifying ensemble piece were the armbands, a pale yellow with a blue growling jira monster spitting flames. These were members of the Jira Clan.

The count was already annoyed, but his annoyance managed to somehow expand. This day was already going to shit, and it was about to get worse. The only reason the Jiras would be causing trouble was because they wanted more money. Lucilous knew this was going to happen, but hoped to some mystical power that he would be spared. Of course he wasn't.

When Lucilous joined the group at the shipping container, his loud footsteps startled the already frightened technician with the clipboard. The poor, pathetic woman jumped in fear, which only pissed the count off even more.

The undersecretary hurried from out of nowhere. "Oh thank goodness, Your Eminence, you're here!" The woman took a few moments to compose herself, for she too was uncharacteristically frazzled, which proved unsuccessful. "I tried to handle the situation myself, but they insisted—"

"What's the situation?" The count's tone conveyed he was not in the mood. "I had to be called away from my important conference. This has better be important." He gave his underling the look of death.

The undersecretary continued struggling for a few more moments to articulate an answer.

One of the thugs in the least amount of armor spoke. His muscles glistened as he gestured his weapon toward the container. "We wanted to personally deliver the package to you, Your Eminence. As stated in the contract." The accent reeked of a poor upbringing, and was full of the wisdom of being raised on the street. This was Radcliffe, the ring leader.

Another thug bumped the speaker with the butt of her weapon, a heavy cannon with a string of ammunition that reached to a pack strapped to her back. "And we weren't happy with the down payment."

"Grint, cool it," Radcliffe spat. His colleague reluctantly obeyed.

The count's heart rate suddenly escalated, and he was growing uneasy. He did not have the time, nor the resources, to negotiate for any monetary increase. "What is that supposed to mean!" The count hoped the anger in his voice hid his true feelings.

"We were promised a certain risk level for this job," Radcliffe answered, creeping closer to the count. "You told us this was supposed to be a clean-cut, go-in-and-come-out with hardly a scratch for anyone."

Lucilous cleared his throat. "That is not at all—"

"Many times we almost met our maker, taken out by the reinforced security that you said *wasn't there!*" Another thug wielding a sniper rifle jumped in. "I counted at least a dozen times where we nearly bit the dust."

"My colleague, Watson, is correct, I'm afraid," Radcliffe added. "We almost didn't fulfill this mission. We don't take kindly to false information, Your Eminence." He was wagging his finger, mere centimeters from Lucilous' face.

"I did not give you false information," the count whispered sinisterly. He slapped the wagging finger away from his face. "Nor did I say there would not be any heavy security. What I said was, that a group with your expertise would have no problem with whatever was there."

Grint, the one with the cannon, shoved Radcliffe out of the way and pointed her barrel at the count's chest. "That's not what you said at all!"

Watson pulled his friend away, cooing her to calm down. Radcliffe crossed his arms and scratched his chin, straining to remember if that was accurate.

"Either way, bossy boy," the gang leader said, "we've decided that we deserve triple the original rate. For all the trouble we went through, you understand."

Lucilous' eyes nearly shot out of his sockets. He grasped the head of his walking stick, about to unsheathe his sword, but returned it to the ground. "Triple!? Are you insane! Why in the hell should I give you more than what we agreed? I have yet to see the merchandise and all you've done is stall and waste my time!" He paused for a moment to look at each one of the thugs' faces. "You know what I think? That you didn't do the job."

The five armed thugs raised their weapons, the clicks of the safeties filling the count's ears.

Radcliffe immediately raised his arms to calm down the fray. "Hey, hey, hey, wait a minute. Oh we did the job, alright. We always get the job done, don't we boys!" They all grunted in agreement. "We just don't deliver until we get paid *as much as we're due.*"

The count wanted to lash out but thought better of it. He would have a better chance at negotiation if he kept face with everyone. More importantly, he wanted to see the merchandise and get going with his itinerary. "Could we discuss this after you unveil the merchandise?" He was never going to tell them that he could barely even cover the cost of the original deal.

Radcliffe acquiesced and gestured at one of his underlings, who ventured into the cargo hold and flipped on the power switch. Lights flickered to life inside the container, revealing the coveted prize.

The kidnapped Ulysses Pircilla, raucous cosmic influencer and son of the illustrious senator, was strapped to a surgical table by electro-bonds. Various tubes of medicine and proteins were sticking out of his body. He seemed to have been sleeping, but awakened as the lights powered on. Once he laid eyes on the audience before him, Ulysses immediately struggled against his bonds, and screamed through the gag in his mouth. He was a caged animal, rabid with anger and the desire to escape.

Lucilous raised his eyebrows as a smile slowly carved into his face. The unease he felt lightened exponentially. This day was suddenly looking brighter. "I'm impressed fellas. I half expected you to bring him dead. The Jira always fulfill their contracts indeed." The count brought his hands together for a light applause.

The thugs were not impressed. Watson presented the captured Ulysses as though they were on a game show. "As you can see, this could have only been done by people with our expertise. He doesn't have a scratch on him, and is obviously unharmed."

The words being spoken entered one of the count's ears and went out the other. Lucilous was focused on nothing else but the person struggling before him. For years the count had loathed Ulysses, not partially because he was jealous of the boy's charisma. The way he so effortlessly mustered up a large following, and so quickly... It was a shame that such perfection did not belong to the Axis, but it was less heartbreaking that the little shit didn't support the Syndicate either. This only gave fuel to Lucilous' hatred. Slowly, but certainly, Ulysses was destroying everything Lucilous worked so hard for.

The count was almost moved to tears. He had hated Ulysses for so long that the moment he finally saw the fucker in person was surprisingly quite emotional. Now that Lucilous was finally in a position to return the favor, he couldn't wait to begin.

"Before I can even consider your proposal gentleman, I'll have to ensure that our guest is indeed *unharmed*." The count resolutely placed his hands behind his back. "After all, it would not be good business to pay inflated prices for an inferior product. And you are dealing with a businessman."

CHAPTER 2

It was Radcliffe's turn for his eyes to nearly go out of their sockets. "What do you mean you have to ensure? Can't you see with your own eyes that he's uninjured? He's as feisty as he can be, and he for sure wouldn't be this energetic if we hadn't kept him hard lined for you. If anything—"

The count quickly cut off the thug leader. "That, within and of itself, is not an indication of his overall health, and we are for sure NOT paying for your shitty, cut rate, energy shots. Only after a thorough medical examination is conducted will we continue our negotiations."

Lucilous turned towards the technician who immediately moved toward the captive. Before the tech could touch the containment cell he was swatted away by a gang member. Once again everyone's weapons were drawn and aimed at the count. The count's security unit, in turn, aimed their weapons at the thugs. The stand-off was so shocking that even Ulysses stopped struggling and watched intently, aware that he was being totally ignored.

Lucilous' face was calmer than his insides, which once again swam in anxiety. Oh how he wanted to unleash his sword at this petulant shit. Instead, he held out his hands. "Gentlemen, why the sudden change in mood? Everything was going so well."

Radcliffe pulled out his pistol and pointed it directly at Lucilous' forehead. "You didn't say anything about a bloody medical. That was nowhere in the contract—"

The count calmed somewhat. "Au contraire, my good man, it is in the original contract, and the one you altered right before I signed it. In order for the deal to be finalized, we must all ensure the merchandise is perfectly healthy. You don't want me to go around telling people you don't like holding up your end of the bargain, now do you?" His voice lowered an octave. "That would cause you an unfathomable amount of problems."

The thug leader's face was angrily grimacing, just waiting for the moment to pull the trigger. The battle of what to do was playing out all over his face. He shook the pistol that was pointed at the count.

"Like I said, you are dealing with a businessman, *and* a politician," Lucilous wryly smiled. "We always get our way."

Deep below the calm visage, his emotions were an absolute wreck. While the count has looked death in the face many times, he was not ready to die and was in fact quite afraid to stop living. There was still too much that he needed to do.

Several seconds passed before the thug lowered his weapon and instructed his associates to follow suit. "Fine. We'll play along with the medical exam. But make it quick. We don't have all day to wait for our damn payment!"

The count's guards lowered their weapons as well. A few beads of sweat rolled down Lucilous' nose. "Oh trust me, everything will come together soon enough."

Moments later the Axis technicians were transporting Ulysses to the medical wing, and there was a general air of peace, though tense. The Jira Gang were furiously looking through every word of the contract to see if the count was right, or if they could use a loophole to their advantage.

Lucilous' wrist unit beeped for his attention. One glance at who was attempting to call him sent shivers down his spine. This person was even more threatening than a band of galactic gangsters. Not even death frightened him this much.

Without hesitation he clapped this encounter to conclusion "Well gentlemen, I have other business to attend to, but we will reconvene in the medical wing after the physical to continue our conversation."

Radcliffe handed the contract data pad to the rest of the team and approached Lucilous. "There's nothing more to discuss, Count. We delivered the goods as ordered, and nearly fucking died in the process, and we want our fair fucking share!"

CHAPTER 2

Lucilous' wrist unit continued whining for his attention. It had been made to wait long enough as it was. His caller is not patient. "We will continue this discussion *later* gentlemen."

The count quickly scurried to the nearest communication shack. He barked at everyone to leave and locked himself inside. Numerous ships in various stages of arrival and departure were all shouting through the radio for further orders. After silencing the main communication channel, Lucilous used the encrypted holo-computer to answer his call.

A cloaked torso emerged in front of him, its face shielded in darkness deep within a large cowl. Even through the green tint of the hologram, the deep shades of the red robe shone through, adding to the creature's menacing air. Even though Lucilous couldn't see them, he could sense the figure's eyes bore into his soul, full of sheer disappointment.

It took almost all of Lucilous' strength to remain still, struggling to not shiver with fear and cower to the floor. Despite that this was a hologram from an unknown number of lightyears away, the figure's fearfully commanding presence was still as potent as though it was here in person.

"You know better than to keep me waiting, Count" The hooded voice was tremulous and deep, seething with disappointment. It spat out the word "count" as though it left a horrid flavor.

Lucilous' throat seized for a moment, unable to form a sound. "My apologies, Master. I was attending to a matter that required my full attention and I couldn't get away."

"And just what could that possibly be, Count?" Every time the voice spoke Lucilous' title, it was punctuated with disdain, as though the title was meaningless and vain. Which it was, in this day and age.

Lucilous was not ignorant of his master's true question—what is more important than he—yet didn't know how to answer it without sounding smug; The reason he was late was because he was doing the other job he was asked to do. "The target has arrived sir, and I was performing its initial inspection."

The hooded hologram twitched slightly, its interest piqued. It leaned forward, its voice sounding more curious than angry. "So soon? They delivered ahead of schedule."

The count took the tone shift as an opportunity to smile slightly. "Yes, my lord. And now they are demanding they be paid triple the original price, which is absolutely–"

"Was the target harmed in any way?" A gloved hand moved into the hood, stroking the invisible chin cloaked in darkness.

Harmed that his master was uninterested in his troubles, Lucilous swallowed his pride and answered. "No, but he is going through his medical examination as we speak, Master. I am confident, though, that the target is completely healthy."

The figure remained silent, stroking its chin for a few moments in contemplation. The count was still on edge. Even though his master was no longer betraying any signs of anger did not mean he couldn't remove that veil at any moment.

"I will depart for your station immediately. Everything is going ahead of schedule, and the Plan is working out perfectly. Get the target prepared. We will begin the procedure as soon as I land."

"Yes, master," Lucilous bowed. A knot was expanding in his stomach. He was already stressed enough with everything else he had to do, and his master's imminent arrival was the last thing he needed. Attempting to convince the figure of the contrary would only be seen as argumentative insubordination. Lucilous learned the hard way that only complete obedience was tolerated.

"Master, how shall I deal with the Jira Gang, the ones who retrieved the asset? I barely have the bluechips to cover the original deal and without another advance–"

The gloved hand shot out from the hood and commanded the count to cease. "Enough about the money! Shouldn't a person of your stature be able to cover any emergency expense without needing to ask someone for help? After all, I'm just another nobody who didn't have any coattails to ride to the top."

Fuck, Lucilous thought. As usual he said the wrong thing. "My apologies, my lord. I did not intend to–"

"Silence! I've heard enough of your voice for today. Tell the retrievers you'll give them whatever they want, then kill them. I'll be there soon to take control of the situation." The anger was once again seeping out of the hooded voice.

It was getting easier for the count to annoy his master lately. No doubt it was the stress of the times, but Lucilous worried that each time he upset his master would be the last.

The count contemplated not telling his master about his other... visitor. It would only upset him even more, no doubt resulting in some more harm for Lucilous. It would be worse, however, for his master to find out later than to just tell him right now. "My lord, before you leave. There is another matter that I'm dealing with that merits your attention."

"Spit it out! We're in a hurry!"

There was no better or worse way, Lucilous thought, than to just go right out and say it. "A Specter has arrived asking if I have any information regarding the abduction that would help clear my name off the suspect list."

Silence fell between them for several seconds. "The Specters? You fool! Why didn't you tell me sooner? You failed to conceal your involvement in the retrieval gang and now we have to work faster! The Specters don't suspect, they *know*!"

Lucilous bowed to the floor in shame. "My humblest apologies, master."

"Those won't help, you idiot!" The figure contemplated for a few seconds. "Kill him, then crash his shuttle against the station and stage it as an engine malfunction." The voice's tone lightened slightly. "Syndicate ships are so unreliable."

Lucilous smiled at his master's dark humor, but was immediately sobered by the hooded voice's angered tone. "Don't fail me again. I will punish you for *this* failure later."

The hologram disappeared, leaving Lucilous shivering with fear and embarrassment. He had definitely failed, but he thought he did a satisfactory job of covering his mistake. The Jira's were hired by his former undersecretary, who was fired and executed a month after the deal was completed when his "familial connections" to the Jiras were discovered. Everything was massively publicized in order to make it look as legitimate as possible. Lucilous figured that level of complexity would have sufficed, but apparently not.

He was also afraid of his upcoming punishment. Yes, he performed well and did everything according to expectations, but this unexpected visitor altered everything, erasing all of Lucilous' progress. And now he had to recreate it in an impossible amount of time. All of the good karma that Lucilous had built up with his master was now all erased. Once one made it to his master's bad side, there was no leaving it. The only solace Lucilous had was that he was still useful—for now.

Eliminating the Jiras was relatively easy, it was luring the Specter that was the trickiest. Lucilous contemplated taking him on a tour of the complex and then stabbing him in the back, but concluded that was impractical. Another option was to have the guards do it, but that always carried the risk of someone leaking the information. The leaks always seemed to originate from the security force. Another option was to crash the Specter's shuttle into the conference room, thereby eliminating everything. But that would cause too much collateral damage, which was currently unaffordable in every way.

The count continued contemplating what to do as he walked to the medical wing to meet with the Jiras. No doubt they had come up with numerous reasons as to why their request should be granted, and could point to many "supporting" clauses within the contract. The one thing Lucilous hated almost as much as Ulysses was negotiating on the losing side.

He waited outside the closed conference room until a full unit of guards joined him. Then they all entered.

The thugs rose as soon as everyone filed in, their hands immediately brandishing their weapons. Radcliffe's face was full of fury. "Alright, enough stalling. We're done with waiting and we want our money now!"

Lucilous wore his calmest face possible. "Patience, gentlemen, patience. You will get everything you want in due time. But pointing your weapons will not do any good for anyone. And before we talk some numbers, I thought we'd all like to see our prize after his medical exam?"

The thugs mulled this over for a moment and eventually followed the count to the medical room, where the captured Ulysses was asleep. He was freshly cleaned and wrapped in pristine bandages. He was heavily sedated but his heartbeat and other readouts were steady.

The count gestured to the doctor studying the readouts. "Tell us Doctor, is he injured?"

"Not from the retrieval. He is suffering from early onset arthritis and has hypothyroidism, which seems to be kept under control by medication. His toxicology suggests he has a drinking problem, and is quite fond of the Herb. But otherwise he's perfectly healthy."

Radcliffe grabbed Lucilous' shoulder and violently pulled. "See, he's perfectly fine as we promised all along. Now give us our fucking money!"

"We're done being patient," Grint threatened, patting her cannon and just itching to use it.

"Absolutely gentlemen," the count responded. "Clearly, you have done an absolutely brilliant job and you of course deserve triple your fee." He inched to the exit. "If you would allow me to retrieve the necessary cash–" But his escape was cut off by Watson blocking the door with his rifle.

"Hold up just a moment!" the sniper spoke. "Why do you have to go get the money when you knew that you had to pay us all along? How do we know you're not baiting us again?"

"We're not falling for that again," Radcliffe said, smirking. "After all, we are criminals." A sinister smile erupted on his face.

Lucilous was sweating, struggling to maintain control. "Please, gentlemen. Please. I have the original amount prepared, but since we renegotiated our terms I need to make the necessary arrangements. It will only take a few moments, I assure you."

Radcliffe considered this proposal, though he still was not fully satisfied. The count added, "After all, it's not every day that we deal in something other than bluechips. Cold hard currency is hard to come by."

The Jira boss was still not fully convinced, but couldn't come up with a counter reason. "Fine. But hurry up. We have other places to be and the clock is ticking."

"More than you know," Lucilous strode out of the room, trying hard to hide his excitement.

Once the door sealed behind Lucilous, the Axis guards remained and raised their weapons. Completely surrounded, the Jira knew what was up and raised their weapons. The doctors ran out of the room as fast as they could. The unconscious Ulysses was completely oblivious to the standoff.

"This isn't going to end well, boys," Watson said. "Even with all that fancy armor, you ain't got a chance against us. We'll blow you and half this station right past kingdom come."

The guard captain snickered. "Right. Only if you can avoid the circle of our gunfire. We're the fastest shots this side of the Meridian."

The Jira Gang chuckled, unintimidated.

Before anyone else could speak, a guard fired the first shot and the battle began. Two thugs collapsed instantly, joined by one guard. The two sides were evenly matched, and evenly armed.

Blaster bolts ricocheted around the room, destroying sensitive equipment which caused sparks to fly in all directions. Broken machines whined for attention, joining the cacophony of noise. The bouncing bolts took a few bodies from each side.

Radcliffe and Grint crouched behind a ventilator, laying a volley of fire on the guards. One, two, three, were felled. Within two minutes, 50% of the guards and thugs were killed.

Awakened, Ulysses opened his eyes to a scene of carnage, the only thing he could make out were flying blaster bolts through the haze of gunfire and electricity. He immediately attempted to free himself from his bonds, yet he was still too groggy from all the sedatives and unable to fully articulate his fingers. His fight was useless, however, because his restraints were metal and activated only by a control button on the wall.

Radcliffe was drawn from his hiding place and locked in a duel with the guard captain. Each shot they fired barely missed the target. The smell of singed hair and skin filled the air. Once the guard lined up a shot, he fired, but the blaster bolt bounced off another bolt and traveled in the opposite direction, eventually incinerating the control of the bed restraint system.

Ulysses was so preoccupied with avoiding the shots as best he could that he didn't notice his restraints were released. One stray laser flew right by his ear, singeing his skin. Instantly, Ulysses jumped out of the bed and crouched beneath it. He interlaced his fingers over his head, creating a rudimentary shield that was only for comfort. Tears streamed down his face, blurring his vision which was already hazy with smoke, sparks, and ozone.

Another blaster bolt rocked the bed, which shuddered the ground beneath Ulysses' knees. A large welt began throbbing on top of his head. He reached up to feel it, and then realized his current location.

"I'm free!" he exclaimed, although the cacophony of noise was too loud for him to hear anything. He quickly searched for a path through the gunfire that would lead him to safety.

There was a momentary pause in the warfare and Ulysses took his chance. He threaded a path across the room, nearly reaching the door before the gunfire erupted again. Quickly spying an overturned medical console, Ulysses took refuge. He could feel the bolts' heat fly across his back. He wished he could just dissolve into the floor.

An armored-clad body flew into the wall right above Ulysses' hiding spot, and suddenly all the air was ripped away from the room, followed by an ear-splitting blast. A sonic grenade was just thrown. Immense heat flooded the room and sparks flew everywhere.

A ball of flame burst the door open, and the sounds of the raging gun battle filled the previously calm hallway.

Across the station, Mycroft was busy debriefing the captain of *The Peacekeeper* about his current visit.

"You think Lucilous is hiding something, don't you?" she asked in awe. She was jealous that she wasn't there but simultaneously glad she was in the escape craft.

"Actually no," Mycroft calmly responded. "Yes, he was evasive and didn't fully answer all of my questions, but that was to be expected. He doesn't appear to actually know anything outside of what the media reported."

"What!?" the captain was shocked. "I don't believe it! For once you're actually taking the suspect's word for it? Maybe the Specter Chiefs were right..."

"Hey! Knock it off, Captain! I'm not losing anything! He genuinely does not know."

The captain couldn't help but chuckle. "Too soon? I'm sorry. That doesn't mean he wasn't involved with it. You know that."

Mycroft attempted to chuckle, for that was a good jibe at him. "Yes I do know that! It's just—"

Mycroft's attention was suddenly taken by a large rumble bursting through the wall. The faint smell of ozone and burning carbon filled his nostrils.

The captain's voice continued trailing through the Specter's ears, but went on ignored. Mycroft's mind was too busy going over the layout of this level, attempting to pinpoint the source of the rumble in relation to his location.

"Mycroft? Specter? Are you listening?" the captain screamed.

His attention returned to the captain. "Barely. There's a gunfight nearby. Gotta go!"

"Wait! Don't blow your cover—" but the comm unit was disconnected before she could finish her order.

Mycroft bounded out of the room in search of the commotion.

The hall was clouded, and full of the symphony of battle. This was more than a little scuffle.

His thoughts wandered over what could possibly be happening. An accident? An attack? No doubt it had something to do with whatever brought Lucilous away from their meeting. But what in the hell would erupt into a full battle?

The Specter brandished his ethellite sword, not yet igniting it in order to conserve the power cell. It was faulty and he only used it when absolutely necessary. He had meant to repair it before embarking, yet life got in the way and...well he screwed up and forgot. But as soon as he was headed back to the *Imperatrix* he would fix it.

The smell of war grew more intense as he turned a corner. The hallway filled with thicker smoke and sparks. Odors of burning electrics and dead bodies filled the Specter's nostrils. Loud explosions erupted before him.

Mycroft turned another corner and found the battle. Two men clad in mismatched gear were shooting at an Axis guard crouched behind a charred medical unit. More people were fighting in the room beyond. None of the fighters noticed the Specter's presence.

He immediately ignited his sword, which illuminated a muted white beam which sputtered and disappeared after a few seconds. Mycroft ignited his sword again, but the blade again disappeared. The sword was officially broken.

An ethellite sword can only hold a charge for so long before needing a new power cell, with the average blade lasting sixty-five minutes of combat. One method of ensuring longer power is to attach a miniature power cell to your bodice, but that becomes quite cumbersome and impossible to hide in an undercover situation.

Mycroft's problem was the power transfer unit, which connects the power cell to the rest of the sword. It would not be an easy fix.

The Specter's constant reigniting of his sword caught everyone's attention, and both the thugs and guards started shooting at him. Mycroft quickly dodged and dove out of the incoming bolts' way. He just barely missed one coming right at his face. He brandished a throwing knife and sent it home, but it bounced off his attacker's heavy armor. Mycroft retrieved his small pistols and fired, carefully choosing his limited shots. These were his last resort weapons.

For several moments the room was a volley of blaster fire, with three separate parts of the room firing at each other. Mycroft could barely make out the pale armband on the nearest enemy.

"Jira," he said to himself. "Of course they'd stir up trouble."

Through the haze of gunfire, Mycroft could see a figure in a medical gown crawl into the hall and crouch behind a charred ventilator.

CHAPTER 2

Everyone was so focused on shooting at each other that they paid no attention to the figure.

Mycroft knew exactly who it was. Why would the count just happen to have a "patient" in the middle of a gunfight? Let alone one that's six foot, eight inches, as tall as Ulysses...Lucilous that sonofabitch.

Mycroft was angry, mostly at himself, for missing all the cues, or worse, misreading them. Now that he looked back, he could see all the parts where the weasel bastard gave himself away. A rookie would have even seen it. Fuck, the Specter thought, he was not in control of himself at all.

The deluge of blaster fire continued over his head, and there wasn't time to contemplate his failure any further. Mycroft peeked around the corner of his barrier to see if there was a path he could take.

Suddenly, the bandaged Ulysses launched to his feet and ran down the hall, away from the fight.

Without thinking, Mycroft bolted from his position and chased after the towering captive. Blaster bolts erupted on all sides, but he miraculously avoided so much as a graze.

Ulysses zigzagged through the corridors, hunting for a way to freedom. He had no idea what he was looking for, or where he was, or where he was going. But he was not going to stop running. Stopping meant death.

Mycroft ran several yards behind, struggling to keep his balance as they turned corners and dodged people. He had no idea where he was in the station, but he knew he had to keep going. Various nurses and medical personnel were shoved out of the way, looks of shock and terror on their faces.

An explosion rocked just behind Mycroft, bringing him to his knees. Just in front of him, Ulysses turned a corner and disappeared out of sight.

Mycroft struggled to his feet, but not before the Jira Gang and guards turned the corner and were in firing range. The shots rained down like a deadly storm. Rather than run forward, the Specter was forced to turn in a different direction, opposite Ulysses.

His pursuers were relentless and quickly gaining ground. Mycroft needed to find another turn to lose them, but the hallway was not breaking off anytime soon.

He spied a large vent in the ceiling a few yards ahead, so he ran faster and leaped off of the floor. He just barely had enough reach to grasp the vent cover and pull it down. He was then able to use it as a ladder and climbed into the vent shaft.

The Specter crawled a few yards until he was sure he was in the clear and paused for a moment to take a breath. His lungs were burning and his bad hip was screaming in pain, yet he was absolutely relieved for the small reprieve.

Unfortunately it didn't last long, because the blaster bolts began stinging through the vent floor, just barely missing Mycroft. He quickly scurried away, trying to avoid the lasers of death.

The fusillade continued. No matter how far he crawled down the vent, the shooting did not stop nor slow. Mycroft only had a couple shots left in his pistols, and firing back would give away his position. The only thing he could do was to continue crawling down the vent, hoping he could outrun the pursuers' walking space.

Lucky for him that happened just as soon as he turned a corner. Suddenly, the floor was no longer ablaze with red and yellow blaster bolts. The serenity of the moment was almost too much of a shock for Mycroft, whose ears were ringing and his muscles were getting sore from trembling so much.

The Specter took a few moments to collect himself, and then peered through the melted blaster holes. No one was in the corridor below. His captors either lost interest in him and continued in pursuit of Ulysses, or tried to find another way to intercept him in the vent shaft.

CHAPTER 2

Mycroft suddenly felt a rumbling further down the vent. He looked and could see the tiny dot of beams of flashlights moving. The chase was on once again!

The Specter traveled further along, pausing at another vent. He peered down and could see a hangar of some sort. A group of guards and technicians were loading carts into a small cargo ship.

Mycroft whispered to himself, "Planet-bound. That's not exactly what I had in mind, but why not take the scenic route?"

He pulled out his comm unit and summoned the captain. Perhaps she could rendezvous with him on the planet before they set off too many alarms. It was, as with everything, a long shot, but one he couldn't afford not to take.

"Captain, do you read?"

Static was his only reply. Mycroft tried again. Still nothing.

"Fuck. Can't someone pick up?"

"Unfortunately, due to your violent behavior, we've had to dispose of your colleagues." The creamy voice of Count Lucilous oozed out of the comm unit. "Rest assured, we will find you and we will take care of you as well."

The Specter growled, "You have no idea what consequences killing me will bring."

The count laughed, "Oh please, a petty little war is not what I fear. It's what I *want*!"

The line went static and another shudder violently shook the ventilation shaft. No doubt that was the final explosion of his ship.

With a heavy heart, Mycroft offered a moment of silence for the captain and the rest of the crew of *The Peacekeeper*. Their loss was not going to be wasted.

The Specter contemplated for another moment, and then acted. He ripped off the vent cover and jumped down into the hangar. Crouching behind a stack of crates, Mycroft searched for his escape route.

He grinned when he found it. "Here goes nothing."

* * *

Ulysses kept running, his numb legs frantically trying to keep up the pace. He was looking for a door, a cubby, *something* that he could hide in, but there wasn't anything in sight. All he saw was another corridor, and he promptly turned into it.

Dodging past the orderlies and patients, Ulysses made quite the distance between his pursuers. He found a slot in the wall that was marked "waste" and without thinking he jumped right in, tumbling down the slimy and grimy shaft.

The pursuing guards ran down the corridor, oblivious to the fact their prize had eluded them.

CHAPTER 3

The frigid snow blew across the frozen desert, magically churning the chilled air even colder. The blowing snowflakes pelted through the air at nearly 100 miles an hour, just begging to have something intercept their path. The snow drifts, most towering nearly ten stories, were worn smooth by the gale-force winds, with peaks that have been sharpened into knives. The towering mountains dotting the entire surface were composed of both rock and ice and snow. The clouds were tens of miles thick, and the sun had never clearly shown through to the surface.

The small moon Ampheres, orbiting the gas giant Coreen, was such a harsh environment that it has no natural indigenous bacterial or plant life. Everything that lived and breathed on this frozen rock was brought to it by humans.

Most of those humans were affiliated with the mining conglomerate JeffCo, which owned Ampheres and the rest of the Coreenian planet group. While the frozen rock lacked natural biology, it contained immense amounts of various precious minerals that made it the single most mineral rich planet in the galaxy. JeffCo advertised the frozen ball as an "Astral Arctic Wonderland" that was "guaranteed to make you rich," but not too many fell for it, making it the company's smallest installation. However, the chance of striking it rich with one of Ampheres' countless illudium or J-m/C deposits was more than enough for the 10,000 brave souls that chose to come to this hell hole.

Those poor souls congregated into the only official human settlement on the planet, the Village. Here the people bonded into an odd community that grew together under the hardships of the environment and untamed desire to strike it rich. No obstacle was too much and no fortune—or chance for one—was too little to pass. Finding a promising J-m/C deposit, the galaxy's most valuable mineral outside of pure Ethellite, was a guaranteed ticket to freedom. Especially since living on the frozen world was expensive enough. Everything had to be shipped in from elsewhere, there were hardly any viable farm and ranchland, and the only crop that could survive on the planet's harsh environment was the main ingredient to the galaxy's favorite recreational hallucinogen, Thorn.

All of this was beside the fact that a miner's wage was barely enough to cover rent in corporate housing and buy food. Miners were also saddled with various "equipment rental surcharges," and an "anticpated-value tax" that soaked whatever the miners could stow away for savings. Transport off the moon was virtually nonexistent and unobtainable.

Striking a J-m/C deposit was the only way to overcome a miner's biggest expense— buying out their service contract.

JeffCo mining installations were run by indentured servants credited with the expenses to mine and buy material up front, who paid the contract and expenses back with their wages and mineral findings. Once a viable deposit had been struck, the company garnished a percentage plus interest and the miner walked away with the remainder of the profit.

The catch was that hardly any mine turned over a profit for the miner after the company took its share. Another was that this job was extremely dangerous, with a forty percent mortality rate and a five percent success rate. The standard contract was forty years, and most miners either died or ended up leaving their contract and then dying weeks later. With the various fees and surcharges, a miner's contract balance continued to expand well above the original amount, rendering a full success all but impossible.

But that was not a deterrent for Ridley Camaro's parents, who came looking to begin a better life. For them, moving to Ampheres was a ticket to financial freedom. Unfortunately, they didn't live too long after Ridley's birth, and he was raised by his grandmother who managed to make this wasteland into a wonderland. For seventeen years, they carved away their meager existence together in this horrid place, finding novel things to enjoy and take pleasure in, making the best of what they had. Neither of them liked the planet, and they most definitely didn't like their jobs, but it was their life, and there wasn't too much that could be done about it.

Ridley emerged from the warm cocoon of the general store nestled in the Village's main street. A half-dozen bags and boxes were precariously brandished in both hands. His grip wasn't too firm and loosened with every step he took. One of his cartons tumbled down the icy steps. He cursed to himself, for that was the *one* package that he wasn't supposed to drop, and let everything else fall from his grip.

He rushed down the steps, nearly breaking his neck, and grabbed the valuable carton. This box contained a fragile part for Ridley's grandmother's medical machine. They ordered this part three months ago, and it took nearly that long to save for it, since it cost half the rent payment. If it broke, they wouldn't be able to afford a new one for a long time, and his grandmother might not make it, for it helped power her spinal fluid dilating machine. They had already let too much time pass already.

Wishing with every bone in his body, Ridley carefully extracted the part from its thick protective foam. It was the size of his pinkie toe and covered in countless, hair-thin wires. To his great relief, it appeared unharmed, but the ultimate test would be after it was installed into the dilating machine. If it didn't work...

"Well, we just won't think about that," he exhaled to himself. "It's bloody amazing how such a small part can cost a small fucking fortune." He shook his head and carefully placed the delicate thing back into its package.

Grumbling about the cold wind biting through his company-issued thermal coat—which they promised was the top of the line—Ridley retrieved his packages and resumed his journey. He walked against the wind, which blew chunks of ice into his eyes. He couldn't see anything and couldn't breathe either, as his breath condensed in his face scarf and froze his nostrils closed.

Even in this horrid weather a few inhabitants of the Village walked about the main street conducting their various errands. At the head of the street was the company administrative office, which was always bustling with activity. Lining each side of the main street were a few stores selling the various necessities of living; grocery, hardware, medical supply, and home goods. Ridley passed the electronics store where he purchased his part, staring into the window at the rat-nosed proprietor busily repairing a computer unit. Next door was the parcel store that was closing up for the day, the weekly ship having departed and won't return again for seven days.

The main road was the spine of the Village, which nestled in between the base of two mountains, making the storm's updrafts especially strong. Past the shops on the main street were rows of small houses, laid out in a neat grid. Ridley and his grandmother, Oz, lived on the far outskirts of town in the original housing units, where the rent was cheapest. The downside was that they lived near an operating thermal drill, and the houses were so old that they needed constant repair.

The storm was so strong that no vehicles were functioning, forcing those brave enough to venture out to do so on foot. The further along

Ridley walked, the fewer people he saw. Eventually he was all alone, the lone dark speck in the middle of the snow. Aside from the howling wind, the place was eerily quiet.

He continued for what seemed like hours. He kept his head down to keep his nose as warm as he could, and couldn't hear anything. His sweat froze to his skin, making his entire body ache. Ridley could barely see anything past his nose when he did look up, and he couldn't see any visible landmarks. But judging by the rising road he was almost home.

Outside of the village the main road rose back into the mountains, eventually turning into the main service access for the larger mining outposts. Ridley's row house was located at the last turnoff near the closest mining post to the Village. Just to go to the store and back was ten miles.

"This place is so far," Ridley said to himself as a huge chunk of ice landed in his eye. "But hey, at least it's warm."

Ridley stumbled on a patch of ice and slipped, his knee collapsing beneath him. A big pop sounded in his knee, followed by a burst of pain. He dropped his packages and cried. He could barely hear himself above the howling wind, even though he screamed at the top of his lungs.

For several minutes he cradled his throbbing knee, the biting wind exacerbating his pain. He still had three miles to walk, and he wasn't sure if he could make it. He was certain he dislocated his kneecap, and if this was like the last time then he was in for a month of throbbing, swollen pain.

A memory suddenly flashed in Ridley's mind, and he rushed as quickly as he could to the carton with the medical part. By now the box was severely damaged, crushed underneath his heavy bag of groceries. Snow was seeping into the package. He quickly retrieved the delicate instrument from inside, inspecting it as best he could. It was still intact for now, but one more drop and it would mostly break for good, Ridley figured.

Giving his knee a final rub, Ridley slowly brought himself to his feet and gathered his belongings. He winced with every movement, for the pain was not just in his knee, but his back, hips, and shoulders.

"Now I know what Grandma Oz feels like all the time." He groaned as he settled his packages in his arms and began his journey once again. He focused on one step at a time, moving slowly and deliberately. The pain increased exponentially with every step he took.

Thick in the blowing snow, just past Ridley's view and above him further along the mountainside, a figure slid down a snow mound, landing just steps behind him. Ridley didn't hear or notice anything, and just continued walking.

On the other side of the path, another figure threw a snowball in Ridley's direction. It just barely missed the boy's head and thunked in the deep snow just ahead of him. Again, Ridley did not notice.

Both figures wore vision-enhancing goggles, and signaled to each other to take positions. They wore heavy fur dyed in crazy, neon patterns. The larger figure took position behind Ridley, matching his footsteps, while the slender one walked side by side with the boy, matching his pace along the trail. Then the man counted down with his fingers, signaling to the other.

Several seconds later, Ridley was ambushed by the bigger figure from behind. The man tackled him like a freight train, launching the boy into the air and completing a full revolution. He landed in a heap on the snow, his wares spread out in a scattered debris field.

The two figures laughed with glee, their giggles floating along the wind into Ridley's ears.

The thinner figure emerged from the shadows carrying a rock. He smashed the rock into Ridley's face, breaking several of his teeth and bending his nose. Blood spread everywhere, dying the pure white snow a deep crimson.

Ridley's vision stung with snow and blood. His ears were ringing and he was on the verge of unconsciousness. He could barely feel his body, for everything tingled with freezing pain. He was struggling to comprehend what had happened. One moment he was walking and then he was suddenly on his back. He thought he had been attacked by an animal, but he realized that the animals big enough to tackle him like that didn't come this close to town. A glimmer of an idea began forming in his mind, but he was too fuzzy to fully function yet.

"Well, well, well. What do we have here," the skinny one asked. He lifted his goggles to reveal yellow, diseased eyes that were sunk deep in his pale-skinned head. This was Siegel, the brains of the pair and a member of the Johns, the local gang that terrorizes the Village and offers "protection" to the various residents and businesses for a nominal fee.

"There's a lot of groceries and things here for someone who told us you were out of money last night. Tsk, tsk, tsk." Siegel shook his head and clicked his tongue. "You know what we do in these situations, right?"

The heavy man, Nelson, the pair's muscle, waved his finger back and forth. "It's not good to lie to us, Ridley. Not good at all. We take care of liars, Ridley."

The two looked down at Ridley, smiling and laughing as though he was a baby in the bassinet. "How could we protect you from this dangerous environment if you don't pay us the costs to do it, buddy?" Siegel sounded genuinely disappointed, as though he was addressing a misbehaving child. "All we're doing is trying to help you out, and you're not letting us, dammit."

"This job ain't cheap, my man." Nelson blew a big bubble with his gum. He then cracked his knuckles. "It's not nice to mooch off of other people, and even ruder to decline an invitation."

Ridley's grogginess finally cleared and he realized what happened, and recognized who was talking to him. He tried to talk but the blood pooled in his throat caused him to cough.

"This was the last of the money we have," he was finally able to say after several moments. "If we paid you yesterday, there wouldn't be anything for us to eat today. We didn't lie to you."

Siegel cracked a bubble with his gum. "Nonsense! There's plenty to eat. You had a very nice spread on the table last night. Certainly there's some leftovers."

"That was the last of it! We would starve if we paid you! How many times do we have to fucking tell you?" Ridley was fired up. This wasn't the first time he'd been beaten up by the Johns, but every time he was always outnumbered and never able to fight back. The previous night, Siegel and another group of Johns harassed him and Oz for protection money. After nearly getting into a gunfight, Ridley thought they all had come to some sort of understanding. Obviously, everyone continued to misunderstand.

Nelson grasped Ridley's collar and heaved him up in the air. The heavy man blew another bubble, which kissed the boy's nose. "Why are you getting so upset, little buddy? All we're doing is trying to help you."

"Beating me up in the middle of fucking nowhere and stealing my shit is helping me?" Ridley countered. "Jeez, I'd hate to see you *attack* me." Blood trickled down his nose, thickening his speech. He spat in Nelson's face at the same time the man blew another bubble, his orange gum speckled with red blood.

This enraged the big man and he shook Ridley. Nelson then spat in his face, but it turned into ice before it landed on the bloody boy. It still stung though.

Siegel rounded out the attack with a hefty smack to the back of Ridley's head before Nelson threw the boy on the ground. Another tooth fell out of his mouth.

"I see more than just groceries, here," Siegel kicked through the debris. "This isn't food. This isn't food." He picked up the carton with the medical part and shook it violently, listening to the contents. "This *definitely* is not edible."

Ridley saw what the gangster was doing and launched to his feet. He primed his arm to punch Siegel in the face but was held back by Nelson, who squeezed his elbows with a vice grip.

The boy struggled against his captor like a rabid animal. He was numb to all the pain in his body. He screamed at the top of his lungs with a rage he didn't know he possessed. "Don't fucking touch that!"

The gangster gave a wry smile. "Why? Is it valuable?" Siegel's eyes twinkled with the anticipation of a major score. "You wouldn't do that for just a bloody box of sweets."

All Ridley saw was red. He struggled harder, even though it was not making any progress at all. "Fuck! No, dammit! It's not mine, it's my grandma's!"

"Ah, so it *is* valuable," Siegel threw the box at Nelson, who missed it. The box tumbled to the ground. One side of it opened and a huge swath of snow blew into it.

Nelson let Ridley go, who tried to rush and grab it, but his body's momentum from struggling made him slip and fall on the ice again. Nelson laughed but was berated by his teammate.

"The fuck, Nelson! Why do you have butter fingers? This is a valuable item that is extremely fragile. We don't want to break away the money we could make from it."

The heavy man stopped laughing and looked down. "Sorry Siegel. I'll try to do better." He grabbed it just before Ridley could reach it and threw the carton back at his teammate.

Ridley made it to his feet, but the two continued playing monkey in the middle with the carton and the boy could not catch it. One, two, and then three rounds. Ridley kicked Nelson in the thigh, interrupting his fourth catch and managed to intercept the carton. He stomped on Nelson's groin, driving his victory home when the man struggled to get to his feet.

Siegel rushed at Ridley, who dodged out of the way just in time. The gangster double backed and was quick enough to punch Ridley in the gut. Ridley collapsed to the ground, but rolled out of the way of Siegel's pile driver. He then bounded to his feet, picked up the stone that was used to hit him, and bashed Siegel over the head, felling the man. Blood poured from the wound, turning the pure snow a deep red.

Nelson recovered from his groin wound and charged at Ridley once again. This time the boy wasn't quick enough and was caught in another tackle. Thankfully it didn't hurt as much as the first, for the snow cushioned his fall. Nelson picked up Ridley, but the man was big enough that the boy was able to maneuver onto his back and squeezed Nelson's neck. Nelson writhed about, trying to breathe and get Ridley off of him. The man found a boulder and turned around, prepared to slam his back, and Ridley, into it.

Ridley flipped off Nelson's back just in time for the heavy man's head to slam into the rock. He fell to the ground, crumpled and unconscious.

Ridley took a few moments to recover from his ordeal. His adrenaline was still rushing so he wasn't yet feeling the full brunt of the pain. He reached for his nose, which wasn't bleeding anymore but was still throbbing. He couldn't breathe through it and it felt warm. He couldn't tell for sure but he thought it was broken, otherwise it wouldn't hurt. Luckily that was something Grandma could take care of.

Siegel moaned and started to squirm, coming out of the dregs of unconsciousness. Ridley rushed over to him.

Rage boiled inside the boy. How much he wanted to continue bashing Siegel's head in with that rock until it was pulp. That would definitely

CHAPTER 3

put an end to *one* of his troubles, which was a rare thing to do on this planet. But then that would also invite another group of Johns to start harassing them all over again, or some other, worse retaliation.

He could report this to the Village constable, but they wouldn't do anything. The only thing JeffCo cared about were profits, and as long as nothing interfered in their making or made them shrink, the company didn't want to be bothered.

Which conversely meant that Ridley really wouldn't receive any retaliation for killing these two fuckers. At least from the official authorities, that is. But this was a small town, and it would not take long for people to notice these two deaths and to start asking questions. No doubt someone outside of the gang had to know that Nelson and Siegel were visiting Ridley's house, and it was only a matter of time before fingers were pointed. And that would cause more harm than good...

If someone wanted to get rid of a fellow employee, all they needed to do was report to the company that they had seen this employee play with company funds. That would immediately open an inquiry that would expose other frowned upon activities that weren't officially against company policy, but would be used against someone to fire them. JeffCo loved firing people.

Ridley could also just leave these two to freeze to death, an accident that definitely happened all the time on Amperes. Someone was always fighting someone else, and this could easily have been a drunken brawl gone wrong...

His conscience started to nag him. Ridley was raised to do the right thing, even if that was not the most satisfying choice. He rushed over to the moaning Siegel and threw some snow in his face. He slapped his face, not lightly, to wake the bastard up. If the man were to remain unconscious, he would be frozen solid in ten minutes.

Within seconds Siegel awakened, attempting to finish the fight he left behind. His hands flailed, too weak to punch but still strong enough to do some damage.

"Hey, hey stop it! I'm trying to *help* you dammit," Ridley restrained the flailing hands. "You'll freeze to death if you stay unconscious."

Siegel wasn't listening and broke his hands free. He landed a punch once again on Ridley's broken nose. Intense pain radiated through Ridley's face, forcing him to collapse to the ground. He rolled his face in the snow to see if the cold would help; it did not.

"Exactly! Payback's a bitch ain't it?" Siegel snickered and kicked Ridley in the stomach before running away. He roused Nelson and the two rummaged through the remainder of the groceries, taking whatever they deemed valuable.

With his arms full, Siegel stood once again over Ridley. "This counts as half of your payment," Siegel snickered, though he sounded drunk. "And we'll be back to take payment for this incident later." He spat on Ridley and rushed away.

Nelson kicked the boy's side one last time before joining his partner.

Several moments passed before Ridley had enough strength to rise to his feet. Surveying the damage, his anger reached new depths. Nothing he could do could rectify the situation. He was so angry he wanted to destroy the entire village. He was fucking tired of the continued ambushes from the Johns. He was fucking tired of living in a frozen wasteland, ten miles from the nearest grocery store and eight miles to his fucking job site. The house he lived in was always half-working, and the days were so cold that he always had to fucking walk everywhere.

His rage consumed every cell of his being. He found a package of synthmeat that had been ripped open, specks of frozen mud stuck within it. Ridley was so mad he kicked it as far as he could and then stomped on it when it landed. He imagined the piece of meat was Siegel's face. Then he imagined it was Nelson's. Then he imagined it was all of the Johns', and he had the sudden urge to murder every last one of them.

With every stomp, Ridley's rage grew. Eventually, the tears and emotion became so unbearable that he collapsed and cried for several minutes. All of his emotions needed an outlet, and crying was the only suitable way. Killing people was inappropriate, he chuckled to himself.

When he finally calmed down, he gathered what belongings he could. The wind was so strong that some of the items blew far away, and he was distracted for so long that some small critters made off with a few scraps of food. After several minutes, he recovered almost one-third of his wares.

The one saving grace in this entire encounter was that the dilator chip wasn't taken, and as far as Ridley could tell, was still relatively undamaged. But only time would be certain.

The remainder of the journey was uneventful, thankfully. Along the way, Ridley fantasized about all the different ways he could take revenge on the Johns. He could just ambush their hideout like an old-fashioned gunslinger and blow up the place. Or he could poison them all with irradiated synthmeat. His favorite method so far was crashing a mining tractor into their hideout, but he couldn't quite determine how to get his hands on one and drive it all the way over here.

"Details," he waved away.

The row house loomed in front of him, shining like a beacon in the pitch darkness. The small, nondescript building was on the end of a row with half-dozen units, and it was the only one occupied, as the company was "actively renovating" the other units. A small trail of smoke erupted from the small chimney, beckoning Ridley to hurry home.

Within no time he was at the door. His fingers were so cramped from the frigid wind and holding onto his packages that he struggled to work the opening controls.

Suddenly the door opened on its own, revealing a small old woman with wild silver hair, wrapped in a heavy blanket. Her wrinkled face was all aghast with shock. "Where the hell have you been? You're late! I was worried sick about you!"

The shocked look on her face was replaced with concern once she saw the welts, bruises, and dried blood covering Ridley's face. "What happened?"

"I got jumped by the Johns, Oz!" he replied as he shoved passed his grandmother and dropped his packages on the floor. He was already not in the mood to talk, and especially didn't want to be interrogated in the doorway. "Bastards took some of the groceries because we didn't pay them last time." He dropped everything but the dilator box on the ground and slumped into a chair, defeated.

Oz closed the door and gathered some healing salve from a cupboard. "We told them all we had was enough for groceries, and they said they would work with us—"

Ridley kicked one of the stray boxes, making a loud, startling noise. "Well this is what they meant, Oz! You know they'll look for any way they can to take advantage and get their money."

Oz approached Ridley with the salve and some cloth. She began applying them to the wounds on her grandson's face. "We should report this to the Village constable."

He flinched as the gauze stung his nose. "Ouch! And what are they going to do? Beat me up some more because they're in the Johns' pockets? If anything, they'll charge us a fucking service fee just answer the damn comm call!"

Another shot of stinging pain erupted from his eyebrow wound. "Fuckin shit! That hurts!" He swatted at her to stop.

All Oz did was roll her eyes. "Boys are such sissies when it comes to pain." She swatted back at him. "Oh quit flinching. It doesn't hurt

CHAPTER 3

that bad."

The boy could barely keep his eyes open. "Yes it does, too!" With every blot of the healing salve his skin stung and burned at a million degrees.

His grandmother continued undeterred. "You've always been squeamish. Ever since you were a kid."

Ridley rolled his eyes at the reference to his youth. She did this so often it was embarrassing, even when they were alone in their own house.

"But you still should say something to the authorities, because this was more than just a little scuffle," Oz continued in her silky smooth voice. Even when she was correcting him, she still sounded loving and caring. "Look at this! They seriously injured you! They shouldn't get away with that!"

"No they shouldn't." Ridley ruminated what he would say to the constable, but a headache soon developed behind his eyes, because every scenario he envisioned ended with him getting his lights punched out. What was he going to say, that he was ambushed for not playing nice with the gangsters that are *also* greasing the hands of the constable's office? No, Ridley concluded, he should *not*.

"And stealing," Oz continued. She stopped applying the salve and looked directly into his eyes. "Ridley if you don't say something I will."

This made Ridley chuckle. "Oh right, like they'll listen to you any more than they'll listen to me, the younger one who can put up a fight."

Oz smiled warmly. "See, that's just it! You're the young, inexperienced one! You'll be surprised at how powerful your grandma is!"

Ridley couldn't help but laugh and embrace Oz in a firm hug. In her arms, nothing could happen to him. It was the safest place in the universe, where everything was right and perfect. For several seconds they just sat in each other's presence, making everything okay, at least for the moment.

When they finally pulled apart, Ridley said. "That's right! And I suggest that before we unleash your powerful wrath on those unfortunate souls we need to see if they've done any major damage first." He looked around for the carton he suffered through all this for.

"What do you mean?" That look of concern only deepened on Oz's face.

He finally found it, and held it gingerly. "The power transfer module for your dilator was severely jostled in the fight. It even got wet, dammit! If that is broken, *then* we'll go over and say something, huh?"

Oz's face contorted into deep fury. "Those fucking bastards shouldn't have been messing with that to begin with! That is ours! We paid for that with our own money and they have no right–"

Now it was Ridley's turn to calm her. He placed his hands on her shoulders. "Grandma, you're right, but that won't solve our problems or change what happened." He loved her to death, but she had a habit of questioning the past in a manner that demanded an answer from the present. And she would then get all worked up over something she had no control over, and then be upset that she had no control over it. Together, they were each other's stress relievers.

The two eventually calmed and continued on with their evening chores. Oz prepared dinner while Ridley worked to install the dilator. Even though Oz was Ridley's grandmother, their relationship was more of live-in roommates, with each working to support one another—which was the only way to survive on this harsh planet. Ridley had the talent to calm her down, and Oz usually let him have the final word. She hated to admit it, but Ridley was usually the only one in the house with any sense. If they followed even half of her ideas, they'd be in solitary confinement.

CHAPTER 3

Dinner was served, consisting of a simple synthmeat stew and the last half of a stale loaf of bread. The conversation turned to the events of each other's work day, which as usual consisted of getting yelled at by the foreman for being too slow, or making a simple mistake.

Once dinner was finished, Ridley returned to work on Oz's spinal fluid dilator. It was a one of a kind machine that Ridley built out of various parts he scavenged when they learned that Oz would need to get her fluid filtered multiple times a week. It was impractical for Oz to travel back and forth to the Village medical center, so Ridley built a machine for her to use at home.

But it was more than just a medical machine, for Ridley soon realized that Oz would need more help around the house. So he constructed the machine as a pocket sized disc that could lift up to 200 pounds, be able to access various types of machines, and just overall keep her company. It was essentially a mini, homemade version of the mine's construction utility units. They called it VERA, which stood for Versatile Robotic Aide, and loved her as a pet.

Usually VERA's personality was vibrant, not unlike a puppy. But lately she's been sluggish in responding to commands, and failing to adequately filter Oz's spinal fluid. Ridley scanned her and discovered the faulty power transfer unit. He replaced the power unit, but that didn't solve the problem. If this power transfer module didn't work, he didn't know what else he could do.

A couple hours passed and the module was installed. Ridley held his breath as he powered on VERA. The small disc erupted to life, bouncing off the ceiling and walls before steadily floating in the center of the room. She emitted the cacophony of sounds that indicated she was functioning properly. She then flew over to Oz's shoulder and implanted herself into the injection point.

Several moments later, she let out a sound that Oz and Ridley hadn't heard in almost three months, the notification of a successful cycle.

Ridley let out a giant sigh of relief, and Oz nuzzled her old companion when she flew off from her back.

"Oh, girl there you are! We missed you! Yes we did! Yes we did!"

It was obvious that the robot was overjoyed to return to its normal state. She performed a series of cartwheels and loop de loops in the air. She flew over and nuzzled against Ridley, thanking him for his work.

Ridley laughed and tickled the machine back. Its fiber optic eyes fluttered in different colors, its version of laughing.

"Anytime, you rascal," the boy warmly proffered. "You had us pretty worried there. For a few seconds I thought you weren't going to make it. Then we really would have been up shit creek!"

Oz lumbered over and kissed Ridley on his other cheek. She embraced him in his arms. "But you came through as always, and that's why we can't live without you. Thank you so much!"

As hard as he tried to hide it, Ridley liked this smothering. He would never get over it. Being in Oz's arms was the safest place he could be. In the comfort of the moment, he closed his eyes. For a brief few moments everything in the universe was perfect. No JeffCo, no Johns, no snow, and no pain. Just total peace. A warmth engulfed his entire being; it was comforting.

The warmth grew in his body, rapidly. So rapidly that he could feel beads of sweat run down his cheek. Soon, Ridley was scorching. He opened his eyes. A large ball of light grew in size and intensity, engulfing his entire field of vision. Suddenly he, Oz, and VERA were thrown into the air, the heat unbearable. For a few moments they were weightless, then landed with a hard bang on the ground.

Suddenly an ear-splitting explosion filled his ears, followed by another surge of energy that pressed them deeper into the ground. The intense heat dissipated, and a steady stream of icy air fell on his face.

CHAPTER 3

Ridley opened his eyes again, but couldn't see anything besides a large dark spot in the center of his vision. He blinked a few times, which didn't make that much of an improvement. VERA had helped Oz to her feet, and soon Ridley followed suit. His ears were ringing and every bone in his body ached. He struggled to stand up straight, his inner ear no doubt affected by the explosion. He was so disoriented he didn't know where he was, or what he was seeing. His head spun so much. It was as though he was standing in the middle of an ocean.

Ridley's vision improved after several moments. When he realized what he saw, he couldn't believe it. The furnace in the corner of the house, which also connected to the stove in the kitchen, exploded. There was a fiery, charred mess of the remnants of the furnace in the middle of the room. In the wall where the furnace used to be was a large hole that exposed the snowy tundra outside. Flurries blew into the room, landing on the carpet. VERA was busy floating around the house, putting out as many fires as she could with the extinguisher she carried. Everything within the immediate vicinity of the furnace, virtually the entire house, was either destroyed, burnt, or currently in flames.

Ridley rushed to Oz who, aside from a few scrapes, was unharmed. Her armchair was right next to the furnace. She got up and moved just a few seconds before...

He embraced his grandmother as hard as he could, vowing to never let go ever again.

Tears covered her ashen face. "All of our stuff is ruined," was all she could bring herself to say.

"At least we're all still alive!" Ridley nearly screamed, for he could only hear a high-pitched ringing in his ears. The intense fear engulfing him transformed into sheer rage. "How can you think about our stuff when we nearly died?"

Oz grew hysterical. "Because now we don't have any warm place to sleep! Nor do we have any warm clothes!" She bundled herself in her smoldering blanket. "We might as well be better off dead!"

"Ah," was all Ridley could respond. That was exactly the way to look at things, he thought. For several moments he remained still, trying to string a single, coherent thought together. His mind was still frazzled. All he could conclude was that they really were shit out of luck.

The boy rubbed his temples and shook his head, trying to get back to one hundred percent. "We'll call the landlord's office. Certainly they'll put us up somewhere until this is repaired." His tongue tingled at the task of talking.

By this time VERA had extinguished most of the large fires, but the extinguisher was empty. It dropped the empty can with a loud thud and flew to rest on Oz's shoulder.

Oz gave Ridley a blank, placid stare. "Now you want to call someone, huh?" A lilt of a smile wrinkled the corners of her mouth. "And you call *me* the crazy, senile one."

It took almost two hours before Ridley could get the comm unit functioning and in contact with a live person at the landlord's office. As much as he pleaded and argued, the office "couldn't be able to do anything until tomorrow afternoon."

He nearly punched the comm unit into the wall. "But where are we supposed to sleep until then? It's fucking snowing in our living room! We'll freeze to death before the shift bell rings."

The bored face on the screen was unmoved. "I've already told you that yelling will not help the situation in any way at all. Damaging company property, or threatening to, is a serious offense, Mr. Camaro." It was typical of a JeffCo representative to always care exclusively about company property while completely ignoring the humanity of the situation. It was practically in the job description.

"And it might behoove you to behave yourself when under a routine security audit." The face of the hologram smirked at Ridley, who immediately understood the reference. A majority of the members of the Johns were the sons and daughters of mid to high-level company employees. Anytime that the Johns did something nefarious, their parents and other company reps would be handsomely paid to look the other way and "not know about anything."

Ridley knew this was a losing battle, but had to stand up for himself and Oz. "That wasn't a routine security audit, dammit! That was getting harassed by a group of thugs who like terrorizing hard-working people, and stealing what they earned"

This finally got an emotional response from the rep and he slammed his fist on the table. The comm screen shook with the force. "My nephews aren't thugs! I have no idea what you are talking about. They are nothing but upstanding, hardworking citizens."

Ridley smirked, which irritated the rep even more. "Hard working my ass!"

"Dammit, they work for a small group that offers the Village a wonderful and effective protection service!" The rep's face was scrunched in anger, his temples pulsing.

Rather than escalate the situation further, Ridley just rolled his eyes. "Terrorizing people on their way home is protection? Shit, I'd hate to see them fight me."

The rep wanted to say something, but held himself back. An evil smile carved into his face and he looked at another screen, keying in some commands. He then exhibited a cartoonish grin as he turned back to the comm screen. "Oh, you know what? I just checked the log. Our earliest available repair slot is in two days..."

Ridley punched the wall and immediately protested, but it was falling on deaf ears.

"...And it looks like we're short on furnaces at the moment, and we won't be able to get another one for six weeks, if we're lucky."

The rep's eyes darkened. "And we're hardly ever lucky out here on Ampheres."

Ridley punched the comm unit again, breaking the screen. He screamed in rage.

"Take care!" and the rep signed off, wearing an exaggerated smile.

Defeated and pissed, Ridley stomped around the room. How he liked to go over and give that sonofabitch a piece of his mind!

He and Oz had given many good, solid years to this shit-forsaken company, and the least they could fucking do was repair their old, dilapidated shit! This was just like the company, to only care about the bottom line. And this was just like the lowlifes who work for the fucking company to always get their hit in too, beating down the lowly worker until there was nothing left but a broken soul.

Just once, Ridley would like to walk up to those greedy assholes and spit in their face. He would love to give them a taste of their own medicine, working them to the bone until they could barely muster the energy to take a breath. Then, only then, would they even know what *one* day feels like in the life of Ridley and Oz. Oh, he just wanted to march right up to that fucking administrative office and tell them what he really fucking means!

In fact, dammit to hell, Ridley was going to do exactly that!

"I'll be back!" he screamed and started out of the room. But he was intercepted by VERA, who blocked his path.

As the boy was about to shove the robot, Oz gently tapped him on the shoulder. "Before you go and get yourself hurt, don't you think it'd be wise to try and solve the problem a different way?"

Ridley turned around, his eyes aflame. "What other way is there? To wait? They won't do anything to help us, and even when they do get here they'll do a half-ass job. This is really the only thing we can do, Grandma!"

"Oh really? Beating the shit out of them is going to fix the house?

CHAPTER 3

Interesting. And you call my ideas crazy?" She crossed her arms and leaned on her hip. Behind her a piece of the ceiling fell to the ground, punctuating her point.

The fire in the boy's eyes dimmed, and finally extinguished. Ridley couldn't help but face Oz's logic. After all, she was right. Beating the shit out of anyone wouldn't help anything about the house. No matter what, they *did* have to fucking wait. "But dammit, it'll feel good! And I can't fix the roof in one night, even with you helping me."

Oz gently touched Ridley's cheek. "Don't worry about that. During your comm call, Nonnie came over and told us we can stay over as long as we need. See, this shithole planet always provides, sweetie. Even when it looks like it might not."

This deflated the rest of Ridley's temper, and he collapsed into her. While this was a consolation, it was far from a full solution. But so was everything else.

Ridley let out a deep sigh. "But why do we have to keep fixing someone else's cheap shit?"

Oz just stroked her grandson's head gently. Even at seventeen, this always calmed him down. "What choice do we have right now, babe?"

That was the question. Ridley had quite a few answers, but none were practical or could get them the immediate relief they needed. He was tired of looking after someone else's property. He was over having to dig his way out of holes others dug for him. He wanted to be in charge of his own destiny, and he wanted to set the course of his life. Ridley had been pandering back and forth for some time, deciding whether or not to make a change; always afraid of the consequences. But if this furnace explosion wasn't a wakeup call, he didn't know what was.

He looked around the charred remnants of their life, desperate for inspiration. Ridley found it in the most unthinkable place.

The boy picked up the flier advertising the Ampherian Gambit, an extremely challenging marathon of surviving in the harshest environments and hunting for the deadliest trophies. Only the strongest of the strongest competed, and only one would win. The grand prize was 250,000 bluechips, which was more than enough to repair the roof and the furnace. Hell, it was enough to buy out both of their contracts, and live their lives the way they wanted to.

An idea Ridley had only contemplated in his dreams ignited in his mind. Its flame engulfed his whole consciousness. This was a long shot, by far the longest shot he had ever taken, but now was the time.

Ridley held up the half-burned flier to the Oz. He barely spoke above a whisper. "This!"

A few seconds of silence hovered over the room as Oz took the flier for a closer look. She looked at it and back at him. "Are you crazy? Or just trying to be funny?"

The boy wasn't so sure himself. "I'm not kidding, Oz! This can be our way out of this! Out of *all* of this. The roof, the furnace, your contract, my contract. All of it!" The more he spoke, the more he convinced himself, but the crazier it sounded.

Oz was still skeptical. "Of course that could be our way out of everything, babe. That kind of money could solve anyone's problems. But that's a contest for professional soldiers, kiddo. You aren't thinking that you can enter, can you? You'll surely get killed either by the contest or by the contestants."

Ridley grasped her by both cheeks. "Oz, if you keep limiting your thinking, we'll never get anywhere except for where we are now. I know you're cautious with everything, and hate anything that is less than a sure thing, but just for once let's take a chance and see if we win. We just might even surprise ourselves."

Her eyes filled with tears. "I'm all about taking chances, Ridley, but this isn't the same thing as gambling on a part from a junkyard. Your life is on the line here. Our life is on the line here! This isn't just some plain obstacle course. Kiddo, this is a multi-day fight for *survival*. You have to battle the animals, terrain, weather, and the final showdown is a fight to the death amongst the contestants.

"Ridley, if you lose, you die!" She looked him directly in his eye, clutching both of his hands in the grasp only grandmothers know. "And that is something I cannot live with. Your life is worth more than some fucking lame contest, and even more so than a damn blown furnace."

He knew what she was saying, but deep down he knew that this was something that he needed to do. He wouldn't be able to live with himself if he didn't try. "Grandma, we'll die anyway if things remain the way they are. If we don't work ourselves to death, living here will kill us, or the fucking Johns will. At this point, Oz, we literally don't have anything to lose. The stakes are the same no matter which way you look at it."

"I can't live the rest of my life without my grandson." Tears streamed down her face. "I just can't."

The two embraced in a tender hug. VERA joined in on the action too. Both Ridley and Oz knew the decision was already made for them.

"Besides," Oz said, breaking up the hug. "You don't have anything to fight with. You can't kill anyone by screaming 'Boo!'"

That hadn't crossed Ridley's mind. But he'd figure it out, he always did.

"Give a person with nothing to lose a rock, and they'll be the last one standing."

CHAPTER 4

Everything was pitch black. He couldn't even see his own hand in front of his face. Not that he would want to, because the floor, walls, and everything he touched were covered with slime, and who knew what else. The bandages wrapped around his body were soaked through with the nasty concoction. The odor was still unbearable, and he dry heaved every few seconds. There was no sound except for his heavy breathing, which fogged up the glasses installed onto his face.

"Not that there's anything to see," Ulysses whispered under his breath.

All he could do was keep going straight—to where, though, he had no idea—and relish that he was not being chased by a barrage of gunfire—again! The only thing that kept him going was the hope that this foul corridor would end in a somewhat safer place.

Ever since he landed in this dark mess, he'd been relatively left alone. He probably could have stayed, but experience taught him to never overstay a welcome, anywhere. As with anything, he just jumped into the first available hole he could find—which is what his old boyfriend accused him of almost daily. If this pathway led to a grinding machine or a fiery furnace, at least Ulysses would die with the comfort that he truly did what he was best at—thwarting everyone's expectations.

Since he was a child, all his parents ever really told Ulysses was how upset they were of him. His mother raised him to join her in the family's mining conglomerate, but Ulysses was dyslexic and unable to read the multitudes of figures on the companies' balance sheets. Despite Ulysses' best efforts, his parents blamed his ailment on a lack of commitment and focus. After spending a majority of his childhood attempting to please her and his absent father with his various exploits, from boring philanthropy to committing petty crimes, Ulysses ran away as soon as he reached legal age and eventually found his niche in the area of disruptive activism. Not only did it bring him fame, but it was the only way his parents would pay any attention to him – they watched the news constantly, and Ulysses was always in the news.

His causes took him all over the galaxy, from the swankiest resort planets to the slummiest backwaters. Despite the rumors, and more often than anyone would give him credit for, Ulysses stared death in the face more than once. A hyped political crowd can go violent within seconds, and one of the first skills Ulysses acquired after running away from home was how to use a gun. On more than a few occasions, it had been the only loyal companion he had.

Ulysses slowly crept along the dark corridor, carefully feeling his way along the blind path. He reached forward and felt the ground suddenly disappear. Before he knew it he fell face first and was sliding down at break-neck speed. His screams were silenced by a huge dollop of disgusting goo flying into his mouth. After what felt like an eternity, Ulysses landed with a crash on the slimy, hard ground. His shoulder and ribcage screamed in pain. All the poor boy could do was whimper.

Another thing his lifestyle forced him to learn quickly, despite his cushy and wealthy upbringing, was that the only person he could depend on, ever, was himself, as things changed in the blink of an eye. The boy that he ran away with those few years ago promised to be with him until "death do us part," until the Senator cut off the credit cards, and the money disappeared. Then Ulysses needed to learn how to take care of himself, starting with the basics, the hard way.

Ulysses' next boyfriend, and the love of his life, was his true mentor. Connery was an ex-SWAT with the Home Fleet, and taught Ulysses everything from how to defend himself to how to kill someone with household cleaning products. On many occasions, those skills came in handy, to both of their surprise. Disruptive activism was more than just posting on the socials and picketing for a plant closing. In order to grab the mass' attention, drastic measures needed to be taken.

For two glorious years, the couple lived a life with immense happiness. Every day, even just a trip to the transport station, was an adventure to remember. They never seriously talked about marriage, but for all intents and purposes they were inseparable. All that came crashing down when Connery was struck by a Home Guardsman's stray laser bolt during a peaceful separation protest.

Ever since that day, Ulysses harbored a deep hatred for the Cosmic Syndicate, and everything it represented. All he saw was loss, greed, death, and broken promises made in the name of "galactic unity." There was nothing unifying about killing people just because you disagreed with them.

As Ulysses slowly dragged his bruised body off the slimy floor, he could still hear the Senator's (the only way he ever referred to his father) words during their last conversation. "If it was peaceful, why was the Home Guard called to disperse the crowd?"

The sad boy wanted to strangle the man through the comm screen. "Because the public is beginning to see how fucking corrupt its leaders are, and how bloody rigged the system is."

Even now, Ulysses' insides churned with the anger of the moment, and that conversation was over a year ago.

Ulysses threw up what little was left in his stomach. He suddenly noticed how hungry he was. "Or the feeling in my stomach could be *this* shit hole," he muttered, looking around the corridor.

CHAPTER 4

Feeling slightly better, he continued slowly down the dark path.

In the year since Connery's death, Ulysses channeled his depression fully into his work, devoting virtually all of his waking hours to his cause. That left very little room in his life for a serious boyfriend, which in turn protected his heart from any potential heartbreak. Of course, there was still plenty of room for sex, yet those relationships were akin to the one with his parents; purely transactional and completely devoid of any real emotion. He had dozens of regular sexual partners, but he hasn't actually climaxed since he'd last made love to his love.

No wonder he was so pissed all the time.

Ulysses crawled along, feeling his way through the nastiness. Suddenly an acrid smell burned into his nostrils, penetrating every cell in his body. It completely overrode every other foul odor, making the man cough so forcefully that he collapsed on the ground. His lungs worked double-time to clear themselves. This, in turn, compelled his stomach to wretch, and Ulysses was coughing and dry heaving simultaneously. The pain from his muscles was unbearable.

An unknown amount of time later, Ulysses finally ceased and calmed. For a moment he thought he was going to suffocate, and the two sensations of his sore muscles and nearly dying made him cry. All the shock and trauma he bottled up from the last 24 hours had finally come to a head, and Ulysses just could not take it anymore. From his cinematic abduction from the political rally to those constant beatings from Lucilous' goons, it was a small miracle he wasn't sold like a slave! Or even raped, though he could see the fire in the eyes of some who were anxious for the opportunity.

This was not what he signed up for, and nothing that he learned could prepare him for this. For the first time in his life, Ulysses wasn't sure he would make it out alive, and he was frightened at the prospect. Despite his attitude, deep down he wanted to reconcile with his family before he died, and try to have that picture-perfect relationship, and give them someone to be proud of. He still wanted them to be proud of him, and to be proud of his accomplishments. All he has ever wanted since the day he was born was for them to be proud of him...

Some time passed before Ulysses cried his last tear and was composed enough to resume his journey. He could hear faint trampling behind him, yet he couldn't decipher whether they were real or imagined. Either way, he figured he had stayed in this one spot long enough.

Soon, he could see small droplets of light bleed into the darkness. A low hum grew louder the closer he crawled towards the light. Was he finally nearing his destination, whether it be an incinerator or air lock to outer space?

Luckily for him, it was the trash compactor chamber, which was a brilliantly illuminated room covered in fathoms of trash and discarded fluids. Even though his senses were jaded from his odorous crawl, the smells in this chamber were strong enough to make Ulysses wretch yet again.

The anti-grime coating on Ulysses' spectacles had been scratched off, yet he could clearly see an opening high above him in the ceiling. Hopefully it would lead to a safer—and cleaner—part of the ship. Although for the moment he felt pretty safe, he absolutely could not stand staying here any longer than he absolutely needed to.

At least he assumed he was in a ship, for surely Count Lucilous wouldn't take him behind the Line of Control. Even the Axis, in all its craziness, wasn't *that* stupid!

After spending a few moments dwelling on the unknown, Ulysses quickly got to work assembling a makeshift ladder. He had to reach the opening, which was at least twelve feet up, but each time the rickety ladder reached around eight feet it would tumble and send him into the nasty sewage. But the young lad was determined to make it. He had no other choice.

CHAPTER 4

After the ninth fall, Ulysses got fed up and threw a random piece of trash hard against the wall. It fell into a pile, and the pile started shaking. Suddenly, a furry creature scuttled from out of the pile, raised itself on its hind legs for a moment, and quickly scurried to another pile.

The one thing Ulysses could never come to live with in the various places were the small rodents that managed to settle in everywhere. Bugs were manageable, but animals crossed the line. He didn't even like pets!

A high shriek escaped from his mouth as he struggled to get his footing and move away as far as the piles of trash would allow. Sewage splashed everywhere, including into his mouth, but he didn't care. All that mattered was moving away from that ugly thing. In his frenzy to move, he unsettled multiple other colonies of rodents who shrieked at the sudden exposure to the bright light. Everyone was frightened at the sight of each other. Combined with Ulysses' screams, the trash chamber resembled the interior of a dog whistle.

Eventually Ulysses managed to climb atop another makeshift pile, just high enough away from those wet, furry pests. The rodents coalesced into one large group, completely covering the little trash clearing Ulysses stood in just moments before. Everywhere the man looked, he saw the yellow-eyed, clawed, screeching monsters. They were absolutely bloodthirsty.

Disgusted, Ulysses turned around and continued his assent, this time reaching a higher point before again tumbling to the clearing. Once he landed in the pile of those rodents, he immediately felt dozens of mouths and hundreds of tiny teeth biting into his skin. The bites weren't deep, yet they hurt like a mother and burned through Ulysses' flesh. He couldn't get out of there soon enough.

Ulysses returned to a high point and resumed climbing. He looked down at the rodents who were determined to catch him. It was as if they had not eaten in years and now saw their chance to feast. Once they received a small taste of him, the rodents couldn't get enough. Kind of like everyone he has ever had sex with, he thought.

The rodents quickly advanced towards the boy, making much progress in a small amount of time.

His unstable ladder collapsed once again, but Ulysses kept a tight grip and only slid down a few feet. The base of the ladder—it was more aptly called a pile—was still very much intact. Ulysses' ankles brushed the advancing pile of rodents, receiving more bites in the process.

One of the ravenous buggers clamped onto one of Ulysses' bandages and crawled up his leg, determined and on a mission. Ulysses jiggled his leg and swiped at the rodent, but it continued unrelenting. He swiped again and received a nasty bite out of his hand.

The boy screamed in pain, but rummaged enough strength to swipe again and knock the rodent off of him. With his renewed resolve, Ulysses climbed the remaining distance and jumped for the ledge of the opening. He was just barely able to grab a hold.

The pile of junk holding Ulysses finally succumbed to the growing weight from the advancing rodents and tumbled to the ground. Ulysses' legs dangled as his fingers slowly lost purchase on the slimy ledge of the opening, which was an outflow vent. He managed to swing his body which allowed him to get a little more grip.

Suddenly a large, tentacled rodent emerged from the outflow vent and slithered onto Ulysses' hands. This was a larger specimen of the legion following Ulysses, perhaps the hive queen. Its gripping tentacles were excreting the same burning and corrosive saliva that accompanied its companions' bites.

Ulysses' grip slipped as the large beast bit deeply into his hand. Another loud wail unleashed itself from the boy's lungs, and his left hand slid entirely off the ledge. The rodent let go, and scurried along his arm, biting him lightly every few inches.

CHAPTER 4

Mustering what strength he had left, Ulysses swung his left arm and grabbed the rodent from his shoulder. Its tentacles gripped with intense strength and refused to let go. Blood seeped through the bandages where the beast ate away at his skin. For several moments, the two were in a tug of war. Ulysses' strength was fading fast, while the rodents' appeared unlimited.

Finally the monster relented just long enough for Ulysses to fling it down to its family below. The man didn't take the time to watch the other rodents feast among their new meal, but hurried through the outflow vent.

The shaft leveled out and provided Ulysses just enough room to sit and not fall back down. But he was met with more, smaller rodents eager to avenge their fallen comrade. Yet their fight proved easy for the boy, and he just quickly threw them out of the shaft.

For several moments, Ulysses gathered his breath and composed himself. That was the first time he had ever been attacked by a swarm of feral animals, no matter how small. He was in such a shock that he was completely numb to the pain of his injuries, even when he looked at his hands and legs, gazing among the hundreds of bloody pockmarks. When he closed his eyes, all he could see was the swarming rodents coming for him. He curled himself into a ball and just rocked himself for a few moments. A single tear escaped his eye.

When he had had enough of waiting, Ulysses continued down his new, dark path, hoping with every cell in his body to never encounter those wretched rats again.

"I prefer Lucilous' goons; at least they don't bite."

* * *

Count Lucilous lumbered through the halls of the planet Chaffee's orbital ring, seething with fury. Everyone he looked at was incompetent and not worth the air they breathed. It had been three hours since Ulysses was last seen, or even registered on the security scanners, and the count was very impatient.

A large knot of dread had consumed his gut since he first heard of Ulysses' escape, and over time it had only grown worse and more intense. Every second that passed without any update as to that kid's whereabouts was a second closer to the count's own demise. Any minute now, his master—no, senior partner, as he tried to convince himself—was going to contact and demand a visual update on the asset, and Lucilous had nothing to offer.

While he strode, Lucilous scrambled to think of how he could cover for this. He wasn't, necessarily, a good liar, as was already evidenced, so it was useless to even try. But that didn't mean he necessarily had to tell the *whole* truth.

His impatience grew, especially at his own weak ineptitude. "For fuck's sake, I'm a politician. I should know how to talk my way out of anything."

His thoughts then crossed to the missing Specter—and Lucilous visibly shuddered. He punched the wall in frustration, sending a small shower of sparks flying.

A concerned security guard moved to ask Lucilous what was the matter. But the count shot him a death glare and ignited his sword, and in one swift movement the guard's legs were severed at the knee.

Wordlessly, a passing cadre of guards moved in and carried their ailing colleague off to the infirmary. The count was left alone to continue brooding.

Soon another officer approached Lucilous, brandishing a data pad and looking terrified. He cleared his throat. "Sir, I have an urgent message."

Lucilous continued staring at the wall.

"Your presence is required, immediately."

CHAPTER 4

Fuck, the count thought. The moment he was dreading was finally here. His insides churned. "Any updates on the asset?"

"The search is still ongoing, Your Excellency. We have multiple teams searching the complex, as well as some on their way to blockade the space lanes—"

Lucilous grasped the officer and lunged him into the wall. The utter look of fear washed over the young man's face. "Don't waste time with the space lanes, fool! Ulysses hasn't left the complex! He's not smart enough to make it out!"

Sweat poured down the terrified face. "But sir, the Specter—" The officer was cut off as the count whipped out his sword, and in one seamless move he sliced the officer's leg off below the knee. The severed leg thudded loudly on the ground while the poor man screamed in pain.

Lucilous snapped his fingers, and two soldiers came and carried the howling man away. The count turned and headed towards the sealed communications room. His mind raced to come up with something to report.

He was growing increasingly irritated with these sudden summonses. After all this was a *partnership* and he was not a servant. But soon he would be the one to demand his partner's presence.

* * *

For the first time in forever, Ulysses was thankful. The shaft he was currently crawling through was immensely cleaner than the trash compactor. A slight breeze blew behind him, giving him an extra shove of momentum. The air he inhaled didn't smell nearly as awful, and it was almost quite pleasant.

The further along he crawled, the more illuminated the corridor became. Soon he was able to make out his hands in front of him, and then he was able to see all the little bite marks dotting his exposed skin. Now that he could clearly see the damage, he could really feel how painful it was. Despite the dull ache, he pressed ahead.

Ulysses encountered a skeleton of one of those rodents, and shuddered with the memory of his last encounter. Directly above the carcass was a shaft of golden light, emanating from a small grate in the floor of the room above. Ulysses saw a lamp hanging from the ceiling, swaying gently in the breeze. Suddenly a foot landed on the boy's face, forcing him to jump back.

Obviously he was beneath some sort of populated area, but he could not distinguish exactly where. Ulysses listened but could hear no voices nor idle chit chat, just a steady cacophony of footsteps. No doors slid open or closed, so it must be some sort of corridor, and a busy one at that.

The boy didn't want to hang around long enough to be noticed, so he continued. A few yards from the first grate was a second one, considerably darker. Ulysses tried to get a closer look into this room, but couldn't see much. All he could smell was old paper and dust, and after several moments of listening didn't hear anything. This was probably a storage room, but the best part was that it was deserted!

Ulysses tried to pull the grate from its casing, but it didn't budge. He then tried to kick it out into the room with his feet, but there was something resting on it that prevented it from moving. He didn't want to press his luck too much by making more noise, so he ventured on, deciding instead to see where the tunnel concluded.

There was a long stretch of the corridor that didn't have any access grates, and the cramped space was once again pitch dark. Ulysses contemplated turning back, but was convinced to keep going when he saw the darkness begin to subside. He crawled for several more feet until the grate openings reappeared, this time directly beneath him.

The grates were just big enough for him to squeeze through, yet

CHAPTER 4

he was once again above another populated room. Two maintenance workers fussed with a gas line while complaining about their current supervisor. One of the workers grew so irate he threw a bolt which then ricocheted off the floor, and bounced right near Ulysses' view hole. Before the two could see him, the boy made a run for it.

The next grate was quite a few yards away, but surprised Ulysses when he arrived and took a look. It overlooked the female guard's locker room.

Ulysses continued along. After crawling a few more yards, he paused for a sneeze. He crawled further and sneezed again. He eventually made it to another vent, and was kneeling over it when he was struck with a hefty sneeze attack. He managed to push the vent out of its casing.

The young prisoner tumbled through the air, landing on his back with a cracking thud in a brightly lit room. Combined with his other wounds, the pain was quickly growing unbearable. Cold drops of water bounced on his face. Soon his entire body was soaked, and he felt... cleaner?

Ulysses opened his eyes and saw a large metal showerhead; the source of the cold water. He was immediately startled by the dozen pairs of eyes staring down at him.

He was in the *male* troopers' locker room!

Men in various stages of undress looked upon Ulysses with a mixture of amazement and curiosity, though mainly confusion, since it wasn't everyday that someone fell from the ceiling in the middle of a shower. Ulysses shared the feeling, and in very different circumstances he would have loved to be in his current predicament. He was, of course, going to take advantage of the situation, but not at all in the way that he wanted.

Ulysses immediately shot to his feet, punching one of his onlookers in the neck. Another half-dressed trooper lunged at him, but the boy narrowly dodged in time. He then ripped off the man's towel and whipped it around another trooper's head and pulled that guy to the floor.

Another soldier caught Ulysses from behind and tried to pull him off his feet, but the boy was strong enough to hold his own and instead scooted his attacker against the wall. The soldier tried to wrap his foot around Ulysses' but the boy managed to knock his attacker's head into the tiled wall, rendering him unconscious.

One trooper tried the same towel trick on Ulysses, but didn't get the angle right. Ulysses grabbed the towel and pulled the man towards him, kneeing him in the stomach and then again in the nose.

For one thing, Ulysses was proud of himself, considering he couldn't really see anything and was running on fumes of pure adrenalin.

While the boy was mentally patting himself on the back, another man grabbed his neck from behind and strangled him. Ulysses' blurry vision suddenly grew darker, and he flailed his limbs hoping to make contact with his attacker somewhere.

He managed to get in a few hits on the legs, but the man's grip continued squeezing Ulysses' neck. He could feel his consciousness fading quickly. He found one of the man's eye sockets and jabbed it with his thumb as hard as he could.

The man screamed in pain, lost his grip and collapsed to the floor. Ulysses gave him one last kick in the face and made a break for it, running as fast as he could. He reached the end of the room-length shower and turned a corner. He was suddenly met with a clothesline to the chest and slammed to the floor.

When he was finally able to open his eyes, Ulysses saw stars, and a fully armored trooper. The cerulean armor twinkled in the misty room, giving an angelic aura to this harbinger of death. The trooper lifted Ulysses up by the throat to eye level. With all of his strength Ulysses kicked and punched, but the poly-durafiber armor made the task futile. The boy punched at the armored throat, which mildly stunned the trooper, but not enough for it to relinquish its grip.

The muffled sounds of wet footsteps filled the space as the others joined their colleague. Ulysses continued pummeling the armored throat, bloodying his knuckles, but the trooper was still unfazed.

The armored man turned to leave the room, but Ulysses' leg was wrapped around his which, combined with the slick ground, made the trooper lose his footing and fall, losing his grip. With that, Ulysses was able to make an escape, running right through the approaching troopers and out of the shower area.

He wound up in the locker room, which thankfully was vacated. Some of the lockers were left open, no doubt by people who rushed when Ulysses fell from the ceiling.

Ulysses spied a rifle and quickly seized it. With this, the deck was more evenly stacked. There was also a full suit of armor, but Ulysses didn't have time to change as the footsteps rushed behind him. He quickly grabbed an ammo clip and hid behind the corner of one of the lockers.

Once the first man entered Ulysses' line of sight, he released a tremendous volley of fire. Immediately several troopers fell to the floor. Amongst the cloud of gun smoke and concrete dust, a slew of rounds careened towards Ulysses.

The firefight continued for several minutes, eventually stopping when the troopers needed to reload. Ulysses took the advantage of the reprieve and dashed out of the area through the back, moving past the bunking area and out into the corridor beyond. The sound of footsteps following him grew louder, and Ulysses released the rest of his clip, just holding down the trigger and blindly firing behind him.

Smoke filled the narrow corridor, giving Ulysses just enough cover. More troopers rushed towards him; he could hear their footsteps. Small explosions erupted out of the wall as shots rained from both directions. The boy snuck behind a nook in the wall, which concealed him just enough to let the oncoming troopers run past him.

Taking advantage of the distraction, Ulysses slunk along the shadows for several yards along the hallway, hiding whenever he encountered anyone. Thankfully the complex was designed with sharp angles and redundant pillars, giving the place plenty of shadows. He passed the mess hall and the armory, and considered reloading his empty ammo or even grabbing some light armor for a disguise. Yet he concluded it was better just to keep moving.

Not to mention that with as much trouble as it took to get him here, Ulysses didn't think Count Lucilous would let his goons kill his new toy.

Once the coast was clear, Ulysses crossed into another hallway. He still had no idea where he was, let alone where he was going, but sensed that this was the right direction. So far his gut had led him to the right places, and there was no sense to stop trusting it now.

He was also surprised that for a complex this large there weren't any direction signs. Perhaps the Axis were smarter than advertised, or this was indeed a small ship.

The hall was completely empty, for an unusually long amount of time. Only the hum of the superstructure and the various machines dotting the surrounding rooms provided the only sound. Even the rooms Ulysses encountered were locked and sealed tight.

The corridor curved, and Ulysses hesitated before continuing. His gut churned, and he suddenly had the feeling that this was a bad way to go. He trusted his instincts, which told him to go this way, yet now they were telling him he was going the wrong way. But if he returned the way he came, he would encounter some of the people he just ran away from. He didn't think they would kill him, yet, but he knew they were just waiting to return the beating he gave them in the shower.

"Now ain't this a rock and hard place," he muttered to himself.

CHAPTER 4

Steeling his nerve, Ulysses ventured forth.

Suddenly the faint sound of talking came towards him. Ulysses leaned as flat as he could against the wall, hoping he would blend into it and whoever was talking wouldn't see him. He remained completely still.

Several seconds passed and no one walked by. The faint voices were as faint as before, which meant they weren't moving. A room must be up ahead.

Carefully, Ulysses crept up the hall and found an open doorway. He peered inside and saw a large communications room, with a grand conference table and hologram projector. One of the voices was Lucilous, who was conversing with a large hooded figure on the projection screen. The conversation was likely important, as the hooded man sounded heated and on the verge of losing control, while the count sounded afraid.

Luckily the room was full of hiding places, and Ulysses quickly scurried beneath the far end of the conference table to hide, and eavesdrop.

"And I'm confident that once we dispatch every trooper, the Specter will be apprehended." The count's voice was trembling, and Ulysses could tell he was doing his best to hide it.

"Why did you lose him in the first place? Don't you know how to keep control of your domain?" The hooded voice was seething with disappointment. It was frightening, even to the boy who didn't know who he was.

The count was quickly losing this battle. "Of course, my liege. I'm capable of controlling what is mine. All I can say is that after the asset's arrival, I was understandably distracted—"

"Understandably to whom?" the hologram growled. "All I understand is that you failed me. All I understand is that my disappointment in you cannot be overstated."

"Yes, my lord," Lucilous sounded on the verge of tears.

"Kill the Specter before he meddles with our plans any further. Each moment he's alive is another moment closer to our failure. I am sure you don't need to be reminded of what will happen if you allow the plan to fail?"

Lucilous audibly gulped, nodding his head slowly.

The hood lowered slightly and silently stared at the count. Even from Ulysses' position the anger was apparent and intimidating. Who was this person? And how important were they that they could threaten Count Lucilous, let alone bring him to tears? After all that man, feeble as he may seem, was the leader of the Axis of Republic Systems, and quite an accomplished businessman in his own right, and he was by no means an easy pushover.

Venom unleashed from the screen. "Show me the asset."

Lucilous once again gulped, but this time his hands fidgeted also. Now he was no longer scared, but nervous as well.

"Yes, um...well, my lord..."

A steady growl rumbled from the screen. "Don't tell me you can't drag that pestilent child out of its cell? For fuck's sake man–"

Lucilous seemed to finally find his nerve. He nearly yelled when he spoke. "My lord, I cannot transport the asset unless it's unconscious. Which is not what my lord wants at the moment."

Another, louder, growl erupted from the screen. Everything, even the specks of dust, remained still, afraid to anger the hooded thing even more.

The voice was laced with poisonous ice. "I will be arriving soon to personally inspect the asset, as well as to ascertain your punishment."

The screen clicked off.

Immediately as the darkness engulfed the room, Lucilous broke down and sobbed uncontrollably.

Ulysses sensed that whatever he just witnessed, the count's troubles extended far beyond looking for his sorry ass. That person, if you could even call it that, was very disappointed in the count, and not afraid to show it. It was quite pathetic seeing the powerful man betray just how weak he truly was, and Ulysses trampled the urge to sympathize with him. Instead he focused on taking this chance to take the Axis leader permanently out of the picture.

Ulysses quietly emerged from beneath the conference table, brandishing his rifle. There was only one shot left in the chamber, and this was the perfect time to use it. He silently moved into range and lined up the perfect shot. He pulled the trigger, and nothing happened.

Hearing the faint click, the count's sobbing ceased immediately. Without looking back, he lifted his head and placed his hands clasped behind his back, a professor prepared to give a lecture.

"It's a pity that even with all of humanity's technological advancements, we still have to deal with gun jams." The pity in the count's voice was replaced with a sinister amusement.

Seething, Ulysses raised the rifle to strike Lucilous in the head. In one smooth fluid motion, Lucilous turned around and gracefully extracted the rifle from the boy's hands. The count offered a deep, throaty laugh.

"Yet humanity will remain the same, always expecting the opponent to play along," Ulysses replied.

Lucilous gracefully smiled and swung the rifle at Ulysses' head, knocking him to the floor. He slowly walked to the boy, clicking his tongue and bending down until he was within centimeters from Ulysses' nose.

"You know, staying with me was the safest option. He'll do everything in his power to get you to do his bidding. I was at least going to kill you. But the Archon will make you wish that you were dead."

With that, Ulysses was knocked unconscious with his own stolen gun.

*　*　*

Elation flooded through Lucilous. Finally something went right, and he could check one thing off of his to-do list. His ass was no longer in complete danger, and he could take a–*single*–breath of relief.

As much as he had wished, though, this didn't really improve Lucilous' circumstances that much. And despite how he'd like to believe it, the Archon would not consider this a success by any means.

Just once, Lucilous wanted that creature to give him his just desserts. To offer even a mere semblance of congratulations for how hard he's worked, and how far they have come together. None of this would have happened without his resources, and the Count was getting tired of the Archon not acknowledging that.

Despite Lucilous' protests, there was nothing he could do to change the fact of the situation;

That fucking Specter was still missing, and that was really all that mattered.

CHAPTER 5

The pain he felt was an entirely new level that he had never before experienced. What began as a minor annoyance had since intensified into a full-blown battle of will. Mycroft was stuffed into a storage cubby in the cockpit of a space freighter. He didn't know how long he had been in there, nor did he know how long he had left to remain. All he knew was that every bone and joint in his body was cramping with intense pain.

Mycroft's small, cramped hiding hole was located directly above the navigation console, where the two pilots navigated the freighter to its unknown destination. The Specter was amazed that no one needed to retrieve something from this cubby. When he defied his own expectations and squeezed into it, all he saw was a smattering of paperwork.

The majority of the ship was devoted to transporting hazardous materials, with only the cockpit safe for human breathing. The compartment was not insulated at all, so Mycroft could hear everything. Yet he was surprised at how silent everything was, with no conversation at all amongst the two pilots. It was as though they wore silencing helmets, or weren't allowed to speak at all.

The monotonous silence was broken by a shrill alarm, violently beeping for attention. Suddenly the ship shuddered and dove headfirst. Inside his cubby, Mycroft was thrust about while outside the pilots busied themselves with pulling the levers and punching the buttons necessary to initiate the landing sequence. Several moments later, the freighter landed with a thud at its final destination.

Mycroft's heart raced in his chest, with both exhilaration and fear. On the one hand he was finally glad to leave his cramped quarters, but now came the difficult part—sneaking out and determining where he was. He started running through the checklist of what to do when one is lost behind enemy lines. There was no easy way to do this, and every option that he could think of all led to the same conclusion.

He had just finished completing the first bullet point on the checklist—assess the immediate location and present peoples—when he tumbled out of the compartment onto the floor of the cockpit. Relief immediately flowed through his outstretched limbs, no longer confined to the cramped compartment. But his relief was soon flooded over with a blast of cold shock as he fully realized his new, current circumstances.

Two helmeted figures gazed at the Specter behind large, dark, insectoid-like goggles. They wore radiation-protective jumpsuits that covered every inch of their bodies, and they had large mouth-coverings that allowed them to communicate amongst each other without anyone eavesdropping.

Mycroft had just enough time to mentally mutter a "No wonder," before the two of them turned into a flurry of swirling motion.

Within a split second, the three were dashing about the cramped cockpit, fighting for their lives. One of the pilots brandished a small stun blade and menacingly swung at Mycroft. The Specter grasped his cape and twirled it into the pilot's face just as the knife was thrust in his direction. The maneuver made the pilot drop his knife and gave Mycroft just enough time to dodge the lunge from the other, larger pilot.

With the two pilots distracted, Mycroft reached for one of his side

CHAPTER 5

pistols. His shot was deflected as the larger pilot accidentally backed into him, and the bullet pierced the wall. There was a fire extinguisher mounted in the corner, and the Specter used it as a club, wailing it into the back of the large pilot.

The hefty man was unfazed and elbowed Mycroft in the stomach. He then turned around and pulled out his own, larger, stun knife. Clearly, he was a man used to his size and not used to being evenly matched, as he left himself wide open. Taking advantage of his opponent's vulnerabilities, Mycroft swung the fire extinguisher at the pilot's head, knocking him to the ground.

The other pilot managed to retrieve his knife and renewed his attack. The cramped space was made even smaller by the large unconscious body of the other pilot laying on the ground. Mycroft's cape ripped from his suit and he couldn't pull the same maneuver again. The pilot lunged, but the Specter swerved just in time.

The two continued their melee, with the pilot lunging but Mycroft dodging just in time. The Specter tried to kick the knife out of his opponent's hand, but there just wasn't enough room. He tried to grab one of his own various melee weapons tucked into his clothes, but the pilot was better trained than its opponent and didn't leave the Specter any room to attack.

Mycroft miscalculated and dodged the wrong way, landing directly into his opponent's strike zone. The knife plunged into his shoulder, sending a charge of electricity throughout his entire body. For several seconds, the Specter was frozen in place, convulsing. All he could taste was blood.

The attacker grabbed his co-pilot's knife and was about to thrust it into the Specter when Mycroft mustered enough strength to counter the move. He was then able to pull the knife out of his shoulder in just enough time to keep the attacking pilot on the ground. Mycroft drove the knife into the pilot's back.

He thought the fight was concluded, but the larger pilot on the floor was no longer unconscious and grasped the Specter's legs, pulling him to the floor. Mycroft lost his knife and tried to kick the goon into loosening his grip, but the hefty man wouldn't budge. Instead the large brute stood and twisted Mycroft's leg, trying to pull it out of its socket.

The Specter flailed around, trying to grab anything that he could use in his defense. His hands grasped a control lever, pulled it out of its housing, and threw it at the brute's face. This stunned the man just long enough that he lost his grip on Mycroft's leg. Mycroft launched to his feet and started laying down a volley of punches. The two sparred for several moments, injuring each other but not enough to conclude the fight.

Mycroft was able to land a punch that knocked the wind out of the large brute. He then grasped the heavy opponent and shoved him into one of the screens in the navigation console. The cramped space was filled with the smell of burnt flesh and hair, and the fight was finally concluded. Peace returned to the smoky cockpit.

"I was shocked to see you too!" Mycroft quipped as the brute's large body collapsed to the floor.

After giving his shoulder wound a minor field dressing, the Specter examined his body and found only minor bruises. Unfortunately, the expensive outfit was completely torn to shreds. He hated that outfit, but felt a little bad that he ruined it. Perks of the job, he supposed.

Mycroft quickly changed into the smaller pilot's uniform, and noticed when he took off the helmet why the two were so silent; their mouths were sewn shut and there were scars gracing their throat, indicating their tongues had been severed as well.

A heavy air came over Mycroft. Such was the life of an Axis slave, he ruminated. And a brutal one it was. The poor wretches were robbed of their abilities to act, speak, or even think for themselves, as they were subject to intense mental conditioning. All they knew how to do was to follow orders, and make sure nothing impeded that task.

The Specter placed the helmet on his head, and was once again met with a heavy silence. His job just became that much harder. Since everyone didn't talk, that meant everyone knew exactly where they needed to be and when. He was about to step into the bowels of a perfectly run machine, and not knowing at all what he was supposed to do or where to go would mean that he would stick out like a sore thumb.

Perhaps the slaves developed their own sign language and he could pick up on it. He took a last look at his two attackers on the floor and shook that idea from his head. He blew that chance when he killed his two teachers. And even then, how would he be able to learn enough to get to a transport vessel, let alone one going in the direction he needed.

Many questions and few answers consumed his thoughts as the Specter exited the ship. The first and foremost being that he was grossly unprepared.

The spaceport was a cacophony of organized chaos with freight, cargo haulers, and workers crisscrossing the vast area with industrial precision. Lines of people and freight sliced through the space in an unstoppable grid, ceaselessly pursuing their destination. Hundreds of cargo haulers landed and took off, delivering and retrieving hundreds of tons of cargo. The number of containers and uniformed workers was limitless.

Aside from the clanks from the heavy machinery, there wasn't a voice to be heard. The workers moved about their tasks with robotic precision, not needing to communicate with each other. For a brief few moments, Mycroft wondered whether he was looking at humans or robots.

"Shit," Mycroft mumbled under his breath. Deciding not to hesitate any longer, the Specter proceeded down the boarding ramp.

He walked no more than a few steps when he was intercepted by a pair of workers. They carried themselves with an air of authority, no doubt deck-officers wanting to inspect the ship. They gestured with their hands in some sign language that Mycroft didn't understand. The Specter remained cool and simply nodded and waved for them to proceed. Apparently this sufficed and the two officers proceeded inside the ship.

Realizing it would only be seconds before the inspectors discovered the two dead pilots, Mycroft walked away quickly. He joined the closest line of moving people and assimilated as best he could.

As best as he could observe, all the lines of people and cargo moved in predetermined lanes that did not waiver or deviate. It was like an expressway, with some workers exiting to join other lines or at the assorted work stations. Mycroft tried his best to not look obvious that he was observing, but it was difficult with the limited view of the helmet. He saw the workers bantering with each other in the same sign language as the inspectors, but what they were saying was still a complete mystery.

The gloved hands of the workers moved so fast, gesticulating beautifully an unknown joke or a long-winded complaint about their boss or family. Mycroft tried to watch what they were saying, attempting to pick out any common or repeated gestures. The Specter was trained to recognize all the official hand languages of the Syndicate, but naturally he wasn't interested in keeping up with his practice. The only repeated gesture he for sure recognized was the universal wave of goodbye.

Suddenly a loud siren blasted through the precision, disrupting the routine. Mycroft was quickly sucked out of his trance of watching hands and bumped into the person in front of him. The line he was in came to a complete standstill. He looked around the vast industrial space, hoping to see the source of the alarm—and hopefully an escape route.

With Mycroft's head frantically turning, he was the only one moving. Everyone else, even the cargo haulers and ships, remained perfectly still.

A soft-spoken voice carried underneath the siren into Mycroft's ears. Only through his Specter training could he even hear the faint noise underneath the siren. "It is the hazard emergency siren. Stop moving."

The Specter's head continued moving, this time looking for the source of the voice. It was the first time since he'd run away from Count Lucilous that he'd heard another person talk, and he was desperate to discover the source.

The mysterious voice spoke again. "It is the hazard siren. That means something is loose and for everyone to stand still."

It wasn't anyone nearby, at least as far as Mycroft could tell. But he couldn't distinguish whether anyone else could hear it.

Feeling that the risk was worth it. Mycroft whispered, "Where are you?"

"In here, underneath the canopy."

The canopy was an arm's length away from Mycroft, and it covered a large crate. The Specter's gut wrenched; of course some of the cargo would include slaves.

Mycroft reached out and touched the crate, hoping to make at least finger-contact with his new rendezvous. "How do you know what that siren is? Who are you?"

"You must remain absolutely still," the muffled voice continued. "You are very noticeable moving your head, and do not look like a worker here at all. I should ask you the same thing, dear sir."

It never failed to amaze Mycroft how people were able, even in the thick of danger, to be wiseasses. And naturally he was always the lucky one to encounter them. "And how do you know I can't report you to the inspectors and have you neutralized for violating the hazard siren?"

"Because without my intervention you would be the one to get neutralized," the disembodied voice spoke from the container. "We are the latest batch of subjects to begin working in the surface plants on the planet Chaffee. However, we have been here for ninety-three hours, forty-seven minutes, and eighteen seconds, and have heard that emergency siren fourteen times."

The person's voice had an odd, modulated rhythm to it, and it answered Mycroft's question a bit too accurately.

The Specter was in the midst of asking if the voice knew of a way out when the incessant siren finally ceased. The silence was welcoming, albeit brief as another whistle chirped through the air. The lines of workers and cargo immediately resumed their tasks as though they had never paused. The emergency was over.

Soon, another alarm blared through the air, this one deeper and more menacing, and a new group of boots spilled onto the platform. Troopers.

Mycroft had a feeling that this was the alarm he was waiting for. The troopers fanned out amongst the platform, hunting.

The voice beneath the canopy spoke, in a matter-of-fact manner. "You are in trouble and need to get out of here fast. You are the one they are looking for."

The Specter was amazed again. Whomever he was speaking to was either an asset, or a hazard. "You know, for being in a crate, you sure are observant. Alright then, do you have a way to help me?"

"Yes I do. If you run you will only call attention to yourself. Stay here and look like you are repairing the crate. There is a ripped seam that is rapidly spreading, and is liable to allow us all to escape. When the real workers arrive to remove the crate, follow them as they leave the spaceport and into the market square. From there you can run to where you need."

Mycroft could only continue to ask himself, who is this person? "Why are you helping me?"

"There is nothing else for me to do," the voice said flatly. "No one in here will talk to me, anymore."

The Specter was going to keep a keen eye on this one. There was more here than the voice was letting on, but there was no time to delve into that right now. Mycroft had to take all of the hints he could. He proceeded to fiddle with the crates and canopies, making it look like he was securing the cargo.

The troopers moved about the unceasing lines of workers and cargo, cutting through the traffic and heading directly for the ship Mycroft departed. Half of them continued inside while the rest scoured the platform for the culprit. The searching troopers lifted canopies and overturned bins, hunting furiously.

The voice inside the crate started screaming at the top of its lungs to be released, complaining they and their companions were being grossly mistreated. Mycroft smacked the crate a few times, playing his part as the brutal prison guard, when a trio of troops approached the crate and shot a few rounds at it. Everyone inside it, including the voice, screamed in fright. Mycroft himself jumped in fright and automatically reached for a wrench to defend himself, but it wasn't necessary.

The troopers' mouths were very much functional and they taunted the slaves in the crate. "Ahh shut up! You spooks aren't gonna last too long anyway. Except for the few of you hot enough to fuck your masters."

The other troopers laughed and added their own spins to the comment, which caused them all to laugh even more. They fired a few more rounds near the crate and moved their attention to Mycroft, who stood waiting for the fight to break out. He lowered his wrench, trying his best to look feeble.

The lead trooper poked Mycroft in the stomach with his rifle. "And just what do we have here? A mineral worker was reassigned to the slave ship? Strange. Show us your credentials."

Blast it! Mycroft didn't even consider that the pilot he commandeered this from was a specialized worker. His brain moved at a thousand miles an hour, thinking of what he could do. The Specter recalled that both of the suit's pockets were empty when he changed into it, and there wasn't any code token attached anywhere else. Frankly he didn't even know what the bloody things looked like.

After several awkward moments, Mycroft decided that not reacting was the best reaction, so Mycroft remained unresponsive. His hand inched back closer to the wrench, slowly and out of the troopers' sight.

"C'mon now, dammit. Show your bloody code token!" One of the other troopers slapped the Specter's shoulder with his rifle.

Nearly losing his balance, Mycroft gestured to his ears and shook his head. He waved his hands frantically, gesturing towards the unrepaired crate. He picked up the wrench and proceeded to return to work.

"Shithead's got a bad transponder. Typical," a trooper chuckled.

The main trooper shouldered his rifle and used the sign language all of the workers were supposedly familiar with. Mycroft remained focused on his task, carefully sneaking glances to find the nearest exit.

The guard signed again, more forcefully and impatiently. The second trooper shoved him with his rifle, and the Specter grabbed it, and countered the shove by heaving it into the trooper's gut. The other two quickly moved in to apprehend the man, but Mycroft swung the large wrench menacingly.

The two standing troopers were in shock. "This isn't a dock pilot. Quickly, call for backup!"

A three-way melee began. Mycroft made contact a few times with his wrench but it was only a few moments before the troopers started shooting. This grabbed the attention of the other troopers who moved closer to the commotion.

Mycroft was able to deflect a few shots with the wrench. The heat of the shots made the metal tool too hot and the Specter threw it at his attackers and ran into the gridlock, which was unceasing despite the loud fight.

The shots followed, ricocheting off the miscellaneous cargo and equipment. Some workers in the moving lanes were felled by the shots, and their colleagues behind them didn't stop to acknowledge them, but just continued on with the work. Stacks of crates and boxes were toppled and exploded, showering their disintegrated wares all over the cargo platform.

The Specter swerved in a serpentine pattern, making his way to the entrance gate. Beyond the towering wall enclosing the vast industrial veldt was the densely shadowed metropolis of factories beyond. There was no more guarantee of safety out there than in here, but Mycroft had no other direction to go. That was the only entrance or exit if one couldn't fly.

As he got closer he saw a swath of troopers move in, enclosing the exit. A half-dozen stood in a firing line with their rifles raised. Mycroft dodged behind a moving loader a split second before the shots screamed across the platform, killing a few workers and disintegrating another batch of cargo. The shots continued as Mycroft ran past the loader and behind a pile of stacked heavy metal crates.

The nearby workers didn't take too much notice of the hiding Specter, who was panting frantically. For a brief few moments the shots seemed to be at a standstill.

"Man, I wished my sword worked," Mycroft quietly breathed through his mask. He peeked above the crate to find a new path and a new shower of shots ran over his head.

"Can't go that way!" The Specter took another glance and dashed to his right, intricately threading his way between hiding places and dodging shots. Unfortunately he was heading back the way he came, towards the rear of the platform, where the ships and machine repair shop were located. There was no exit back there, as the cargo platform was on the edge of a deep, craggy ravine. Only one exit would keep you alive.

Shot after shot rang out behind him, pecking closer and closer to his feet. The hiding places were quickly disappearing as the Specter continued carving his path. He took refuge behind a stack of repulsor-block casings, which wasn't very sturdy at all. In the split second before the stack evaporated into a thousand pieces by the troopers' fire, Mycroft spotted his getaway and went for it.

He dashed into the repair bay unnoticed and snagged a portable blow torch resting on the workbench. It was the closest thing to a weapon he could grab without having to look. Then he climbed into the cabin of a ground-freight carrier, which was one of the largest pieces of machinery in the repair bay.

A large, complicated dashboard lay dormant in front of him, full of a hundred knobs and buttons that did....things. Mycroft found the starter and turned it, but nothing happened.

He looked up, noticing that the carrier's loading arms were still hanging on chains. Mycroft took a deep sigh. "I hope you're fixed and not waiting to be, my darlin'. Now how in the hell do I turn you on?"

By now the troopers had caught up to Mycroft in the bay, and were furiously shooting at the freight carrier, which effortlessly repelled the attack. The piece of equipment was essentially a giant suit of armor, with two long grasping arms capable of carrying 50 tons. As long as the troopers continued using their small-arm fire, Mycroft would be just fine.

CHAPTER 5

Undeterred by the shots, Mycroft continued pushing random buttons and pulling random levers in an attempt to bring the rig to life. He found a set of four pedals at his feet, but was still unable to make any progress.

He looked up as a shot ricocheted off the windshield, leaving a giant carbide smear. Mycroft gazed out to his side, and saw a trooper attempt to pry the door open. The Specter tried to barricade the door, but the trooper succeeded. The trooper got in and tried to pull Mycroft out, and the two engaged in a tug-of-war over the trooper's rifle.

A few bolts emanated from the rifle, but only shot holes through the thick windshield. Mycroft's ears rang with the loud volume in such a small space and he could no longer hear a thing, but he continued holding his own. The Specter grasped his blow torch and sprayed directly into the trooper's eye port. The trooper collapsed out of the freight carrier's cabin, and Mycroft got to keep the rifle.

As soon as the one trooper left, another barged in from the other side. Another fight and tug-of-war ensued, with the trooper having the advantage of attacking Mycroft's rear. The armed figure managed to position his rifle over the Specter's neck and pulled his airway closed.

Mycroft punched and flailed his arms, trying to get purchase on his attacker's head. As his vision darkened due to the lack of oxygen, Mycroft kicked his feet wildly. In the midst of the scuffle, either the rifle or Mycroft's foot hit the correct switch and the freight carrier rumbled to life, immediately lifting a few inches of the ground on a nice cushion of air. The cabin and dashboard erupted in a flurry of beeps and lights.

Mycroft kept kicking as he struggled to take a breath. His vision was nearly completely black and he was losing consciousness. He grasped the rifle and pushed with all of his strength against it, but it wouldn't budge. His foot kicked another button, which closed the doors. In a split second there was a light shower of blood and a loud crunching noise as the door sliced Mycroft's attacker in half.

The rifle at Mycroft's neck went limp, and the Specter slithered his way free. He scrunched his nose at the gruesome sight.

"Get your own bloody taxi."

Now that the fight was concluded, Mycroft had to teach himself how to operate this lumbering vehicle. Meanwhile a barrage of troopers attempted to enter the freight carrier, but were unsuccessful thanks to the rig's automatic locking mechanism.

In the few moments that Mycroft spent teaching himself how to get the machine moving, the troopers at the entrance to the repair bay had set up a large tri-barrel cannon and aimed it at the rumbling rig.

The rig began moving when suddenly the roof of the cab blew off in a fiery ball. The troopers immediately reloaded the cannon. Mycroft had barely missed losing his upper body.

"Damn, what a bunch of hotheads."

Mycroft steered the freight carrier in the direction of the gate. The giant thing easily obliterated the cargo crates and work benches in its path, and made mincemeat of the pitiful barricades the troopers had set up. The large machine cut through the lines of production like butter, throwing the well-organized order into absolute chaos. The shots continued following the machine, but all they did was bounce off the heavy plating. The freight carrier was virtually unharmed.

The firing squad at the gate procured some of the same tri-cannons as their colleagues in the repair bay. The three large barrels pointed directly at the Specter's head. Mycroft jammed the accelerator as fast as it would go and ducked under the dash.

The shots landed on the rig's front loading winch, sending the apparatus into an enormous ball of flame, which traveled along the body of the freight carrier. One of the linkages to the arms caught fire, and one of the two large loading arms collapsed to the floor. Despite the damage, the cab remained intact and Mycroft was unharmed.

CHAPTER 5

A few moments later, the rig struck the entrance gate barrier emitter, sending the machine into a cloud of sparks. The yellow laser barrier, which can disintegrate anything that passes through, extinguished, leaving the path free and clear. The firing squad couldn't get out of the way, and disintegrated amongst the flames.

The freight carrier escaped the cargo platform and made its way down the main boulevard of the metropolis. Various refineries and factories lined the street, while various sized vehicles clogged every lane of traffic. The sun tried to shine through the thick smog, but was barely successful. There was never a sunny day on the planet Chaffee.

Despite the fire burning along the severed arm connection, the freight carrier traveled rather well, as though taunting the vehicles on the road just to prove it can still function. Inside the cabin, the ride was as peaceful as in a luxury yacht. Mycroft didn't feel any of the bumps or collisions at all.

The Specter sat up and stared out the windshield. For the most part, the freight carrier remained in a straight line with no influence on Mycroft's part. The scurrying vehicles swerved and collided with each other to avoid crashing into the large machine, which was clearly the largest vehicle on the road. For the briefest of moments the Specter was able to relax.

Ahead, another large cargo hauler turned onto the boulevard, its 100-foot long trailer stretched across the entire road. The other vehicles slowed to a stop to give the hauler enough room, yet Mycroft's rig was barreling straight ahead.

Mycroft took over the controls, but they were unresponsive. All of the Specter's relaxation disappeared and he was engulfed with a sense of panic. Collision was imminent.

"Blast! Apparently you aren't indestructible, my friend."

He kept trying with all his might to move the control yoke, but the damn thing wouldn't budge. The Specter tried to maneuver the vehicle towards a group of speeders in an attempt to use them to slow the rig down, but the freight carrier was determined to maintain its trajectory.

Through the blue and pink flames emerging from beneath the hood of the freight carrier, Mycroft saw the cargo hauler get closer. The hauler itself and the rest of traffic slowed to a halt as the signals above the boulevard indicated a train was approaching.

The Specter panicked and reached for the door to jump out, but it was sealed shut by the intense heat emanating from the front. He kicked at the window, but all it did was crack into a web-like pattern.

The Specter was trapped.

Ahead, the barriers raised around the track, flashing their warning about the speedily approaching train.

All Mycroft could really do was wince. "This is going to hurt."

In seconds, the rig met the rear of the hauler, sending it forward to jump the barrier and collide with the train. Both pieces of machinery met in a loud explosion of smoke and molten metal. The parts of the hauler's cab that didn't immediately disintegrate upon impact flew through the air and landed on a group of waiting vehicles. The force of that explosion rippled through traffic, and was strong enough to send Mycroft's rig sliding across the boulevard, coming to a dramatic halt by crashing into the chemical extraction center lining the street.

The smoggy atmosphere was further clouded by the final explosion of the train crumpling and colliding with a nearby smelting facility.

The smattering of witnesses who were watching the traffic jam were in absolute awe at the sight. Suddenly their ordinary day turned into something to talk about.

The crowd barely recovered before another explosion erupted from Mycroft's crashed rig, engulfing the chemical extraction center in a barrage of purple flames.

The troopers from the landing platform reached the wreckage at the same time as the fire and emergency crews. The task of extinguishing

CHAPTER 5

both large fires and the dozens of small ones took the better part of 18 hours, during which time no one was concerned about finding any survivors. When everything was all cleared, the rig and most-everything around it was an unrecognizable mound of molten metal. The train was a metal interpretation of a used snakeskin, no longer useful and only a fraction of the size it used to be.

The troopers searched everything and everywhere and found no escaped pilot amongst the wreckage.

CHAPTER 6

The dusk sun cast a gorgeous purple and orange pallor over the planet Chaffee. The geometric shadows cast by the industrial metropolis created beautiful and meticulous visual sculptures on the surface, lending the area a macabre attractiveness, with the rusted and grime covered machines lending to the aesthetic.

A dozen blocks from the crash site, an old dockyard foreman shuffled into the alley, loaded with four heavy bails of waste. He grunted with each step, as the pain coursed through his old, tired joints.

He approached the dented and rusty dumpster and dropped his bags with relief. The dumpster was too tall for the man, so he climbed on a stack of unused crates to be able to reach the door to open it. After a few attempts, the man heaved open the door. The smell was unbearable, and a few of the trash rodents scattered away at the sign of light.

The man left the ladder and heaved two of his bags into the dumpster. As he was heaving the third, one of the bags flew out of the dumpster. The foreman was flabbergasted, but grabbed the bag and threw it in once again, thinking nothing of it.

He proceeded to heave in the third bag when both bags flew out of the dumpster. The foreman rubbed his eyes in surprise. He knew the rodents were capable of immense strength, but throwing out three giant garbage bags? He had to take a peek.

The man peered over the dumpster, when suddenly a giant shadow

CHAPTER 6

quickly approached him and engulfed him in darkness. Startled beyond belief, the poor old man clutched his chest, lost his balance, and fell off the unsteady pile and crashed to the floor.

The black mass emerged from the dumpster, covered in an amalgam of trash. The mass let out a deep, hoarse wail as it collapsed to the ground. It was the epitome of every monster that is featured in children's bedtime stories.

The mass laid motionless for a few moments, then wiped its face clear. Mycroft breathed heavily through his charred pilot's mask, which instead of filtering out the stench, contained it close to his nostrils. He ripped the mask off and relished the cleaner air. His lungs worked overtime, having been nearly suffocating for 36 hours.

After catching his breath, he stood up and assessed himself. What remained of his gray flight suit was a molten black mess. It was a miracle, even to him, that he made it out of the wreckage unharmed. The collision blasted out the window, giving him the perfect escape route to make it to this dumpster. His hair was now full of unmentionable liquids, and every joint in his body hurt from being in that cramped dumpster.

He moved the kinks out of his jaw. "If only my nose would stop working, this wouldn't be so horrible." Mycroft nearly gagged when a gooey substance made its way into his mouth.

It was the most unbearable smell he had ever experienced. Worse than the time he infiltrated the despot battle station, in one of his first assignments as a Specter.

Slowly, but still faster than his body wanted, Mycroft rose to his feet. Try as he might, he couldn't help but let out a painful grunt as he stood. A weaker sound entered his ears, calling out to the Specter.

Mycroft turned and ran to the foreman on the ground. The man's face was turning a deep shade of purple, and he clutched his chest. A trickle of blood dripped out of his nose, and he struggled to take a full breath.

The Specter proffered the man a bright and generous smile and grasped the man's hand. "My savior! I don't know how to thank you. Certainly giving you a fatal heart attack was not what I had in my mind."

When the man looked at Mycroft's smile, his eyes were no longer fearful and looked upon the Specter with a warm sense of relief. He took comfort in knowing it was not a mutant rodent but rather a hiding human. It was as though that fact alone was going to make the man's crossover much easier.

The man's hand released his chest and caressed Mycroft's face. The two shared the intimate connection that exists when one witnesses another's final moments. The two gently smiled at each other, with the man winking subtlety.

"If I was thirty years older, you'd have to run from me," Mycroft responded, causing the two to chuckle.

The man's laughter transformed into a violent coughing attack. Speckles of blood covered Mycroft's hands as they warmly clutched the dying man's. Tears caressed slowly down Mycroft's face. The man pointed to the bulge at the side of Mycroft's waist—his sword.

A defeated look crossed the Specter's face. "I'm afraid she's out of commission. Believe me, I would if I could, mate."

The light flickered in the man's eyes. Mycroft was doing everything in his power to keep himself together. He was so overcome with emotion.

It was a natural part of the life of a Specter to have to kill for mission success. Thousands of hours of psychological training and technical exercises were required for each member, but frankly weren't necessary. When one views killing someone as a mission objective, each Specter was numbed to the act by their third victim.

But dealing with a collateral damage killing, one which resulted

CHAPTER 6

due to a mistake or via completion of another mission, was *not* in the training and the most difficult to deal with. Each time Mycroft encountered this situation felt like the first time.

A Specter's purpose is to control the flow of events and consequences without revealing themselves or the mission. Losing this control, even for a micro moment, leads to more situations the Specters must insert themselves in, compromising the immense security of their make-up. The Specter's success relies on their secrecy being maintained, and the less chances of that secret being exposed, the better.

Simply put, Mycroft was trained to never have to do this.

He looked deep into the eyes of the man, tears flowing down both their cheeks. The man's eyes silently begged for the Specter to end his misery immediately.

Mycroft looked up at the twinkling stars breaking through the dusk. His eyes burned with tears of anger. He stole one last look at the man.

"I'm very sorry, Old Boy. This might hurt you now, but it will hurt me forever."

The Specter closed his eyes and whispered an ancient prayer, the only semblance of any of the ancient Scriptures that Mycroft bothered to remember from his Specter teachings. He encountered the prayer in one of his ancient studies classes, and it stuck with him for reasons that the Specter could not explain. It just comforted him to offer some sort of farewell to those leaving too soon. He didn't know if it worked, and he certainly didn't feel any of the intended religious sentiment, but for some reason his gut just always told him to say it.

Once Mycroft finished reciting the prayer, he twisted the man's neck. The Specter felt the expected subtle pop, and then the body he held went limp.

Unable to contain his emotions any longer, Mycroft broke down sobbing. He clutched his new companion tightly like he held his husband in his final moments. The similarities between the two instances were too numerous to ignore. The Specter felt like he was reliving that moment again, right now in this odorous alley in an industrial metropolis. It was at this moment that he cursed himself, for being the only survivor; for being the murderer; for having to exist in this realm; for being a Specter; for telling his superiors that he was capable of this mission; for failing himself.

After an indeterminate amount of time, the Specter finally stopped crying and fell into a sleep for a few moments, finally allowing his troubled soul to get some rest.

In the distance, a loud boom shook the night, throwing the Specter out of his emotional trance. In a split second his conscious replayed everything that happened up to that point, and Mycroft jumped up to action. He crossed himself with the gesture borrowed from the same place as the prayer he recited over the old man, and dragged the body behind the dumpster. In a flash of inspiration, Mycroft exchanged outfits with the old man. The troopers were searching for a runaway pilot, not some old hobo in dirty, threadbare fatigues.

Once he changed into the outsized clothes, which were thankfully cleaner than the flight suit, the Specter bid a final farewell to his new companion and marched out of the alley, just another person slumming his way through life.

The night had fully set in, and the warm globes dotting the avenue gave off barely any light through the thick smog. Mycroft walked amongst the shadows, careful not to draw too much attention to himself, and to act like a local. This was a small residential district, and thankfully there was hardly anyone in sight.

Mycroft passed by a stand on the corner. The owner was loudly hawking a disgusting looking animal skewered on a stick. The Specter's stomach growled intently at the sight of even the essence of food. It had been hours since he'd eaten, and he was starting to feel weak.

CHAPTER 6

He almost approached the stand to buy one skewer, when a passing industrial vehicle's exhaust backfired. The loud blast startled Mycroft, as it resembled a blaster shot, and the Specter sped away as fast as he could.

The Specter turned another corner and encountered another main street. This was the brightest area of the entire industrial metropolis. Blast furnaces, factories, and plants lined the road. Inserted in any sort of nook and cranny they could find was a smattering of shopping stands and store fronts, selling everything from spare parts to interesting knick-knacks. The sidewalks were not packed, but significantly busier than anything Mycroft had yet seen. It was here that he looked out of place, as most everyone around him wore some sort of uniform or safety gear. Mycroft almost looked like a tourist.

Another loud explosion ripped through the air followed by a large ball of flame reaching into the sky. One of the gas exhaust towers behind a processing plant was engulfed in flame, and large pieces from the superstructure billowed to the ground. Streams of people, in various stages of panic, ran away from the inferno. Within seconds, a squadron of fire trucks arrived at the scene.

Interestingly enough, the firefighters weren't wrangling any equipment from the truck, but wrangling some of the poor souls running away from the blaze. The workers were no doubt slaves, and getting hastily reassigned from working in the factory to suddenly saving it.

Mycroft was just across the street, witnessing this terror. He turned to run away from the blaze, hoping to use this distraction to his advantage. He looked for a speeder to steal and made towards one, when a heavy blow struck him over the head.

Within a split second the Specter was thrown to the ground, staring at the business end of a rifle.

A deep voice growled at him. "Damn, Spook! What are you doing all the way out here?"

"Looks like we got another runner," the other firefighter sneered. He bounced a crowbar threateningly in his hands.

The first fireman clicked his tongue. "We don't like runners, especially when there's such a large conflagration just across the street. Don't we, Tamor?"

"Right-o, Hudson. We don't care for runners at all. Makes things harder than they need to be." Tamor touched Mycroft's forehead with the crowbar, and pressed it hard into the Specter's skin.

Mycroft attempted to struggle, but Hudson cracked his legs with the rifle. "Ooo, lookie here, Tamor! The little myx likes to squirm! We'll just have to fix that then."

Tamor released the crowbar from the Specter's head and whacked it across Mycroft's legs as well.

Mycroft screamed and kicked, fighting back as hard as he could. The fight was short-lived, however, when the firemen hit him over the back and smashed him in the gut.

"This one needs another tongue burned out," Tamor commented.

Hudson spat in Mycroft's face. "Fucking myxs. Great in bed but otherwise nothing but problems."

The two firemen dragged Mycroft to the edge of the inferno, near the other slaves fighting the raging blaze. Scantily clad slaves ran about, gathering hoses and douse foam canisters from the firetrucks. A few of the poor souls were already charred to a crisp, collapsing right where they stood. As soon as one fell, another slave was shoved into its place.

Rather than immediately join the front line, Mycroft was thrown into a locked van. Apparently this was some sort of reserve corps that wasn't immediately needed. A few of the other slaves rushed to the greet the newcomer, but they immediately realized he was not one of them, and retreated back to the shadows without so much as a mumbled greeting.

CHAPTER 6

The Specter took a few moments to gather his breath and assess his surroundings. He couldn't see anything, as his eyes hadn't adjusted to the pitch darkness, but he could hear faint whispers. He figured at least a half-dozen people were with him. Pain erupted throughout his whole beaten body, but he could not lower his guard.

Suddenly, a loud shout erupted through the van. "It is you!"

The surprise outburst startled the Specter, and he jumped and slammed his head into the ceiling. He still couldn't clearly see much, but he could definitely hear a plodding footstep rushing towards him.

Within seconds, Mycroft saw a pair of glowing light blue eyes staring at him. They were bright enough to illuminate the contained area, and the beaming smile on the wearer's face.

Mycroft immediately recognized the man's voice—it was the same one from the landing platform container. The Specter didn't know whether to be nervous or relieved.

"Me? It's...you?" Mycroft was still unsure about this guy.

"Correct! And I am pleased to tell you that I am unharmed!" The man—boy was a better descriptor, but he appeared too old—looked Mycroft up and down, occasionally poking him with a cold finger.

The Specter seized the boy's wrist, which was strong, cold, and felt unnatural, even though it was real skin. "Just what the fuck do you think you're doing?"

The young man was not shaken at all, and remained oddly too calm. He spoke in a tone that implied the question was silly. "Giving you a medical check of course. A rudimentary one, I am afraid, but it still detects all the common maladies one might be inflicted with in this environment."

He tried to move his wrist, but Mycroft's grip only tightened as the Specter's suspicions rose. "Who in the hell are you, anyway?"

The boy ignored the Specter and instead frantically looked him up and down with his glowing blue eyes. The eyes roved around so fast that they were a swirling blue blur.

Mycroft grabbed the boy's throat and slammed him to the ground. The others within the container slunk further away from the fighting couple.

The Specter screamed at the top of his lungs. "Stop whatever the hell you're doing. Just what the fuck *are you* pal?"

The boy wasn't as out of breath as he should have been, nor did he seem afraid. He picked up the conversation exactly where he left it. "And I am happy to announce that you too, are relatively healthy. But medical attention would soon be necessary for your concussion, and two of your spinal discs are almost fully herniated."

The other slaves in the van crammed into the far corner, trying to get as far away from them as possible. Clearly they didn't trust the man with the glowing eyes either.

The young man continued. "I am Elio. What is your name?"

There was something odd about Elio's voice. It wasn't necessarily artificially modulated, but it sounded like it was speaking in three different tones simultaneously.

Mycroft only grew more confused, which exacerbated his anger. "What the hell are you?"

Without hesitating, Elio responded, "I am currently pinned to the floor by a stranger holding my neck. This is no formal greeting I am familiar with, though I admit to not knowing the customs of every culture in the galaxy. It is actually quite uncomfortable."

It was becoming increasingly apparent to the Specter that this man was not normal. "You aren't human."

The blue eyes just blinked at him, calmly and expectedly.

Mycroft shook Elio's head. "Well?"

"Yes?" the young man queried.

The Specter's frustration mounted. "I said you aren't human!" He screamed a bit louder.

"I heard you, as well as everyone else in this van. And probably the people outside, since you are screaming so loudly." Elio spoke in a very matter-of-fact tone. "But with the fire and other ambient noise, the firemen most likely did not hear what you said."

Mycroft lifted Elio's head and slammed it to the floor repeatedly. He couldn't grasp what was going on here, but he was getting frustrated at the games. All he wanted was a fucking straight-forward answer, and this was the first person he encountered that was moderately helpful. The Specter was not afraid to beat the answer out of this...thing if he had to.

When the beating was finished, Elio looked annoyed and slightly uncomfortable, but didn't appear to be in any pain.

This frustrated Mycroft even more. He got within centimeters of Elio's face and screamed, "Are you a robot?"

Elio remained silent and his glowing blue eyes remained blank for a full five seconds before answering, "Not exactly."

Before the Specter could continue his questioning, the van's doors burst open. Two firemen reached into the van and grabbed the first pair of bodies they grasped—Elio and Mycroft.

"Time to refill," one of the firemen snickered as he dragged the two men into the night.

Even from the distance of the van, the heat from the fire was intense. The exhaust tower was nearly completely destroyed, and the fire spread to engulf the entire facility. The effort from those fighting the fire was not enough; almost half of the original fighting force had been depleted.

The two men were taken to a fire truck and handed hoses and foam canisters.

"Now go put out the fire," one of the firemen patted their back and sent them on their way.

At the front line, the wall of fire was an intimidating tower of rage.

Glowing embers of the exhaust tower's superstructure careened to the ground, crushing a few unlucky souls. Mycroft navigated the obstacle course of debris and dead bodies, careful to avoid the flying sparks as well. The closer he approached the conflagration, the more he could feel his skin singe. His lungs burned with the inhalation of the countless acrid chemicals floating amongst the embers.

Firemen were scattered throughout the line, shoving the poor slaves closer to the inferno, and death. One gave the Specter a shove, nearly throwing him to the ground.

Elio stuck to Mycroft like glue, only he didn't need to be encouraged and happily trotted closer to the flames. He was not too affected by the intense heat, and actually seemed to be enjoying the experience of discomfort.

"The fire has expanded forty-three percent since our relief van arrived," he said. "Nothing we can do alone will put it out. We might as well run into the flames! It would be a better way to use our energy, frankly."

Mycroft turned away from the flames and looked towards Elio in awe. "Do you always have a comment to make?"

Elio looked genuinely confused. "What do you mean?"

The evidence was too apparent to ignore. Robots were rudimentary machines that were capable of performing simple, specific tasks such as manufacturing and construction. No one had yet developed an artificial intelligence that was even remotely comparable to human functionality. The best AIs in the galaxy were still only capable of answering basic questions and sorting through prearranged algorithms.

Mycroft now knew that someone, somehow, was able to integrate a robotic intelligence with a human brain. And the result stood next to him.

"Are you going to answer me, or continue this staring contest?" Elio inquired.

CHAPTER 6

Biting back a retort, Mycroft embraced his circumstances for what they were and asked a serious question. "Do you know where the closest ship to us is?"

Unbothered by the sudden shift in the conversation, Elio just blinked. "Of course, it's approximately twelve thousand yards south, southwest of us, in the asset processing complex."

The inferno flared, and a large sword of flame shot out into the night. The large tower buckled under its own weight, and toppled over like a broken toothpick. A large cloud of dust, dirt, and ash ballooned out of the ground. No one could see past a few inches in front of them. Reinforcements were brought in to control the blaze, which continued to grow despite their best efforts.

Elio rushed to join the new offensive, but was held back by Mycroft. "Take me to the ship."

"But we have to fight the fire," the young man protested. "That is our main priority."

The Specter's grip on the boy's arm tightened. There was no time for this. "Not mine, it isn't. I have to get out of here, and you're going to have to come with me." At least as far as the ship, then he might have to kill the poor lad.

Realization flooded Elio's face, yet it still remained rather stoic. "You are not from here. You are not a pilot, nor are you a slave. It all makes sense now. You are on the run from someone! And you probably have someplace important to be! Now if you do not mind me asking, just who are *you*, sir?"

Mycroft was taken aback for a moment. The man was right. Mycroft had demanded so much information and assistance from this...Elio, yet he had barely given any in return. The Specter admitted that Elio had been helpful since they met, and the least he could do was offer some information.

"Listen, I'm Mycroft," the Specter truthfully admitted. Lying wasn't worth it, just yet. "But we don't have time for me to tell you everything. Can you just lead me to the ship, and I promise I'll explain everything you need to know?"

Elio paused, not entirely convinced. "But why should I go with you? How do I know that you are going somewhere safe?"

The Specter's irritation grew. Precious time they didn't have was fleeting. "Any place can be safer than here! Look kid, the choice is yours. Trust me and come with me, or stay. Do you really want to stay here? Surely you have a home to go back to?"

A roving fireman came by and harassed them for not working. After shoving them closer to the flames, the man started beating them with his rifle. Mycroft managed to slam his head with the foam hose, and Elio grabbed the fireman's rifle.

As soon as the guard hit the ground, the conflagration flared again. Another piece of the structure fell to the ground, trapping a half dozen firefighting slaves underneath. Everyone in the immediate vicinity rushed to save the people trapped underneath the large piece of metal.

Taking advantage of the opportunity, Mycroft and Elio ran unnoticed towards the processing center.

* * *

The entire local trooper corps was assembled in the military launch hangar in the habitable ring orbiting above the Planet Chaffee. Each trooper stood at attention, dressed to precision in their gleaming armor, and listening intently.

At the head of the room was Count Lucilous, slowly and menacingly pacing back and forth. He passionately addressed the assembly, frequently gesturing towards the six people kneeling before him. They were the six garrison leaders of the Trooper Corp, all handcuffed and hanging their helmetless heads in shame. The firing squad stood close by, awaiting their cue.

"Unlike the Cosmic Syndicate, we the Axis have no tolerance for failure. We only have a tolerance for excellence and accomplishment. Everyone in this room is here because you all have the capacity to accomplish everything. You were all placed in your roles because you always demonstrate excellence. You were given this assignment under the specific expectation that you ALWAYS succeed!"

"But, Your Excellency," one of the kneeled leaders protested.

Count Lucilous kicked the disobedient soldier hard in the back. "Silence! The Axis has no room for charity cases and no tolerance for empathy. We are aiming to align the stars to greatness, and each failure is one more distraction for our limited resources. If failure is permitted to permeate throughout the organization, our entire existence can be compromised. Only by excising the infection can we ensure it will not be repeated, and we can remain on the path to greatness."

Rather than summoning the firing squad, the count ignited his ethellite sword and held it high above his head. He was going to personally deliver this lesson, so that everyone would understand that only success will be accepted.

He looked down his nose at the scum before him. Some of them were fully crying. Pathetic. The Axis never showed weakness. He spat on the blonde head beneath his sizzling sword. "Any final words?"

One trooper replied, "We deserve this, for we earned it."

The count smirked. He truly enjoyed seeing people learn the lesson. All of their lives were in his hands. "Yes, you do."

In a single and smooth acrobatic move, Count Lucilous's sword sliced the heads of the six guilty garrison leaders. The light bounces of the bodies hitting the hard ground punctuated the demonstration. The air in the hangar was heavy with dread, tension, and fear.

Lucilous loved this. "Unfortunately, their realization does not correct the mistake."

He dismissed the troopers and made his way back to the command center. The ten-minute power trip was a nice reprieve, but it wasn't enough to release the tight knot of anxiety in his stomach. The count had made as much progress finding that little shit Ulysses as he did in locating the Specter. And his partner would be imminently arriving to personally examine Ulysses...

There was another lesson to be taken away from his demonstration; all of his trooper's lives were in his hands, but his life was not at all in his control.

As the count entered the command center, one of the planetary surface operations officers rushed to speak to him. She was clearly worried and her voice trembled. "Sir, we have a problem."

Lucilous grew immediately annoyed. He always addressed his subordinates and the public with the collective we, for everyone was invested in the Axis' success. But the Axis failures were an individual problem that needed to be dealt with. "You mean you have addressed the problem and are apprising me of the situation. Now, what is it?"

"The central exhaust complex combusted, sir. The safety seals finally shattered like we warned."

The count remained silent, gravely staring at the officer.

After a few moments, the officer weakly asked, "Sir?"

"I'm still listening for what the problem is," Lucilous yelled.

Flustered, the woman continued. "Well count, our production will be held back for months until we can—"

He grasped her neck and pressed her against the wall. "You interrupted me for this?"

The officer tried not to show how terrified she was. "No, Your Excellency. We have an unauthorized take-off from the asset processing center."

Lucilous paused and turned, looking deep into the woman's eyes.

CHAPTER 6

"It could only be..."

The count whisked away to the security office, allowing the officer to collapse in a heap on the floor.

* * *

"I do not like this."

Elio and Mycroft sat in the cockpit of a small slave ship. It had been over ten minutes since they took off, yet they still had not left the atmosphere. The planet's airspace limited all ships to trolling speed, making any hasty escape rather difficult. To make matters worse, the ship's interspace controls weren't operating. Now the two were frantically rewiring the controls, which neither of them really knew how to do. Apparently, the escape from the fire to the hangar was the easy part.

Elio was crouched beneath the cockpit control board, providing Mycroft some light as the Specter spliced different wires together.

A spark shot through the wires and burned Mycroft's finger. He yelped in pain. "Fuck! To tell you the truth, kiddo, I don't blame you." He licked his sore finger. "Our escape has so far been too easy. No one's contacted us on the radio or anything. Odd."

Elio was searching around, the soft blue from his eyes casting a soft, pale pallor over the cramped space. "What? Oh, no I was talking about the layout of the controls." The young man's attention returned to the control board. "The shield diffuser is located next to the forward battery launcher, and the throttle is way out of arm's reach from the control yoke. I am going to find out who the designer was and give them a scathing product review. This is absolute madness." Elio reached for the ship's data manual and vigorously searched for his answer, abandoning the Specter.

Mycroft asked himself for the hundredth time already why he let this...*creature* come along. His original plan was to kill the boy once he reached the hangar, but the young man had risked his life twice to help him, and that meant a lot to Mycroft. The kid even gave him a rudimentary medical scan. It didn't seem fair to trick the poor boy with false hope. And his new companion had proved immensely valuable when the two encountered the state of the interspace unit.

The Specter didn't know what he was going to do with his new friend, given the nature of his assignment. Perhaps he would knock the kid out and leave him on some outpost somewhere in the corporate sector, but he couldn't think about that at the moment. Like everything else, life will eventually sort out, Mycroft hoped.

Right now though he was glad Elio finally found something to occupy himself with. The silence was a welcome reprieve.

Suddenly the ship lurched from side to side, shuddering as heavy blaster shots pounded into the hull.

Mycroft smiled to himself. "The other shoe is finally dropping."

For the first time since meeting the Specter, Elio seemed surprised. "They are firing at us!" It was as though he had never encountered this before.

The Specter roved the cockpit, looking for some sort of defense control. "Correct. Do me a favor and see if you can get the guns to fire, huh. I have to get us outta here." He returned beneath the control board. The ship shuddered with a blast hit and he smashed his head, screaming in pain.

Elio sat in one of the two seats on the control board, deliberately studying its layout. "Why are they shooting at us? We are on an Axis ship in Axis space."

"They aren't that stupid!" Mycroft dropped his wiring and sat in the pilot's seat. He gripped the controls and forced the ship to perform acrobatics it was not designed to do. More rounds flew into the ship's hull, but the quick maneuvers reduced their effectiveness.

CHAPTER 6

The slave ship was mercilessly pursued by four spit fighters, with speed and agility far superior to its weak prey. The chase continued above the twinkling lights of the industrial metropolis, with the stars growing more visible as the ships traveled higher into the sky. The blasts from the spit fighters relentlessly pummeled into the slave ship.

Mycroft struggled to keep the ship rising into the sky while following a random serpentine pattern to avoid the shots. "Why aren't you shooting at them? I'm running out of quick maneuvers here."

Elio clicked various switches with his left hand while his right flipped through the ship's data manual. "The weapons system is disabled, but I first had to find out what I was seeing. I need to do a spacewalk to reconnect it in order to see if I can fix it." He quickly jumped out of his seat and rushed towards the exit ramp.

The Specter looked back and shouted at the top of his lungs, "No! Stay here. Leave it. We'll just have to make do as long as we can." Panic grew inside him, and he wasn't sure if he was going to live to see anything once again.

The five ships ceased climbing as the slave barge dived to evade a series of shots. The chase wound its way through the canyons created by the towering exhaust and outflow tunnels reaching above the smog layer. Mycroft drove the ship into the smog layer, which completely obscured the ground. A few of the fighters followed, and Mycroft tried to evade them but was unsuccessful. The slave barge just wasn't very maneuverable.

The Specter lifted the ship above the smog and resumed the climb to space. By this time, Elio had returned to the cockpit. "See if you can finish connecting the jump drive and program us out of here."

Elio disappeared beneath the control board, and resumed only a few short seconds later. "Done. You were almost finished."

Mycroft didn't have time to be surprised. "Start programming the navigator to get us out of here."

Elio was already keying in the commands. "Where is the target jump destination?"

A shot crossed the cockpit, blackening the view right in front of Mycroft's face. "The farthest place we can go!"

The young man once again sounded surprised. "Your plan after stealing this space ship was just to go the farthest place possible?"

After several harrowing minutes the slave barge finally exited the atmosphere, and was rapidly approaching the orbital ring. Several more shots erupted at the barge, this time originating from the ship's security systems. Soon, a half-dozen more ships joined the chase, eager to get a fresh kill.

"I guess the cat's out of the bag," Mycroft mumbled.

The ship shuddered violently as multiple shots ricocheted off the hull. A siren blared and a triage of lights erupted on the control board. The slave ship's controls started to become unresponsive.

The Specter was doing his best not to panic. "Just pick a place Elio, c'mon! We have to get the fuck out of here!"

Elio stopped entering commands into the navigation computer and looked at Mycroft. "Oh, ok, now I understand. We just need somewhere to disappear for now. Do you care which sector it is in."

Mycroft was mere seconds from killing that boy right then and there. "Choose a random one. Now!"

"You got it." He closed his eyes and randomly keyed in a destination.

More shots punctured the ship, compelling a smattering of the interior panels to dislodge and fall onto the two pilots. The Specter's view was obscured by a tangle of hanging wires.

"Forty-five seconds," Elio announced, counting down the time to jump.

The Specter ripped the obstructing panel out of his way. "We don't fucking have forty-five seconds!"

The Specter flew the barge between floating satellites, following a

CHAPTER 6

random astral obstacle course. The barge still didn't have any weapons and there wasn't any way to kill any of their pursuers without some creative flying.

The chase circled around one of the large satellites, its dish nearly a mile wide. Mycroft flew the barge as close to the large dish as he could without clipping it and killing him and his companion. There was a sudden piece of the superstructure that jutted out, and the barge just barely missed it, however one of the pair's pursuers wasn't so lucky.

"Twenty-five seconds."

A blaring alarm split through the cockpit. To add to the pair's troubles, a small fire erupted in one of the hydraulic lines within the control panel.

"That's not good!" Mycroft exhaled.

"One of the afterburners exploded. That is what the siren is." Elio moved to extinguish the fire, but he couldn't find an extinguisher, so he ripped his shirt off and fanned the flames by hand.

All Mycroft could do was keep the ship from hitting something. "Definitely not good!"

A fiery piece of the ship flew in front of the cockpit window. It was hard to identify, but was definitely large enough to not be cosmetic. Another ear-splitting alarm joined the chaos. The ship shuddered as if it rode along a rough cobblestone path.

"Ten seconds."

The ship flew a corkscrew through one of the orbital rings' support beams, which took out another pursuer. Mycroft kept trying to get the ship as far away from the station as he could to make a clear jump, otherwise they'd travel right into the ring. The pursuing fighters, however, refused to let the ship have a clear getaway, and tried to box him in.

More pieces of the ship fell off as the shots kept pummeling into the hull. Inside the cockpit, multiple sirens and alarms fought for the

Specter's attention.

Mycroft made a final corkscrew and managed to get clear enough of the orbital ring.

Deep in the bowels of the ship, the jump drive rotors whined to life, and the red corona of the interspace surrounded the remnants of the cockpit window. Soon the corona enveloped the entire ship, and splatters of interspace broke through to this dimension. Spacers called this in between the "clutch."

Within seconds there was an ear-splitting crack of matter and an immense flash of light.

* * *

In the command room aboard the orbital ring, Count Lucilous observed the chase readout on the main view screen. Blue fighting dots pursued a red dot to the edge of the radar field. The red dot sputtered after a few seconds and eventually disappeared.

Fury erupted within him, then immense fear. He was not the only one that was going to be punished for this. That much was certain.

CHAPTER 7

Mere moments after the slave barge disappeared into the black ether of interspace, a sinister and sleek looking corvette manifested itself on the other side of the orbital ring. The red corona of the straggling interspace left a living, wiggling trail in the wake of the modified guerilla ship. Despite its bulky appearance, the *Rakkis*, could outrun the best of either the Syndicate's or Axis' navy, and outgun a heavy battle cruiser. Its owner valued only two possessions, their life, and this ship.

The *Rakkis* glided quickly and smoothly through the orbital ring's space, resembling a bat blissfully swimming amongst the stars. A few of the ring's security satellites activated onto the target and prepared to fire, but once they received the clearance code the *Rakkis* transmitted every few seconds, the weapons stood down and deactivated.

An assembly of the Axis' innermost political and military personnel awaited the *Rakkis* in one of the landing hangars. Everyone was dressed in their finest livery, displaying glistening medals and twinkling jewels. Count Lucilous was with the group, dressed in an iridescent purple and black gown that was tastefully understated, not too grand yet not too plain.

Whomever the group was waiting for, they were immensely important.

The *Rakkis* silently rested on the ground, and the mood in the room immediately darkened. The count carefully approached the ship as the landing platform descended and bowed upon the sound of heavy footsteps. Everyone else bowed as the footsteps grew louder and closer. The entire hangar grew still, not even a pin dared to make a sound.

The owner of the footsteps wore heavy, dented battle armor that clearly had seen many encounters, yet was lovingly well cared for. A thick cape cascaded down his shoulders, covering a collection of small knives, grenades, bombs, and various other weapons of destruction. The figure's skin was completely covered, with a heavy, bright red cowl obscuring its face, resembling a militant monk.

The aura about the figure was both terrifying and prophetic. It simultaneously gave the impression it wanted to tear away your limbs, and then help you cope with the aftermath. The Axis leaders bowed before it because they believed it (or He?) was the Cosmos' own messenger to bring the galaxy absolution. They were specifically chosen by him to carve their own path, away from the distracting sins of the Syndicate, armed with a renewed appreciation and conviction to the "Scripted Way."

The figure before them preached that only by studying the documents believed to be created by the founders of the galaxy, the Twelve Scriptures, could one harness all the powers of the universe and live a truly complete existence. This belief was in line with the original mission of the Specters, before they were conscripted to a lesser existence.

But where the belief diverged between the figure and the Specters was in the application and use of this power, or what the Specters deemed, *knowledge*. The Specters focused on living up to the Scriptures to the best of their ability, and applying their knowledge for benevolent purposes, albeit deeply behind the scenes.

The figure, ergo the Axis, believed this knowledge was in fact a *power* that could only be utilized by a chosen few, otherwise it would be diluted and wasted away on pettiness. It was only through the careful selection of each choice could one truly achieve a meaningful existence, but that existence was only made whole if one possessed the power.

The Axis was obsessed with finding this power, and it was only through this terrifying, and compelling, prophet could they achieve it. Weakness, failure, and complacency were not tolerated.

One thing was for certain, this was not a person to cross or question.

The hooded figure stopped at the kneeling count, and spread his arms wide. He addressed the crowd with a sensual and comforting voice that carried an immense and compelling power.

"Thank you very much my friends. It is with a great honor that I finally meet you all in person, for our final chapter before Redemption. I am pleased to say that everything has gone perfectly according to the Plan, and all remain completely faithful. Faith and trust remain strong, with no doubt amongst any that our success is anything but certain."

The loud, husky voice reached every corner of the hangar, yet still felt soft-spoken. The man sounded as though he was incapable of raising his voice in anger, yet possessed a tone that implied it never needed to. His arms gracefully waved through the air, as though beaming its benevolent power to all within reach.

The speaker's face was completely obscured, yet sounded like it wore the biggest smile of gratitude in the universe.

"Now my friends, please. Rise and pay respects not to me, not to the Script, but to *yourselves* for being untiringly faithful. Without your never-ending zeal, none of what we have accomplished would have happened. And it is only through your continued perseverance that our absolution will manifest."

The crowd rose slowly and broke into a light applause. Everyone watched with rapturous attention at the towering figure before them, who even with his dark and dented armor appeared to be full of nothing but powerful and intense love.

The prophet carefully lowered his arms and lightly touched the count's forehead. Lucilous dared not to break the salute, and remained as still as his muscles would allow. His forehead burned at the sight where the gloved finger met his skin, and the count tried to clear his mind of all thoughts. The power of the prophet was being channeled into Lucilous, and he needed all that he could receive.

"*Only through faith can we achieve*," the prophet spoke so only Lucilous could hear.

"*And all who achieve are faithful*," the count whispered. His throat was dry and full of sawdust. Every breath he took was labored, and in fear.

The prophet removed his hands from Lucilous' forehead and put them at his side. "Rise, my friend."

Slowly and deliberately Lucilous stood, careful to keep his gaze directed at the ground. His entire body filled with anxiety and fear, and the count tried his best to not betray it.

The prophet stood mere inches in front of him, breathing heavily and hungrily. Even without looking, the count could sense the seething fury, a fact that was hidden to all the spectators just feet away.

The figure placed its hands on the count's shoulders, silently waiting. Lucilous slowly raised his gaze to meet the glowing eyes hidden deep within the crimson cowl.

With every ounce of strength he could muster, Lucilous loudly proclaimed, "We are honored by your presence, Archon."

The spectators raucously cheered, "All hail the mighty Archon," and erupted into a thundering applause. Before them stood their greatest celebrity, their biggest influence, and their *true leader*.

Still speaking loud enough so only the count could hear, the Archon whispered, "Like I said, without you, none of this would have happened." The menacing displeasure was obvious and unabated. His grip on the count's shoulders tightened, and the pain increased to a near unbearable level.

The Archon released Lucilous from his grasp and proceeded to the crowd, interacting and schmoozing them with his greatness while leaving the count alone to wallow in fear, anticipating the true punishment to come later, and in private.

Sweat poured down Lucilous' face as his thoughts raced at a million miles a second. Thankfully, the Archon's attention would be mostly consumed by Ulysses, which would give Lucilous a bit of extra time to get an update on the missing Specter. And he could then carefully go over each of the Axis' administrative updates with the Archon...but that would only delay the inevitable.

Hours later, Count Lucilous was alone with the Archon in his private quarters, the most opulent area on the entire station. The Archon had remained completely silent, not uttering a word since entering the room, and had remained still, staring out the window, deep into the cosmos beyond. Lucilous at first attempted to get the Archon to tour the orbital ring, and even suggested they immediately view Ulysses, but nothing broke the hooded figure out of his trance.

The count filled the silence by providing the administrative updates that he knew his partner was not interested in knowing. But Lucilous could not bring himself to sit in the devastating silence. He was currently spouting off some miscellaneous figures regarding the latest trade shipments.

"With this final shipment of THAAD missiles, we have finally reached the quota and the reserve forces are officially fully stocked. We are ready to proceed at your order, sir."

The Archon stood with his arms behind his back, staring out the window, emotionless.

Lucilous gulped, but the lump in his throat remained. Sweat poured down his face, and his suit felt like it was strangling him. Each breath he took was shallower than the last. For a brief moment, the count thought the Archon was making this happen, but he immediately dismissed that as silly nonsense.

Desperately wanting a drink, Lucilous continued through the talking points on his conversation sheet.

Just as the count was starting the discussion about the preparedness of the Axis Military Intelligence, the brooding Archon finally broke the silence.

"What was that large fire on the planet's surface? Western industrial quadrant? It's so large it's visible from space."

Lucilous cleared his throat to buy himself time to collect his words. "One of the larger exhaust towers failed, erupting into a fire which spread throughout the entire block. The firemen have identified a safety failure as the primary cause, although I predict that a full investigation will uncover evidence of deliberate sabotage."

The Archon turned away from the viewport and stared at the count. There was no other movement from the cloaked figure, but there was no denying what the creature thought.

"Why do you waste my time, believing I am only interested in the Axis' military capability? Do you think I do not want to hear about each of the other realms within the Axis?"

The count struggled to articulate the response. "My lord...I never assumed at all..."

"Wrong. You have in fact assumed quite a lot. You have assumed that I would not notice the decrepit state of the planet Chaffee's industrial metropolises. You assume that I have no knowledge of the Axis' other, hidden failures that are indeed of a greater magnitude than even you can foresee."

With each sentence, the Archon crept slowly towards the weakening Lucilous. The count was using every ounce of his strength to keep himself from trembling visibly.

The prophet's voice never rose above a whisper, yet possessed the strength of an enraged army.

"You assume I would not have noticed your conspicuous silence regarding the uncovered Specter, which I know is still missing."

The Archon was only inches from the count. He moved his arms and Lucilous collapsed to the floor, bowing as low as possible.

"I have failed you, my lord," Lucilous was on the verge of tears. "I have failed you by choosing a staff that is inept and pathetic, capable of nothing but failure. They have neglected the Axis way and have failed me, in turn failing you." He started crying, unable to hold it in any longer. He did not care at all about how embarrassing this looked.

Silently watching the pathetic escapade, the Archon's arms finished their movement and crossed in front of him. While quite abundant in patience, the Archon was not an unlimited well of it.

"The garrison leaders were executed at once, for their incompetence. And as punishment for their insubordination, no other trooper is to rest until that Specter is found." Lucilous continued spouting off words he hoped the Archon wanted to hear, yet careful not to include the highly probable fact that the bastard had escaped on a slave barge and was probably halfway to the *Imperatrix* by now.

Finally fed up with the act, the Archon grasped Count Lucilous by the throat with one hand, lifting him in the air high enough that his feet were level with the monk's armored knees. Red lightning bolts erupted from the count's body, covering him entirely like a fishing net. The man screamed loudly and convulsed with pain.

The voice that seeped from the cowl was ripe with fury, and hungry to kill. "Do you take me for a fool, you miserable being? Do you think you can hide the truth behind incompetence? Your failures began not today, but the moment I allowed you to be the face of the Axis, the moment I invited you into the faith. And your failures continue to this moment. No matter how much you try to shield behind others, your failure will always be apparent.

"Your incompetence allowed the Specter to escape. He utilized your under-resourced planetary industry to cloak your attention and slip away undetected. All aided by your negligence. No doubt a similar set of events occurred when the Specter eluded your weak grasp and escaped off the station."

The lightning ceased, but the count still writhed in pain. The one handed grip clenched the count's throat, squeezing the life slowly away. Lucilous struggled to fight the armored grip, desperately gasping for air. The Archon was undeterred by the pitiful struggle, and even less so by the count's pleas for air.

"You are a disappointment to the Script, for if you were a member of the truly faithful, you would accept the fate bequeathed you.

"Do you know why I told you to kill the Specter?" the murderous prophet queried. "Do you know why it is imperative that the bastard doesn't make it back to his headquarters alive? Because he already knows too much. What do I mean by that? Well, the Specters already have a hunch that you are involved in the senator's son's kidnapping. That alone is enough cause for your execution. They don't reveal, even under disguise, unless they're certain of who they're talking to.

"No doubt you humored his suspicions by giving him a tour, in an attempt to prove your innocence. Once again you were mistaken. In not showing the Specter what he was looking for, you *did* reveal to him the sheer size of the Axis' resources and operation, tipping our hand before we get to play it. Specters don't have to know too much to connect the dots to the final conclusion, but their failure rests in the fact they usually connect the dots incorrectly."

By this time the count's face was turning blue and his attack on the Archon's powerful grip waned. Lucilous' vision was darkening, and he felt a series of uncomfortable cracks in his neck. A hint of the familiar copper flavor of blood creeped into the count's mouth. His hearing grew increasingly muted as the last drop of consciousness sped away.

The count suddenly made contact with the ground, and the comforting sensation of rushing air filled his lungs. His throat was on fire, and his entire body felt like it was baked in an oven. For several seconds he just inhaled the lovely air, relishing in this brief moment of comfort. That was all that he could look forward to.

Towering above, the Archon clenched his fists and intently stared at the pathetic pile before him. "By seeing only what you showed him, the Specter will still be able to easily guess our plan of attack. Our element of surprise is completely shattered! The Specter can extrapolate our plan of attacking a stationary target, which his train of logic will lead him to search for a surface dome station or a land-heavy planet. Do you know, dear Count, that only a select few locations near the Line of Control fit those categories? The Colfax Shipyards, the Illunium system, LaMere Station, and the Coreenian Industrial Complex!"

The Axis' war strategy was quite simple, which made it so effective. By attacking and destroying the Syndicate's major industrial centers, the Syndicate's economy will be crippled and the main reason any of the planetary systems to remain in the political pact will all but evaporate. When the money was affected was when any real action was taken, and if the money disappeared, then so did the incentive to pool resources.

The industrial centers were the epitome of the Syndicate's cooperation, but if the shared profits dried up, that eliminated the incentive to pool resources and the allied star systems would soon realize that it is economically better to remain alone. The galactic economy would implode within days, and the pain would retaliate far beyond the economic centers of the Syndicate, affecting everyone in the whole galaxy. The level of destruction would be spectacular, unmatched by any bullet or battleship!

This was the Axis' favorite part of the Plan.

"Now, none of what is meant to be will happen, thanks to you!" The Archon delivered a heavy kick into Lucilous' stomach, punctuating the point. Another round of red lightning coursed through the count's body, compelling him to scream out in pain.

"Because of your constant need for attention," the Archon kicked the count's stomach again, "and due to your reckless carelessness," another kick in the face, "the Specters will alert the Home Fleet, who will increase their security at the targets we especially chose because they were relatively unguarded!"

The Archon gave a final kick to the count's nose and then paced the room. His breathing was heavy for a few seconds, but then grew silent as the militant monk regained his composure. He once again returned to the viewport, his arms returned to their position behind his back.

The red lightning ceased once the Archon finally calmed. Lucilous could not feel or move anything. Even breathing was immensely painful.

The Archon's tone returned again to a near whisper, resembling a father coaxing his child to quit having a tantrum. "How did this Specter introduce himself to you?"

It took several seconds for the count to muster enough energy to form a thought, let alone stand and address the Archon, and when he spoke his words were flavored in burnt blood.

"He claimed he was an ambassador from the Syndicate, sent on a goodwill tour to find any information about the senator's son kidnapping. The scans showed he was carrying no weapon, and he was thoroughly searched multiple times. He was impeccably dressed..." Lucilous let his hands fall helplessly at his side. "...Nothing about him indicated he was not who he represented he was."

A light, evil laugh emerged from the viewport, and the hooded figure shook his head slowly. "Of course he wouldn't have a weapon that appears on the scanners. 'Nothing about him represented he wasn't who he was,'" the Archon mocked. "Of course you would be taken by his performance, for you can't see anything past the end of your nose. No one who ever was truly threatening ever looked the part.

"Describe him to me."

Lucilous proceeded to give a very thorough description of the Specter. Despite his injuries, his memory was still sharp. Nothing about the Specter's appearance, from the man's face to his outfit, was forgotten or left unobserved. That was perhaps the count's greatest asset, aside from his family's vast wealth. His memory allowed him to access the innermost circles of the Syndicate's industry, for he retained those little snippets of gossip that many thought were revealed in the utmost confidence. It was amazing how valuable information was to the highest bidder.

At the conclusion of the count's recitation, the Archon placed his hand under his cowl, gently stroking his chin in deep contemplation. A deep rumble erupted from the man. "Doesn't sound particularly familiar, but quite frankly that describes nearly every one of the male Specters of that breed, for they all look the same."

The room fell silent for several moments as the two contemplated the facts before them. A sudden burst of inspiration befell Lucilous

"The Specter did mention that he was sent on personal invitation of the Primarch and Senator Pircilla. No doubt that task would not be trusted to anyone besides a close personal friend. Sir?"

The silence hung for a few moments longer, growing uncomfortable. "Perhaps we're not entirely without answers," The Archon turned to look at the count. "Ulysses might be more useful than we realize."

Memories of the intense pain coursing through his body flooded through Lucilous when the cloaked figure stared at him once again. He could feel the intensity of the glowing eyes, boring deep into his soul. The count struggled to hide how much pain he felt. "What do you mean, my lord?"

"That young man may hold the answers to this Specter's identity. No doubt he's been under their watch since his privileged life began. He's most likely seen his watchful guardians, and that's who this personal friend is, and why he was sent on this mission."

Within moments the cloaked pair were entering the small holding cell with their prized asset. Ulysses was his usual nonchalant, carefree self, despite being strapped to the chair and the numerous cuts and bruises dotting his body. One of his eyes was swollen shut, and his lower lip was twice its size when he smiled, genuinely amused to see them.

"My, my, my. Nice to see you again, Count, and so soon! And you brought friends. Please excuse me while I grab another place setting." He punctuated the greeting by scowling. The young man's voice was strong and jovial, albeit quite hoarse.

The Archon remained still, hands behind his back, not betraying any emotion. Lucilous completed the triangle, eyes darting back and forth between the two men, waiting to see what atrocities were in store and who would begin first.

A heavy silence hung in the air, its presence growing ever apparent as the seconds ticked away. The count remained silent, for if he were first to break the tension he would surely be killed immediately.

"Do you know who I am?" the Archon queried, his voice just barely audible.

Ulysses looked the hooded, armored figure up and down for a half a second longer than usual. Despite his best efforts to conceal it, he could see this was an immensely powerful man and was immediately afraid.

"No. You look like an Axis politician, or a priest. Probably just another of the count's fanatic followers." The boy struggled to look directly into the hooded face, and let out a nervous laugh. "Honestly,

I don't know what you fools see in this dolt of a human," the boy gestured to the count. "I mean look at him, he's nothing but a bunch of nerves."

Ulysses leaned in and loudly whispered, "It's the cane isn't it?"

The Archon and count looked at each other, with the former releasing a hearty, "Hmm." In one swift action the Archon ignited his sword and held it threateningly close to Ulysses' face. The boy's smirk vanished, replaced by the wide-eyed look of intense fear. He tried to move his face as far away from the pulsing line of pure, white-hot, energy.

"Oh? Nothing to say, have you?" The Archon taunted. "No more confidence? No more arrogant retorts? Afraid you'll get hurt?"

The Archon raised his sword to strike, and the boy closed his eyes in preparation. But the cloaked figure stopped the swing just millimeters from Ulysses' skin. The sword hesitated for a few seconds before singeing a scar into the pale young skin.

Ulysses had never released such a scream, nor felt this much pain. He could feel every cell being scorched by the intense energy. He tried to move his neck out of the way but had stretched his muscles as far as he could.

The white sword moved from the neck, and was swung again with a furious force that nearly struck the count's face. The holding cell was so small that even Lucilous was made uncomfortable by the blades' piercing heat.

The Archon's blade struck the panicking prisoner in the cheek, stomach, shoulder, back, chest, calf, and inner thigh, leaving a small, inch-long, burnt kiss each time. The smell of burnt skin and hair filled the cramped space, accompanied by Ulysses' howling screams.

The young boy struggled against his restraints, suffering from pain and fury. The Archon broke into a maniacal laughter, completely enamored with the macabre scene. Count Lucilous didn't know what to make of the situation. Despite his best efforts, he was not taking any sort of pleasure from the boy's pain. Granted, the kid was a piece of shit, but Lucilous could not help but see himself in that restraining chair, being slowly killed by the one promising to bring salvation to the galaxy. Lucilous tried to tell himself that this was just for Ulysses, but somewhere deep down, the count couldn't help but feel disgusted.

Laughter continued to fill the cramped space. It was terrifying, dreadful, and poisonous. "The golden child cries out in fear. The hell raiser wants his father to come and save the day. The galaxy's crusader can't handle a few ethellite cuts. Pathetic! The strength you so brazenly display is in fact nothing more than a charade, the veil to hide your true self. Beneath the facade you're nothing more than a weak pile of nothing! If only *your* devoted following could see you now!"

He lifted the boy by his throat, ripping him straight out of his restraints with a super human strength. The Archon then squeezed Ulysses throat before throwing him into the wall. He pummeled the hilt of his extinguished sword repeatedly into Ulysses' stomach, and then struck the boy in the face.

The Archon let the boy crumple to the ground in a bleeding, heaving heap. Ignoring Lucilous, he crossed to the control panel on the outer side of the door and turned a dial. The weak boy, who was naked save for a light terry cloth wrap around his waist, jumped into the air, howling in more pain as he hopped on one foot and then another. The metal floor and walls had increased to a scalding temperature, instantly developing blisters on Ulysses' skin.

The two men couldn't feel a thing through their boots, and they silently watched the naked boy hop from one wall to the other, shrieking in pain from the intense heat.

After several seconds the hooded man extinguished the heat and allowed the poor boy to once again crumple to the ground. Ulysses'

CHAPTER 7

howling transformed into a weak whimpering, barely audible among the sound of sizzling flesh. The air was filled with the thick ozone layer from the Archon's ethellite sword, and the smell of burning skin.

"Who is your rescuer?" the Archon asked in a bored tone.

Ulysses could barely open his eyes, and he was panting vigorously. It took every ounce of his strength to turn his head to face his torturer. "My what?" His voice was barely audible.

The Archon ignited his sword once again and poked Ulysses in the side, giving him a new scar just above his kidney. "Who came here to rescue you?"

"Someone came to rescue me?" The boy's voice grew just a bit perkier. "Who? I have no fucking clue. I don't even know where I am, other than in pain."

The Archon stabbed Ulysses again, this time more forcefully in the shoulder blade, careful not to drive the blade too deep. "Please cooperate. I'd hate to have to use force. Just tell me who your protectors are and you will remain unharmed." The voice from the hood was immensely calm, almost bored.

Ulysses had mustered enough energy to yell, raising himself a bit straighter. "I don't have any protectors! I haven't been under any authority's protection since I ran away from home for the third time. The only fucking attention I get from any authorities is when they think I'm in trouble. No one would be looking for me!"

The Archon remained still for several moments, growing increasingly irritated. He turned the heat in the room on once again, taking pleasure in seeing Ulysses dance the waltz of torture. After a full two minutes, the hooded prophet switched the mechanism off and repeated his question.

"I told you there isn't anybody!" Ulysses screamed at the top of his lungs. "My father never paid attention to me, even when I was on his good side, do you think he would bat an eye now that I'm missing? To him I'm evil incarnate, and he wouldn't even be paid to expend any sort of energy finding me! Fuck, he'd probably pay *you* to keep me locked here forever."

Lucilous lightly chuckled, for the first time since this encounter began. He had to admit the boy had a sense of humor, and also a point. The acrimonious relationship between Senator Pircilla and his son was famous and well-covered by the entertainment tabloids. The count would actually be surprised if the boy was lying about that particular fact.

The Archon raised his sword to strike Ulysses again, and the boy cowered against the floor. But the prophet extinguished the blade. The boy was telling the truth.

He lowered his sword. "If your father wouldn't organize a rescue for you, then who would? No one is ever totally alone, despite what they might feel. Someone in the galaxy has to love you enough to want you alive, otherwise we wouldn't be here."

Ulysses looked the Archon directly at eye level, and spoke with a strong voice full of deep conviction. "Many people want me alive, but none with the resources or clout of my father."

The Archon chuckled deeply. "Is that so? Either way that doesn't necessarily mean you don't know people who can't figure out how to be resourceful enough, or are even foolish enough to attempt your rescue."

The boy managed a mischievous smile, its effect only intensified by the scars and bruises on his face. "I've got a lot of friends like that." Ulysses looked at the two men carefully, then gazed intently at the Archon, studying every inch of the creature. "You're not just some goon of his. You're more important. You mean something."

Lucilous' fists clenched, he was incensed that even this lowlife of a prisoner would dare comment on the difference in status, no matter how perceived it was. The count stepped forward, now anxious to have his turn at torturing the loud-mouth little shit.

The Archon held his hand in front of the count, stopping him from going any further.

"Thankfully your inherited wit is undamaged." With another blow to the head, the cloaked prophet knocked Ulysses unconscious.

The two remained still, watching the battered body breathing in deep sleep before them. The air in the cramped cell was heavy with dread, fear, and anger. Not to mention the horrid concoction of smells.

After getting his bearings back, Lucilous spoke quietly, barely above a whisper. "His resistance to the traditional methods is considerable. It will be some time before we can extract any information from him. We might have to employ more creative methods of persuasion."

"On the contrary, we learned a considerable amount. His father has zero interest in his well-being, which means there's a mountain of unharvested potential in this situation. We also learned he hasn't been guarded in years, at least officially, which narrows the list of potential suspects, and obstacles."

"But he said he didn't know who the Specter was," the count protested.

"That doesn't mean anything. He wasn't lying, necessarily, but that does not subtract the possibility that he has an idea of who it might be. It is obviously someone whom Ulysses thinks highly of, despite his troubled past. And I still suspect that this savior is not necessarily the best of the Specters."

The Archon crossed his arms in contemplation and remained silent for a few moments. "If we act quickly, we might be able to lure this Specter back here once more!" There was a rabid hunger to the prophet's words.

Lucilous was growing fearful, and confused. For a man who possessed infinite wisdom, what the Archon just said was a bit silly. "Lure him back? You really don't believe that the Specter will return here for another rescue attempt? That would be suicide."

The Archon turned to look directly into the count's eyes. "No, I do not believe that. For once you are correct. That is why I am taking Ulysses with me. I will lure our prey out of hiding by baiting it. Then, like a wise hunter, I will use the dolt's own strength against him."

Lucilous erupted into a full panic. This was not at all something he had prepared for. The longer the Specter remained alive, the higher the chance of the plan failing. Which translated into the death of Count Lucilous.

"But, Your Eminence," he nearly screamed, "time is of the essence. The Plan is ready to be initiated and if anyone were to discover–"

"Which is something you should have considered before you lead us to this moment," the Archon yelled, his booming voice echoing off the cell walls. "It is only because of your carelessness that we have to use valuable resources on this in the first place! I'll take possession of the asset and weasel out this Specter. You continue preparations and contain your ineptitude. Nothing will be delayed."

"But sir–"

"Would you prefer I leave you to answer for your crimes in the middle of interspace? At least there you won't have anyone to disappoint." The Archon ignited his sword, the blazing energy filling the area with dusty ozone.

Looking at the glowing sword, the count weighed his words carefully. "I will obey your commands, my lord."

"Oh right you will. And you won't continue your trend of failure, for if you do, death will be the benefit you wish you could enjoy."

The count audibly gulped. There was no more delaying the inevitable. This was his last chance.

The Archon looked at the unconscious Ulysses, his voice once again dropping to a whisper. "This boy is the key to our future, Lucilous. He guards the entrance to prosperity and the end to our trouble. Without him, our work is wasted. Instead of grooming him, I must be distracted by finding his savior. That Specter is the Axis' prime threat. He can destroy everything and very nearly has.

"Lucilous, together right now, you and I control the fate of the cosmos. Our very existence rests upon our actions over these few short days. For your sake, pray you find the Specter before I do."

The Archon summoned a guard to carry Ulysses to the *Rakkis*, and left the count alone in the small dark cell. It was an ironic foreshadow. Perhaps, if the count had succeeded in *every* way, he might have spent the rest of his life in a cell like this. Alas, in this very moment, even in the best of circumstances, there was only one destination for the count.

He wanted to cry, but that wouldn't have solved anything nor made it better. His world was quickly coming apart, moments after it was looking as if it was coming together. The partnership between him and the Archon was clearly anything but, and even the fucking decrepit prisoner could see that obvious, painful fact.

All he could do was pray his luck would turn around. And to quit worrying about the more important question of "how," as that would only distract him from the current task at hand.

He left the cell and headed for the command bridge. As he traveled the halls, various troopers and personnel saluted him, boosting his confidence. Like the Archon said, one is never alone despite how they feel. There were always people who would look up Lucilous as the center of their world, and would always be in his corner. In fact, as he traveled the halls, the count was made more aware of just how much support he had, and this got him to rethink the balance of the partnership.

He couldn't help but smile to himself and let out a little laugh.

After all, he *always* lands on his feet.

CHAPTER 8

The slave barge glided through the interspace with relative ease, considering how damaged it was. Multiple hull panels were either severely compromised or completely missing. The engines were operating at less than fifty percent capacity and were emitting a thick smoke, and the viewport was cracked in multiple places. By all appearances this vessel was not space worthy, but like its inhabitants, it still defied the odds.

Inside, Mycroft was monitoring the status of the ship, watching each vital system go offline every few seconds and growing increasingly worried that they wouldn't make it out of interspace. His companion, Elio, monitored the navigation computer and simultaneously composed his complaint to the ship's designers for its poor layout and weak construction.

A light whistle cried for attention, and Elio studied the navigation screen intently. "That was an alert I set. We should be well outside of Axis territory now. Shall I take us out of jumpspeed?"

The specter was in a trance in the pilot's seat, intently staring at the various readouts. He mentally urged all of them to not fail and to continue working as best they could. Mycroft knew this was a futile effort, but it was really all he could do.

It took a few seconds to realize what his companion said. "Huh? No, no! Just because we're out of Axis space doesn't mean we're safe at all. What did you set as our destination?"

Elio had dropped his letter, devoting his full attention to the navi-computer. "I did *not* set one, since you told me to not to, remember! I just put us in the closest jump lane and set the barge to follow it."

Several interspace corridors crisscrossed the galaxy, creating a web of vital trade routes. They were known colloquially as jump lanes. The slave barge was currently headed into Syndicate space, but the travelers were on the very edge of it, where the gangsters and outlaws outnumbered even the traversing traders.

"Clever!" was all Mycroft could say. "We're headed in the right direction then, but we're still deep in gang territory. On this edge of the galaxy, the Syndicate only exists in small pockets, and even those can be influenced with enough bluechips."

"Shall we increase our traveling speed and select a final destination?" Elio moved out of his seat, but was waved down by the specter.

"We seem to be safe enough for the time being. Let's just stay the course for now and catch our breath." The specter felt the weight of all of his previous exploits, and grew incredibly fatigued. Even the few moments he had with nobody chasing or trying to kill him were enough to make his body demand rest.

A huge yawn escaped his mouth, and Mycroft could barely keep his eyes open. It had been nearly two hours since their interstellar journey began, and the two men spent the time finding and disabling all of the location trackers. Being that this was an Axis barge, their location was transmitted back to the planet Chaffee every few seconds. Elio managed to rig the beacon to scramble its location code after each transmission, so every few seconds the ship was marked to be in a completely different area of the cosmos, making it impossible to track.

The travelers' relief was short lived however, as the ship continued to fall apart around them, constantly shuddering as one vital piece after another broke off and disintegrated in the stars. Alarm after alarm rang, begging for attention to tell the men about the increasingly failing health of the ship. Nothing could be done, however, except pray they made it to wherever they were going.

"Will you finally tell me where we are going?" Elio asked a few moments after Mycroft closed his eyes. "We cannot just follow the jump lane until it ends. The troopers following us no doubt have already planned for such thinking."

Mycroft was too tired to get angry at the question, and even too exhausted to lie. To be honest, even he didn't know where they should go. He still hadn't found Ulysses, but did have plenty of intelligence to deliver to his superiors on the *Imperatrix*.

"Well for right now, we need to find a place that's out of the way enough so that we can lay low for a while," the specter finally said. "So why don't you scope out a couple of options that could work, huh? I'm going to rest my eyes for a few minutes. You should too, actually."

The specter tried to doze off, for his aching body desperately pined for slumber, but Elio's constant commenting on the navigation readouts made that impossible. After fifteen minutes, Mycroft had finally had enough.

"Will you please quit that?" Mycroft jumped to his feet. "There is no need to keep constantly reading the screen aloud, or to make comments on every damn thing you fucking encounter!"

The young man's face showed a hint of emotion, but his voice was as stoic as always. "I am stressed. I hyper focus on things when I feel overloaded and over-stimulated."

A memory entered Mycroft's mind. He had asked Elio about this before, but he only now had the chance to really start the conversation.

The specter calmed his tone, at least as best as he could. "Earlier, when I asked you if you were a robot, you were coy and evaded the question. Now that we're in a relatively safe space," the man held out his hands, "would you care to elaborate?"

A silence hung in the air for a few moments. Elio's blue eyes blinked slowly, staring deep into Mycroft's. "Would I care to elaborate as to why I answered that way? Or do you want me to elaborate on if I am actually a robot or not? You are a bit hard to follow, you know. You *do* need some sleep."

Mycroft took a breath and closed his eyes. All of his misery could be ended with a twist of the neck...As calmly as he could muster, he said. "Please, *please* just answer my questions! Who are you? Where do you come from? Are you a robot?" His patience didn't last until the end of the sentence.

"I was born forty years ago on the small asteroid, X311, in the Atraxis belt. I have no memory of my parents, but I can recall that the first roof I lived under was in a juice farm."

Juice was the galaxy's most addictive substance, and arguably most valuable. It affects one's mind by making them think time has slowed to a quarter of its speed, and numbed one's pain for days. There were two types, Wak, which relaxes the body to within inches of death, slowing your heart rate and breathing to twice an hour; and Yak, which gives the user immense amounts of energy and strength, keeping them awake for 180 hours straight and giving one a wild sex drive.

Manufacturing and distribution of juice was illegal, yet possession in small amounts was not, because it was so widely available. It could be smoked, inhaled, vaporized, eaten, injected, or snorted. Detecting it was impossible unless it was in massive quantities. The Syndicate government predicts the juice market alone is larger than the entire galactic economy.

Powerful gangs controlled the market, from manufacturing to distribution. Manufacturing the stuff was a dangerous process, depending on the strain and the intensity. It was a large industry with zero oversight and regulation, and many who manufactured it died in so-called "cooking accidents," as the stuff was highly explosive. The

Axis military was currently researching juice's ballistic applications.

Elio continued his story. "I quickly grew up the ranks to become the gang's top product mover. I remember being popular for going undetected, and being able to easily squeeze by when I did get caught. Another memory I have was traveling from the Ring to the Meridian in less than ten days, which at that time had never been done before."

Mycroft was stunned, and blinked his eyes several times to make sure he was seeing correctly. "You were born before the TAL? But you still look like a kid!"

The Trans-Astral Spacelane was the galaxy's largest interspace lane, connecting the Meridian with the Ethenian Ring and crossing the entire galaxy. It was the cosmos' largest construction project and took 100 years to finish. It was completed over 25 years ago, and made trans-galactic travel within five days possible. Without the TAL, the galactic economy would only be half its current size.

The young man continued uninterrupted. "During a run, my ship crash landed on a small construction outpost. There I encountered a rival gang's juice farm, and fought my way back to my ship. My last memory was them plucking my eyes out before shooting me in the heart.

"Somehow I did not die, and supposedly I was returned to my home base, and left there as a warning. The asteroid's local surgeon was the only one who believed what little life I had left was worth salvaging."

All Mycroft could do was swallow the lump in his throat. His entire body was frozen listening to this horrid story.

"Replacing and repairing the damaged limbs and tissues was the easy part. Getting my heart to beat on its own was impossible. A module powerful enough to work was not small enough to get internally installed."

The specter worked up the courage to interrupt. "That's impossible! Any medic in the Syndicate is more than equipped–"

CHAPTER 8

Elio gently raised his hand into the air. "Remember, we were not in the Syndicate. Out in the middle of nowhere, everything is hard to come by. And we could not afford Syndicate material to waste on some science project. This surgeon was not a medic at all, but the closest thing we had.

"After months of failed attempts, the man finally made it work, by splicing my heart with the capable hearts of seven healthy men. It was the only way to get my heart strong enough to withstand the bio-computer.

"But then the immense power was too much strain on my nervous system. Every beat of my heart would send me into a seizure. I do not remember much from that time other than pain, intense, terrible pain, and the heavy taste of blood. We were back to square one.

"Years of experiments, years of pain, years of failure. The sounds will haunt me forever, shadows of a pain no longer felt, yet never forgotten, and still always present." The poor young man shivered, and hugged himself. This was the closest the specter had seen him to being genuinely scared.

Emotion welled within Mycroft as he was truly moved by the story. His eyes filled with tears and his face grew warm with anger and compassion. Never did he expect this to be the answer to his question.

Despite being obviously disturbed by the tale, the young man pressed on. "My first experience as Elio occurred one hundred twenty million hours ago. The darkness was lifted from my eyes and my vision altered completely. Everything was simultaneously in and out of focus. Multiple spectra of light made themselves visible to my sight, and everything just looked and felt different. Sounds from hundreds of meters away crept into my ears as though they were occurring in my same location. My mind was no longer only mine. Memories, sounds, and images passed before my consciousness that I had never seen before. Smiles that were not directed at me filled this body with warmth. Frowns and shouts came at me from the ether of memory, yet they were not for...me.

"I knew something was wrong when the surgeon asked me to recite the year, and the planet on which we were located. Suddenly dozens of ghosts entered my head, competing for attention, and all providing a different answer to the question."

A tear cascaded down the specter's cheek, and his whole body shook with anger and a hint of disgust. "Good grief! You were fused with a computer and spliced with other people..." Mycroft's mouth hung open in sheer shock.

Ironically, this was the point where Elio shrugged his shoulders, apparently not bothered by the sheer horror. "I have identified seven hundred and fifty-nine separate entities, all compiled to make Elio- the world's first Electronically Inbred Living Organism."

All Mycroft could do in response was cover his mouth with his trembling hand.

"My creator fell victim to ill health," Elio went on, "and I was forgotten by my original family long after I first died. Elio was not completed until fifteen years after my original death, and there was no one left to take me in. My abilities and make-up intimidated everyone on the entire asteroid. No one wanted me to work for them, or be around them. Multiple times they tried to kill me and sell me as scrap metal, but the junk dealer would not pay; said it was not right parting off a dead body.

"One night, I was ambushed and kidnapped off world where I was sold to the highest bidder, who took one look at me and shoved me in the back corner of the slave cage. I only made it to Chaffee because we were traded to a rival dealer for a new ship."

The specter was a well of tears. Where many saw a freak of nature, Mycroft saw a beautiful being who didn't belong anywhere, yet desperately wanted to. Yes, the young man was a bit eccentric and clearly mentally altered, if not outright *damaged*, but Elio was really no different than any other human in the galaxy that just wanted to be part of a tribe and feel that they belonged somewhere. It wasn't the boy's fault that he was biologically, severely, different.

Mycroft was internally torn. He wanted to continue being apathetic about Elio, as that was one of the cardinal rules in his line of work. A Specter could not form any attachments in the field, as they would only lead to disappointment and heartbreak. The more he resisted, the more Mycroft's heart loved the damaged, lonely young man before him.

The Specter's original plan was to leave Elio at the first outpost they found and go on his merry way. But now Mycroft didn't have the heart to abandon the boy again. What would happen to him? He did possess skills, but no one appreciated them—Mycroft included. No doubt the poor kid would only be sold back into slavery, or worse.

But what could Mycroft do with the boy? He didn't really need a helper, although without Elio Mycroft probably would still be on the planet Chafee. But Elio wouldn't be allowed to join the Specters, let alone learn of their existence. Just because someone helped a Specter didn't mean they would get any type of special treatment.

A heavy silence hung between them for several moments, giving the men the necessary time to process their emotions.

"I never did thank you for saving me, Mycroft," Elio said. Raw emotion dripped out of his modulated, stoic voice. "I do not know what would have happened if I had stayed in that cage. We were waiting to get our tongues removed."

Mycroft had almost forgotten that the boy was just barely spared the inhumane dangers of the galactic slave trade. Body mutilation was a common practice, used as an incentive to comply with one's masters.

"Of course," the Specter responded. "But to tell you the truth, that's not the worst that could have happened to you, kiddo."

Elio smiled uncomfortably. "You are correct, but the buyers had no idea what they bought." He opened his mouth, revealing an amalgamation of organic and mechanical material. A round vocoder box blinked at the back of his throat. "My tongue is only decorative."

The Specter nearly gagged. He'd been in countless conflicts and seen numerous bodies in each stage of injury and gore, but this phenomenon was too much for him to handle at the moment. Mycroft could barely look without cringing. "You can put that away now."

Suddenly an ear-splitting alarm cut through the air, begging for everyone's attention. Another emergency. The two rushed to the control desk, eagerly searching for the genesis of this current crisis.

Reading from one of the blinking status screens, Elio shouted, "Power loss in thrusters one and three."

Mycroft had found the switch that silenced the alarm. His ears were still incessantly ringing. "Loss of what, where? Why? What's going on?"

Elio turned to the Specter and said, "The thrusters fell off the ship, Mycroft."

"Oh, brilliant," was all Mycroft could bring himself to say. The slave barge only had three main power thrusters, and if two weren't functioning...

A new sense of panic engulfed the Specter. He gripped the controls as hard as he could. Their lives depended on it. "Well, it looks like we're approaching our exit. Is there a place for us to land in this neck of the woods?"

Before Elio could answer the ship squealed and violently shook. Every light on the control board blinked, every siren blared loudly, and the controls grew increasingly unresponsive. Everything was going haywire.

The red corona of interspace disappeared, and the viewport displayed the countless stars of real space, twinkling peacefully. The ship was in a freefall, with multiple pieces of varying size breaking off the hull and engine mountings. Blazing green flames covered the entire engine bay.

Inside, the temporary peace was broken by another blaring alarm.

"Power has been completely lost in all engines," Elio announced. "And we have a major fuel breach."

Mycroft gave a nihilistic, deep throated chuckle. "Just what we need. Is there any place for us to drift, before we're left in the void?"

The young man searched through the navigation mainframe, typing faster than any natural human could. "Two options. There's a habitable ice moon or its jungle twin."

At least something was looking up, the Specter thought. "Set course for the jungle. It's harder to sweat to death than it is to freeze."

Together, with great effort, the two men were able to maneuver the limping barge to head in the intended direction. The pitiful thing limped along, slowly and precariously, across the stars.

"I am surprised we have not had a hull breach," Elio said several minutes later. "Considering two of our three engines are gone."

Struggling with the controls, Mycroft loudly hushed his companion. "Shut up! It might hear you."

Suddenly, the ship shuddered and bounced violently, lurching to the side. Within seconds the barge had turned one complete revolution and entered another one before stopping upside down. Everything that wasn't strapped down cascaded on top of Elio and Mycroft's heads, as the gravity wells failed. The loud, distinct sound of crackling glass filled the cockpit. The viewport was cracking in multiple places, slowly eliminating the thin barrier to the deadly vacuum of space.

Mycroft just turned and stared intently at Elio, who could only blink slowly in silence. The Specter was fuming. "See! What did I tell you?"

"You are frustrated that I stated an observation that was proven wrong just seconds later," the young man replied. "That is not my fault. I did not force the ship to suddenly—"

"Never mind! Just forget it and shut the fuck up!" The man's anger only grew at the fact the young man didn't fully understand a rhetorical question.

Elio's attention was brought back to the status screen. He looked at the readouts, then at the fuming Specter staring intently at the viewport. "Before I comply with your request, I must inform you that we will not make it to the jungle moon. With the fuel levels being so low and the barge's sheer lack of power...the viewport will fail before we reach the moon's atmosphere."

Mycroft sighed heavily and shook his head. "Of course this has to get harder."

The barge continued its slow, tumbling journey. The ship was close enough to get pulled by the ice moon's gravity field, but the fires and small explosions constantly erupting all over the surface only worsened the tumbling. The ship resembled a poorly thrown football, with pieces of varying size and importance falling away from it, like rats fleeing a sinking ship.

A new, smaller fire erupted directly beneath the viewport, but extinguished within seconds due to the leaking fuel. However brief, the conflagration was still hot enough to add a new series of deep cracks in the viewport.

As the barge entered the moon's atmosphere, more pieces broke away as the crumbling ship was fully engulfed in heated air. Multiple tiles from the hull flew away like a scattered deck of cards. Within seconds the barge's inner skeleton was completely uncovered and visible, with everything glowing red, pulsing with immense heat. Small fires erupted both on the remnants of the outer superstructure and within the bowels of the ship.

Inside the cockpit, the intense temperature was unrelenting. Beads of perspiration poured down the men's faces, while their clothes

CHAPTER 8

doubled their weight, saturated with sweat.

Elio seemed relatively unaffected by the temperature, but Mycroft was struggling to remain conscious, with his lack of rest mixing with the heat to make the perfectly dangerous combination.

In front of them, the viewport was a clear wall of purely intense blue heat. "One hundred thousand meters until touchdown," Elio announced.

A new lesion appeared in the viewport, punctuating Elio's announcement with a piercing shriek.

The sound was so loud, it broke Mycroft out of his descent to unconsciousness. All that met his gaze was the new crack in the window. "We might not make it."

The intense flames dissipated, giving the pilots a clear view of more pieces of ship flying in front of them. An intense draft seeped from the cracks in the window, as well as from the seams in the wall paneling behind them.

"That's a welcome breeze!" the Specter enjoined, braving a smile.

Elio's eyes flashed a brighter blue, in what was the young man's version of panic. "That is pure butane gas. It will kill us in two minutes."

"Everything always comes with a catch," Mycroft punched the control board in disappointment. "No wonder my headache was getting worse."

"Eighty thousand meters to impact."

Inside the cockpit, the air grew cloudy and thick. Mycroft was heavily panting, his lungs unable to get a sufficient amount of oxygen. His eyelids drooped as he struggled to stay awake. The air was so dense that all the Specter could see were Elio's glowing eyes.

Outside, a giant square flew in front of the viewport. A new high pitched siren added its contribution to the cockpit's symphony of death. The interspace engine was no longer attached to the ship.

The blue wall of flame dissipated and the window filled with a pure blue sky, with craggy peaks jutting above the thick cloud layer. The barge's tumbling worsened as the full gravity from the icy moon came into effect, and the ship plummeted through the sky. A heavy trail of smoke followed the flaming vehicle, making it look like an incoming missile. Once the ship dipped beneath the clouds, a collection of mountainous valleys emerged, spreading their veiny reach across the entire landscape. There wasn't a smooth surface to be found anywhere.

Inside, Mycroft was fading fast as they butane replaced the oxygen. He could barely keep his eyes open or hold up his head. Elio continued reading the altimeter and monitoring the map, still relatively unaffected by the lack of air.

The ship tumbled through the air, but still remained relatively airborne. However, it was low enough to clip the peak of one of the towering mountains. The main thruster engines sheared from the barge's main frame and crashed to the ground. The sudden loss of all that weight relatively stabilized the ship and prevented it from revolving, however the nose was now heavier than the rear, and the ship was diving directly into the ground.

The Specter finally fell unconscious, releasing what little hold he had on the controls. Elio tried to keep the ship steady by himself, but after a few moments the controls wouldn't budge, despite how hard he pulled them. Impact was imminent.

Thinking fast, Elio hoisted Mycroft over his shoulders and ran towards the rear of the ship as fast as he could. He opened a hatch leading to the rear hall and encountered a wall of flame. He hesitated for a few moments, then ran as fast as he could through the fire and jumped out of the crashing barge.

Seconds later, the ship impacted into the side of a mountain.

CHAPTER 9

Hours later, the two men were lying in a heap in a patch of melted snow. Scattered and flaming debris encased the little clearing. The pristine blue sky was filled with smoke, steam, and musty exhaust.

The first thing that Mycroft felt when he came up from the depths of his unconsciousness was the immense pain. Every muscle, joint, tendon, and nerve hurt. Even thinking about moving made him hurt even more. He finally mustered up the energy to open his eyes and was blinded by the blazing white snow. He was in a clearing, with the skeleton of the ship encasing the small area. Rubble was everywhere and he could barely move. A faint muffled noise came from across the way, deep in the shadows. The Specter's thoughts immediately went to Elio and he started panicking.

Mustering his strength, Mycroft lifted some of the rubble and cleared himself a path. It wasn't easy moving his stiff body, but within moments he was crossing the clearing in search of the sound. It wasn't occurring at regular intervals, like an alarm or siren, which led Mycroft to believe it *was* his companion. But it was incredibly difficult to see, with the scattered rubble everywhere and the dark shadows that refused to be visible to Mycroft's snow-scorched eyes.

He knew he was getting closer, as the sound was growing louder. He started moving piles around, looking underneath for his missing companion. Soon he uncovered Elio's hand, and entwined their fingers together, searching for a pulse. But the hand was motionless.

Ghost images started floating into Mycroft's mind, flooding his already fragile psyche with gruesome images of the worst. "No! No! No!"

Frantically, he ripped apart the rest of the rubble covering his friend. After an eternity, Elio was finally unearthed. The poor man's eyes were closed. His skin was charred in places, with a pronounced spot on the neck. He looked dead.

Elio was cold to the touch, which made Mycroft panic, but then the Specter remembered who—*what*—Elio was and figured he must always feel like that. Armed with the vestige of comfort, Mycroft lightly slapped his face to rouse him awake.

Garnering no results, Mycroft shook Elio. "Come on. C'mon. Give me some life here. You can't have only come with me to go only this far? We just got started."

Tears streamed down his face. This was as exact a reenactment of the death of his husband. The pain was too much for his heart to bear. Mycroft tried to keep shaking Elio, but he soon broke down weeping, rocking the cold body in his arms back and forth.

He kissed Elio warmly, apologizing for failing to make his life, at least this small piece of it, worth something. Like the rest of his body, Elio's lips were cold and dry, but his lips were the softest the Specter had ever felt.

If it wasn't for him, Mycroft thought, Elio would still be alive. The words stumbled from his mouth. "I'm sorry."

While the Specter kept weeping Elio's eyes slowly opened. They were completely black, with the soft blue outlines missing. He blinked a few times and the eyes grew to a light gray, and slowly the blue outlined iris returned, albeit only in the right eye.

The young man looked around his surroundings, taking everything in. He noticed his companion's weeping apology, and grew confused. In a husky, gravelly mechanical voice, Elio asked, "What are you sorry for?"

Mycroft didn't hear his companion, and his weeping continued unabated. Elio continued as well. "I am the one who should apologize. I was not able to steer the ship, which led to us hitting the mountain. I could not carry you through the fire, which got us to this point. Are you listening to me? Why are you still crying?"

The Specter finally stopped weeping and embraced Elio, holding him for several seconds. "Don't ever trick me like that, again! Next time just die quickly so I can hurry up and move on." Mycroft's voice was still full of tears, but a light smile slowly carved itself onto his face.

"Trick you? I did not trick you. When my core temperature drops too low, I enter into automatic shutdown. I should be okay, just a little slow moving until my systems return to normal temperature. But I will say that my left optic is completely ruined. I will need to visit a repair bench soon, and procure the necessary materials. Allow me to perform a body scan for you."

The young man extracted himself from the Specter's arms and rose to his feet. The movement was not smooth, and Elio nearly stumbled a few times. His head moved up and down as he performed Mycroft's body scan, but the Specter could hear the rotors grinding in the poor boy's neck.

Elio's one working eye flickered as it performed the scan. "Unable to complete scan. I am sorry, but I require my other eye. I am truly no use without it."

A pang of guilt sliced through the Specter's heart. All of Elio's injuries were because of him. "Well, we'll just have to jury rig something and get you back into shape, now won't we."

The warmth of the moment was completely lost on the young boy.

"Yes, we will. That is exactly what I just told you."

The Specter couldn't help but smile. His reality brightened exponentially, even though they both were still lying on Death's doorstep. Despite none of this being a part of his original intentions, Mycroft warmly said, "For once, something went right."

The men gathered themselves and looked for a clear exit. The musty air smelled of burnt flesh, which intensified depending on their location within the ship-covered clearing.

Mycroft wrinkled his nose. "Fuck man. Was that you? How much skin did you burn? It reeks."

"This smell was not caused by me," Elio responded. "There is a wild element to that smell, and it is not entirely human."

The Specter immediately found a remnant of the beast, a large chunk of hairy, scaled flesh. It was reptilian and rough to the touch. "Here's our culprit right here. Big mother." He held the piece of skin towards the light to get a better look.

"Not one!" Elio picked up another remnant, this time it was a small head, severed just at the neck. The hair, while matching Mycroft's specimen, was lighter and finer "Many! Small offspring by the looks of them. The place is covered with them."

Hundreds of small reptiles covered the floor, with bits of their mangled bodies here and there. The white snow was stained orange with their blood.

"We must have landed on a nest, or some colony," Mycroft pondered.

The snow shifted around and beneath them, as though it was alive. The ship creaked ominously, as though it could fall over a cliff at any minute. Underneath the creaking, the men could hear the faint slithering of the creatures beyond.

Elio examined his specimen more closely. "This one still has baby teeth. I think this is a breeding ground."

CHAPTER 9

More anxiety welled within the Specter. The gravity of their situation once again made itself apparent in the most dangerous way.

"Wonderful," was all he could bring himself to say. "Really, the only thing we can do is hurry and get out of here before mom gets home." He looked around the immediate area, disappointed. "We don't have any weapons, and the last thing we need to do is play with the local wildlife."

Elio unceremoniously dropped his severed head. "Oh I do not think they will be playful. On the contrary, I think the adults will be quite furious."

Eventually the men made their way out of the clearing and found the outer hull, which completely encased the area. The overcast sun beckoned them through a small hole in the ceiling.

Slowly, the men climbed, taking the painstaking journey as carefully as they could. Suddenly, a violent force shoved Mycroft up a few feet.

"Hey! Cool it down there! I'm going as fast as I can."

The force shoved him again, more violently. Mycroft lashed out at Elio, "I said cool it!"

Suddenly both men were shoved completely out of the hole and tumbled down the snow bank. A giant serpent emerged out of the snowy ground, obliterating the fragile remnants of the slave barge. It towered many feet into the air, with the hood around its head flared to the frightening maximum. The creature hissed menacingly at them, with 12-foot long fangs just waiting to devour the duo.

"See, I told you it would not be playful!" was all Elio said.

The mother snake lunged at them but they rolled out of the way just in time. Again the serpent struck, leaving a gigantic crater in the soft snow. The two once more just barely avoided meeting their maker.

The gigantic beast continued striking as the two men struggled to find cover. The ship crashed into a narrow, rocky valley and there was nigh a tree nor cutout in sight. With tremendous force, the serpent carved deep craters in the powdery snow, destroying any hope of using that for cover.

Thinking quickly, Elio led Mycroft to a large boulder and the pair climbed atop. This tricked the pursuing beast for a moment, as it continued striking at the spot they had just left. Once the beast sensed their new location, most likely by smell, it altered its attack. The beast lunged into the boulder, forcing the fragile rock to fracture. A burst of pebbles exploded with each of the beast's lunges, cascading atop the men's heads and walloping them with fresh bruises. The beast was injured by the rock as well, receiving many deep, large abrasions with each lunge.

The beast struck the boulder, cracking the large rock in half and damaging one of its eyes. This caused the beast to howl in immense pain. Its growl penetrated every cell of Elio's and Mycroft's frigid bodies, and even visibly moved the air. Then it doubled down on its attack, each strike was closer and stronger than the last. The men ran out of space on the rock, for the fighting beast cornered them.

The serpent reared back for its final death blow, a smile seemed to crack its horrid face. Mycroft and Elio looked deep into the beast's ruby red eyes, determined to look their killer in the eye. The beast dove into the attack, but out of nowhere a bright yellow blaster bolt shot directly into its chest. The beast was stunned momentarily, but it was just long enough for another shot from a different direction to land in the serpent's side.

The beast turned to attack the new front when a trio of shots punctured it from another side. The dying giant was confused as to where to attack first, but it was also too weak to keep up the fight.

It reared back its head to deliver the final death blow, but another volley of shots from all directions pierced its body, and the beast tumbled to the floor. Its bright orange blood stained the pristine white snow.

Huddled together on the boulder, Mycroft and Elio were stunned. They didn't know what to believe and looked at each other in astonishment.

"How did–?" Elio began

"I have no idea," Mycroft cut in.

"Do you think we are next?"

All the Specter could do was shrug his shoulders. "Most likely."

A breeze gently blew across the landscape, wiping the smell of freshly killed carcass in Mycroft and Elio's direction. The two carefully peered out from the shadow of the boulder, in the direction of the shots. All they saw was the empty wild beyond.

Suddenly a small boulder moved, shaking off its snow covering and rising a full six feet. A large rifle was holstered on its shoulders. It had large, black goggles and a furry hood covering its face. It walked towards the carcass, seemingly human.

Soon eight other boulders rose, turning into men and walking towards their kill.

Elio's one blue eye brightened at the view. "Oh look! Humans! We are saved!" Elio jumped and started waving his arms and screaming. "Over here! We are alive! Over here!"

Mycroft immediately pulled the boy down and slapped his hand over his mouth. "What the blazes are you doing? We have no idea if they're hostile or friendly. For all we know they could be the ones Lucilous sent to look for us!"

Effortlessly the boy pulled the Specter's hand away from his mouth. "But they killed the beast and helped us," Elio said with a confused look on his face. "How could the hunters be hostile towards us if they have already helped us?"

All the Specter could do was shake his head. Boy this kid had a lot to learn. "They are *hunters*! Just because they killed that thing means nothing! We were probably just in their way and could be next!"

By this time Elio had uncurled himself out of Mycroft's clutches. "But you have your training and weapons to protect us. We have nothing to fear."

The Specter paused for a moment, taken completely aback. He had not told Elio anything about who he was or what his mission was. How could the boy notice anything? "What is that supposed to mean?"

Elio kept trying to stand up, to once again get the hunters' attention, but Mycroft kept pulling him down. "I figured you were some sort of military as soon as you hotwired the ship. Only people with access to the high-clearance materials can even begin to hotwire that barge's encryption level. Plus, the fact that everyone is always chasing you, even when I met you."

The boy looked deep into Mycroft's eyes. "I just know you are not some regular person."

Mycroft searched for words, but was unable to find the appropriate ones. Elio wiggled out of Mycroft's grip and once again attempted to get the attention of the hunters. The Specter subdued him again, but not before a few of the hunters took interest in their direction.

"Great! Now they are coming towards us!" Elio exclaimed as he returned to sit.

Mycroft just pinched the bridge of his nose. "No, it's not great. We don't know who they are, and they don't know who we are."

"What does it matter?" Elio, still being stoic, was quite flippant over the whole situation. "They are the only humans for miles, and our only way to civilization. If they cannot take us to the nearest spaceport then we will freeze before we walk there."

Just then a loud screech pierced the air. The wind picked up and suddenly a large, dark shadow appeared on the ground. In one fell swoop, an enormous winged raptor touched down on the valley floor, picked up the carcass with its massive claws, and departed, squealing into the crisp sky.

CHAPTER 9

Everyone, from the two men on the boulder to the hunters on the surface, were completely still, silent, and stunned beyond belief.

No one uttered a sound for several moments. Finally, Elio asked, "Now do you see those people differently?"

Before Mycroft could respond a shrill whistle came from the direction of the hunters.

"Whoever you are, you best come with us if you want to live. That ice hawk is looking to feed its nest with anything that moves, and it *will* be back."

"See, I told you," was Elio's response. He immediately descended the boulder to join his new companions. Mycroft hesitated for a few moments, then caved and ran after Elio, struggling to keep up.

"My partner is so timid to meet people," Elio was telling the hunters as Mycroft caught up with them. "He is afraid of everything and everyone. But I told him you were the only help we had. See, that is our ship's wreckage, just over there—"

One of the hunters stepped forward, with a large, ice covered mustache. "We're frontiersmen, just chasing our paycheck. We've been out here for four days tracking that sonofabitch snake. But with the weather so warm, the hatchlings were born early and that fucking hawk took all our game." He flipped off the sky. "But we'll come get that piece of shit. Oh boy, we'll get him!"

As if it heard them, a loud screech from the raptor skipped across the air. The beast was returning for more, sooner than originally thought.

The hunter squinted as he surveyed the horizon. "Quick. We only have so much time to leave. It's a five-mile hike to the transport. Like I said, you're more than welcome to join us—but you can stay if you'd like."

Without hesitation, Elio followed them. He looked back at the still waiting Mycroft and beckoned the Specter to come. For the briefest of moments, Mycroft considered killing all of the hunters and stealing their transport, but that would raise questions. No matter which path he chose to follow, each led to an unbearable deluge of questions.

Sure enough, once the eight reached the speeder and were headed back to town, the stream began.

One of the female hunters that sat next to the pair asked, "So where are you all from?"

"We took off from the planet Chaffee," Elio blurted without hesitation, and was promptly elbowed in the stomach by Mycroft. Clearly discretion was not his strong suit. "What? We did! That is the truth!"

Mycroft struggled to keep his irritation from graduating into full blown fury. "I know, but that doesn't mean they need to know anything, dammit! You found us a ride, now shut up and let me do all the talking from now on!"

One of the hunters watched the confrontation anxiously. He gently elbowed his seating companion, another female, whose hand inched towards her rifle. Mycroft noticed the slight movements and thought quickly.

"Sorry, you all had to see that. He's still not one hundred percent after the surgery." Mycroft pointed to Elio's eyes. "And the crash didn't help at all."

The first female hunter slowly shook her head and gave a nervous smile. "I can see that. Is that why you two were in the Axis?"

Mycroft cut Elio off before the young boy would get them into more trouble. "Yes. Black market medicine is cheaper on that side of the control line. But as you can see, you get what you pay for."

The first hunter, with the mustache, was driving the transport, and looked back through the rearview mirror. "So what brought y'all out to this shithole? We're out on the edge of nowhere, and not many ships venture this way on purpose."

Mycroft gathered the driver was the one to watch out for. The Specter needed to watch what he said. "Our ship was damaged during the interspace jump. We were going back to work in the Talfus Gates, but the damage caused the navi-computer to malfunction and brought us here."

The female with her hand on her rifle loosened her grip a bit. "Yikes. What caused the damage? Damn thing looked like it was missing all the engines."

"We were being chased by the security team!" Elio blurted before the Specter could intervene. Mycroft just gave Elio a stern look rather than elbow him again. The young man looked at the Specter with the classic expression of "What did I do?"

Gently, Mycroft patted Elio's head. "Poor thing. What he means is that our jump convoy was intercepted and our slow piece of shit was caught in the crossfire." The Specter gave the boy a death glare, but the kid was still ignorant that he was doing anything wrong.

"Intercepted by whom," the driver asked, not bothering to hide his curiosity.

Mycroft again considered killing everyone in the van and going his own way. But then he returned to his senses. He'll just deal with what comes when it comes. *A Specter is always present, but never seen*, he remembered.

"A group of attack ships," the Specter finally said. "They were painted with Syndicate colors but that doesn't mean anything."

All the hunters in the transport sighed in disbelief. "Fuckin A, what are you hauling?"

"Slaves from the Coreenian Ring," the boy added.

Maybe the best decision was to just kill *Elio*, the Specter pondered. Since that was part of the original plan.

"Shit! Then there must be survivors back there! We have to go look for them," the driver said as he slammed the brakes. The transport lurched to a stop and proceeded to turn around.

"It's no use!" Mycroft exclaimed. "The cargo has a failsafe that separates it from the ship in the event of an emergency. It's floating somewhere in the interspace right now."

"It was probably smashed into by another trading barge," Elio added, finally catching on to the story. "So there would not be any survivors."

A tense silence hung in the van. The hunters looked at each other, soundlessly communicating. Mycroft found a pressure point in Elio's back and pressed it as hard as he could. A normal human would be fainting in pain. Instead, the boy simply turned his head, mildly confused.

"Why are you doing that?"

Mycroft's face was contorted with the struggle to keep Elio quiet. He spoke through gritted teeth, "To keep you from stressing out any longer. Once we get into town, we'll find you a place where you can rest."

One of the bearded hunters looked at them with disdain. "How the fuck can you smuggle human beings and still have any semblance of emotion?" He spat onto the floor. "You two are fucking monsters! We should dump you out right here."

An argument broke out amongst the hunters, in a language completely foreign to Mycroft. The driver of the rig and three other hunters seemed to gang up on the bearded hunter, the two females, and another, with both sides talking over each other. The two travelers were suddenly ignored.

The Specter leaned over to Elio, whispering "Do you know what they're saying?"

Elio raised his eyebrows, and his modulated voice rose a couple octaves. "Oh, now you want my help? Are you going to inflict pain on me again? Or *try* to?"

Mycroft gave him another death glare. "Not unless you don't answer my fucking question!"

"They are arguing over what to do with us. Those two want to leave us here, while that one wants to kill us now. The one in back thinks we should be turned in, while the driver insists they take us to town because he made us a promise."

Mycroft underestimated the nosy man. He never figured the hunter to have integrity. The argument escalated, graduating to a full shouting match. The Specter intervened before a fight broke out.

"Listen fellas, we don't want to cause any trouble. We're just like you and chasing a paycheck. If you can just take us to the nearest space harbor, we'll leave you alone and still be greatly appreciative."

The hunters were silent long enough to hear what Mycroft had to say before launching back into the shouting match.

Elio translated for the Specter. "Now they are all thinking of turning us in. One right there thinks there is a reward on our heads."

Mycroft raised his eyebrow. "So that means they're not exactly legal themselves, huh? We might be able to use that."

He stood up again to address the hunters. "Hey, folks. Maybe we can cut a deal that benefits both of us?"

The bearded man who wanted to turn them in feigned a look of shock. "Oh? And just what are you considering?"

Mycroft nearly jumped with giddiness. For once, something was actually going right. "Do you have a ship? We have plenty of bluechips—"

"That's all?" One of the females shoved her rifle into the Specter's stomach. "We're going to need more than just money."

Shit, of course, Mycroft thought. "Well, what do you have in mind?"

The bearded one pointed at Elio. "There's something special about your little lover here."

Another hunter poked the boy with his rifle, but Mycroft shoved it away. "Out of the fucking question."

"Then we have no deal." The woman raised her rifle to fire.

The mustached driver intervened, and pointed his rifle at her. "Enough, Sams. Put the gun down. We'll just take them to the station and go our way. Enough said."

"No!" Sams was nearing a full conniption fit, for she jumped up and down and could barely keep still. "We could get some serious coin – and better – if we make them take us to their shipment. Screw them, let's get paid."

The driver was resolute. "We're not slave traders, dammit."

Another hunter stepped into the standoff. "Which is why we're poor and stuck in this shithole."

Sams was so nervous that her trigger finger twitched, sending a shot through the cramped van. The shot ricocheted off the ceiling and exploded a storage control panel. In the commotion, Mycroft took the opportunity to distract Sams, disarm her, and break her neck. Within seconds, like a blur, the Specter moved to the bearded hunter and shot him in the chest with Sams' rifle.

The cramped space grew silent for several moments. Everyone remained still, waiting for their opponents' next move. The driver moved to un-holster his weapon, but Mycroft shot the hunter in the shoulder and took him into a chokehold. The other five hunters aimed their rifles at Elio.

"Now, I don't want to cause any more trouble, and just like you all, we just want to leave this freezing place. So can you please drop us off in the nearest town and we'll leave each other alone after that? Or do I have to injure your leader?"

The others hesitated a moment and then lowered their weapons.

"Deal," one of the female hunters declared.

Mycroft released the driver and returned to sit next to Elio, who was twitching erratically every few seconds. His one working eyeball looked around the room, as though the poor boy was drunk.

Concern flooded the Specter. In just a few short hours he had become attached to the strange young man. "What's wrong with you now? Did you get hit by a shot?"

Elio's lips vibrated as he spoke, and his voice rose and fell many octaves within a few short breaths. "The cold is affecting my operating temperature and I can no longer compensate for the difference."

A piercing pain shot through Mycroft's heart, but now was not the time for affection. The boy was the only person in the van without any coat or jacket to wear. "You're cold? Me too! Well you're just going to have to deal with it until we get to town. Unless you get us in trouble again." The Specter took the cold young man into his arms, sharing what warmth he could.

Elio's eyebrows raised. "I, get us in trouble? You are the one who fought everybody and killed those two hunters. All I did was get their attention and answer their questions as honestly as possible."

Mycroft began to speak but held his tongue. No matter what he said, he wouldn't change anything or improve the situation. He wanted so much to knock the young boy unconscious, but knew he couldn't punch hard enough. "Just do me a favor and shut up until I tell you to talk."

"But–"

"Shut it!" The Specter enjoyed the newfound silence, and kept a vigilant eye on the hunters for the remainder of the journey.

The town the transport arrived in was small and dreary. Every building looked exactly the same save for the plain, nondescript signs that advertised what was sold inside. A smattering of freight carts and vehicles dotted the tiny roads, and the few people out looked as miserable as the sore and battered Mycroft felt.

"Where the fuck are we?" the Specter asked after the hunters dumped him and Elio out of the van and sped off into the horizon.

Elio looked around at the snow covered squares surrounding them. "I cannot locate any identifying markers, but I can tell this settlement is full of miners."

Mycroft noticed that as well. "Yeah, it looks like a corporate-owned settlement. But at least that means it has facilities. C'mon, let's find a harbor master."

The pair set off in a random direction, hoping to be lucky on the first try. They walked three blocks and didn't find anything. The Specter turned back to talk to Elio, who was a full block behind and ticking worse than before, and urged him to keep up. Mycroft felt bad for being hard on the poor fellow, but time was of the essence, and this place was dangerous. If a group of hunters would nearly kill them, who knew about the townspeople's attitudes.

Mycroft took a blanket off a nearby ox pulling a cart full of pottery and wrapped it around Elio. "Will this help you move faster?"

A small smile of relief replaced the obvious discomfort on the boy's face. "Marginally, but yes it shall. Now that you are here I can finally tell you. The harbormaster is back the way we came."

Mycroft fumed with annoyance. He resisted the urge to pull the kid's head off of his neck.

Elio remained relatively stoic. "I tried to tell you about the direction sign but you had already stormed off this way."

The Specter just cracked his knuckles, attempting to calm. "For fuck's sake why didn't you scream, or get my fucking attention? Bloody hell, now we just wasted so much time. We could freeze to death out here!

Elio's face contorted into a look of confusion. "Why do you always get angry with me? You hate it when I tell the truth. You hate it when I do not lie. You hate it when I tell you things. You hate it when I do not tell you things. You want me to talk, then you get upset because it is too late and now you do not want me to talk anymore."

The Specter was thrown off guard for a moment. This was the most emotional Elio had been. "I'm not always mad at you. I'm—"

"Well you could have fooled me." Elio's voice broke in and out, modulating in different tones.

"I just get frustrated because you don't always have common sense."

"What is that?" The young man's face contorted into a look of confusion.

Once again, Mycroft restrained himself. This was by far the hardest challenge he had ever faced. "You just don't know better. Sometimes you say things at the wrong time, which makes our situation harder than it needs to be."

"I am only telling the truth."

"Yes, but that's not always the right thing." The Specter placed his arms around Elio. "Our success in getting back to the *Imperatrix* rests in as *few* people knowing the truth as possible."

Elio remained silent for a few beats. "I do not even know your whole truth. I have noticed secrets are very important to you."

Mycroft pulled the boy in closer. "You have no idea. So do you think you can do me a favor and work on not telling everyone we meet who we are and where we came from, or where we're going? It will help both of us out immensely."

"And will you not be mad at me all the time?" The boy's voice was as full with sadness as mechanically possible.

"I promise I'll work on it." The Specter was genuine about that, but also confused as to how to fulfill his promise.

The harbormaster's shop was small and cramped, with piles of junk haphazardly stacked everywhere. Canyons of shelves filled every walkable inch of the space. Lone lightbulbs left most of the room encased in darkness.

A faint triangle of light highlighted the sales desk, and the fat slug of a man behind it. The harbormaster was filthy and disgusting, with a smell so pungent that no one could stand near him for very long. A thick cigar smoldered in his mouth, underscoring the obvious frown covering his face.

He immediately took a dislike to the two travelers. "Can I help you gentlemen?"

"Why yes you can," Mycroft responded, as politely as he could. "We are in need of a ship."

Elio wandered off, having taken an interest in something on a nearby shelf. A hound appeared from behind the counter and followed him, with a low growl erupting from his mouth.

The harbormaster chewed the stogie, contemplating. "A ship, huh? Just what exactly did you have in mind?"

"Nothing too fancy, just something that can take us from point A to point B. We're in a bit of a rush actually, and can't really afford to be picky. Can I look at what you have in the yard?"

The man continued to roll his cigar around his mouth, uninterested in the Specter's plight. "Ah, before we do that, do you have sufficient funds?"

Mycroft didn't bother to hide his annoyance, but played it off as taking offense. "Of course. That's not a problem."

"Mind if I...take a look-see?" A smug smile flashed on the disgusting pig's face.

Annoyed, Mycroft pressed his fabricated identicard into the reader. According to it, Mycroft was an intergalactic bond trader with a game hunting hobby. There was *plenty* of money available.

The harbormaster's eyebrows raised, clearly impressed. "Nice. Very nice. Let's go out back."

In the back, the dog barked loudly as a bunch of heavy things crashed to the floor. Suddenly, Elio spoke loudly, "Oh shut up, you infernal thing. I am not stealing, I was just seeing if it fits."

The boy came from the bowels of the shop, the hound following his every move. Both of his eyes now glowed their brilliant blue. A small smile overcame Elio's face.

CHAPTER 9

"I found some of the parts! We still have to go to another shop, but I already found most of what I needed."

Mycroft grabbed the young man and pulled him closer, making sure he never left the Specter's sight. "He's no harm at all, and of course I'll pay for everything he took."

The harbormaster was not amused, "See that you do." He whistled loudly and the hound quit barking.

It was lightly snowing when the four entered the shipyard. That was a loose description, as it was mostly full of an amalgamation of junk and spare parts. When they walked down the "sales floor," as the owner called it, Mycroft struggled to not look disgusted.

All four of the functioning ships for sale looked in worse shape than the one the travelers came in. There were two freighters, which didn't look space worthy at all, a small, and very old, corvette, and a touring ship that was rustier than the piles of junk surrounding it.

The harbormaster spread his arms widely, and proudly. "I don't usually have this much of a selection. But it's all high quality, guaranteed." The smug smile carved onto the fat man's face again.

Elio kicked the corvette's landing leg, and a large piece of the mechanism fell to the floor. "It is?"

The harbormaster scowled at the remark, and the hound growled as well. "Feel free to take a look, but don't touch anything. If you break it, you buy it."

Mycroft scowled at Elio, who wrapped his hands under the blanket. The Specter inspected the corvette, careful not to anger the harbormaster further. "Can we see the inside of this one?"

Reluctantly, the man opened the small ship and escorted the travelers inside, with the hound guarding the rear. The corvette was small, yet laid out in a way that didn't feel cramped. It smelled old and dirty, with everything likely outdated if not broken. Wires from jury rigged appliances and mechanisms stuck out from the walls and consoles. In the cockpit, half the control board was singed from an old fire. All of the monitors and control units were at least 45 years old.

Mycroft looked at the pitiful sight. He focused on a particular switch in the ceiling and it fell to the floor as though it sensed his presence.

"Hey, I told you not to touch anything," the harbormaster yelled.

"I didn't," the Specter calmly replied. "The quality of this vehicle really shows…Impressive. Does it run?"

The salesman looked offended. "Of course it does. Who do you think I am? A crook?"

Well he never did say where he got it from, Mycroft pondered. "May we take it for a test flight?"

"Afraid I don't have any time for that," the fat man shook his head, the fastest movement he's ever made. "Time is money, you see, and I have another showing this evening. But take my word for it fellas, which is all you need around here, she runs like a clock." He lovingly patted the wall and one of the screens tumbled to the floor. The harbormaster took no notice at all.

A small smile carved onto Mycroft's face. Here was the part that every salesman played either so well, or so poorly. "Well I can't buy a ship I haven't flown. It's not good business. You know that."

The harbormaster frowned. "I don't do good business, I just do *my* business. Do you want to buy it or not?" The silence hung amongst the men for several moments.

Mycroft tried to hold out, but eventually folded. "How much?"

"Well," the harbormaster looked around and leaned, lovingly, onto the wall, every second-hand dealers' signature move. "Seeing how many extra installations it has and the rarity of the model…This is a valuable craft. You don't see too many around anymore, especially in such good condition."

Mycroft rolled his eyes and refused to hide his irritation. "How much?"

CHAPTER 9

The harbormaster continued his spiel. "There's been a lot of demand for this 'vette. Nicest one we've had in a long time... forty-five thousand."

Elio busted out laughing. It was maniacal and uncontrollable, and quite startling. The hound barked loudly as it was startled. The harbormaster furrowed his brow, and Mycroft pinched the bridge of his nose.

"This craft is not even worth one-tenth that," the young man said. "The structure has not been inspected since its isotope half-life checkup, which was who-knows-how long ago. The repulsor modules are corroded and need replacing. The illudium coils are failing. The extra installations have short-circuited the electrical board. And we have not even turned on the thing or looked beneath stuff."

Elio continued listing the litany of issues with the vessel. The dog growled as if it was being attacked. The man chewed his cigar vigorously, and swallowed it, clearly angered. Mycroft reached for the back of Elio's neck and squeezed. He knew it wouldn't hurt, but it worked in silencing the young man.

Fuming, the harbormaster said. "Alright you little shits. I'm done dicking around with you people. Forty-five is my final offer. Take it or get the fuck out!"

The boy was now adept at squirming out of Mycroft's grip, and somehow pried away the Specter's fingers and bent them backwards. Now it was the Specter's turn to be silenced in pain.

"Do you think we are stupid? It will take triple that to get this rust bucket off the ground. Even if demand for this was as high as you claim, it would still only be worth fifteen hundred. Frankly, you should sell it for scraps and part it out. It would be worth more!" Elio looked around a bit more. "Actually, by the looks of things, you already have a few times over."

"Get out!" The harbormaster screamed at the top of his lungs. The hound bit Mycroft's leg as the dealer shoved them out of the small ship.

The two men ran from the shipyard and took refuge in a small side alley. They continued scuffling for a few seconds, but all it amounted to was a shoving match.

Mycroft was livid, and unable to restrain himself anymore. He was done being nice. "Why? Just, for fuck's sake, why?"

Elio just remained still when the shoving match ended. "You knew that trying to strangle me that way would not work. All it does actually is make *your* life harder in the long run."

"Fuckin A, you can say that again." The scuffle resumed with Mycroft landing a few critical hits in Elio's stomach, kidneys and chest. Elio was able to counter and trip Mycroft, yet didn't try to punch him. The Specter countered and punched the boy right in the face, breaking his nose. This was only the second time Elio expressed any pain.

The boy returned the punch into the face, and dislocated the Specter's jaw. The ruckus continued for several minutes, grabbing the attention of a passerby.

"Hey, hey, hey! Knock it off! Knock it off!" Ridley dropped his wares and rushed to intervene. The fighting continued, with Ridley getting a few hits to the face. After a few moments he got hold of Mycroft and pulled him away from his opponent.

"Stop it! Just what the hell happened with you two?" Ridley struggled to restrain the man who only wanted to continue fighting.

Elio straightened himself out after he picked himself up from the floor. "He keeps getting furious with me because I keep following his directions. He punches me for telling him the truth. He gets mad at me for telling him things, or not telling him things."

Fatigue had overcome Mycroft, for he could have easily broken free from the hold, but he didn't bother, for it wouldn't be worth it. "No! That's not true. He doesn't follow my directions. He goes against

CHAPTER 9

everything I say, and does the exact opposite of what I tell him to do!"

Elio interrupted. "That is only because you tell me one thing and do not tell me the change of plans. Then you get mad at yourself for not saying anything and take it out on me."

Mycroft lunged at Elio again, and it took all of Ridley's strength to hold him back. "And you always fucking do that!" the Specter said. "You haven't any inkling of common sense."

"Hey, cool it! You don't have to kill him just because he pissed you off," Ridley said.

Mycroft continued to lunge at his prey. "Oh, you have no idea how better my life would be if he wasn't in it."

"He wants to kill me, but he has not yet figured out how," Elio said.

Ridley chuckled. "My grandma says that's the only thing husbands know how to do well."

Mycroft stopped struggling, utterly appalled. He turned to the boy. "We are NOT married, or together! *Thankfully!*" The Specter was genuinely offended.

Elio continued in his trademark stoic tone. "His attraction to me makes him that much more upset, and he struggles to reconcile that within himself."

Using the last ounce of strength. Mycroft broke from Ridley's grip and swung at Elio. He missed and collapsed on the ground in a heap. Mycroft had finally hit his wall.

"His lack of rest and need for sustenance makes him angrier as well," Elio added.

Ridley looked at the two men before him, amazed that a weird disabled kid and an enraged brute made it this far without killing each other. But his curiosity only deepened. "Where did you guys come from, and how the fuck did you end up here?"

"Well, well, well. Look at what we found here." Five Johns appeared, each brandishing their own makeshift weapon, just itching to use them. "A bitch and a couple of thugs."

"Oh is that what your name is?" Elio asked Ridley. "Nice to meet your acquaintance."

"Just what do you creeps want?" Ridley stood at attention, his fists clenched. He was done taking shit from them. "I only have the replacement of what you took from us yesterday in my bags."

The lead thug sniggered. "Nah, little bitch. We're not looking for you. Those two runts stole some parts from the harbormaster and we've come to take them back."

Ridley's temper rose as he stood his ground. "These two didn't steal from that crook!"

Mycroft joined his new companion. "Actually we were chased out by him and that scraggly hound."

"But we did promise to pay," Elio said triumphantly. "And you said you can afford it."

The Specter waved Elio quiet. "He's right. A deal is a deal. How much do we owe?"

"Oh no, no." The leader wagged his finger. "You see, the harbormaster was greatly offended by you two. So much so that money alone won't solve the problem." The gang slowly approached the men.

An uneasy feeling welled within Ridley. "What else did he have in mind? All he ever wants is money."

"I think I know what they had in mind," Mycroft said, cracking his neck in preparation.

The two biggest thugs went after Elio while the others rushed Mycroft and Ridley. A pair of bolos flew through the air. Mycroft caught them and threw them back at the attacker, immobilizing him. The Specter ran towards the thug with a mace attacking Ridley. Mycroft kicked him in the kidneys, but caught the full force of the mace swing and crumpled to the floor. The Specter's sword rolled out of one of his pockets.

CHAPTER 9

The sword's hilt caught Ridley's attention. Before he could grab it, he was pulled by the goon leader into the air and was repeatedly socked in the face. Ridley managed to kick the goon in the crotch, but that only stopped the punches. The goon squeezed Ridley's neck, and the boy in turn pressed in the goon's eyes. The two danced around in pain.

Mycroft was kicked into consciousness by another goon, but the Specter grabbed his ankle and broke it. The thug fell to the ground, howling in pain, but turned to pummel Mycroft. The scuffle continued for a while, but ended with the Specter getting kneed in the throat.

The thug fighting Mycroft saw the sword, picked it up and threw it at the goon holding Ridley. Ridley fell to the ground and punched the goon, but it hardly stunned him. Mycroft finished off his thug and rushed over to help Ridley.

Another goon rushed and knocked both of them to the floor. Mycroft rolled and missed the goon's lunge, but was able to give him a quick roundhouse in the back. Ridley, in turn, kicked the goon into final submission.

Somehow, in the midst of the fight, the sword was ignited, and remained on the ground. No one had noticed it, and Mycroft quickly brandished it and rushed to aid Elio.

The poor boy was no match for the two giant thugs, both trying to grab him and take out his eyes. Elio mostly dodged their lunges, but every so often he'd miss and take a punch. His face with the broken nose was covered with blood.

The Specter masterfully swung his sword, a dance partner joining him in the ballet of death. Quickly he dispatched the first giant goon, slicing his limbs off before silencing his screaming head.

The other thug stood in awe of what happened. When Mycroft attempted to slice the man with the sword, the blade extinguished, not damaging anything. The goon was virtually unharmed and slammed into Mycroft, ramming him into a wall. Ridley grabbed the mace out of the goon's hand and swung it into the man's back. The goon prepared to punch the Specter's face, when Elio came out of nowhere and bit him in the jugular.

The giant thug fell to the floor, howling in pain. Elio reached down and pulled out the howling man's eye.

"I told you it was painful, but you did not listen." Elio shouted. He looked at Ridley and Mycroft who were shocked. He straightened his nose and remained still, just staring at his two companions.

"Ok, who the fuck are you guys?" Ridley asked in complete shock. "And what the fuck is with the ethellite sword?"

Mycroft's body hurt all over. He was bleeding from a few stab wounds and in no mood to talk. He was in desperate need of some minor medical care. "Is there a warmer, safer place to answer questions? I promise we have nothing to hide from you."

"He says that to everyone," Elio quipped.

Hours later, the trio all sat around the table in Ridley's house. Everyone was warm and fed, and Mycroft's wounds were bandaged. Oz was threading Elio's facial wounds with steel nylon. For all things considered, the place felt cozy. Mycroft had just finished the tale of how they crash landed on the planet.

"Well, you picked the worst place to get stranded," Oz said. "The only things here are snow and misery."

"And creatures that enjoy fighting," Elio said.

"What is the name of this moon anyway?" Mycroft asked. It had been four days since he'd last contacted the *Imperatrix* and needed to send a status message immediately. He had no idea what events had transpired since he'd departed.

"Ampheres," Ridley said. "The pocket book of the galaxy."

"You can say that again!" Oz quipped, expelling a deep, phlegm filled laugh.

CHAPTER 9

"Without us mining this iceberg, the entire *galactic* production schedule would shut down," Ridley continued.

"What do you mean?" The Specter was suddenly intrigued.

"Mostly illudium," the boy went on, "which is the essential ingredient in power cells, propulsion modules, and computing blocks. The galaxy's largest deposit is underneath our feet. We couldn't mine it all if we wanted to."

Oz laughed. "Supposedly JeffCo wants to mine it all, but they're too cheap to fully automate the process. It's too cold, and the same amount of people would need to maintain the machines, making it too expensive to be profitable."

"So instead they work us to death, and let us freeze!" Ridley shouted in the direction of the hole in the ceiling.

"Are you employees of JeffCo?" Elio asked.

"In name only. We're officially contract players, with the standard contract lasting forty-five years," Oz stopped sewing Elio. "Ok, I think we're done! Looking good, kid!"

Elio smiled at his reflection in the mirror. "Thank you very much! Your stitches are incredible," He looked less boyish, and seemed more expressive.

Oz laughed. "Why thank you, handsome."

"How long do you have left on your contracts?" Mycroft asked.

"Forty-three years. I started when I was fifteen, with the training unpaid for three months," Ridley replied. "And Oz has seven."

"Actually, I'm overdue by nine, but I can't afford to move off-planet, let alone live outside of corporate housing."

Mycroft pulled his identicard from his pocket and pressed it with his thumb. His spending chip popped out of a slot. He handed it to Ridley. "Thank you for breaking up our fight, and for getting us out of another, and for all the hospitality. There's more than enough here to buy out your contracts and move to a tropical climate. All I ask is we keep enough to buy a ship out of here."

"And I will patch your roof, and repair the furnace, in exchange for you giving me scars," Elio said. "It is the least I could do."

Oz and Ridley were hysterical. At first they tried to refuse, but after that proved unsuccessful they were overcome with extreme gratitude.

"How can we ever thank you? This is too generous." Oz was crying so hard she could barely be understood.

Mycroft gave her a big hug. "You've been more than generous. All we ask is that if we could stay until we can buy a ship from that piece of shit?"

"Once Chrysler hates you, there's no getting back on his good side. I'm afraid you won't be able to do business with him, or be seen in town until you pay off his debt," Ridley said.

"You poor thing," Oz said as she stroked Elio's face. "He hurt you because he's a greedy motherfucker. Can't he see that you're something special, who deserves as much help you can get? It's a wonder he didn't try to sell you for scrap."

"Yeah, I've never seen anyone with bionic eyes before," Ridley said, in awe of his house guest. "Or anyone else like you. Or you," he pointed at Mycroft. "You never did answer my question. And how did you learn to wield a sword like that?"

The Specter contemplated how to proceed. Even Elio didn't know, and one wrong move could let the wrong people get the upper hand. He still didn't really know who these people were, and while they were very polite, that did not mean they were intending to keep Mycroft's best interests at heart. He promised he wasn't going to lie, and these nice people didn't deserve it, but it never did hurt to omit certain facts.

"I was sent by the Cosmic Syndicate from the *Imperatrix* to negotiate a peace deal with the planet Chaffee. I used to serve in the Home Guard, which is how I learned to fight with a sword and why I have one"

"So you're an ambassador?" Oz asked with astonishment.

"No, more security to the ambassador. That's all. I'm afraid it's not that glamorous, until I crashed here. This is really my only interesting story to tell"

Elio had a contemplative frown. "Then how did you come to meet me in a pilot's uniform, and get chased by the security force?"

Fuck, Mycroft was tired. If he'd been a little more rested he would have caught that hole in the story. "The negotiations didn't go as planned. My team was ambushed, and I'm the only one left. Which is why I need to get back to the capitol as soon as possible. Ridley said there is an interlink we could use?"

"Not in this dump, I'm afraid. We can barely afford food, and have no one to call," Oz said. "And the signal from here is so poor, and the capitol is so far away, that your message will take a week to get there. It's quicker to fly there yourself."

No doubt, the Specter thought. But it was worth a try anyway. There was no other option. "Do you know where the nearest one is?"

"The control tower at the spaceport," she replied. "Or any of the company facilities and plants, really. But only the control tower is reasonably close."

"Brilliant," was all he could say. Disappointment flooded his entire being.

"Let's all take a good night's rest," Oz declared. "It's been a busy day and it's pretty late already. We'll come at this with a clear head in the morning."

Reluctantly, Mycroft followed the rest and adjourned to bed. The journey was small, as they moved just across the room to a more securely covered part of the house. Mycroft wanted to get going and send his message, but fell asleep as soon as his head hit the pillow.

Hours later, Mycroft jolted awake. The house was dark and only the snoring from Oz and Ridley filled his ears. Even Elio's breathing was heavy with sleep. Mycroft felt his sword at his side. It's cold metal beckoning him.

Quietly, and as quickly as his sore body could move, he gathered his few belongings and left the house, wishing his new companions well.

At the shipyard, Mycroft snuck past the guard cameras and that pesky hound and broke into the corvette he was going to buy earlier. He was going to steal the ship and make it back to the Syndicate capital. Elio was left in safe hands, and Ridley and his grandmother were well taken care of. It was time for the Specter to go back to his main mission.

After several attempts, the ship's rockets wouldn't start. The Specter summed it up to an installed immobilizer, and he commenced searching the ship for the correct circuits to cut.

Mycroft made his way to the engineering bay. It was cramped and he could hardly move. He fiddled with the wiring, but it was useless without any tools. Sparks flew as he ripped wires out of the console and spliced some together. Lights twinkled and a few of the ship's systems came to life.

As soon as he crawled out of the cubby the lights went out and the ship returned to its dormant state. Everything was pitch black.

"You know it will never work, right?"

Mycroft jumped with fright at the sound of a new voice. Instinctively he reached for his sword, its brilliant white blade igniting Ridley's smirking face.

The surprise that the Specter's blade worked was not hidden from Mycroft's face.

"And I fixed your sword," the boy said.

"How—"

"Did I find you?" the boy completed. "I slipped you your sword and then went to bed. You're stirring woke me; I'm a light sleeper."

Mycroft lowered his sword. "How did you know where I was?"

"I followed you, and waited outside for the ship to take off. But when nothing happened I figured you'd need a hand. The ship won't turn over until it's warmer. The night's too cold and depleted the power core."

Mycroft slouched in defeat. He was losing his touch worse than he thought. He extinguished his blade. "Where's there another shipyard?"

"There isn't. This is the only settlement on the planet."

Mycroft growled in frustration and punched the wall.

Ridley was intrigued with the man before him. He knew the person was important, but there was something he didn't yet know. "Where do you need to get to? Honestly. Even your friend didn't believe your story."

The Specter considered lying some more, but was too tired to contemplate a good one. "I need to get to the capital as soon as possible to prevent the outbreak of war. The Axis stole a valuable Syndicate treasure, and if I don't locate it the galaxy will erupt in a conflict no one has seen in generations."

"What is this treasure?" Ridley wanted to know.

"A living one—at least it was before I broke out of Chaffee. What's the quickest way I can get to a ship that's operable?"

"It's not going to be easy," Ridley said.

"Hardly ever is," was all the Specter could say.

"And I'm gonna need to borrow your sword," Ridley added, "and you'll need to teach me how to fight like you do."

Mycroft was unamused. Everything came with a price, but the Specter didn't think he heard correctly. "Come again."

He and Ridley then discussed the upcoming competition, the Gambit, and how it could solve both of their problems.

CHAPTER 10

Immediately after taking possession of Ulysses, the Archon departed Count Lucilous' domain and headed for the planet Chaffee's main freight port. The ones that actually do the work are the possessors of the most knowledge, and the Archon knew exactly who to ask.

In the port's control tower, the Archon tortured the duty officer and learned that a slave ship was stolen and severely damaged before jumping into the interspace. The barge's last radar ping was from the Antilles System, and the Archon headed there next.

Upon arriving at the system, the mysterious monk learned from the control tower officer that his quarry made a course correction and headed toward the Calphalon cluster.

Despite his best efforts, and torturing to death nearly everyone he encountered, the Archon couldn't get any more information and the trail went cold. The stolen slave barge crossed into unaffiliated corporate space and was officially out of the Axis, but that didn't mean it was safe. There were 1,000 different places the ship could have gone, with the only saving grace being the poor state of the ship, which limited its reach. Even then, the options were quite numerous.

For three whole days the Archon traversed the cosmos, searching for the missing Specter. It didn't usually take this much time for the prophet to succeed, and he struggled to restrain his tempestuous frustration. Success was reached as easily as the root of a blade of grass for the Archon, and he was not used to working so hard.

This in turn proved quite terrible for Ulysses, who had to bear the brunt of his captor's temper with repeated beatings, each growing in severity. The Archon always beat Ulysses to within inches of his life, but took great pains to not kill him. No doubt there was some reason that only made death the most appealing option.

CHAPTER 11

"The task is simple. Make it from the drop point to the finish line. The terrain, the animals, and the pain you'll endure, however, are not so forgiving." The warden told the 18 contenders assembled on the stage before the sky glider. A small crowd made up of the contenders' relatives and a few fans, gathered outside in the crisp morning. Today was the beginning of the Ampherian Gambit.

"To help you," the warden continued, "halfway is a checkpoint mark, where you can find a fresh survival pack to replenish your supplies. But the catch is that there is only enough for one of you!"

Ridley shook in his boots. He was the smallest contender, the youngest, and no doubt the least experienced. For most of the people here, this was the last day they would see their loved ones, and the last time they would set foot in this hellhole of a settlement. But this was nothing compared to the hell he would face out there in the wild. He gripped Mycroft's sword so hard his knuckles cracked. But it was the only sense of security the poor boy had.

He remembered what the mysterious man said during their brief training session the day before: "The sword knows where it needs to go, just use your body to guide it there. Fighting takes little effort from your part. But the sword does the easy part, while you have to use their rage against them. The sword is nothing more than an extension of the tool, which is you. That is the only answer to victory."

Looking around, the other contestants intimidated Ridley, for they were made exclusively of rage. How was he supposed to channel that against them? The poor boy's mind raced at a million miles an hour. Beads of sweat poured down his forehead and instantly froze in the frigid air.

Oz was right, he concluded. This was a mistake. The danger he was about to face was by far not worth the reward—even the *idea* of it. He was facing impossible odds against people who were better equipped and prepared than he ever could be. All he really was doing was wasting what precious few hours he had left standing here and acting stupid.

Ridley looked back at the crowd, which was roughly half the town, and found his companions, Oz, Mycroft, and Elio. They were the only support he had in this entire universe. Oz was crying into her scarf and Mycroft looked at him with a fatherly pride, while Elio was keenly observing the entire spectacle. A feeling welled with Ridley when he saw the expression in their faces, especially his grandmother's. They believed in him, despite how much they were afraid for his safety. Ridley remembered that he wasn't doing this just for his own future, he was doing this for Oz, who had been through a hell of a lot more than he could ever imagine.

The warden's voice interrupted his train of thought. "Not all of you will make it out of the veldt, but the one who makes it home gets a hearty reward and the best bragging rights this side of the Meridian!"

The contestants howled, ready to go, and the crowd clapped and whistled. A renewed resolve grew inside Ridley. While he couldn't ignore the possibility that he would die, at least it wouldn't be in vain. At least he would die trying to improve his life rather than just waiting around for it to fix itself. Oz taught him to be the change he wanted to see in the world, and this was him living that lesson. Ridley knew it within his heart of hearts that this was the right thing to do.

The contestants proceeded to the sky glider, saying their last goodbyes to their loved ones. Ridley waved at his family and friends, a beaming smile on his face. His gut told him everything was going to be okay, even though his mind and heart were screaming the exact opposite. Oz tried to return his smile, but struggled to do anything besides wail into her handkerchief. He once again thought that this was the last time he was going to see her.

Ridley's attention turned to Mycroft, who gave the boy a stiff salute. The boy could see the intense trust in the man's eyes, and Ridley's resolve was steeled a bit more. Elio applauded vigorously, seemingly caught up in the hype of the moment.

The glider took off into the crisp air, slicing its path through the icy sky. Ridley bundled his flimsy snow wrap as tightly as he could to stop shaking; the glider was open walled. But his shakes were not because of the cold. There was no turning back now, and this was the literal do or die moment. To distract his mind, he took in as much of the scenery as he could. This was a bird's eye preview of what was to come, and he could at least try to do some preparation.

The icy veldt was flat and barren, completely desolate of plant life, with only the occasional ghost wolf scurrying across. Snow swirled across the landscape, fooling the wandering eye into seeing an animal. An ice raptor flew in the distance, howling its cry into the sky. From the distance of the sky glider, it looked rather peaceful, even beautiful. But even a young Ampherian native like Ridley knew that the most beautiful covering disguised the most dangerous.

The game warden paced along the sky glider, looking at the view and checking in with the contestants. He shouted from one of the window wells, "Don't let the serenity of the scene fool you. It's a two-day trek through this shit after the checkpoint. And...Ah, here it is."

Below, a nondescript orange pole rose into the air, making it the tallest structure in sight. Its neon color made it stand out amongst the pure white plains, and it looked completely out of place. The sun glinted off the tip of the pole. It was the silver box full of fresh survival gear, just beckoning each of the contestants to take it.

Beyond the checkpoint pole, the terrain rose into rocky hogbacks and lowered into deep, narrow valleys. The smoothness of the veldt was completely gone, as though a giant monster erupted from the ground and disturbed the earth. Miles long crevasses cut through the landscape as though ripped open by giant claws. The sky glider descended into one of the deeper ones and hovered over a large, pitch black hole.

"Alright, gentlemen, here we are!" A large smile carved onto the game warden's face. He was giddier than a child with a new toy. "Fellas, from this point on, the people around you are your enemy, along with the rest of your surroundings. Trust nothing, and be wary of every animal you encounter. Even the most unassuming can still incapacitate you, and leave you to the cold. Which is only waiting to kill you."

The warden smiled. "Have fun!"

Before he realized what happened, the floor dropped out from under Ridley's feet, and all 18 contestants cascaded into the black hole. After several seconds the surface appeared, covered in sharp rock and icy outcroppings. A few of the players impaled themselves on the sharp spears of ice, ending their competition before it could really get started. Others met the ground with enough force to break several limbs and bones, while some were able to make it from the fall relatively unscathed.

Ridley and a few contestants broke through a thin area of the icy floor and continued sliding into a cavern at high speed. The tunnel twisted sharply, dizzying the boy and compelling a few more of the contestants to crash into the wall, their bodies turning into broken, unconscious ragdolls.

The tunnel continued removing contestants from the gambit before abruptly ending in a small cavern, with walls and ceiling covered in long, sharp spears of ice. Two of the contestants impaled themselves in the chest. Ridley entered the room at such speed that he would have impaled himself also, but bounced off the body of the unfortunate soul who beat him to it.

The young man was nearly knocked unconscious, and when he brought himself to his feet he realized he stood in a pile of human bones. No doubt contestants of long past, or some animal's old dinner. Ridley gave himself the once over and was pleased to find himself relatively unharmed, and with most of his supplies still intact. Already the young man had faced more than he had ever dreamed of, let alone prepared for, and he didn't know if he would even survive past this...entrance exam. His tomb might very well be this frozen tunnel into hell.

A faint light peeped from the tunnel that Ridley entered through, bathing the small space in gloomy semidarkness. The cavern split into different directions, each leading into their own separate dark path. There were no other living contestants in the cavern, and Ridley could hear his own breathing, and see the mist of his own faint breath.

"Well, shit. I made it this far. But now what the fuck do I do?" His words bounced off the uneven walls and assailed his eardrums. A few loose pieces of ice fell from the ceiling.

Ridley rummaged through his rucksack for a glow rod. There was no use remaining in the darkness. The boy struggled to see what he was grabbing, and kept picking out the wrong thing. His fingers grasped the hilt of Mycroft's sword.

Mycroft's words drifted through his mind. "The sword is only an extension of the greatest tool, which is you, yet it is useful in most situations. Especially ones with limited supplies."

The boy set the sword aside and continued rummaging, eventually finding the glow rods and additional power packs for the sword. There were only two working glow rods, as the others burst open during the fall from the sky glider. Ridley weighed whether or not to use them now or wait, because he figured this could be only the first of many dark caverns he'll encounter. He could use the sword as a light source, and that would give him the added security of being able to defend himself.

"Ah shit! You know this is the right decision! Just do it!" Ridley was growing frustrated with his internal vacillations. He ignited the sword, flooding the small dark cavern with a powerful white light. The smell of dead carcass was replaced by the intense odor of burning ozone and ethellite, yet the former odor was still incredibly pungent.

Armed with his light, Ridley slowly inched forward, searching for the way out. Over the hum of the pulsing sword, a soft, padded pitter patter entered his ears. The boy looked around frantically and saw a pride of silver ghost wolves cascade into the cavern from a concealed nook in the wall. They immediately made a beeline for the fresh carcasses dotting the cavern's floor, paying no attention to the breathing Ridley.

The boy was frozen in shock for several moments, unable to move any muscle in his body. He had never been this close to one of these dangerous creatures, let alone ignored by them. That realization broke through Ridley's shock, and he resumed his trek for a way out. He crossed the room carefully, but the further he moved, the more aware the wolves grew of his presence.

At first only one wolf started growling at him, its loud, deep rumble filling every inch of the empty space. The long fangs were still pearly white despite feasting on a bloody carcass. Within seconds, a third of the entire pride was focused only on Ridley, desperate for their next meal.

They crept closer to Ridley, barking and growling at him to back up. Ridley waved the sword at them threateningly, but that only aggravated them more. Their fangs reflected the brilliantly bright blade, daring it to a fight.

The ghost wolves backed Ridley into an icy corner. He had nowhere to turn, and his only two options were to kill or be killed. His pounding heart nearly burst through his chest, and drowned out all the other sounds coming through his ears. This was only his second brush with death, and his first with animals, and he was already nearly dead. Despite his timid swinging with the sword, the wolves continued their advance.

Mycroft's voice once again echoed into his head. "When you need to make the kill, don't hesitate, just do it. Clear your mind and take action. It's the only way to survive."

"Yeah, easier said than done, you piece of shit!" Ridley screamed, but that didn't make him feel better. With as much force as he could muster, Ridley swung the sword at the advancing wolves, but he missed his target each time.

One of the wolves had had enough and lunged at Ridley, who slammed against the wall and forced a few pebbles of ice to fall to the ground. The wolves were hungry.

"Ah! It's only a fucking animal," Ridley screamed to himself. "C'mon Ridley, you chicken shit! This is what you signed up for! Fucking do it!"

Intense fear filled his soul each time Ridley looked at the hungry wolf pack, which had doubled in number. The dead carcasses were no longer edible, yet the wolves were still hungry.

Oz's face flashed in his mind, reminding him of the real reason he was doing this, and it steeled his weak nerves. He swung the blade with all his might, effortlessly cutting through a couple of the ravenous wolves. He closed his eyes to hide the hideous sight, but the animal's warm blood oozed over his skin. The warm cloud rose from the body in Ridley's direction, giving him a brief reprieve from the frigid air,

CHAPTER 11

and carrying the pungent smell of fresh death. Once the odor made it to his mouth he immediately threw up. He had never killed an animal as large as wolf, and for some reason he felt it was akin to murdering a fellow human being. Even the thought of it being in self-defense was not comforting.

Most of the remaining wolves were suddenly no longer interested in Ridley or the ethellite sword, as they had a more enticing new carcass to devour. A smattering of the wolf pride still maintained some interest in the boy, but they were too far away to be any real threat, for now.

Ridley was relatively left alone once again, and he was able to sneak out from the corner and make his way to one of the cavern's exits. He decided to follow the wolves' tracks and found himself in an icy tunnel, just tall enough for him to stand up straight. The tunnel twisted and turned for several hundred yards, but remained relatively level.

He came to a fork, and chose the path that rose to the surface, but after several yards of walking the tunnel lowered into the earth once again. He walked back to the fork and chose a different tunnel, but that ended in a dead end, before forking into another direction.

After two hours of walking, Ridley had still remained underground and made very little progress. He was growing restless that he was only getting more lost, and that the wolves would find him at any moment to finish the fight they started.

Another memory from his training session drifted into Ridley's mind. "Nature will always point you towards the right path, you just have to be patient enough to listen to her."

This only exacerbated his frustration. "But what the fuck does that mean?" Ridley screamed. Remembering quotes of silly wisdom didn't do him any good when he was fucking lost in an underground maze. Ridley was getting increasingly convinced that he made the wrong decision, which in turn was making him angrier, and more scared.

He quit walking and kicked at the frozen ground as hard as he could.

Ridley lost his balance and slipped on his ice, giving his tailbone a loud crack.

The pain and frustration were so immense that Ridley broke out crying, unable to keep himself together any longer. He didn't care if the ghost wolves caught up to him, for he would soon be dead anyway. He might as well get devoured by a hungry animal.

Oz was right, and he should have listened to her. All Ridley could ever do is focus on what was wrong and what he didn't have and how shitty things were. It was as though he liked to complain, she would always tell him. He wasn't going to take that from her, and he was going to prove her wrong. But then he had to prove he had a pair of balls and do something that was not only really stupid, but immensely dangerous, all because he saw a fucking bluechip sign on a silly ass poster.

The tears streamed down, burning the scars of shame into his face. Doing the Gambit was not the way to improve his and Oz's life, but there was nothing he could do about it now.

After several more minutes, Ridley's crying finally subsided and he tried to choose his next move. The ethellite sword was steadily pulsing, its bright light illuminating virtually every inch of the cramped tunnel. He noticed some strange markings leading straight into the wall and was intrigued. He moved closer and saw that they were various animal tracks, some not that old, leading in a direction perpendicular to the tunnel. The icy wall was a recent addition, and relatively thin.

A small smile crossed Ridley's face. "So that's what that means. Remembering stupid quotes is useful after all."

It took several minutes and bruises before Ridley was able to break through the thin ice wall to continue following the frozen animal tracks. The path took an initial decline, which lowered Ridley's spirits, but then it dramatically inclined, so much so that the boy nearly had to climb a sheer wall of ice.

CHAPTER 11

Ridley guessed it took him an hour before he felt a slight cold breeze blow across his face. The surface was closely approaching! With this newfound enthusiasm, Ridley increased the speed of his climb, not taking as much care to get solid footing. Within minutes the breeze was stronger.

Beneath his feet, Ridley could hear the ghost wolves' padded feet growing closer. They were hungry once again, and not afraid to climb a wall of ice to get food. Slowly a few of the ghost wolves began ascending the wall, catching up to Ridley. The boy increased his speed as much as he could, but he was starting to slip on the rocks and fell a few feet. He could feel the nips of the wolves at his feet, and he struggled to climb faster.

He swung his sword at the wolves to give himself some distance, but all he succeeded in doing was burning his already sore legs. No matter what Ridley did, he could not outrun a four-legged animal.

If it hadn't been for some of the ghost wolves losing their footing and slipping to their deaths, the rest of the wolf pride would have caught up to Ridley and cleaned off his bones.

By the time he had finally made it to the surface, the moon had replaced the sun and the stars twinkled under a cloudy veil. Ridley checked his competition stopwatch and learned the Gambit had entered its ninth hour. Ridley had no idea where he was or how far he needed to go, not to mention where the other contestants were, but the one thing he did know was that he was losing.

* * *

Across the veldt, Mycroft snuck into the Village's spaceport control tower. He effortlessly knocked out the night duty officer and was currently hacking into the communication system. Since the outpost was the only habitable one on the ice moon, and there were hardly any security breaches, the passwords were quite rudimentary.

The Specter hadn't been in the control room for even five minutes when he successfully reached through the mainframe and dialed in the Specter communication code.

A static-filled image of an artificial operator appeared in the view screen, her words breaking in and out, barely audible. "Thank you for contacting the Warner-Tojira customer review hotline. Your comments are very important to us. Please clearly state your comment and our quality assurance team will be in contact with you. Thank you again for contacting Warner-Tojira."

This was the way any Specter abroad could relay their message to the *Imperatrix* without needing a secure line. As soon as Mycroft's message was received, a team of comm officers relayed his message through the necessary channels, and—hopefully—action would be taken. All Mycroft had left was hope.

He took a breath and began his message. "Specter Chiefs, this is Mycroft Zebulon. I have confirmed that Ulysses Pircilla is in the possession of Count Lucilous. I cannot confirm the status of the asset, nor his current location, as I was nearly terminated by the count. I crash landed on the mining moon Ampheres, in Corporate Space, and am alive, but I will require some time to secure transport, due to the remoteness of this system.

"I have also learned that, despite what Military Intelligence suggests, the Axis is more than adequately equipped for a full-scale assault, and is actively preparing for war."

Mycroft's shoulders dropped with the weight of the situation. He hadn't failed, exactly, but there wasn't much he could do to fulfill his mission.

"I expect to be in Syndicate Space within seven days. Communications on Ampheres are centralized and highly monitored, and it's likely you won't get this message for several days. This will be my

CHAPTER 11

final correspondence. If you do not hear from me within seven days, proceed with the Protocol. Specter out."

Mycroft nearly collapsed to the floor with grief. The galaxy was going to see a civil war. It was unavoidable. The Protocol was the Syndicate's operation to strike the Axis in response to the kidnapping and murder of Ulysses. The operation was intended to be covert, but the Axis' retaliation would be swift and mighty. It was Mycroft's ultimate goal to find a reason to justify either proceeding with the Protocol, or scrubbing it.

The Specter reached for his sword, and his hand met an empty belt.

"And now the fate of the galaxy is in the hands of some backwoods kid playing around in a survival competition. Fuckin A, I need a drink!"

* * *

Since the moon Ampheres was on the edge of the galaxy, communications took a long time to reach their destination. The further the signal traveled, the more it weakened, thus it was necessary for signal boosters to be placed in every known settlement to help send the comms signal along.

Deep in the darkness of space orbited the small agro-mining rock Atreon, which was known for nothing other than being the smallest outfit for its company. In the small shack that operated as the rock's control tower, the Archon was finishing beating the controller's face. The ignorant and incompetent woman refused to comply and only wanted to make things more difficult. Time was absolutely of the essence, and the Archon needed to forcefully show her that.

The hooded monk slammed the woman's body to the floor, and overheard the end of an incoming transmission. The image was missing and the sound was barely audible over the scratchy static, and every third word sounded like it came from another recording, which indicated the sender was trying to cloak the signal. Despite this, the Archon was able to make out the final two words:

"...Specter out."

A menacing laugh escaped from the red hood, echoing across every corner of the small shack. It was a deep and evil bellow that was completely satisfied.

As always, the Cosmos shows you which way to take, the Archon thought.

The armored priest tracked the source of the transmission, yet the signal was still too weak to give an exact location and provided three possible planetoids, all within a relatively short distance from each other.

The menacing laugh grew deeper and slower, eventually turning into a growl.

"Here I come."

CHAPTER 12

Ridley didn't get one second of sleep the entire night. The air was too cold and the snow was too wet for his wimpy tent and sleeping bag. His muscles were sore from shivering so much. Then the ghost wolves kept entering his camp, despite the fire ring he lit. At least four times Ridley had to leave the tent and scare the wolves off with the sword, and even then that was barely a deterrent for more than a few minutes, and they grew braver with each encounter. To top it off were all the noises in the night he had never heard before, from an unceasing flapping to a high pitched whine to a growl that sounded near-human.

Still, against all the odds he could see, Ridley survived the first night of the Gambit, and his first real night in the wild. That alone gave him enough energy to tackle this day.

After quickly packing and eating a handful of his provisions, Ridley set off hiking the icy tundra. The land was still scarred with crevasses and valleys, some only knee-deep and others appeared bottomless. On multiple occasions Ridley nearly slipped and fell into a few of them, but his quick reflexes managed to keep him alive thus far.

Hours upon hours of hiking later and the terrain had metamorphosed into really high mountains. The checkpoint was nowhere in sight, and any animals Ridley did see immediately scurried away upon hearing his footsteps.

Ridley stopped at the base of a mountain, its top hidden underneath a veil of clouds. There was no visible pass around the towering peak, so he took the time to have a bite of lunch and survey his next move.

He found a boulder and took a drink from his canteen. There was only a liter and a half of water left, so he couldn't drink as much as he needed and had to preserve it for as long as he could. His foodstuffs didn't appear any better, so he only ate two bites from his vitamin bar.

"Now I might fucking starve to death! That's just bloody wonderful!" Ridley punched the boulder and cursed in pain as he dislocated a finger. "Fuck you too, you piece of shit!"

He took out his compass and terrain map, which conveniently only labeled the village and checkpoint and left everything else blank, and surveyed where he was. Ridley calculated he had hiked eight miles, but traveled twelve vertical miles. His legs and feet were burning with soreness, and he wasn't even close to the checkpoint.

All he could do was chuckle lightly. "At least I'm finally getting what I wanted and going up instead of down!"

Suddenly the wind whipped up fiercely, as though a storm was rushing in. A familiar loud screech pierced the air, followed by a large and menacing shadow.

Ridley barely moved off the boulder before the raptor dove and snapped it up with its beak, like it were a pebble. Disappointed in its flavor, the ice raptor crushed the boulder and a tumble of rocks cascaded from the sky on the place Ridley used to sit.

The barren land provided no place to hide, so Ridley stuck close to ground and moved as fast as he could in random patterns. He ducked this way and dipped that, running away from the pursuing shadow in a zigzag, yet his speed was still no match for the raptor.

Ridley tried to take cover under another boulder, but it rolled away as soon as he hid there. The boy didn't have time to react before he felt the strong grip of leathery talons wrap around his shoulders. Ridley

CHAPTER 12

could feel himself being lifted off the ground. He quickly grasped the ethellite sword and in one swift motion ignited it and sliced the talons off above the ankles.

The raptor howled in pain and quickly descended to the ground. The large wings knocked over the fragile boulders surrounding the landing zone.

Ridley tumbled to the snowy ground, quickly rushing out of the way of the huge bird, its large wings flapping wildly. The boy tried to rush the bird with the sword and get in a few hits, but the whipping air was too strong for Ridley to stand up straight, let alone walk.

The raptor recovered enough to charge at Ridley with its fiercely chomping beak. Ridley swung the brilliant white blade and chipped away a few chunks of the bird's face, stunning the beast enough for the boy to run out of the way before another lunge.

Ridley ran as fast as he could, quickly hunting for a hiding spot but came up empty. The bird quickly caught him, its strength no match for the boy's feeble speed. The raptor snapped repeatedly at Ridley, and managed to draw blood.

The attack continued unabated, with Ridley struggling to continue to fend off the gigantic bird. He could feel his strength fading fast, yet the bird seemed to just be warming up.

Suddenly the ground collapsed from underneath Ridley's feet, and the warring duo careened into an icy cavern. The space was shallow, just a few feet beneath the surface level, yet there was hardly any room for Ridley to run away from the raptor's relentless attack.

The boy managed to keep the piercing beak at bay with the ignited ethellite sword. There was barely any room to move, yet Ridley swung the sword as madly as he could. He managed to stab the raptor in the eye, causing the gigantic bird to screech in pain. The sound waves coursed through the small icy cavern, causing the fragile walls to cave in. Mounds of half-frozen slush filled the shallow space, threatening to drown Ridley. As he was climbing out, the raptor struck him in the shoulder and embedded the tip of its beak inside his flesh. The raptor soared into the air with a howling Ridley in tow.

The bird leveled off at roughly 50 feet, desperately chomping at the body suspended on its beak, mere inches out of reach. For his part, Ridley swung at the bird but kept just barely missing the target.

The raptor lowered altitude and started scraping the boulders. Ridley's body thrashed and swung wildly, but still desperately clung in place. With all the flying debris, the ethellite sword suddenly flickered out, extinguishing. Ridley tried to reignite it, but the blasted machine would not cooperate. It was done for.

But the raptor was not. It continued chomping at the hanging boy, desperate for its prey.

Ridley beat the beast's beak with the sword's hilt, but the beak was too hard and the raptor was unfazed. The bird scrapped itself against the rocks again, but this time it inadvertently injured its one good eye. Soon after the bird lost balance and tumbled to the ground, skidding in a useless heap.

The force of the impact sent Ridley tumbling away from the giant raptor, the tip of the beak still embedded in the boy's shoulder. After taking a few seconds to gain his footing, Ridley made for the closest boulder and took refuge behind it.

Blinded, the bird listened to Ridley's movements and kept lashing out for its quarry. Within seconds the boulder Ridley hid behind was obliterated, and he struggled to make a clear getaway.

The bird's attacks were relentless, yet Ridley was successful in evading the raptor's lashings. He picked up small rocks and threw them at the bird, but the beast was unfazed. Ridley attempted to retrieve the sword's spare battery from his backpack, but kept having to avoid being killed.

Ridley threw a larger rock, which landed in the raptor's mouth and blocked its airway. The bird swallowed it and started choking, giving Ridley just enough time to open his pack. The noise attracted the bird and it lunged at the boy. Ridley ran as fast as he could, forcing everything in the pack to spill out in a small debris field.

The chase continued, with the choking beast desperately attacking the fleeing Ridley. The boy had nothing to throw at the bird, forcing him to just run as fast as he could. The chase circled back to the debris field, giving Ridley another chance to retrieve a weapon.

He grabbed the first thing he could in between strikes from the beast's beak; it was an emergency shelter in an explosive can.

This was not at all what Ridley wanted or needed to grab, but it was all he had to use.

"Here goes nothing." Ridley pulled the pin and threw the can into the bird's mouth. Excitedly, the bird closed its mouth as the can exploded in a giant puff of steam. The orange fabric tent erupted in the bird's mouth, decimating its face. The tent's support beams pierced the raptor's cranium.

The giant ice raptor fell limp to the ground, finally dead.

Ridley spent several moments standing still above the bleeding carcass, in total shock. His muscles shook and his eyes didn't blink. The only thing moving was his hair blowing in the wind.

"I just killed an ice raptor," he whispered, just barely audible for his own ears. He genuinely could not believe it.

For several more minutes Ridley stood in awe of his kill, the shock fully consuming him. It was only the distant siren of another ice raptor that broke him out of the trance.

Quickly, Ridley gathered his belongings. The tent he used to fell the ice raptor was his last shelter, and it was unsalvageable.

"And there isn't another snow cave within reasonable walking distance. Fuck!"

Ridley surveyed the mountainous tundra. Dusk was quickly approaching, as was a storm. The fierce wind whipped straight through his bloodstained clothes and froze every cell in his body. The mountains were still miles away, and even in his best shape would be quite difficult for Ridley to traverse.

The wind changed direction, channeling the raptor's dead stench directly into his nostrils. The smell was unbearable...but felt warm.

Ridley contemplated his options. "Fuck it," and got to work.

He separated the carcass' skull from its body and dragged it a few feet away, and then proceeded to hollow out the brain to make a shelter. There was plenty of room for him to lay comfortably and, ironically, plenty of food to eat. Ridley then set fire to the skull to dry up the blood, as well as the rest of the body to both ward off the ghost wolves and keep him warm for the remainder of the night.

The sun set just as the storm rolled in, and Ridley settled in for the night and tended to his injured shoulder as much as he could.

The third day was no easier, coupled with his injuries and the extensively difficult terrain. Ridley had to hike ten miles back to the base of the mountain ridge because the flight with the ice raptor took him so far out of the way. He managed to find a pass between two towering peaks, and nearly lost his life a few times since the deep snow covered the slippery ice.

That night he made camp underneath a small overhang, struggling with the pain of his shoulder and his dwindling supply of food. Tired beyond comprehension, Ridley barely got any sleep due to the wolves making fiercer advances, this time joined by other dangerous predators.

He ran out of water on the fourth day, and barely had food to last him through the night. Hunting an animal wouldn't be of any help as the other animals would steal it from him, and kill him in the process. Even if he managed to keep his kill, Ridley would have no way to cook it, since he no longer had any snow-proof fire fuel, and it was impossible

CHAPTER 12

to get a fire hot enough to burn without some insulated shelter.

Provided he was reading the compass and charts correctly, Ridley was only five miles from the checkpoint and could make it there in roughly twelve hours. But without any food or water he was moving quite slow, and he was bound to be caught by the wolves that pursued him, just waiting for their next meal.

But the taste of victory was making Ridley salivate, and he was just too close to stop trying now. So the young boy buckled down and continued along the treacherous way.

After eight hours, Ridley checked his progress and for once actually felt hopeful he could make it. The mountain range was ending and he was approaching a relatively open plain. In the far distance he could see a bright orange pole. Ridley was so excited that he increased his pace to a full run.

Ridley continued hiking through the night, taking 20 minute catnaps in between fighting with the ever braver wolves. They were growing increasingly impatient, unwilling to continue to wait for Ridley to die and hoping to speed up the process themselves.

At sunrise Ridley woke up from his latest nap, beyond exhausted. His throat crackled with thirst yet the snow was too cold to melt, and it was full of mining pollutants that needed to be boiled out first. Ridley finished his remaining foodstuffs and noticed strange shadows on the ground. He looked up and saw vultures circling above him.

"Fuck, first the wolves and now you guys want to join the party?" Ridley flipped the bird with both his hands at the vultures. "Kiss my ass and take a number." He wasn't going to let some dumb birds intimidate him.

With his nerves steeled, Ridley hiked on. The orange checkpoint loomed ahead, yet Ridley was still too far away to notice if the survival pack was still attached to the pole. All of his struggles would have been for not if one of the other competitors already took the one saving grace he had. Ridley hesitantly held out hope, though he was starting to grow doubtful.

After what felt like an eternity, Ridley finally reached the towering beacon. Its bright orange paint blinding in the cloudless sky. Shimmering like a diamond at the top of the pole was the survival pack, unclaimed and unopened.

Ridley was so excited that he screamed as loudly as he could, his voice echoing in the frozen nothingness. He spent several minutes just celebrating the fact that he made it to the checkpoint and that the survival pack was still ready to be claimed. He almost felt like he was going to win the Gambit!

Once he got the celebrations out of his system, Ridley began studying how to get to the survival pack. There were no instructions, and no clear way to climb the pole. He couldn't see any footholds and there weren't any rungs to grasp.

He was suddenly startled by a loud growl. "Get the fuck away from that you little shit. That pack belongs to me."

The largest of the other contestants slowly approached Ridley. His face was freshly scarred and his eye was missing. He walked with a heavy limp and wore bandages soaked in blood. A large staff was brandished across his shoulders. He looked completely pissed off and was ready to kill any living thing he confronted.

Utter fear coursed through Ridley. This was by far the deadliest creature he'd so far encountered. "We don't even know if it's even still in here," Ridley thought quickly. "Let's at least open it first before fighting over nothing." After all, the boy thought, this was no different than fighting with one of the Johns back home.

"Dammit kid, you really are fucking foolish," the bald man growled, showing his teeth. Even those were stained with blood. "Don't you get it? Everyone else is dead! The ones who survived the cold and the wolves were killed by me. I thought I was all that's left, and then I fucking see you here. And you're just some fucking kid! Just who the fuck are you to make it this fucking far, huh?"

The man was not only angry at Ridley, but actually jealous of him. Ridley was genuinely surprised at this, especially coming from that large and dangerous man. He was confused as to what the man was jealous about, for Ridley did not do anything special to survive as long as he did. All he did was all that he knew how to, rely on his instincts, and his ten seconds of training. Ridley had absolutely no idea that he was the only one left, and thought that surely someone else besides him would survive. If anything, Ridley thought he would be the *last* to reach the beacon.

The survivor swirled his staff and stabbed it in the ground. "Well? Fucking answer me!"

Ridley just casually shrugged his shoulders, not hiding his confusion at the situation. "Just beginner's luck, I guess."

The large survivor laughed menacingly. "That's a good one! Well that luck ends today, you little shit."

Without hesitation, he swung his staff and lunged at Ridley, who ignited his sword and blocked the incoming weapon. The man swung the staff again, but Ridley jumped just in time. He elbowed the man in the chin, but the survivor quickly spun and Ridley made contact with his shoulder instead.

The large man was quick and agile for his size, and he was giving Ridley's limited swordsman skills a run for their money. Every time Ridley swung his blade, the man would counter with his staff and dodge in the other direction. The boy did manage to get in a few hits, but not enough to severely damage the survivor.

"You telegraph your moves, rookie!" the survivor growled. "And yet you still made it this fucking far!" The man's anger grew, and he doubled down on his attack.

The two engaged in the battle dance for some time, both unyielding and willing to die. Ridley was frankly surprised he was able to keep up, considering he only had a day's lesson with the ethellite sword and this was his first duel. Somehow, using the weapon in its intended fashion came naturally to Ridley. He didn't get much practice from fending off all those wolves, yet he couldn't fully discount that that was not "experience."

Ridley was completely unafraid to die. He knew well in advance that that was a high risk going into this Gambit, and the fact that he wasn't killed yet from the wolves, raptors, or other ferocious beasts was a feat within itself. If he were to die now, at the hands of this angry contestant, Ridley would not have any regrets. He at least tried to improve his and Oz's life, and he tried to live up to everything he believed in and was raised by. He would never give up, especially since he made it this far.

The only true fear Ridley had was not being able to return Mycroft's sword. Maybe his new companion would see it hanging from this contestant's belt and seek vengeance.

Relentlessly, the large man continued his attack, but Ridley could tell he was weakening. The staff's heavy swings were becoming too erratic and the man was struggling to lift it. Ridley danced around the struggling brute, swinging his sword. But the brute kept up the fight, and swung his staff heavily. Ridley dodged it and took advantage of the hole in the survivor's defense and sliced off the man's leg mid-thigh.

The survivor was heavily panting on the ground, his red blood staining the pristine white snow.

Ridley held the sword, waiting to strike. His heart pounding in his head, vibrating his entire body.

"What's wrong boy?" the survivor sneered. "Don't have the courage? Don't have the guts! You don't want this enough. A better life means nothing to you. You are just a weak little nothing who got lucky. You will never be able to do what it takes!"

CHAPTER 12

Mycroft's words echoed again in the boy's head, but letting go and just doing the deed was easier with an animal. This was a human, capable of talking and thinking and loving and hating. Killing him felt wrong, even though it really was the right thing to do.

Ridley swung, but his heart wasn't in it and he let up at the last second, grazing the man's chest. The survivor coughed violently and convulsed. The wound had partially burned his lungs, but he wasn't dead.

The poor man's eyes were bloodshot with pain, and he gasped inaudible curse words. Ridley's stomach couldn't handle the sight and vomited all of its bare contents.

Several moments passed before Ridley could look at the man. The survivor's eyes bored into Ridley's, looking deep within the boy's soul. The eyes weren't asking to be released from their suffering, they were daring Ridley to do the deed and become a man.

With a determined final swing, Ridley drove the sword into the survivor's chest, and immediately collapsed into a heavily sobbing heap.

Ridley cried until sundown. His entire body and soul ached, and his very existence seemed to implode. His heart burned in his chest, attempting to jump out of its unworthy body. He felt emotionally empty, physically drained, and absolutely exhausted. Every cell in his body cried in pain, struggling to reconcile with what he had just done.

As the sun set into dusk. Ridley had cried his last tear. The frozen wind was too cold to ignore, and the young man rustled up his strength to climb the checkpoint and gather his much-needed supply boost.

* * *

Two days had passed since the last surveillance drone reported discovering the last body, a one-eyed man whose leg was sliced away. All of the contestants' bodies were accounted for, but Ridley's whereabouts remained unknown. At the finish line, in a small cabin, the game warden was repeatedly pressed to call the Gambit closed and the final contestant dead, but he resisted until Ridley's whereabouts were known, and his mortality confirmed.

"The kid was probably eaten by the ice raptors," one of the family members of the survivor said. "That's why he'll never be found. The Gambit is a draw. Call it over and split the consolation prize among the survivors."

"Yea, it's the least you can do," another family member shouted, joined by the rest of the mob. Soon a chorus of voices were calling for the contest to be concluded.

The warden banged his fists on the table and rose. "Goddammit, shut up! For the thousandth time, the rules are solid on this one. Until we know for certain he's dead, he's still alive and the Gambit is still on. Period. The consolation prize will remain untouched until we know for sure he's dead, even if that takes until next fucking year!"

The chorus of voices continued, but a small group of people remained relatively quiet. Oz stood in the corner sobbing into a handkerchief, looking out on the horizon and desperately trying not to listen to the talks about her grandson being dead. She'd hardly moved from the spot since the last body was reported found. Mycroft and Elio kept vigil with her, silently looking at the horizon and willing the young man to return home to his family.

The Specter remained relatively silent and somber after hearing the game warden call off the chorus of dissenters. However, once Elio heard the comment about how long it might take to find Ridley's body, he immediately started spewing out statistics.

"The probability of the drone finding him alive is four hundred eighteen thousand, to one. And the chances of him being alive is–"

"Shut your mouth," Mycroft ordered, fury in his voice. "In five

CHAPTER 12

minutes you'll be sent to go search for him. Alone!"

Elio wasn't the least bit perturbed or threatened by the Specter. "I will not last more than ten hours in the cold before my core will shut down, and then I will freeze over. I certainly will not be able to find him by then."

Mycroft lunged at Elio, but Elio dodged out of the way. The Specter grasped the man's throat and started squeezing when a loud siren pierced the air, bringing everyone to a halt.

"They found him!" Oz declared, her voice immediately showing signs of hope. She ran towards the game warden.

"Most likely not alive," Elio blurted. Mycroft threw him on the ground and followed Oz.

Everyone rushed out of the game warden's cabin to greet the incoming drone, their faces a mix of dread and delight. Some would finally get the answer they wanted, and a big paycheck, while others would get the worst news of their lives.

To everyone's shock, an injured and frail Ridley limped towards the town gate, dragging the remnants of his backpack behind him. The crowd cheered, simultaneously out of joy and disappointment, for now there was a declared winner – and keeper of the prize money.

Oz rushed to embrace him as well as Mycroft and Elio. All of them were relieved and surprised he made it back and they couldn't believe it. Hugging him was not enough, and they all squeezed the weak Ridley as hard as they could.

The warden pulled the boy out of his grandmother's embrace and presented Ridley with the trophy and bluechip worth 125,000, the grand prize for winning the Ampherian Gambit.

It was more than enough to get both of them out of their contracts and Mycroft a ship, and get everyone everything that they wanted.

Ridley, although exhausted, felt on top of the universe. He had never won anything in his life, and he was all but certain he wouldn't survive this. But fuck, he won! Everyone present at the finish line, which by then had ballooned into the entire town, looked up at him and congratulated him. His friends and enemies alike looked at him in awe, for this young man survived the stone cold wilderness for days, and came back alive to claim the prize. For ten whole minutes it seemed as if the world was as it should be, and Ridley was finally at peace.

He could get used to this, Ridley told himself. Everyone asked him to tell his story, and he found himself surprisingly enjoying the attention. He was the town hero, and he loved that.

In the back of his head, he wanted to always be the hero and be looked up to. The Gambit showed him that there was more to life than always waiting for your shift to end. More than complaining about how bad things are and how better they should be. The tournament was the first time he felt alive, and he wanted to experience that feeling again—and constantly. He liked feeling important, and wanted to matter to people's lives, and his own. He wanted to have this feeling constantly; the feeling of being important, of mattering to more than just your small family.

Ridley knew that this would be the beginning of something huge, of something important. Today was the beginning of the rest of his life.

CHAPTER 13

The Archon's *Rakkis* tore through the ice storm engulfing the entire atmosphere of Ampheres, piercing through the turbulent air as smoothly as the pummeling ice crystals would allow. The ship shuddered as it landed on the rough outskirts of the Village, with steam emitting from the hull as though it was angry at being challenged.

The Archon's mood mirrored the anger of the ship. He was beyond furious that his plan had been interrupted by this petty hunt for this miniscule Specter, and especially furious that this minute individual could single-handedly destroy his life's work. Time was quickly becoming an ally of his enemy, and this was by far the most daunting test the Archon had ever faced.

The angered prophet bundled into a heavier cloak, grumbling to himself while he contemplated on how he was exactly going to approach the Specter once he found him. While the Archon would love to gloat and relish the pain in the man's face, there was simply not enough time for anything more than a quick beheading, unfortunately.

He visited Ulysses, who was still safely secured in the corvette's holding chamber. The young man was angrily glaring at the Archon. The landing must have jarred him awake. "The bruises have faded nicely. Now it looks like you're only recovering from a sunburn."

Ulysses remained silent and spat in the face hidden beneath the dark hood.

"The pain will only get worse the longer you continue to not cooperate," the Archon replied calmly, almost bored. "Soon you will have no choice but to comply. Once I've eliminated your final hope for salvation, you will be mine to control and design."

Ulysses spat in the hooded face again. "Your childish persistence is a joke! Frankly, my darling you're wasting your time with me, and all this searching of yours. Just give it up already and get to the good part. You already seem so determined!" Ulysses flashed a mocking smile. "What's the fucking point of torturing me to the *brink* of death? Just fucking kill me already. Satisfy yourself!"

The Archon slapped Ulysses across the face. "Despite bringing me immense joy with every breath you take, keeping you alive gives me leverage and the upper hand. The Syndicate will waste all its resources looking and bargaining for you that it'll end up ill-prepared for the storm that is to come. You are a detrimental ingredient to the entire recipe, dear Ulysses." The monk's voice oozed anger and sarcasm.

"But the key to all of this is timing," he continued. "And killing you now will derail everything, and result in too many unnecessary lives lost."

"Ooo, your heart just expanded three sizes," Ulysses quipped. "Detrimental ingredient, huh? So I just belong right here, forever in the torture chamber?"

"Oh no, I have quite a few plans for you. While your looks are above average, driving public opinion is your only talent. Once you grow more submissive, you will become the face and voice of the war. With my tutelage, you'll fuel the fires that drive the conflict, adding to the vitriol and turning everyone against each other. You will ensure the battle spreads beyond the war theater, and continues indefinitely."

Ulysses glared at the pure evil standing before him, baring his teeth. "You'll never get me to join you."

CHAPTER 13

The Archon released a half-chuckle. "Oh? Even when I am no more, you and your work will continue long after I fade from memory." A smile was heard in the menacing voice. "You're further along than you think."

"You won't win," Ulysses shouted as the Archon exited the chamber. "Even if everything right now happens as it should, you won't win."

The Archon remained motionless, staring at Ulysses silently for several moments. Suddenly the armored monk raised his finger slightly and red lightning coursed all through Ulysses' body. The boy screamed and lurched with immense pain. His body convulsed violently, straining at the tight bonds holding him to the table. Blood seeped out of his rug-burned wrists and ankles.

This was by far the worst pain Ulysses had ever experienced.

"That's just a taste of what is to come." The Archon stomped out of the chamber, leaving the young man smoldering.

The angered monk's first stop was JeffCo's administrative offices, as that was the village hall. He found the company executive in charge and questioned him about any strange new arrivals within the last couple of weeks. The interview proved fruitless and ended in a bloody mess. The underlings were of no use as well, and the Archon cleaned out most of the office. Deep in the bowels of the building, one of the custodians offered a lead, and the Archon showed his mercy by sparing a life.

That led the Archon to the spaceport dealer, who tried to take him for an average fool, and refused to offer any real information but rather attempted to sell some junk at an inflated price.

After some violent persuasion, the foolish dealer described the Specter and told the story of him and his slave companion.

"Where are they?" the Archon asked, his voice dripping with menace.

"I don't know, sir." The dealer's face was a bloody mess, and his voice was thick with blood and hard to understand through the broken jaw.

"Don't make me choose between your eye and your hand," the Archon squeezed the brute's neck harder and ignited his sword, enticing the dealer with the brilliantly flickering blade.

Tears streamed down the dealer's face, and his voice rose many octaves out of pure fear. "I told you a thousand times already, man, I don't know! My nephew tells me they're always seen with that Camaro boy and his grandmother. They live on the outskirts, in the old housing unit."

The Archon spared the dealer's life, and organs, but promised to return if the information wasn't accurate. Everywhere the monk went, he could smell the foul essence of the Specter in this village.

He was close, very close.

Soon the Specter would be eliminated and the presence of the Hyde won't be discovered until the Syndicate is on its knees, and the Specters won't be able to save it. That moment was inching closer and closer, and the Archon was almost certain it would be today.

CHAPTER 14

It was the day after the victory and the mood in the Camaro hovel was beyond cheerful. Oz and Ridley spent their time making lists of all the things they wanted to do, the places they wanted to go, and the knickknacks they wanted to get with their new fortune. Mycroft was planning his departure and thinking about which ship he could buy while Elio tended to the temperamental furnace. It was so cold in the hovel they could all see their breaths.

"Don't bother fucking with that, Elio!" Ridley exclaimed. "Buddy, soon we'll be outta here and buying people to fix those things for us! The fuckin company can fix it, leave it alone!"

"Well the first thing we have to do is buy out our contracts," Oz said as she laid out breakfast. "Once we get that bullshit out of the way, then we can focus on tackling that list. But he's right honey, don't fix something that ain't ours."

"Let's all go right now," Ridley shouter. "Show that chief shithead what two free people look like! They're going to buy a ship today anyway," he gestured to Mycroft and Elio. "No sense in wasting time."

"I share the boy's eagerness as well. Time is of the essence for everyone," Mycroft added. "If you don't mind, I think we'll skip breakfast and get going." He closed his pack where he stowed his ethellite sword and rose to gather his cloak.

Oz nodded, a defeated look on her face. She half-hoped they would change their minds and stay awhile. "I understand. But look at that weather. No one has any business being out in this."

The furnace rattled as the wind shook the house, sifting soot all over Elio. "This soot is terribly difficult to work with. It gets everywhere and is bloody hard to clean." He threw the piece of furnace he was working with unceremoniously on the floor. "I am finished with this project."

The Specter looked out the window at the fiercely blowing snow. He could barely see the structures across the little street. He very much did not want to go out in this, for he had already had it with snowstorms in his brief stay here on Ampheres. But duty called.

"Unfortunately, madam, I cannot allow the weather to dictate my actions. Come Elio, let's get you outside. The snow will clean you off on the way to the yard." Mycroft nodded at Oz and proceeded to leave.

Ridley hurried to follow them. "Are you sure you don't want to come with us?" he asked, desperately. "It won't be as fun without you there to tell those bastards to fuck off!"

"Duty calls, young friend," Mycroft said and patted him on the shoulder. "But I don't see why we can't stop by the contract officer before the junk dealer." He smiled lightly, but calculated how long this would exactly take, for he still had to figure out what to do with Elio before returning to the *Imperatrix.*

Oz scoffed. "You guys are still going out in this?" She waved her hands and shook her head. "Y'all have at it! While I'd love to see the look on that snake, venturing out in this nastiness isn't worth it. You guys go ahead. I'll stay behind and start packing!"

Mycroft and Elio exchanged goodbyes with Oz and ventured off into the storm. She grabbed Ridley by the shoulder as he was leaving, "Try to convince them to take us with them!" she whispered.

Ridley looked at his grandmother, completely puzzled. She just smiled widely and winked at him. "It's what you want, ain't it!"

He struggled to form words. This was so unlike her, to convince him to take a risk beyond her pain tolerance. But the smile on her face and the twinkle in her eyes told him that she was being completely serious. She finally trusted him, and he was touched beyond words.

Oz hurried him along, and watched her grandson chase after his future.

At the space yard, the three travelers were surprisingly greeted by a more polite, albeit severely beaten, junk dealer. One of his arms was wrapped in a dirty sling, and he shivered not from the cold, but from fear. When he first made sight of the men, he started to hide in the back, but thought better of it.

The dealer nervously smiled at the three men, and would not make eye contact. His voice was raspy, as though he was recently strangled, and was terribly sing-songy, another sign of a recent beating.

"Gentlemen. Welcome back! How can I help you today?"

"We're here to finish the deal you stopped them from making the other day," Ridley said, cocky and all guns-a blazing. He was getting himself more worked up than anything else. "But today, we're not taking any more of your bullshit." He slammed his fist on the counter, a shiny new bluechip card twinkled under the light. The holographic engraving displayed a very impressive number, and disappeared after a few seconds.

A flash of recognition sparked in the dealer's eyes, just to be replaced fractions of a moment later with utter fear. His upper lip trembled. "I don't understand...I've never seen these two men before in my life." The dealer's voice quaked and tears welled in the man's one un-swollen eye.

Mycroft's senses spiked the moment he walked into the shop, noticing the evidence of a fight. Originally, the Specter surmised it was from a typical angry customer who was a bit sick of the dealer's sense of humor. But the intense level of trepidation coming from the dealer was evidence of something beyond typical. And the fact that the man would lie and say he's never seen the Specter before was puzzling.

Something else was going on here, and the Specter suddenly felt uncomfortable—and in danger.

Mycroft raised his eyebrow. "Get a taste of your own medicine, mate?"

The dealer found something interesting to look at on the floor, refusing to make eye contact. A heavy tear fell down his face. "Like I said, I've never seen you guys before. So what do you guys want? Just state your business or get the hell outta here!"

Not wanting to press the issue, Mycroft let Ridley continue bargaining for a ship while he observed the store's disarray a little closer. Images of an Axis trooper popped into the Specter's mind. It had already been a week since he'd crashed here and it wasn't out of the ordinary to see troopers this close to the Line of Control. It wouldn't be entirely impossible for them to search for a missing Specter out here.

Suddenly, Mycroft spied a large scar along one of the shelving units, everything beneath it was burned and melted into its surroundings.

This was made by an ethellite sword, the Specter surmised. And Axis troopers didn't carry swords...

Mycroft needed to get going...before it was too late.

* * *

Oz hummed to herself as she packed the bags. She gathered the clothes from the various drawers and folded them neatly before placing them into the rucksack. Behind her a group of pots bubbled, cooking delicious smelling food. The cooking unit made so much noise that Oz didn't hear the window creak open. She was moving around so much, back and forth between the dressers and the rucksacks, that she didn't see the form slink around the room, inching closer to her.

The Archon entered silently, slithering like a snake towards his prey. In one fluid motion, he ignited his sword, grabbed her by the ponytail and rotated her to face him. He held his blade mere centimeters from Oz's neck, the heat from the sizzling ethellite scorching her fair skin.

She was scared silent, her eyes wide open and completely focused on the faceless person in front of her.

"You are seen with two men that aren't locals. Where are they?" The Archon's voice exuded pure authority.

Oz's voice was unwavering. "Not here," she said matter-of-factly.

The Archon wasn't amused. "Don't. Lie. Tell me, woman, or your precious life ends. Where are they?"

Her eyes moved to look at the sizzling blade, then back at the faceless creature. "Even if I knew, I would never tell the likes of...you." The word left her mouth like a cough, and she spat on him.

"You will never realize how more dangerous they are than I, woman. You do not realize what they are, or how much destruction they will cause. Be the patriot you are and stop trying to protect the enemy. Please."

Oz's face contorted into a look of fury. "Fuck you!"

The Archon slowly backed away as red lightning engulfed Oz's body. Oz convulsed and writhed in intense pain. The smell of burning flesh and hair filled the room. Her body slowly lifted into the air, still writhing and screaming loudly and intensely.

For several seconds she remained this way, completely suffering. The Archon cocked his head as he watched the torture. In some ways he was taking pleasure, but he mostly wanted someone to just *fucking* cooperate with him. He had no intention of killing people who had no reason to die—at least as far as he was concerned—and all he wanted was to get back to what he intended to do.

The Archon sighed and swung his sword in a gentle arc. The room fell silent after the dead body thudded to the floor.

The armored monk felt disappointed, because this was not what he wanted to do. But alas, *the pathway to the truth is never the easiest to take.*

He proceeded to search the hovel, which did not take very long, and found evidence of the Specter's stay. He might return, but the Archon surmised that would be unlikely.

The search continued.

CHAPTER 15

With a ship in hand, Mycroft and Elio were anxious to leave the frozen wasteland and get going, but it took all of Ridley's conniving to convince the pair (mostly Mycroft) to say a final goodbye to Oz. Along the way, Ridley attempted to broach the subject that he and his grandma could come with the traveling pair, but all he could do was go on about the meal Oz was (probably) going to make.

"I'm telling you, her seasoned wolf tenderloin is the best on the planet. Everyone who's ever had it only has good things to say. The town always requests it for the quarterly bonus celebrations."

Ridley didn't want them to leave. They were his first glimpse at the universe outside his meager hovel, and he wanted to go with them. From an early age, Ridley knew he had always wanted a life of adventure, and Mycroft's arrival was proof that that was possible. The daily routine was stale and slowly killing him, Ridley knew even though he was only 17. He would never live a long life if all he could hope for was living forever in this frozen hell hole. Repeatedly, Ridley pondered how in the hell Oz was able to do it for so long.

Oz. She was the one who definitely deserved better than this. She's had a long life of working constantly and had earned the right to spend the rest of her days doing whatever the hell she wanted to do. Ridley knew she would never be able to join him on his crusades across the stars, she would always be waiting to hear his stories when he came home. Ridley had never known a life without her, and all he had ever wanted was for her to be as comfortable as possible.

As much as he wanted to, Ridley could never live on his own. He was always lonely, forgetting important things, and always looking forward to the next best thing. Living with her yet still being able to do things on his own was the best medium, where he could be himself out there but still have a grounded home to return to. While she might have turned over a new leaf of letting him do whatever he wanted, Oz was still going to be the boss.

But Ridley was afraid of what Mycroft would say. He had been nothing but nice and agreeable so far, and there was no reason to think he wouldn't at least understand where Ridley and Oz were coming from with their request to join him. But the rejection would be the hardest to deal with. A busy man like him wouldn't have time to ferry around a kid and his grandmother, and at the end of the day that was all Ridley and Oz were.

By the time the three reached the row house, Ridley still hadn't breached the subject. He fumbled entering the door code, still looking for the right way to ask. "I've had it a thousand times and won't miss it if I can't have it again."

"I will not get to taste it," Elio said. "And I am not sure that I am missing out on anything. Wolf is not the most flavorful of meats, nor the most edible."

"Elio, you don't always have to interject the unrelated truth into the conversation," Mycroft said. "And besides, you've never eaten Ampherian wolf. It might be the exception."

"I have not eaten anything, actually. And that is highly unlikely. Like humans, wolves are part of the same group of genes that share collected genomes across the entire explored universe, rendering the differences amongst them minute."

CHAPTER 15

The trio was stunned to silence once they entered the home. It was completely destroyed. Every piece of furniture was upturned and ripped to shreds. Scars of scorched destruction dotted the walls, floors, and ceiling. Oz and Ridley's belongings were scattered about and destroyed beyond recognition. Blaster bolt holes and sword marks covered virtually every surface. Elio's roof patch was destroyed, allowing a delicate dusting of snow to fall inside. Beneath the snowfall, almost in a pose, was Oz's body. Her closed eyes and delicate face gave the impression she was asleep.

Mycroft and Elio stood back as Ridley approached the carcass. Tears streamed down his face as he lifted her head and placed it against his chest. He remained completely still in this position as he cried silently.

The other two stood still in respect, silently surveying the damage. The Specter was analyzing the damage, trying to determine just exactly who made all this destruction.

Suddenly, Ridley expelled a blood curdling scream, releasing all of his emotions. Fury, depression, anger, desperation, fear, jealousy, hatred, and want. It was so powerful it changed the direction of the snowfall, as though it were the wind. The scream lasted for an eternity.

***

A few hours later, Ridley had mostly collected himself and joined the others in analyzing the row house's devastation.

When he spoke, his voice was hollow, as though an integral piece of his soul was suddenly ripped away. He seemed dejected, defeated, and exhausted with every breath he took. "The Johns did this, no question. Look at this mess. All the copper and precious metals stripped from the wiring and electronics. Every valuable thing, stolen." His voice got thick for a few moments and he nearly cried again, but somehow held it together.

Elio sorted the destroyed belongings into neat trash piles. "But what is the reason for all the blaster holes? Did another group disrupt the first? Look at this," he held up the body of the destroyed VERA, "This still contains perfectly functional parts, and no doubt worth a pretty penny in these extreme environments. No smart looter would leave this behind unless he's working under a time pressure."

Mycroft looked around the place with his hand underneath his chin. "Elio makes an excellent point. There is so much needless destruction that makes me wonder if this wasn't staged."

"The Johns are the only gang here. And they shot the place up because, why the hell not?" Ridley said. His face grew redder with each word he spoke. Redder with anger, redder with fear, redder with sadness.

"They cause trouble and destroy lives because that's what they do." His fists clenched as tears slowly streamed down his face. "They've been fucking with us my entire life. Not once giving us a break, always taking it to the next level. Fucking A!"

Mycroft sensed the boy's anger, and while it was appropriate, found it misplaced. "Look closer at Oz. She wasn't shot by these rifles or bludgeoned to death. See there, that's a sword wound. Do the Johns wield swords? An expensive, highbrow weapon for a backwater corporate world."

Ridley wasn't convinced. "They use whatever they find."

"But you yourself said that mine was the first sword you've seen outside of a picture. And this destruction looks too systematic to have been done by some hood rats." Mycroft tried to get the boy to see reason. To open his mind a little more and see beyond the veil of fury.

Ridley's fury, however, grew insatiable. "But there's no one else here! Who else would come here and beat the shit out of our lives?"

Mycroft thought of the dealer's strange behavior, and of the count's pursuit. He started to tell Ridley about them when the boy interrupted.

CHAPTER 15

"I'm giving them a taste of their own medicine." He grabbed a broken piece of furnace pipe and stormed out of the house.

"Wait. Ridley! It's too dangerous! Don't do this!"

But it was too late, the determined boy was off to take revenge. Mycroft rushed after him, but couldn't find him after hours of searching. He eventually gave up, determining the fate of the galaxy wasn't worth chasing after a back alley kid.

CHAPTER 16

All Ridley saw was red. His eyes were bloodshot with anger and tears. He ran as fast as he could, and still couldn't burn off his energy. Even in the violent winter storm, he was burning hot with a fever. Every cell in his being was consumed with fury, and there was only one thing on his mind: Kill.

He hadn't gone far when he encountered two of the Johns pilfering parts from an abandoned speeder.

"Well, lookie what we have here," the shortest gangster said. "The new Gambit champion!"

The taller one chuckled heavily. "More like the Gambit *cheater*."

Without any words or hesitation, Ridley pummeled the shorter guy with his pipe. The beating was continuous and unrelenting.

The victim's companion tried to intervene and stop Ridley's attack, but it was a futile effort. The furious boy's strength was too much to handle.

Blood splattered everywhere, staining the pristine white snow with the deep shade of pain.

In mere moments the first John's brain was pulverized to a pulp. Ridley moved to attack the other one, but the man was fleeing off into the snowy distance. Ridley's strength, though, was no match, and he caught the running man easily, striking the man's knees and ankles with the heavy pipe.

The man screamed in pain and tried to crawl away with his useless legs, but Ridley blocked his path.

"Where are the others?" The boy's voice no longer sounded the same. He had lost that last sliver of innocent hope that had kept him going for so many years. Now all was left was the beaten, raw soul of a man who lost everything, and was willing to take some of it back.

All the squealing gangster could do was howl in between the tears streaming from his face. "The fuck man? The fuck's wrong with you?"

Ridley swung again, this time at the small of the man's back. The crunch of the spine was blood curdling, yet Ridley found it oddly satisfying. An evil smile appeared on his face, displaying pristine fangs, hungry for blood. "How many bones do I have to break before you'll start cooperating?"

Despite the pain, the gangster was not folding. "Kiss my ass, you piece of shit!"

Ridley swung, breaking the man's shoulder. "It's okay. We can break them one by one." He hefted the pipe again, preparing to strike.

"Fine, fine, fine. Alright I'll talk." The John put his hands out for mercy.

Across the frozen tundra, on the other side of the Village, stood the old plasticum factory. It had been abandoned for nearly a decade, since the construction of the larger plant closer to the mining fields. The structure was decommissioned and abandoned, but the company was too cheap to tear it down and just left the building there, still full of its old equipment and chemicals, to rot under the ice.

The space was perfect for the Johns, who used it as their lair. They claimed the toxic fumes were euphoric and offered them a special clairvoyance. While the fumes did provide the inhalants with immense levels of strength and increased stamina, they also gradually decreased the brain's thinking capacity and processing power, leading the Johns to frequently cause needless mayhem. In some sense, the Johns' environment is what led them to be who they were.

There was a calm, easy atmosphere in the common room, with the gang members scattered about the room having sex, smoking and ingesting drugs, or just catching a heavy nap before the next event. The hazy smoke filled the air with the pungent scent of yak and wak, combining with the odorous chemical fumes that would give any entrant to the room an immediate headache.

The calm was abruptly interrupted by Ridley, who stormed in through the loading door and started attacking everything in sight. No living creature was spared the boy's murderous wrath, as he moved gracefully about the room performing the ballet of destruction. Vicious swings of the heavy pipe turned sturdy skulls into crinkled paper, crushed bones to dust, and snapped necks as though they were twigs.

No gang member had enough time to retrieve a weapon, as the drug-filled haze impeded their reaction time. Even those who did possess some type of weapon on their person were caught off guard by Ridley's intense assault, and they only had enough seconds to see their life briefly pass before their eyes.

In no time at all, he cleared the Johns from the entrance and advanced to the barracks.

It was another sweat and drug filled haze. Bodies of every gender were intertwined with each other in various, and in some cases unnatural, lovemaking positions. The few who weren't procreating were fast asleep, dead to the world. Hardly anyone noticed Ridley's entrance, as the sex was too enthralling to interrupt.

Ridley didn't appreciate the lack of attention because he was so focused on his mission to inflict pain. The angry young man effortlessly cleared the room. No one put up a fight, and one couple even tried to bring him in for a threesome.

Deep in the bowels of the facility, the gang's leadership huddled at a large conference table, looming over the latest cache of stolen goods.

CHAPTER 16

They seemed to be arguing over how to equally split the kitty when the blood-soaked Ridley stormed into the room.

For a few moments the two sides just stared at each other silently, both equally surprised at their current predicament. The gang's leaders took one glance at the blood covering the boy and knew immediately what happened. But rather than show anger or even sadness, they all started lightly chuckling.

The head member stepped away from the table and moved closer to Ridley, very amused and even impressed. "Well, well, well. If it isn't the runt-turned-champion here to grace us with his presence. To what do we owe this pleasure? Come to pay off your debts, kiddo?"

The rest of the group cackled loudly. Despite all that Ridley had gone through to get into this room, and all the blood covering him, they were not going to take him seriously. He was outnumbered seven to one.

Ridley's grip on his dented pipe tightened, and his fury grew to a new degree. "No. Actually I've come to collect what you took from me. Or at least the equivalent."

The laughing only increased. "What *we* took from you? Ha! And just what might that be?"

The boy whispered, barely audible even for himself to hear. "Oh, you fuckers know damn well what!"

Ridley charged the goons, swinging his trusty pipe as hard as he could. The goons barely had time to get out of the way, and one of them was struck in the face and knocked unconscious. The others rushed to pull out their weapons, but the attack was relentless.

One of the goons fired his rifle, but missed Ridley and hit a rusty pipe in the wall. The pipe immediately burst into flame and quickly spread, engulfing the entire ceiling. Lightbulbs burst from the heat, raining down on the fight below.

The fight continued, with the six remaining goons giving Ridley a run for his money. One of them hit Ridley's shoulder with their staff, leaving a large gash. The boy hardly felt anything, his rage was so immense. He managed to block another blow from the staff and threw the pipe at the wielder's head, which burrowed itself into the man's left eye. Ridley grabbed the staff and pushed the dying goon to the floor, then turned his attention to the others.

The others were felled in a relatively short time. Every time Ridley made contact with a head with his weapon, he only felt hungry for more. It was an insatiable hunger, increasing with every kill and slowly shielding over the wound left by his murdered grandmother. Nothing would ever replace that piece of his being that was ripped away from him, but at least he could feel some semblance of healing.

Tears streamed down his face, filled with intense anger, immense hate, tremendous sadness, and the titanic fear of knowing there is no returning to the way things were. Ever.

Soon only the gang leader remained, blocking every blow that Ridley gave. The leader tried to launch a counter attack, but the boy gave no opening in his anger-filled fight. Ridley pushed the leader into a corner and disarmed him, but the coward ducked away to the other side of the room and pulled out a small six-shot pistol from his boot.

Most of the bodies were either killed or unconscious. Only the gang leader was left, and he cowered in fear, brandishing his pistol.

"What the fuck man? All we ever did was steal money and shit from you and your old lady." His face was full of nothing but genuine fear and panic. "We never killed anybody."

Ridley raised his staff to swing, but hesitated. They never killed anyone? Mycroft alluded to the same thing. But was this shithead before Ridley just saying things to save himself? Was it the drugs, or did the fucker really mean it?

Could Ridley have done all this for nothing? Was he taking out his anger on the wrong people? And was there another party that was responsible for killing Oz?

The gangster started crying, bringing Ridley out of his trance. "Why are you doing this? Please have mercy." The pathetic man couldn't even hold his pistol steady.

And that's what sent Ridley over the edge. With all the trouble the Johns caused him and Oz throughout the years, not to mention the rest of the Village—not once did they show him mercy. They never showed Oz mercy. Why should Ridley give the Johns the very thing they denied to everyone else?

In one swift motion Ridley bashed in the gang leader's brain. Gray matter splattered everywhere, adding another stench to the multiple foul odors in the room. The body reflexively shot its gun, and the bolt ignited another conflagration along the wall, and soon the entire room was engulfed in flames.

Ridley ran out of the building just as it was fully inflamed. It was barely seconds when the large exhaust column collapsed, bringing the roof and the Johns down with it. Soon the blaze was the brightest point on the entire planet, attracting the entire Village to watch the conflagration.

Ridley collapsed on the ground, every ounce of energy exhausted. He couldn't keep his eyes open, and had to remind himself to keep breathing. He would have been fully content to die right then and there.

In what seemed like an eternity, he heard the muffled sounds of someone kneeling beside him. He felt a soft, warm touch on his chest, and his ears were filled with the nicest, yet angriest sound he ever heard.

"Has your hunger been satisfied?"

Ridley opened his eyes to see Mycroft gently staring back at him.

"You know that nothing will ever make you feel complete. Even if you killed the exact person who took Oz from this world. Nothing can ever bring back the dead. The pain will follow you forever, never going away. The only thing you can do is channel it into something beneficial to us, the living."

The young man's eyes were puffy with tears, and he struggled to speak. "I have nothing to live for. She was everything I knew."

"And is this how you want to honor her memory? By vanquishing her enemies, which actually were yours? Do you think she'd approve?"

Ridley chuckled. "She wouldn't approve of anything."

Mycroft smiled lightly, fondly remembering his late husband. "Our loved ones never do."

By now Ridley had gained enough strength to sit up and stare into the Specter's eyes. "Let me come with you. There's nothing for me here, and I have nowhere else to go."

Mycroft waved the idea away and stood "But you have the entire galaxy at your feet. Why do you want to come with some old space cop? You're a champion fighter now. Travel the circuit, increase your winnings." He started back towards the shipyard, for he was already late enough as it was.

Ridley ran to keep up. "I think we both know this was a one shot deal. I won't stay in your way. I promise. And I can fix everything. Honest. Please! Let me help you."

Ridley grew excited and began ranting about all the things he's fixed and built for Oz.

Mycroft struggled to silence him. "You can't, kiddo. The work I do isn't for the untrained, and the life I live is dangerous. You'll be in the way by virtue of your lack of experience."

"Then why is Elio tagging along? He certainly isn't trained."

Damn, the kid had a point. "Touché. Elio helped me and I owe him repayment." Mycroft struggled to look Ridley in the eye.

The boy stopped the Specter in his tracks. "Well there you go! You owe me then."

CHAPTER 16

"Incorrect. I taught you how to use the ethellite sword, as well as lent mine to you. It is because of my help that you won. Ergo, we're square." Mycroft moved the kid out of the way and continued on his journey.

"So you're really just gonna leave me here?" Ridley used the most pathetic tone he could, and shot the biggest pouting face when Mycroft looked back at him. The same expression worked on Oz, why wouldn't it work now?

Mycroft fought long and hard against his heart. His better judgment told him to leave both the kid and Elio here to fend for themselves. They were with civilization and had plenty of bluechips. Mycroft had a war to stop and a galaxy to save from implosion. He was not a fucking taxicab!

But the truth also was that these two kids had no one at all, and he was truly the only person that was on their side, let alone could trust.

"You can come as far as the *Imperatrix*, the galactic capital. After that, you and Elio are on your own, and I return to my work. Deal?"

Ridley hesitated for a few seconds, then erupted into a big smile. "Deal! But I'm sure you'll be convinced to let me stay during the trip."

Mycroft only rolled his eyes as the two returned to the small row house.

Loaded with what few belongings they had, the trio embarked to the ship. The weather had turned for the worse, with visibility so bad they couldn't see more than a few inches in front of their faces. Elio's eyes weren't affected by the storm and led the pack.

"Are we almost there? I can hardly breathe in this wind," Mycroft asked.

"We have another fifteen hundred meters." Ridley removed his wind mask and handed it to Mycroft. "Here. You take it for the last leg."

"No thanks," the Specter shook his head. "I can manage."

"Stop being stubborn and accept help when you need it!" Ridley slammed.

"Help yourself before you run out of resources. I'm not being stubborn," Mycroft countered. "I'm following my training."

The two stopped walking and erupted in a small argument. Elio continued on, ignoring them. He didn't get more than 20 feet when a mountain of snow cascaded on top of him. Within seconds, Elio was buried up to his chin.

The snowfall was so thick and the argument was so intense, that Mycroft and Ridley didn't notice the dark figure land between them, ignite its sword, and kick them to the ground.

The Archon moved in on Mycroft to make the kill, but Mycroft ignited his sword just in time to block the blow.

The dancing swordsmen moved expertly, blocking and parrying each attack with such grace it was almost beautiful to watch. The men's movements were so intense and focused, each swing intended to be the last. The two danced so quickly there was just a blur of moving light.

Apparently unconscious for a few seconds, Ridley opened his eyes to see two brilliantly bright blades of light clash with each other. His first instinct was to immediately rush in to help, but he hesitated because he didn't know exactly what help he could provide. Perhaps the cranky Mycroft was right, all Ridley would do was get in the way.

Amongst the swinging blades, Ridley heard a faint whimpering. Elio's face popped into his mind, and the boy rushed to save his other companion.

Mycroft was completely astonished. This was the first time he had an actual sword fight with anyone in a non-training capacity, let alone with a non-Specter. While the ethellite sword was a fairly common weapon, very few actually knew how to appropriately wield it. Mycroft's opponent was an expert swordsman, with the weapon acting

CHAPTER 16

as an extension of the figure's body. It was as though he possessed the deep knowledge of the Specter teachings, but there was absolutely no record of anyone ever defecting from the organization.

Thinking back to the rest of his schooling, Mycroft had some faint recollection of an organization that rivaled the Specters and wielded the sword as their primary weapon. But that group's history ended at the formation of the Syndicate, 5,000 years ago.

The dueling swordsman circled each other, their swords embraced in a deadlock.

"You're not with Lucilous," Mycroft declared.

The hooded figure laughed menacingly. "Quick on the uptake, I see. Very good!"

The deadlock broke and the Archon lunged at Mycroft, who deflected the attack with an easy twist of the wrist.

The Specter was sick of playing around. "Who are you!?"

"Your teacher."

The Archon charged his swing and launched into a new offensive. Mycroft struggled to fend off the attack. While the two were equally as strong, his quarry was considerably faster and younger.

"Where's Ulysses? I know you know"

The figure laughed. "Wouldn't you like to know?"

Mycroft launched into his own offensive. It was deflected in less than three seconds. "Tell me, or die."

"Phfft. An empty promise. Your precious Syndicate is so consumed with finding that brat that it's neglecting the actual threat...*me*."

The Archon leaped onto a snowy ledge, away from the fight. A hidden pistol slid into his palm and he shot at the fragile snow. An avalanche developed, rolling down the steep mountainside straight for the Specter. Mycroft jumped out of the way just in time, joining his opponent on the mountain ledge and continuing the fight.

Ridley had just dug out Elio when another snowy cascade threatened them. The boys managed to run a fair distance away, but still ended up buried to their waist.

Neither Mycroft nor the Archon were willing to surrender to one another. The fight to the death was relentless.

The Specter was quickly losing his energy. He struggled to keep himself alive, let alone to probe for information. "Why are you doing this? What do you want?"

The voice beneath the hood didn't sound tired at all. "To teach you"

"Teach what?"

The Archon kicked at the Specter, which gave him an opening to strike Mycroft's shoulder. "You'll soon find out. Just follow the pattern and open your eyes."

Instead of killing him, the Archon extinguished his sword, saluted Mycroft and dove off the ledge into a deep crevasse below.

Mycroft looked for a trace, but only saw swirling snow and ice. He wanted to remain still and revel in what just happened, digesting every little detail while it was still fresh in his mind, but time did not allow. Mycroft rushed to his colleagues, who were still digging themselves out of the snow.

"Who was that?" Ridley asked, dumbfounded and excited to see action.

Mycroft remained silent for several seconds. "I have my suspicions but unfortunately no facts. All I do know is that the sooner we get going, the better." All he wanted was to get on his way and delve deeply into contemplation.

***

He should have killed the Specter, the Archon thought to himself as he boarded his ship. That was the original plan and he should have followed through with it. Now he had to make adjustments, and not

CHAPTER 16

any minor ones.

But his emotions got the better of him and he just couldn't help himself. This was the first encounter between his kind and a Specter in almost 5,000 years, and he got a bit carried away in the moment. No point in eating the best cut of meat all in one bite, you want to savor every last drop of flavor.

The Specter was no threat to him or the Plan, the Archon concluded. The man's mere existence was inconsequential.

Then why did the Archon have an uncomfortable feeling in his stomach? Was it excitement, or fear?

He contacted Lucilous who immediately started bumbling around like a fool. "My lord! Have you found the Specter? Despite our efforts, we still haven't located—"

"Launch phase one. Now!"

CHAPTER 17

The Kulaki were a peaceful people, devoting their lives to producing and developing medical technology. Their planetary system of two stars, three habitable planets, and a moon produced the entire galactic supply of Pirin, the universal pain reliever and disinfectant. Every single medical kit in the Syndicate, Axis, and everywhere in between contained the stuff.

Given the exclusivity of this valuable resource, the Kulaki tightly restrict the entrance of goods and people into the system, which makes it extremely difficult to smuggle anything, or anyone, in or out. They do this with the star gate, a large shield that encompasses the entire border of the system, which can only be entered via designated points.

The Kulaki have no geo-galactic or political enemies, as they are universally respected by all, because of their valuable Pirin. Locally, however, a few families control the largest conglomerates in each of the star system's industrial sectors, while the rest of the planet's people are relegated to the working class.

Violent flare ups among the two castes are common, but have never grown intense enough to warrant any outside attention. However the peace is far from fragile.

The south's largest port was bustling away, with hundreds of thousands of tons of freight and humanity going in and out. There was so much commotion that one couldn't focus on any particular thing, even if they tried.

Amongst the hustle and bustle, a nondescript gang of workers transported ordinary freight pallets to the awaiting haulers. It was a normal day.

Once loaded with the precious cargo, the ships embarked on their journeys across the stars. As they approached the star gate, all 18 ships spontaneously combusted, destroying the invaluable shipment of Pirin. It was the largest terrorist event in Kulaki history.

Fervor erupted within the Kulaki government, who blamed the attack on the age-old caste feud. The government's opposition party, and most of the public, didn't believe the story because the feuding parties have always avoided damaging the Pirin. *Always.* Immediately, rumors began circulating that an outside force was to blame.

To bring down the fervor, the ruling party started pondering the idea of ceasing Pirin exports until the mystery could be solved, or an apology was offered.

* * *

Corporate Space is a collection of semi-close star systems that provide the bulk of the galaxy's economic resources such as banking, building materials, and jumpspace fuel.

The Kulaki refuse to be a part of Corporate Space because they are philosophically against making profits. The Corporate Conglomerates, on the other hand, thrive on the profit margin, and serve anyone willing to pay the price, Syndicate or Axis. They control and regulate the galaxy's standard currency, the bluechip.

Both the Axis and the Syndicate reviled the Corporate Conglomerates, but understood the necessity to tolerate their business practices. An attack, politically or militarily, would elicit a devastating response for everyone, and be counterproductive to either side's goals.

Mere hours after the surprise attack in Kulak, an armada of battleships bearing the Syndicate's colors blockaded the banking planet, Depew, demanding it cease serving the Axis and only recognize the Syndicate.

In retaliation, a battalion of Axis frigates barricaded the main jump route into Corporate Space, claiming it was annexing the territory.

Frustrated and growing helpless, the directorates in charge of the Corporate Conglomerates chartered the services of their own mercenary force to take military countermeasures. Both the Axis and Syndicate pleaded for them to not strike, and negotiated for peace.

For now, everyone was prepared to fire the first shot.

* * *

The newest independent system in the Coreenian sector was Alcyon, a small agrarian planet that, until a few years ago, knew only great suffering. The civil war with its sister planet, Zaylon, lasted for millennia and peace was a relatively new concept for both peoples.

Even after Alcyon joined the Syndicate as its own independent member, the skirmishes between the two planets were still common and very violent. Both planets still struggled to recognize each other's independence, but it was no longer an all-out war. But after the Syndicate intervened, the two planets shared an understanding that they would never attack their homelands, meaning they would only have space battles or fights on disputed territory.

Which is why it was so surprising when a tremendous explosion rocked Alcyon's surface, destroying its largest city and cultural hub. All signs pointed to the Zaylons as the aggressors, so in response the Alcyons launched an offensive, destroying Zaylon's food supplies.

This was the first all-out battle between member states since the formation of the Syndicate.

CHAPTER 17

* * *

Aboard the space station *Imperatrix*, the capital of the Cosmic Syndicate, the Senate was erupting into sheer chaos. There hadn't been a crisis requiring the lazy senators' attention in over a generation. Every corner of the Syndicate was erupting into violence, with everyone blaming each other for causing the problems, or not doing enough to prevent them. The one thing that everyone in the room seemed to agree upon was that the time had come to hold an official war declaration vote.

Senator Pircilla had certainly never seen a crisis like this in his life, yet understood the magnitude of this moment. However, he was still undecided as to declaring war on the Axis. As far as he could see there was no direct link from the Axis to the current troubles, and all the zeitgeist to finally go to war with them was mainly the result of old prejudices finally coming to a boil. He definitely did agree that the Axis was somehow involved with this, but he was not sure a full-throated military intervention was necessary.

The senator received pleas and threats from all sides of the chamber, the same number in favor of war as against it. Pircilla was the ultimate deciding vote, and for his part pleaded with the others to be patient enough until more details from the attacks came to light, but no one listened. All he could hear were the hearty chants of "Vote now, vote now."

The Primarch was the leader of the Syndicate, yet had been virtually powerless and ineffective since his election. He was too busy wringing his hands and desperately trying to come up with something to say, rather than do anything of substance. But even then, he kept being distracted by all the attractive junior senators. Even on the eve of war he was still a sex-crazed maniac.

The Primarch was not the only one distracted. Pircilla himself was still reeling over the disappearance of his son Ulysses. It had been 10 days of silence and he was starting to lose hope in the Specters, or that his son was even still alive. Despite the past the two shared, Pircilla really missed the boy and never wanted him to come to any harm. In fact, the senator was ready to leave and go look for himself that very day, had it not been for the summons for this current emergency session.

Pircilla was furious and terrified, just like his colleagues in the room. Unlike them though, it was not about the current matter at hand.

"It is our right to retaliate! We must strike back against the Axis!" One senator screamed. He was joined by a loud chorus of support from half of the chamber.

"The Axis didn't attack us, the wretched Alinians did! Death to them!" came a cry from another representative. Another chorus of support erupted, this time from the other half of the chamber.

"Gentlemen, please!' the Primarch pleaded. "Listen to what you're suggesting; one Syndicate member attacking another? That goes against the very foundation of the Articles of Allegiance."

"Attacking a peaceful, non-party system goes against Syndicate principals as well." The first senator, a representative from Bogartha, bellowed. "Small interplanetary militia squabbles are not responsible for this destruction, it's the Axis!"

"Why, then, would the Axis attack the Kulaki, when it benefits from them just as much as we do?" Senator Pircilla tried to be the voice of reason in all situations. "It makes no sense that they would shoot themselves in the foot.

"So then you're suggesting there exists another threat to us that is *not* the Axis?" The Primarch asked. "Whom do you suggest that is?"

Ever since his son was kidnapped, the Senate has viewed Pircilla's judgment as skewed, and never listened fully to what he was saying.

"Perhaps it's the same party that kidnapped my son," was all he could bring himself to say.

The entire Senate erupted into boos and hisses.

"Senator Pircilla, may I be the first to suggest that you seek outside counsel. It's been nearly two weeks since your son was kidnapped, and even the secret police haven't concluded the act was done by the Axis. It's looking more and more likely that your son either was a poor victim of circumstance, or he irritated the wrong group of thugs. You did recently cut him off financially, did you not?" The Primarch was irritated to address this again. "Now, if we may return to the matter at hand."

"The Corporate Space blockade shows no signs of abating," the commerce secretary reported. "Syndicate construction projects are at a standstill, and the funds in the treasury will be depleted in nineteen days."

A representative from the Conglomerates approached his speaking platform. "Honorable Members of the Cosmic Syndicate. Until the situation in neutral Corporate Space has abated, and in order to protect its own interests, the Conglomerates are suspending all transactions with all customers until further notice."

Fervor erupted in the chamber. Everyone was protesting the action and begging for the Primarch to do something.

The previous irritation displayed by the old Primarch was immediately replaced with the pathetic expression of the powerless. "As they're not members of the Syndicate, there's nothing I can do. They're not under Senate jurisdiction."

Most of the Syndicate's members joined solely for the access to the various guilds and societies that had an exclusive deal with it. The most-coveted of the Corporate Conglomerate's resources were not available to members outside of the Syndicate, and since the resources were no longer available, the incentive to remain a member instantly disappeared.

Some of the star systems began debating about whether or not they should remain in the Syndicate or secede.

"Since we no longer have incentive to stay members, there's nothing barring us from defending our own personal interests anymore," the Alinian senator declared. "Since the only thing the Syndicate truly cares about is economics. We the Alinians revoke our membership, effective immediately."

"Do you know what you'll cause?" Pircilla asked. "Like it or not, you're safer in the pact than out of it. Leaving us leaves your people to defend for themselves. The Home Fleet won't come to your aid when the Axis comes to annex you."

The Alinian shot a death glare at Pircilla. "Senator that is the exact position we are in now."

Pircilla continued his pleas. "The Axis will not hesitate to invade and take control of your system, leaving you in a worse position than now. Please, man, see reason!"

"All the reason we see is that we have power and no resources. Which is worse, Senator, resources abundant with no power to use them, or the power to control a limited amount of resources? The Syndicate is turning into the very thing its abundance of rules swore it wouldn't, a powerless, bureaucratic, monstrous waste."

"At this rate, joining the Axis is looking rather desirable every minute," another senator declared. "I move we call a vote."

"A vote? For what?" The Primarch was befuddled. "It is against Article Forty-Three to secede from the Syndicate without a unanimous vote from the full Senate. Even with a situation we all can agree, unanimous votes are nonexistent. At least in my twenty-five years as Primarch."

It was the Loraxian senator who quipped, "I don't believe my government is *requesting* to leave, Primarch."

Chaos erupted in the chamber. Many other star systems joined the chorus of wanting to leave the alliance pact. Voices shouted over each other in both opposition and support of the move.

Conflicts erupted almost immediately, with the senators transmitting to their home governments to launch attacks on various adversaries for various reasons. Thousands of star systems declared their independence effective immediately, and launched hundreds of small skirmishes by the conclusion of the day.

The Primarch watched silently as his control of the situation disappeared.

Senator Pricilla, unable to gain any conversational traction, left to converse with the Specters. They were the galaxy's only hope.

* * *

Deep in space, restrained aboard the *Rakkis*, Ulysses watched the news with rapturous attention, witnessing the galaxy crumble in slow-motion.

The Archon's laugh was full of satisfaction and menace. "See? This is the culmination of the Syndicate's strength; expounding an already existing problem until there remains only one option, implosion. I have done nothing but want for your precious Syndicate to undo itself, and have received it."

Ulysses couldn't bring himself to look at his captor, and tears slowly streamed down his face. "Your plan won't succeed. You'll be stopped before you even get started. The Syndicate will never bend to you."

The hooded man bent and stared directly into the boys' face, filling his entire field of vision. "They already have, my boy, by bringing themselves to my ideals. It's only a matter of time before they give me the victory."

The voice emanating from the hood changed dramatically in tone. "But the one who has the power to stop all of this is you."

Ulysses was completely taken off guard. "Me? Bullshit. How?"

"Emerge from hiding and urge the galaxy to come to peace. The answers don't lie within the Syndicate. We've seen how far blind faith takes you. How weak it makes you."

The boy spit in the Archon's face with all that remained in his dry mouth. "Never! Your weakness is your blind faith that everyone *won't* come to their senses."

"Your weakness is assuming your opinions alone are the correct ones." He slapped Ulysses hard across the face, drawing blood. "Soon you'll be brought to heel. Perhaps mailing an appendage to your father will help your learning?"

Through gritted teeth, Ulysses said, "I am numb to your pain!"

"Then you will witness the suffering of others, knowing full well only you can put an end to it!"

Ulysses' loudest blood curdling scream echoed through the small ship as the Archon resumed the torture.

CHAPTER 18

The ancient corvette from Ampheres sped through the interspace lane toward the capitol. Despite the ship's great age, the ride was smooth, with only the slightest tremor felt inside. The silence in the ship was comforting, providing a necessary reprieve from such an action-filled day.

Elio was preoccupied designing his version of a new control board layout, currently obsessing over where the pressure monitoring dial should be placed. Ever since he entered this ship that was the only thing he could focus on, and nothing else. It drove his fellow companions crazy, and they threatened to harm him unless he kept quiet about it.

Ridley was fast asleep, his energy spent taking in all of the new sights and sounds. As soon as the ship left the atmosphere, Ridley was in absolute awe of everything he saw. The sheer depth of the black void of space, the brilliant yet faint twinkling stars dotting every single centimeter of vision, and the bird's eye view of the only universe the boy had known was overwhelming for Ridley. He had never seen anything like this, and it was well beyond his imagination. Even the red corona of jump space was an awesome sight for the young man.

At first, Mycroft was annoyed at all of Ridley's exclamations, but he quickly grew to enjoy it. He sat at the table nursing an empty cup, deeply contemplating the possible identities of the hooded attacker back on Ampheres. The bloody man–creature–was certainly more than a member of the Axis, yet there was nothing too distinguishing about the thing's appearance. Except for the extraordinary mastery of the ethellite sword...

As he sat twirling the empty cup, Mycroft's mind rolled through the various theories of who the elusive creature could be, yet he kept circling back to the same one. And it was too crazy even for him, the history buff, to believe.

Ridley awakened at the sound of an alarm from one of the cockpit's computers. He tended to it and joined Mycroft at the table with two new cups of coffee.

"They're hard to drink when they're empty, ya know," the boy smiled. "Besides, you can use this more than anyone else. How long have you been awake, anyway?"

"About ninety-six hours, give or take a day." The Specter took a large swig of the coffee. "Thanks kid."

"Why don't you get some sleep?" Ridley asked.

The Specter slammed down the mug on the table, spilling some coffee. "There's too much to figure out before I reach the capitol for sleep!"

Ridley jumped at the outburst but then let out a large yawn. "And are you any closer to figuring it out?"

"For fucks' sake no!" Mycroft threw the mug across the room, and the coffee exploded on the viewport.

Ridley raised his eyebrows. "Well now it doesn't taste that bad. Hey, perhaps I can help you. Talk through all of your ideas with me and maybe we can narrow down your options. Oz always said things make more or less sense when you say them out loud."

Mycroft just glared at the kid, who shrugged his shoulders. A surprising sense of pride welled within the Specter, who noticed this was the first time Ridley mentioned his grandmother without welling with tears.

Ridley couldn't stand the seconds of silence. "Obviously what you're doing now is working so well." He loudly sipped his coffee in hopes of soliciting a response.

The Specter resigned, and figuring he had nothing to lose, shared his theory.

"Well, that man, if that's what it even was, fought as though he was trained in the ancient martial arts. My organization is as well, but he clearly was not a Specter. Nor was he some run of the mill Axis grunt either."

"Maybe he defected from your side years ago and joined the Axis as an elite assassin," Ridley interjected.

Mycroft nodded his head. "At first that's what I thought, too, but there haven't been any defections or terminations in decades."

Ridley pointed at the tired old man. "Perhaps he did it years ago? When was the last defection?"

"Two hundred years ago," Mycroft answered in a grave tone.

The young man nodded his head, slowly at first, then gradually picking up speed. "Well, then...are there multiple organizations like yours? After all, the galaxy is quite large."

"No, there aren't. Yes, there are mercenaries and paramilitary groups that claim to know the ancient arts," Mycroft postulated as he spoke, "but we Specters are alone nowadays."

So that's what he was, Ridley thought, a Specter. Judging by what Mycroft taught him, a Specter's job must be really cool. But whatever they did sounded dangerous, and those that did it must be a rare breed. "Nowadays? What do you mean nowadays?"

"Hundreds of years ago, around the creation of the jump drive, there were many disorganized tribes scattered throughout the galaxy. They each believed they had the claim to rule the whole galaxy, and for years war was all the stars had known.

"The two most powerful tribes were the Specters, and the Hyde, a group of acolytes who believed they possessed supernatural powers that gave them divine right to rule. The Hyde believed their power came from these ancient texts that were written by the founders of the galaxy, the Twelve Sacred Scriptures. Once the Hyde fully studied each one of the books, they would rule the galaxy. However, the texts were scattered throughout space and lost in antiquity.

"Ultimately, the Specters won the ancient war, inadvertently by retrieving some of the sacred texts the Hyde was looking for. The Hyde was consumed with internal conflict and ultimately fell into the memories of antiquity. Even their most ardent followers grew disillusioned with them. Now, the Hyde is all but extinct, and the Specters remain around in some form as the Syndicate's secret police, guarding the stars in the event of the Hyde's resurgence."

Mycroft fell silent, lost in the magic and despair of his own story.

Ridley was awestruck. "So, you're all prepared for this then? This Hyde bastard will be taken care of, lickety split, right? That's what you said!"

"Not necessarily." The Specter tried to temper the boy's naive expectations. "The Specter Corps' attention has been increasingly consumed with the Senate's most trivial matters, including the one that sent me to meet you. Our original goal has all been but forgotten. It will take a miracle to convince the Specter Chiefs of this theory. That's why I've been wracking my brain to look for another possibility, otherwise I'd be laughed at as a fool."

"This doesn't sound foolish to me at all," Ridley protested. "Oz taught me that the planet was larger than only what you know, so it only makes sense that rings true for the rest of the galaxy. She would always say that the universe doesn't have to make sense." He grew teary eyed and looked down at the floor.

Mycroft's first instinct was to comfort the boy, but admittedly he

CHAPTER 18

wasn't very good at that, nor did the boy need to be coddled. Life wasn't supposed to be easy, and Ridley was smart enough to understand that.

"I wish the chiefs were as open-minded as you and Oz. Unfortunately, losing one's common sense is a prerequisite to leadership."

"Can't you tell them that this Hyde is a bigger threat than the Axis? Surely they can see that?" Ridley looked out at the traversing space for a few moments. "I've never heard of them and I see how threatening they are."

Mycroft looked out as well. The two men saw different things from the same image. "In the twilight of war, nothing is more dangerous than your opponent. It will be hard to dissuade them to think anything is more important than that."

Suddenly another alarm blared through the air, demanding everyone's attention. Elio and the others raced to the cockpit as the ship suddenly came out of jumpspace.

Filling the viewport was the capitol station *Imperatrix*, the seat of the Cosmic Syndicate. The station constantly traveled throughout Syndicate space, surveying the realm, and was currently orbiting the Pircilla Nebula, a beautiful purple starburst.

Unfortunately, the picturesque background was obscured by the armada of starfighters, frigates, and battle cruisers orbiting the capitol station. More battle cruisers and fleet carriers were in various stages of being loaded, and a few garrisons were jumping out into the interspace, going who knew where.

"This is the twilight of war?" Ridley asked.

"The war has already begun," Elio said as he patched in the battlecruisers through the loudspeakers. Multiple reports of battle casualties flooded the speakers, as well as various deployment commands.

* * *

After landing on the station, which was only possible thanks to Mycroft's security clearance, the trio arrived at the nearest transport depot. The Specter intended to leave the two young men here to go their separate ways, wherever that was, while he continued on to Specter Headquarters. Mycroft told Ridley and Elio that he would get them as far as the *Imperatrix*, and he kept his promise. The babysitting was now over and he could go onto concluding his mission. Elio was removed from slavery and Ridley was given a slew of new opportunities. Priorities fulfilled. Check and done.

"Well gentlemen, this is where we say farewell," Mycroft declared in the middle of the concourse. "Thank you both so very much for all that you've helped with on the way here. It is because of all of our collective work that we all made it here alive. Truly, I could not have done it without you. Allow me to return the favor." He reached into his pocket and pulled out another pair of bluchips. He handed one to each of them.

"Now they're empty," Mycroft continued, "but by this afternoon, after I return to headquarters, there will be enough money for both of you to get a start at making a decent life for yourselves."

The two just stared at him in silence. Elio in his usual stoic way and Ridley with the least amused expression on his face.

"That's it? After all we've done to get you this far, that's the end of the road? Here's your money, thanks, goodbye." Ridley asked. "The fuck?"

"It does appear as if you are intentionally trying to get rid of us," Elio added. There was a hint of disappointment in his voice. "As though you do not want us to be with you anymore. After all, you have been trying to get rid of us since Ampheres, and me since the two of us met."

"That is not true at all," Mycroft protested. "Well yes, I have said I'll leave you eventually, I'm at least leaving you in the capitol! It's not like it's the middle of fucking nowhere! But I have never tried–"

"We've come this far, dammit, I want to see what will happen next." Ridley pleaded. His face was pleading for belonging, and his eyes welled with tears.

Mycroft could tell this was more than the look Ridley used to get his way, he was desperately searching for somewhere to belong.

"War is what is happening next," was all Mycroft could say. "And here comes a time where everyone instinctively looks after themselves. It's best you do the same, son."

"And all the more reason for us to come along with you" Elio pleaded. "Soon a draft will be imposed and we will have no choice but to join you. The military won't accept me. If anything they subject me to testing and–"

"I don't think that will ever happen," Mycroft interjected.

"War is unpredictable, you told me that," Ridley said. "Everything we've done up to this point has only succeeded, right. So why waste a winning streak?" Ridley grabbed the Specter by the collar. "C'mon Mycroft, we're volunteering now, before shit hits the fan."

Mycroft was cornered, literally and figuratively. Everyone had great reasons to come, he had to admit. It was hard for him to come up with any real reason to not allow them to come along, other than it was a certain death wish. He knew they were both capable of learning the ropes, and learning them quickly. Mycroft was just afraid that all their zeal would get them killed.

The aged Specter closed his eyes and lowered his head, defeated.

"I can't guarantee that you'll be allowed to help, let alone be allowed to join. We are a well-funded operation, with immense amounts of training required. That means we can afford to be picky. Actually," his voice quavered for a moment, "I wasn't supposed to allow you to learn my true identity." He swallowed a large gulp. "All I can do is ask that they not kill you. I have no control."

Ridley smiled, and Elio replied, "That is all we can ask for!" in his most emotive voice possible.

Traveling via the interstation transport, the trio ultimately arrived at an exquisite, very fancy high-end instrument dealer that sold handmade, top of the line pianos. Hardly anyone other than the workers dressed in nice suits were in the store, and the trio entering were the filthiest things in sight.

Passing by dozens of high-end pianos polished to a mirror finish, Mycroft bee-lined for the rear service entrance, ignoring and being ignored by the suited workers. Behind the doors lay a filthy workshop where the pianos were repaired and manufactured. Here the trio fit in just fine along with the dozen other filthy workers. The workers cordially greeted Mycroft, but glared at his traveling companions.

Through the workshop, the travelers entered a small corridor which terminated into an elevator. Inside the elevator, there were only two buttons, and Mycroft pressed down.

Within seconds, the three were looking upon the headquarters of the Specters.

One giant chamber was filled with stations of computers and data screens as far as the eye could see. Multiple levels of balconies circled above them to the vast, dark ceiling above. Ridley lost count after eight levels, easily each 12 feet high. People, agents, of all shapes and sizes and dresses crisscrossed the area, coming to computers, going from computers, each traveling in a haphazard manner, yet all with a purpose.

"What is this place? A piano dealer/galactic police station?" Ridley asked. He wandered to a data kiosk and started scrolling through the information.

Mycroft quickly pulled him away. "The information contained here is extremely sensitive and highly classified. Don't look at anything or talk to anyone."

CHAPTER 18

"That did not answer his question," Elio added.

Dammit, Mycroft thought. He didn't want to give any more information than absolutely necessary. "The piano shop is our front. Think about it. A dealer in a high-end product wouldn't get a lot of foot traffic, because not a lot of people buy a piano every day. And as long as a dozen or so pianos are sold each month, no one asks any questions or thinks anything out of the ordinary. It's the perfect setup."

"Which government branch is this?" Ridley asked. "The Senate protection agency?"

"Not exactly," Mycroft was suddenly interrupted by a fellow agent, who wore a smug and disgusted look on his face.

"My, my, Mycroft, you are losing your touch. Prisoners and witnesses are to be brought *unconscious*, remember?" The man broke out into a disgusting sounding chuckle.

"The fuck you calling us prisoners?" Ridley grew immediately defensive. He didn't care where he was or who he was with. "No one calls us fucking prisoners."

Elio placed his hands on the angry boy's shoulders, prepared for what might happen.

The smug agent raised his eyebrows and could barely bring himself to look at Ridley. "Why else would you bring in living guests to headquarters, Mycroft? Certainly your trauma hasn't forced you to forget all of our protocols!" The piece of shit broke into a heartier laughter, unable to control himself.

Mycroft took his time in taking a deep, calming breath. "No, Thurgood, I haven't lost my touch nor forgotten the protocols. These two helped me during my latest mission and I believe they're not only worthy of a commendation, but they will play an integral role in the next phase of my mission."

"Helped you?" Thurgood sneered. "A veteran Specter needed help from the public? Jeez, is this what we get to look forward to in old age, old man? You need help just to *not* get the job done and go to war? Might I remind you, old man, that Ulysses' body hasn't been found, and we now know for a fact he's not alive anymore."

Mycroft lunged at Thurgood, pummeling his fist into the smug man's face. The fight lasted for two minutes, stealing everyone's attention that was nearest to them. Ridley tried to assist Mycroft, but was held back by Elio.

"They do not need us to get in the way," Elio told the young man. Still, Ridley struggled against the tight hold to assist his friend in any way he could.

A booming voice echoed over the room, ending the fight immediately as well as bringing everyone's attention to halt. The fighters halted and stood at attention, their bloody and bruised faces struggling to remove the lingering hatred for their opponent.

"Now that the homecoming party is over," the Specter Chief declared, "Mycroft, report to the main audience chamber immediately."

Mycroft saluted. "Yes, sir." He set off in the direction at once.

"And take your friends to the medical bay," the chief ordered, "where they'll stop distracting my men."

"Absolutely sir." The Specter summoned his companions with a wave of the arm, and the three quickly trotted out of the room.

Staring at Thurgood, the Specter Chief sneered. "And you, acting in a manner unbecoming of an officer. You should be ashamed of yourself."

Thurgood saluted crisply. "Yes, sir." Although he couldn't fully remove the smile from his face.

This got the chief especially angry. "Ah, I see just how ashamed you are. Perhaps a few months on custodial duty will drive the point home. Report to Davis at once and *request* latrine duty, on my command."

The formally smug officer lowered his chin and weakly saluted before obeying his orders.

CHAPTER 18

Once Thurgood left his sight, the chief turned his attention to the rest of the chamber. "Doesn't everyone have work to do?" The chief turned on his heel and left. The murmur and movement of the room only returned after a few seconds.

The nine Specter Chiefs seated above Mycroft at the head of the audience chamber were the best of the best, together containing almost 1,000 years of collective knowledge. These figures had seen pretty much everything there was to see in the line of duty, and had learned enough to be able to finally make the hard decisions. It was every individual Specter's goal to survive long enough in their career to achieve the rank of chief.

Listening to Mycroft's report, the chiefs grew less and less amused with each passing sentence. Not only was the retrieval a failure, but getting intercepted by any foreign party—an enemy, as far as the chiefs were concerned—was not a means to celebrate. And deliberately going out of one's way to achieve some other, unaffiliated party's goal, was on par with dereliction of duty.

"Do you dare to insult us, Mycroft?" Albus, the senior Chief Specter, questioned. "Not only do you bring the uninitiated into these hallowed halls, you have yet to locate Senator Pircilla's son, nor are you any closer to negotiating a pause in the already exploded tensions. The war is mere seconds from *officially* beginning, and you, the illustrious Mycroft, have the nerve to stand before us and suggest that an extinct, ancient tribe has made a comeback and is attempting to fulfill its divine, age-old mission to control the Twelve Sacred Scriptures that will allow them to finally control the galaxy? That suggestion alone is prime evidence for expulsion, sir!"

Mycroft knew he was fighting an uphill battle in convincing these aged men to believe his story, which he admitted himself was crazy and hard to believe. But if he hadn't seen it with his own eyes...

"Gentlemen, if I may implore you all to just hear what I have to say," he pleaded. "I know it sounds unbelievable—"

"Damn straight it does," said Latiolais, the chief that was always the hardest to win over in an argument. "The mere suggestion that an ancient force is controlling the Axis is asinine. Your abilities have been impaired by your husband's death more than we thought, Mycroft."

"I do not think it's appropriate to merely dismiss Mycroft's assertions. If he's to say there's ample evidence of this group's return, it behooves us to do our duty and investigate." Silas was Mycroft's old master, and was known for flouting procedure and simply doing what he wanted to do. He always gave everyone the benefit of the doubt. "After all, he's never lied before. Why would he start now?"

"Mycroft is our best agent and a consummate professional," Silas continued. "We know absolutely nothing of this being that attacked him. If we were to simply ignore this, it could fester into a greater problem than what we currently face, and for all we know blow up into a bigger problem than the war."

"Silas, you are as delusional as your apprentice. Nothing is more pressing than the war," Latiolais said. "Which is only made worse by the senator's son still missing. Without him, we have no bargaining chip to negotiate a cease-fire. Mycroft's failure has—"

"I have no doubt that Ulysses Picilla is still alive," Mycroft interjected. He was mildly insulted that his integrity would be questioned like that, but Latiolais was not above such a low attack. "Without him alive, Count Lucilous has no negotiating piece either. That boy is as important to both sides. There isn't any reason to kill him."

"The senator has proceeded to employ a smear campaign against us in the Senate," Albus said. "Because we haven't fulfilled this mission, he claims, we are incapable of carrying out the rest of our duties, rendering us useless. He's calling for an end to our funding and for us to be disbanded immediately."

Mycroft struggled to contain his anger. He knew the chiefs were smart enough to not believe such hogwash. The Specters always fulfilled their mission, just not always in the desired timeline. But the craze of war shook everyone's thinking, even an experienced Specter.

"Of course," Albus continued, leering at Mycroft from the corner of his eye. "This has only been made worse by you, I'm afraid..."

"I'm telling you," Mycroft struggled not to yell. "Ulysses is still alive, and will be used as a poster child for the count. He won't be killed immediately, if at all."

"Unfortunately, that won't satisfy the matter at hand." Albus's tone was that of a school teacher scolding a misbehaving student. "There are too many threats facing the galaxy, and even mentioning that another, illogical, enemy is in fact in control of the man that kidnapped a prominent senator's son will be the final nail in the coffin, for the Syndicate and for the Specter Corps."

"Pircilla is the tie breaking vote for the war declaration," Latiolais interjected. "He is all but certain to vote yes given the current state of affairs. Every ten seconds we get word of another attack amongst the Syndicate."

"The only thing we haven't given Mycroft credit for, is that he confirmed the boy was in Lucilous' custody." Silas said. "We must admit that the mission wasn't a complete failure."

"But since you mentioned the other threats," Albus added, "the senator's security has been compromised by domestic gangs, both in support and against the war. They feel that nothing will happen and the stalemate will continue as long as there is an even number of votes in the Senate. In response, the Senate has moved the vote for the war declaration to tonight."

Mycroft was truly shocked to hear this bit of news. "Tonight? No, they can't! The Axis isn't the one with Ulysses. It's the Hyde, or at least someone who worships them. Give me more time. I can find them."

This time Albus was the one to look disappointed. "There isn't any more time left, I'm afraid. Despite our pleas, the Senate is moving ahead. And despite my instincts, you're ordered to go over to guard the senators during the vote."

"This is a mistake! I can't go protect the senators. I have to go looking for that thing I fought on Ampheres, and he'll lead me to the boy!" Mycroft pleaded. He looked like a lunatic but he didn't care. "There are plenty of others who can guard—"

Silas intervened this time. "The rest are quelling the gang uprisings and supporting the troop build ups. There is no one left, Mr. Mycroft. You will report to the Senate chambers immediately, Specter. This is the only thing in the galaxy that matters."

Resigned that his protests would get nowhere, Mycroft remained silent. He had no choice but to accept his fate. His only hope now was to convince Senator Pircilla to vote against the war declaration. There was ample evidence to suggest peace could be reached before any more blood was spilt.

But he needed time to find his mysterious enemy, and the only way to do that was to postpone the war for just a few more days.

The Specter was about to leave the questioning podium when his mind flashed to his two companions. "Sirs, if I may inquire. What is to happen to those two sentients I arrived with? Truly, the help they provided to me was invaluable."

"They'll be processed and re-mitigated back onto the station with their memories wiped," Latiolais interjected. "We do acknowledge the service they have provided to the Specters, but there still remains the overarching security risk."

That was not the answer Mycroft wanted to hear. But there really wasn't much he could do about this, even if he wasn't already in trouble. "Allow me to say that the tall one with the eyes, Elio, is technically enhanced, and won't likely respond to the standard memory wipe."

Latiolais met him with a steely death glare. "Then he will be exterminated."

"Allow him to remain employed with the Specters," Mycroft pleaded. "Elio's technical enhancements would be an invaluable asset to the organization and the war effort. Ridley too. He is as equally as brilliant as any current Specter and a tremendously hard worker. They both have tremendous potential and will only serve us well during the war effort."

Every Specter Chief looked at this idea with a tremendous lack of amusement. The room was dead silent for several seconds, making even Mycroft rather uncomfortable.

"What are we supposed to do with a teenaged recruit?" Albus was the one who finally broke the silence. His points were pragmatic, but a bit abrasive. "They're too old to become experts in practically any of our skills, especially fighting and swordsmanship. They're too old to begin learning anything really, for their questioning and believability quotients are too strong. They're also too young to be a real useful informant, as they're clearly rather inexperienced."

Latiolais joined in on the questioning. "Where do their loyalties lie? They're clearly too old for reorientation as well."

"I promise you, Mycroft, that I will personally see to it that your companions are taken care of," Silas declared. "You have my word."

That was the closest thing to an answer to his request that Mycroft was going to get, but it was definitely better than termination. "Thank you, sir."

After the meeting was adjourned, Mycroft rushed to the infirmary to visit Elio and Ridley, and to offer them his final goodbye before they really go their separate ways, and their memories get wiped. The Specter was surprised to find Chief Silas there as well.

The two patients were lying in bed, freshly bathed and bandaged.

Elio was busy blabbering away to Silas, while Ridley just watched. Clearly the introductions had been made.

"For being a secret police force, you all are pretty easy to spot," Elio said as Mycroft entered the room, "Now that I know what to look for, I have seen you on literally every planet I have stepped foot on. All nine hundred eighty-seven of them."

"Now I understand what you meant about this one's special skills," Silas said to Mycroft. "Don't worry. I've arranged it so they won't get processed."

Mycroft's heart leapt for joy, and a large smile carved onto his face. He shook his superior's hand vigorously. For once, something finally went Mycroft's way.

On the other hand, Ridley suddenly turned into a hysterical mess. "Processed? What the hell does that mean? They're gonna kill us, huh? Wipe our memories and kill us. Well they're not gonna get me!" He ripped off the monitor pads attached to his body, which set off an alarm and summoned a group of nurses with the crash cart.

Once the nurses realized that Ridley was just losing his cool, they immediately moved to restrain and calm the man. The boy had a large athletic build and proved too strong for the nurses, so they summoned the guard who struggled as well.

Mycroft and Silas finally joined in to assist. "Will you calm the fuck down, Ridley!" Mycroft ordered. "You're going to be fine. Nothing is going to happen to you unless you quit fussing around. You're not going to die or get your memories erased. Just calm down. Everything will be fine."

After several minutes, Ridley was finally calm and sedate, with the helping of a few doses of medication the doctors injected into him. The young man once again looked upon the room before him, this time with heavily lidded eyes.

"You are stronger than advertised!" Silas spoke to Ridley, beaming with a large smile. "And you can quickly infer the true meaning of something without being told or provided any hints. Mycroft was right, you should join this organization. You'll make a fine Specter!"

Ridley beamed with a large smile. "Really?" He looked at Mycroft. "See there, I told you." He turned his attention back to Silas. "This dummy said that we'd only get in the way."

Mycroft merely rolled his eyes with annoyance while Silas lightly chuckled. "Don't take it personally my dear boy. This cranky sot is like that with everyone. According to him, everything is in his way. He's been that way since he was my apprentice. But what he still struggles to realize is that most of what he claims to be in his way are his own struggles that he doesn't want to deal with."

"We don't need to talk about this anymore," Mycroft said. "And actually, I have to get going." He made his way to the door.

"You were his trainer?" Ridley asked. His eyes grew wider and he was clearly in awe of the old Specter Chief before him.

Silas nodded his head softly. "He hasn't changed at all, since before he was your age. So much passion, so much fury, so much love. Of course when his husband came into the picture, his edge softened a bit."

"That is surprising, considering how stubborn he is." Elio said from the bed next to Ridley. "But I suppose there is someone for everyone to fall in love with."

"Love can do powerful things. It's the only force in the universe that can hold you together," Silas said. "Sometimes despite your desires."

"Wait a minute, you mean old Mycroft had a husband? I can't believe someone would find you loveable, let alone attractive," Ridley said. "What happened to him? Did he finally realize what he was missing and scram?"

Everyone laughed while Mycroft struggled not to cry. His instinctual response was to bite everyone's head off for even mentioning his husband, but his heart hurt too much to even put up that much effort. Everyone in this group was heartbroken in their own way, and who was he to claim he suffered the most. And despite his best effort, Mycroft struggled not to laugh, himself. "I better head out. Don't want to leave the senator unattended."

The mood amongst Ridley and the rest shifted when Mycroft left. The joviality was gone, cast over by a heavy shell of doom.

"What's the matter with him?" Ridley asked. "All we were doing was razzing him."

Silas looked at Mycroft's vacant space, and pondered for a moment. "Life has a way of taking the humor out of you, sometimes quite brutally.

"C'mon, let's get you out of here and see what we can discover about this mysterious duelist."

CHAPTER 19

The highest point of the *Imperatrix* station was the Chamber of the High Senate, where over 100,000 star system representatives argued over the most mundane, yet highly consequential, decisions that made the Cosmic Syndicate function.

In the office of the one senator who was still undecided as to whether or not to formally declare war on the Axis of the Republic Systems, Mycroft watched Senator Pircilla get accosted by the senior representatives of both sides of the vote.

The poor Specter could only pinch the bridge of his nose as Pircilla stared at his steepled hands while the two representatives talked over each other. Mycroft wanted to shoot all three of them.

"They have your son!" Senator Rand of the Yes-bloc yelled. "That should be reason enough to declare war! Not to mention all the embargoes, and trade disruptions, and planet blockades that have since been instituted. At what point are you going to say enough is enough and do the right thing?"

"Right thing?" stormed Kingsley of the No-votes. "We have yet to see an aggressive act that is one hundred percent certifiably caused by the Axis. At this point, all either side is doing is grand standing and flexing their muscles. The Corporate Conglomerates have embargoed both sides out of panic, and all that has happened has been in anticipation of the first shot—which, again, hasn't happened yet. Do the right thing, Pircilla, and vote no and let us get started on the path to reconciliation."

Pircilla pinched the bridge of his nose. "Senators, while I appreciate your last minute entreaties, my opinion will be private until the vote, in twenty minutes time. I'm sure you both want to make your final preparations, so I'll excuse you now."

He rose, and the two reluctantly left the room. Mycroft admired how well Pircilla carried stress, as well as how smoothly he cleared an unwanted audience without having to lift a finger.

"I envy you, Specter." the senator spoke as soon as the door closed. You can easily silence your adversaries, while I have to let them say what they want to say and pretend to listen."

Mycroft couldn't help but smile. "Unfortunately, I feel both of our jobs are equally as hard in their own way. For the record, though, I don't envy your job at all."

"Not many do, and those that actually want this job are genuinely sick in the head." Pircilla sunk into his desk. "This is, hands down, the most difficult decision I've ever had to make."

Mycroft simply bowed his head. "No doubt, sir."

"Tell me, Specter, what are the chances you can retrieve my son alive?"

"Actually quite high," the Specter was honest. "But even higher if you vote against the war. Your son is definitely alive, Senator, but for how long remains, right now, up to you. The sooner you act, the better."

Pircilla's brows furrowed with interest. "In what way?"

"The Axis wants your son to influence the public to join their side. He's the most influential celebrity in the galaxy, after all, and they need that—at least for right now. But if you declare war, then his usefulness rapidly declines."

"So I'm damned if I do and damned if I don't. Typical." Pircilla

CHAPTER 19

slammed his fist on the desk and poured himself a drink.

"The Axis has your son, yes, but they are not the real power behind the war effort." The Specter explained his encounter with the duelists, and the story of the Hyde.

The senator looked dumbstruck while Mycroft completed his theory. "Attacking the Axis only feeds into their overall plan. This vote will lead to the end of the Syndicate, let alone your son's life."

Pircilla poured himself another drink, contemplating what he had just heard. "Why aren't the other Specters investigating this...group?"

"The others are too preoccupied with securing the fragile alliance than searching for the genesis of the war. The Specter Chiefs feel that that is the Senate and Military Intelligence's responsibility."

Mycroft ran up to the senator's desk and planted both of his wrists with a heavy pound. "Please, sir. As the one who personally searched for your son, and was on the front lines, vote no on the declaration. The Specters can find your son. *I* can find your son! They are just overworked with this deadly dick contest."

The senator was visibly affected by Mycroft's words, and the Specter could tell that he had swayed the man. Suddenly, the comm on the desk flashed and the senator answered it.

The voice of Pircilla's assistant filled the room. "Sir, you might want to see the news."

Pircilla switched on the monitor, and nearly choked.

Ulysses' face filled the screen, the camera shook as he held it. His face was covered with bruises and scratches. Both of his eyes were black, and a few of his teeth were missing. The poor boy's nose was exceptionally swollen.

"My former Syndicate brethren," his voice was slurred and mechanical. He was highly sedated and most likely under the threat of a rifle barrel. "Now is the beginning of the change you so desperately seek. Gone are the days of stagnation, ignorance, and waste. Today brings the glorious rise of our future. Join me as we witness the ascendancy of prosperity, of our new epoch. Leave the Syndicate, forget the pestilence of the past and embrace the triumphant future under the Axis!"

Mycroft's face hardened. He could tell all of this was done under coercion. He saw Pircilla's eyes flooded with tears, and the man's knuckles shook so much they started bleeding.

"In celebration of our new independence, here's a pyrotechnic display."

The camera feed cut to the stand-off zone at the Line of Control. Ships from both sides assembled at the disputed border, just waiting to make the first shot.

Suddenly a searing red bolt of rocket plasma arched in the sky. In a silent few moments, the red turned into a deadly rainbow and struck the assembled ships, which erupted into a glorious series of explosions. In seconds, a large fraction of the Syndicate's fleet was destroyed. Shots erupted on both sides.

The feed cut back to Ulysses' battered face. He had been crying. "The only thing standing in the way of prosperity is my father, Senator Pircilla. Daddy, please do the right thing. Uphold your duty and say yes to progress. Stop wasting the valuable time that we don't have."

The feed suddenly cut and was replaced by a stunned newscaster. The senator's commlinks started ringing off the hook. Everyone wanted to talk with the representative whose son declared war on his own people.

Pircilla looked gravely at Mycroft. "It appears my hand is forced."

The civil war was officially declared 12 minutes later.

CHAPTER 20

All of the available Specters on the station assembled in the War Hall, aptly named but seldom used for its actual purpose. Those who could not appear by person arrived via hologram. Before them, the Specter Chiefs elucidated a grand speech about politics and duty, and how the Specters must rise above it all to fulfill their oath. It wasn't too inspiring, but in times like these one took what they could get.

In truth the Specters were excited to see more than a petty crime, they were seeing a war!

"This may be the last mission imparted to us, as the Senate's faith in our organization has reduced rapidly," Chief Albus spoke to the assembly. "While the allegations are unfounded, that does not mean we don't know what the fuck we're doing. We will succeed, but to do that we need to be better than we've ever been. Got it?"

"Oorah!" The Specters all saluted.

"We have been conscripted to spy on the Axis and gather intelligence. No front is too far, no fact is too mundane. Now, due to the vast area to cover, and the secrecy of the project, we all have to work solo. I'm confident you all can bring home a win. Not everyone will survive, but your sacrifice will not be in vain."

The group saluted once more and disassembled to receive their first orders. Forces were gathering at the Sargasso Cluster, and

Mycroft's mission was to assess the geographic layout and ordnance configuration. The plan was for this to be the first and final battle of the war, hopefully ending with the enemy's forces getting scared into submission.

Despite his protests, Mycroft's pleas to go after the Hyde went unanswered. No one believed that they were any real viable threat.

Left with no choice, the Specter returned to the boys to tell them the bad news and to say goodbye.

Silas was too excited to let Mycroft get a word in edgewise. "While you were away, I took advantage of Elio's superb research skills and combed our archives on what we contained of the Hyde. We only have three texts, all of which barely mention the bloody folks."

"They weren't completely useless though," Ridley chimed in. "We learned a lot actually. They were the largest group of people outside of the Specter's sphere of influence, and at their peak numbered fifty billion people. They had multiple bases and holy sites scattered throughout the galaxy, with each being dedicated to one of the Twelve Sacred Scriptures."

"Each one of those scriptures," Elio continued, "the Hyde believed, would provide them with certain powers. And if one fully studied all of the scriptures, they then can take over the whole galaxy. One scripture offers a sense of clairvoyance, another provides a method to inflict pain without touching your opponent, and even one scripture is rumored to allow you to manipulate another's mind." Elio spoke in his usual monotonous tone, but he even seemed fascinated by the subject matter.

Mycroft put up his hands before anyone else could speak, otherwise they'd be there until the end of the war. "That all sounds fascinating, and not unlike what I already told you. Do we know anything about their home world? History is great, but the present is what I'm concerned about."

CHAPTER 20

"Dotsero is their oldest known settlement," the young Elio answered, "and the literature says it is also home to the most powerful temple. While the majority of the planet was destroyed from the countless conflicts throughout history, many sites, and temples still stand and provide their energy for study. It is located on the edge of the Correenian Cluster, in the Tarturus Systems. It is extremely difficult to access, and since the planet is so near its sun, a ship can only stay in the atmosphere for a few hours. The fleet would find it near impossible to get there in time."

"But that's, no doubt, where that bastard is," Mycroft fumed. His temper was already boiling. "The fleet is wasting its time with the Axis, and they want me to scout the upcoming battlefield. Idiots!"

"That's clear across the galaxy!" Silas said. "It would be impossible to do both in a timely manner."

"I know, which is why I'm focusing on this," Mycroft declared. "If we can retrieve Ulysses back and kill this piece of shit, then we won't need to fight that battle. I know it's the longest shot but it's the only option that won't kill too many lives."

"I'm with you, every step of the way," Silas declared. "I know that I'm technically breaking my oath to the Articles of Allegiance, but I am convinced that this is the right way to go. I'll take full responsibility as far as the chiefs are concerned. When do we take off?"

Mycroft was stunned speechless. He never expected his mentor, who was the second most senior chief of the Specters, to flagrantly flout a direct order from his fellow council. Yes, the man was known for charting his own path but that was always within the parameters of the rules and mission objectives. Not once had he directly disobeyed an order.

But times were changing with every passing second, and Mycroft needed to adapt just as quickly. "Immediately, sir. Once we say our last goodbyes to these two."

Silas remained silent, looking at Mycroft with a twinkling half smile, while Ridley devolved into another conniption fit.

"What? You're just gonna let us do all this work and nearly die for you, just to dump us when the fuel hits the thruster? What's wrong? Haven't we proved we're not useless?"

Ridley's eyes filled with tears and he looked genuinely terrified as to what will happen next. Elio blankly looked on, but his glowing blue eyes began wandering the room.

Mycroft couldn't see anything else other than a pathetic pair of lost, lonely boys floating in the middle of the most brutal place in the universe.

He sat beside Ridley. "No. Look, you've helped out in more ways than I could possibly imagine. I wouldn't be alive if it weren't for you two. But this is the part where the experienced ones need to take over. You must understand!"

Tears of anger flowed down the boy's face. "I understand that you dragged me across the galaxy and now want to leave me all alone out here on a bloody space station!" He slapped the Specter as hard as he could.

"You won't be alone, you'll have Elio," Mycroft retorted as he grabbed Ridley's hand in midair.

"Actually, he should come with us. We could use that brain of his," Silas muttered under his breath. He was suddenly fascinated with something on the ceiling and didn't look anyone else in the eye.

"I wonder if leaving Ridley has to do with your sexual attraction to me, Mycroft" Elio declared suddenly. "After all that is a well-known... secret."

"No!" Mycroft protested. "It's because I care about your safety."

Ridley grew even more irate at that remark. "Is that supposed to make me feel better, you piece of shit? You'll use me as free labor, but you care so much about me that you'll leave me alone in the midst of a

CHAPTER 20

war? Fuck you!"

Mycroft couldn't take anymore and clapped his hands to silence everyone. "Now will everyone just shut the fuck up? I'm not jealous or bitter or angry about anyone, so let's everyone get that out of their minds. Second, yes, both of you are absolutely capable of any task thrown at you, and you two are frankly the first two beings beside my husband that I care about. I want to keep you alive, which is why I want to keep you *here*."

"I'm not leaving a loved one alone to defend themselves again," Ridley said. "Last time I did that they died."

A heavy silence hung over the group for several moments. Mycroft was thoroughly exasperated and defeated. He didn't know what to do that would keep these kids here and out of harm's way. The Specter looked at his old mentor, Silas, who stared directly through his eyes into his soul. There was really only one answer.

Mycroft let out a heavy sigh and closed his eyes. He knew this was the wrong decision. "If I let you come, will you promise to do exactly what I tell you?"

"Yes!" Elio and Ridley said in unison.

"When I say run, you run." Mycroft nearly whispered. "When I tell you to stay, you'll stay put, got it?"

"Yep!" This time Silas, Elio, and Ridley all spoke in unison.

Mycroft rolled his eyes as he proceeded to the hangar. "C'mon then dammit."

* * *

Across the stars, Ulysses struggled against his restraints aboard the Archon's ship. He had just completed the propaganda video and threw up all over his bed. The camera had just shut down when Ulysses sent it crashing to the wall.

"Naughty, naughty little boy." Archon's voice emerged from the shadows as he examined the pile of wreckage. "That was an expensive piece of equipment." He slowly turned his gaze towards the captive. "You'll have to pay for that."

Tears streamed down the boy's face. "You killed all those soldiers! You promised me that you wouldn't kill anyone if I agreed to make your video. You fucking monster! I have family stationed at the Line of Control."

The Archon slowly moved closer to the restraining bed. "Pity. No doubt your father was thinking of them as well, while he heard his son preach for the Axis. As far as I'm concerned, you haven't any family left."

Ulysses managed to wrench his elbow free and scratch the Archon's face, revealing a heavily scarred, or tattooed, cheek, bleeding purple blood. The creature retaliated by giving Ulysses a swift backhand. The young man spit out a broken tooth.

"You will pay for this!"

Red lightning erupted around Ulysses, who screamed loudly in intense pain. The lightning didn't have a source, as though it emanated from the young captive's body. Ulysses writhed in agony, his restraints barely keeping him in the bed.

The lightning ceased after several seconds.

"I'm growing quite impatient with your attitude," the Archon spoke just above a whisper, each word tinged with intense anger and fury. "I've tried to re-educate you with kindness, persuasion, brute force, but it seems pain is the only way to reach you."

The lightning once again engulfed Ulysses' body. His screams grew louder with each passing second. Once it stopped, smoke and the smell of singed skin enveloped the small cell.

The Archon wiped at his cheek, the purple blood staining his bright red gloves. "You see, up until the missile strike you were quite valuable to me alive, but now that the deck has been played, your usefulness has been reduced to but one task. I was hoping to save it for after the victory, but your misbehavior has left me no choice."

The Archon gathered a syringe and injected Ulysses with its mysterious contents, but not after another bloody struggle.

"The sole purpose of your life, now, is reproduction. I know that you are a Myx, one of the few human variants capable of giving birth to humans with DNA and RNA divergents. You Myxian males, especially, give tremendous results regarding passing on variant traits to the fetus."

The monster made a dramatic flourish. "I am one of the last of my kind, and you, dear boy, are the catalyst to continuing my legacy."

Ulysses tried to speak, but he was too weak from the pain and the sedative was already taking effect. He felt oddly aroused, and had a sudden urge to have sex with everything he could see. The boy developed the most intense hard-on of his life. Ulysses realized he was just given a date-rape drug.

"While you don't possess the most ideal traits," the Archon continued. His voice developed a sinister and evil sensuality. "They can easily be trained and bred out after a generation or two. All we need from you is a good foundation to build upon."

More lightning ran through Ulysses' body as the Archon climbed on top of him. The pain was still excruciating but the rape drug diluted the effects, and Ulysses' strength. The poor boy kicked his legs with all of his might, but they barely moved more than a few millimeters.

Conversely, the Archon moved with ravenous speed, ripping off the few rags Ulysses wore. He kissed the boy's body all over, the creature's slimy and scarred lips instantly developing blistering welts on the poor boy's fair skin.

The monster kissed Ulysses' mouth. The poor young man tasted nothing but disgusting, terrorizing, fear.

"You taste amazing! It's too bad," the Archon said, as he inserted himself in Ulysses, "that you won't live long enough to become a prophet. Then I could taste you every day during prayers."

This was the first time in the entire turn of events that Ulysses truly wanted to die. The pain he felt at this moment was immensely worse than all the beatings he'd ever experienced.

Words could not describe this experience, so much so that he didn't even scream. His mouth was wide open with pain but no sound came out. Tears streamed down his face like a waterfall. Ulysses had never cried like this in his life, and all he desperately wanted in that moment was for his dad to come save him.

Ulysses tried to lose consciousness, but it didn't work. He was emotionally numb, and after the first ejaculation was completely physically numb as well.

Five ejaculations later, the Archon climbed off its victim.

"You are the first being in millennia to bear a new member of the Hyde, a species that will one day claim its rightful place in the galaxy. Our powers are unmatched, and nothing can stand in our way.

"With that being said, if you fail to deliver this child, or if it's not born with the necessary skills, you will be executed by your own precious soldiers."

Ulysses didn't hear a word, all his mind could focus on was his desire to die immediately.

As he left, the Archon said, "Next time, I draw blood."

The Archon went to the ship's cockpit and contacted Count Lucilous, who was at a meeting with the Axis military chiefs.

"Gentlemen, today is the moment we've all been waiting for. Soon our forces will be looked upon with fear for the first time, and our supremacy will be cemented in history forever."

The holograms clapped, and uttered muted congratulations. While the Archon displayed appreciation, he was in reality unamused and went right back to business. "Lucilous, what is the status of the battlefield?"

"The Syndicate is still reeling from the missile launch, sir. Everyone on that side of the Line of Control is paralyzed. They can't help but be distracted, enough so that a surprise offensive now will eradicate them forever!"

"No, Count, we'll save that for the first battle. It is not fun to have a complete shut out," the Archon lectured. "The other side needs a fair chance as well."

Lucilous was visibly embarrassed and tried to save face. "But sir, we can easily—"

"That is all." Even through the hologram, the violent glare of the glowing red eyes showed through and terrified everyone watching.

"It will be done my lord," was all the count could say.

* * *

Across the stars, the Archon's hologram disappeared, and Lucilous took several seconds to calm himself. He was shaking all over with fear, anger, and embarrassment. He slowly turned and stared warily at the generals. The trust between the two was already fragile, and now was severely compromised. The count was not prepared, either mentally or tactically, for the long war ahead, but all he could do was focus on one battle at a time.

This was the first.

"Will the Archon join us at the battlefield?" one of the generals asked. "After all, this is his war."

That was actually a good question, Lucilous had to admit. One that he'd asked the man himself. "The Archon is preoccupied with his prisoner and...personal projects. Frankly, I don't know what he is going to do until after he's done it."

Lucilous was curious though, as the Archon never really explained the reason why *Ulysses* was chosen. The popularity aspect couldn't be the whole of it. What could that creature be doing now, all secluded in his ancient temple on the outskirts of the galaxy?

Suddenly, an inkling of fear dribbled into Lucilous' mind. What if the Archon was grooming Ulysses to depose him as leader of the Axis? He immediately dismissed that out of his mind. The Count was still too valuable to the Plan for such a dramatic move.

"Typical of you, Lucilous, not knowing more than what you're told. It's a wonder why you're still kept around," the general said, taking the count out of his trance.

The count moved closer to the general and placed his hand on his sword, prepared to strike. But Lucilous wanted this war to end soon – and to keep his own life – so he refrained. Instead he just sneered at the man and ordered everyone to prepare for the first grand assault.

He was going to visit the Archon to see what he was missing.

* * *

Across the stars, at the Line of Control strike zone, the Syndicate was still preoccupied with their own personnel and materiel losses to instigate any sort of counterattack. The amount of damage was astronomical, and nowhere near fully assessed. Chaos was everywhere.

In the midst of their enemy's preoccupation, the Axis launched a full offensive.

A small squadron of Syndicate fighters moved to engage the attackers, managing to divert the fusillade away from the main damage area long enough to evacuate what survivors they could find. Unfortunately, this mission was not without heavy ship casualties. Within the first half hour nearly half of the Syndicate squadron was lost.

Despite the squadron's calls for help, no one was close enough to

CHAPTER 20

arrive in time. The entire Syndicate fleet at the Line of Control was all but decimated, creating a border of flaming wreckage between the two fighting powers.

The Primarch of the Syndicate watched the conflagration unfold on the screens in his office aboard the *Imperatrix*, joined with the Specter Chiefs, and the military generals. He was silent and scowling.

"Did we make the correct decision in starting this war?" He asked while tapping his steepled hands on his chin, his nervous tick. "Are we the ones in the right, or do they have a point?"

"Your Excellency, that line of thinking is an insult to all those victims' memories," one of the generals said. "The best way to honor them is by annihilating them all at this battle and the next. That is our one and only chance."

The Primarch nodded in silence, watching the chaos unfold, while the generals proceeded to tactical planning.

The Specter Chiefs merely watched and waited for their next orders.

CHAPTER 21

The junky corvette from Ampheres lumbered along through the interspace, steadfastly heading to its mysterious and unknown destination. Inside, the navi-computer continuously beeped, begging to be fed the destination coordinates.

The two Specters inside didn't even really know where they were headed. Mycroft simply ordered the autopilot to travel in a straight course. All the information the passengers had were some old books, even older legends, and a helpful heaping of blind faith.

The mood was tense, yet jovial. While everyone was well aware of the danger before them, they all desperately tried to not think about it for the time being. Ridley's enthusiasm to be a part of a galaxy saving mission was contagious, and even Mycroft couldn't resist feeling less anxious about the approaching danger.

Eventually though, after several hours of chatting, the group ran out of mundane conversation topics and the conversation drifted to the upcoming mission. Elio and Ridley immediately asked the questions that required details the Specters didn't have to answer.

Mycroft's irritation quickly returned and he flippantly said, "This fucking place might not even be there."

"What do you mean this place might *not be there*?" Ridley asked incredulously. "I thought you guys were supposed to know everything about these Hyde people and where they come from!"

CHAPTER 21

"Even the wisest of our Specter sophists argue over certain details of the past. This is one of them," Silas said. "After all, we're talking about a place that was last *intentionally* visited a millennia ago. So many natural events could have decimated the planet's surface. An asteroid could have struck the temple and now the whole place is covered in lava. The sun could have expanded so large it set the entire surface aflame."

"The damn planet might not even be there anymore," Mycroft repeated. "And if we're lucky, it *won't* be."

"According to the latest celestial charts, that area of the galaxy remains, albeit unstable," Elio said. His nose was buried in the technical manual, scrutinizing the navigation terminal's design. "Still, the last update to the chart was over one hundred years ago. Mycroft might be right, the temple might not be there."

Ridley scurried over to the terminal and pulled up the star chart. " What was the planet's name again, Dotsero?" He studied the map, searching for the smallest detail.

"That was the settlement. The planet is Tartarus Prime, and boy does it live up to its name," Mycroft said. "It's surrounded by celestial storms and the remnants of an eons-old supernova. Not to mention volatile minefields and all the wreckage from the countless wars fought near it. There is no direct way to the system, with the pathway ever-changing."

"The *Imperatrix* cannot travel to it, which is one of the reasons the system has not been added to the Syndicate," Elio chimed in. "There are not any geological or economic reasons for the Syndicate to even fully explore this section of the galaxy."

"Even the Corporate Conglomerates don't want anything to do with this place," Mycroft added. "And that says a lot." He shook his head in slow, solemn disappointment, "This place is pure evil."

"Which makes it the perfect place to harbor a galactic takeover,"

Silas declared. He also shook his head, not disappointed but ashamed. "Why didn't we notice this sooner?" He bowed his head and contemplated his failure.

"What's supposed to be on this planet? Besides Ulysses and this Hyde fellow, I mean?" Ridley asked.

"Once upon a time there was a vast array of temples and abandoned military forts. A shit-ton of old bones and mountains upon mountains of rubble," Mycroft added. "Frankly, nothing that is really that important to us at the moment."

"The Scriptures," Silas offered. "For all we know they could be in this duelist's possession. They might even be the reason why this creature is even alive. There are far too many things, which we do not know that are there, that are equally as important as the heart in your chest."

Everyone was silent for several moments, stunned at what Silas just said.

"You mean to tell me these scriptures are real, and can bring people from the dead? That *can* be useful," Ridley said. His voice was barely audible and lost some of its energy, yet held out hope for a sad idea.

"It's a selfish thing to want to bring someone back from the dead, for they chose, subconsciously, to go in the first place." Silas rose from his seat and placed a warm, loving arm around Ridley's shoulders.

"It upsets the natural order and places too much power in the hands of the incapable human. That is truly what the Hyde's way is—ignoring the natural way in order to get what they want, disregarding anything that they hurt. That is the fundamental difference between us and them. We do what is right—they do what is easy."

Silence hung once again in the cockpit for several moments. Aside from the navi-computer's incessant beeping, the only other sound were Ridley's heavy tears plopping on the solid metal floor.

Mycroft stewed Silas' words in his head and thought of his husband.

CHAPTER 21

He didn't want to die, that choice was *made* for him. Anger immediately swelled inside the veteran Specter, yet he quickly quelled it and remained silent.

"If the Hyde were to find all twelve of the Sacred Scriptures," Silas continued, "they could possess a power that humanity has never seen before. If you think the galaxy is ripping apart now, under the Hyde's reawakening the discord will get tremendously worse. Their leadership breeds only one trait, selfishness, and there's too much of that in the galaxy right now as it is.

"It has always been the Specters' mission to prevent the Hyde's rise, even though we have been constantly preoccupied with petty political squabbles over the past few centuries. We have always ensured that at least *one* of those Sacred Scriptures was protected."

"And ensured to eradicate the Hyde," Mycroft interrupted. "Which we thought we did already."

"So then there really is such a thing as magic?" Ridley asked. His crying had stopped but his voice was still fragile. His demeanor was a mix of confusion and defeat, as though he had finally realized the missing piece of his soul was gone forever.

"Supposedly, but only if you ask one of them," Mycroft answered, putting all of his cynicism on full display. "We Specters think the Hyde's 'magic' is entirely psychological. Given the widespread fear of them, it makes perfect sense that everyone who has ever seen a Hyde would give in to hyperbole and rumor. After all, that's all anyone is ever afraid of, rumors. But honestly, kiddo, don't believe everything old Silas here tells ya. Aside from the brutality of their fighting tactics, the Hyde are no more powerful than we are."

Silas looked deeply at Mycroft. He didn't say a word, but his eyes said everything. Hurtful disappointment flooded the old man's face, and for once that twinkle in his eye dimmed. "You never cease to surprise me, Mycroft. *All* magic is real, all you have to do is open your eyes."

"But the more your eyes open," Mycroft retorted, "the more you realize that magic isn't everything you think it is."

The two Specters stared each other down for several painstakingly silent moments. All Elio and Ridley could do was watch uncomfortably.

Finally, Ridley had had enough and asked in the most obnoxious way he could, "So what do the Specters see in the Twelve Scriptures? What powers do they get?"

The stare-off continued for another half-second before the two looked away. After all, it was difficult to ignore an obnoxiously naive teenager.

"The power to be a wholesome person, one who serves himself by helping others. One who is content with the status quo, for they are constantly growing into the universe," Mycroft said. He threw the piece of paper he'd been doodling on away. "Disappointing, ain't it?"

"That's not true!" Silas intervened, gently correcting his student. "They're guidelines by which we all can learn to live by. They're more useful than anyone realizes. If only you people would take the bloody time to actually study!"

The last comment was clearly directed at Mycroft, who merely sneered at the old man.

Ridley's brows furrowed. He just could not understand what the hell was going on. "Why is there such a disagreement between you two? Are these books actually useful or not?"

Silas and Mycroft stared at each other again. Not angrily this time, but as though they were both sharing a telepathic statement. They both looked at the young Ridley after several more seconds.

"That's the question, isn't it?" Silas said with a large, warm smile on his face.

A blaring alarm pierced the air as the ship quickly shuddered out of interspace. The navi-computer detected the end of the interspace lane. The easy part of the trip was over.

Elio rushed to the controls, and everyone filed into the cockpit after him. A swirling mass of cosmic debris, wreckage, and other unidentifiable detritus rose like a wall before them. The black void of space completely disappeared and there were no twinkling stars in sight. There seemed to be no clear way through the cosmic storm cloud.

"This is the border to Tartarus," Silas declared. A smile grew on his face. "See, the star charts are accurate!"

Elio rattled off the cloud's make-up, a litany of carbonized gasses and plasma. "It is, in essence, a collapsed black hole, blowing out matter, not swallowing it."

"Can you find an entrance?" Mycroft asked. He peered through the viewport, taking in as much as his aged eyes could.

"There are all kinds to choose from," Elio countered, "but they appear and disappear so fast it is near impossible to enter."

"Another reason the *Imperatrix* never ventures over here," Silas chimed in.

"See if you can use the ship's sensors to aid in the search," Mycroft ordered.

"Those are virtually nonexistent," Elio started to say but was interrupted by Silas.

"Trust your senses and your instincts. Don't keep doubting yourself. You have abilities the three of us could not even fathom. You'll be able to find us a safe passage."

For the first time, Mycroft noticed Elio emote doubt. This was the most human the old man had ever seen the mechanical boy, and it broke his heart. A sense of protection welled within Mycroft, his duty.

He moved to Elio and laid a comforting hand on his shoulder. "Yes. Don't doubt yourself, son. We'll be fine, just believe that we will. That's all we can do. You have what it takes to get us through safely.

You just have to believe!"

The Specter could tell Elio was getting some confidence back, yet there was still the overwhelming sense of doubt.

"Ridley will help, won't you?" Silas gripped the young man's shoulders and forced him into the co-pilot's chair. "If you learn how to fly evasive maneuvers in this, everything else will be a piece of cake."

The two Specters then left the cockpit, leaving Elio and Ridley alone to frantically search for a path forward.

In the mess hall, the Specters began a more honest conversation.

"Do you really think we stand a chance against this thing?" Mycroft asked bluntly. "After all, from all that we know and with all that's happened, it's a miracle we haven't died already."

"If you keep doubting your abilities like our companions in there, then we will certainly lose." Silas solemnly said. "Optimism is the most powerful force we know—"

Mycroft grew exasperated and started flailing his arms and pacing the room. "What abilities? I'm a trained fighter and an experienced killer. I can't negotiate with him using diplomacy! I already used all my skills against that fucker and here we are!

"The Hyde looks at those books and gets the ability to harness lightning in their opponent's body, and all we Specters get is a code of honor." Mycroft slumped down into a chair, his energy spent. "How am I supposed to see what isn't there?" He placed his head into his hands and squeezed as hard as he could. Hopefully he'd crush his own skull.

Silas smiled lightly, and shook his head. He wasn't the least bit perturbed. "You still have that impatience from childhood. Will you ever learn?"

Mycroft rolled his eyes. "Silas, now is not the time for—"

"How do you think the Specters beat the Hyde the first time, all those millennia ago? The odds were exactly as they are now, with our opponents only that much more powerful. If anything, the collective back then was weaker than the two of us are right now. They didn't get any more help than we did, yet still pulled out a victory."

Mycroft was beyond annoyed, yet remained silent and listened as intently as he could.

"Sheer will, hope, and the power of believing in themselves was really all the original Specters had," Silas continued. "There was nothing that could hold them back because they had nothing to lose. And that's the secret, Mycroft! To those Specters, they had to prove it to Fate that they were worth the time to create in the first place. There was nothing to prove to anyone, but there was *everything* to prove to themselves."

Mycroft was unamused. "Gee Silas, that's *all*? *That's* what the secret sauce is?"

As Silas answered, Ridley and Elio yelled for their attention in the cockpit. As the Specters entered the cramped confines, the ship lurched violently forward, sending them into their seats.

"In roughly twelve seconds we won't have an opening anymore," Ridley said as he struggled to keep the control yoke steady.

"We cannot wait any longer," Elio said as he expertly maneuvered the ship into the mass. The ghost of a smile came upon his face. "I had to make an executive decision."

"Good thinking, Specter," Silas patted Elio's shoulder.

The ship lumbered into the cloud as fast as it could, where debris pummeled the weak and aged hull. The cosmic storm created massive turbulence, shaking everything within the ship that wasn't bolted down. The passengers bounced around, as though the corvette flew through a fierce tornado. The terror was punctuated by the impact of a large rock into the viewport.

"Here we go again," Mycroft retorted. Flashbacks raced through his mind.

"How do we know where we're going?" Ridley asked. "I can't see a damn thing and can't tell which direction is which."

"The central planets are on the scope," Elio replied. "As long as they are in front of us we are heading in the right direction. It will be obvious once we get there, the storm will dissipate."

"How far away are we," Silas inquired. "Will it take us long to get there?"

"It will take as long as it will take," was all Elio replied.

The heroes' corvette painstakingly zig-zagged around the treacherous cosmic maze of terror. Gigantic masses of carbonized gas and large asteroids nearly collided with the fragile craft.

Scattered about the natural obstacles were large fragments of ancient war frigates, floating aimlessly through the tempest. Elio's expert piloting got the corvette passed several close calls, each more harrowing than the last.

The long minutes turned into an innumerable amount of hours as the corvette carved through the storm. While the passenger's resolve was stronger than ever, the ship itself was rapidly falling apart. The viewport cracked even more, and dents appeared in the hull. Interior walls buckled and panels fell from the ceiling, as the storm caused intense pressure that the ship couldn't handle anymore. The various computers alerted them to several chemical and pressure leaks, but the pilots ignored the constant, annoying pleas.

On the navi-computer, the map showed the planet clearing inch closer and closer, but even after hours of travel, they still hadn't cleared the storm.

Suddenly, a large impact struck the left side of the ship, compelling it to lurch off course. Elio struggled to keep the ship steady, and everyone else inside all jostled around.

"What the fuck was that?" Ridley exclaimed, as he struggled to assist Elio in controlling the ship.

"Another asteroid or ship wreckage," Silas mused. His eyes showed intense fear, even though he tried to hide it.

The ship was struck again, this time from beneath. It lurched upward and nearly collided with another large piece of starship wreckage. It was only by Elio's superhuman reflexes that the corvette survived the close encounter.

"Something hit us," Elio said. "It is not reading on any of the scopes or scanners."

"Nothing organic can live in this, can they?" Ridley asked, referring to the cosmic tempest. "Let alone in the vacuum of space."

"Statistically," Elio began, "there is a near certainty that creatures live in the interspace atmosphere. Stories from freight pilots have provided ample evidence, and the few confirmed sightings have only solidified the certainty. However no official literature has been published on the subject."

"It makes sense that something can adapt to exist in here," Mycroft said. "And since we're traveling through, of course it's going to give *us* a hard time."

He ran to the engine electrics closet. "If we turn off all power it'll leave us alone. But we have to be fast, otherwise the ship will get caught in the current and get crushed by something."

"Try to move us to that debris clearing." Silas pointed to a large void in the storm that provided just barely enough room. "We should have just enough time to make it there and lose the creature without getting swept up in the current. Mycroft, wait for my mark."

Elio nodded and directed the ship towards the clearing. Several more impacts from the unseen behemoth slammed into the ship, nearly tearing it apart. The seconds it took for the ship to reach the clearing felt like hours.

"Here!" Elio declared.

Silas screamed at Mycroft to cut the power. The Specter complied and the ship lurched once more before going still. The interior lights, screens and sirens all went black. The only semblance of light came from the storm's green luminescence.

The ship floated along the strong currents and the passengers could hear the small debris pound into the fragile hull. The viewport cracked some more but the ship remained largely still. The creature ceased ramming the ship, and unleashed a tremendous howl.

The howling continued for several more minutes until the creature finally retreated back into the storm.

"Good grief. I'd hate to have to hunt that sucker," Ridley commented, shuddering as the creature's growls faded off into the distance. "Damn thing must feed off of rocket fuel."

"And all the other shit that's in here," Mycroft said. His eyes roved around the damaged interior, assessing just how terrible the state they were all in.

Just then a massive shadow exterminated what little light entered the ship, and the creature's howl was louder than ever. A large, dark mass filled the top of the viewport, slowly creeping into sight. The creature resembled an alligator crossed with a shark, only the size of a sports stadium. Its four large eyes rolled around in its head, hunting for the vanished prey. The creature roared, revealing a tremendously ugly mouth filled with millions of flaming teeth.

The whole ship shook at the volume of the sound, and a few bolts tumbled out of the ceiling. No one dared move, as all they could really do was be entranced by the creature before them.

"How long do we wait?" Silas whispered. He wiped a curtain of sweat off his brow.

"How long *can* we wait?" Mycroft countered.

"I estimate another two minutes, on the generous side," Elio added. His grip on the ship's controls was so strong, his knuckles were white as pearls.

"Can we outrun it?" Ridley asked.

"Not likely," Silas said. "As soon as we restart the ship, he'll be after us again. He'll catch us in two seconds."

"Actually, less than seven-tenths of a second," Elio added.

"How far away are we to the planet clearing?" Mycroft leaned in to get a better view of the creature, swimming lazily. "If we cross the storm veil, the monster likely won't follow us out."

"Because chances are we will not make it," Elio countered.

"Come now, my little friend. What about that self-doubt we've been talking about," Silas patted the pilot on the shoulder. "All we can do is trust that we'll do it, and we will."

"Perhaps you would like to fly the ship," Elio added. He was clearly nervous and unsure about their chances of success.

"If I remember correctly we didn't have that far left to go until the clearing," Ridley said. "We won't really know for sure without turning the navi-computer back on, though."

"And if we do that, then we'll attract that thing to come back and get us," Mycroft said.

"That is inevitable, dear Mycroft," Silas said. "All we can do is to continue until we can't anymore. Yes our options are limited, but–"

"But it does not matter because we will fail anyway," Elio said. "It is practically inevitable." He was in a full panic, as his blue eyes roved around madly, not focusing on any one thing for longer than a millisecond.

"Dammit, Elio, will you quit that bullshit!" Ridley grabbed his companion's collar, ready to punch him.

"Look!" Elio pointed out the viewport, unfazed by the assault. "A wreckage is heading straight for us! ETA twenty seconds and counting."

Ridley released his grip and joined everyone else looking out the viewport. A large section of an old frigate's superstructure headed straight for the ship. There was no avoiding it.

Mycroft immediately ran back to the electrical closet. "I'll restart the ship on five. Ready? One!"

"Wait!" Ridley panicked. "We'll have to program the navi-computer for another trajectory, and it'll take at least thirty seconds. We can't just go flying off in any direction we want!"

"Fifteen seconds to impact!" Elio screamed, staring as the wreckage came closer.

"Two!" Mycroft yelled from the electrics closet.

"We can't wait, Ridley! We'll just have to take a chance," Silas screamed.

"Three."

"Wreckage ETA, ten seconds," Elio said.

"Where are we supposed to go?" Ridley screamed. "How are we supposed to be going in the right direction if the computer hasn't found a route?"

"Just follow your instincts. That's all we've really been doing up to this point," Silas said. "We're going to die any way you look at it, the question is just *when*? Now or next time! I vote for next time!"

"Four."

Elio was frantically looking for a path as he kept watching the impending doom. "Wreckage impact in three... two..."

"Five!" Mycroft pulled the switches and the ship came back to life. Once the lights returned inside the cockpit, Elio pressed the throttle to its limits and the corvette launched with speed into the cosmic storm. Thanks to its pilot's superhuman abilities, the ship effortlessly moved through the incoming wreckage without sustaining major damage, and was able to carve a path through the churning mess.

But as the ship traveled further into the storm, the more difficult it was to avoid the ever-appearing obstacles. A small asteroid clipped

CHAPTER 21

the edge of one of the wings, sending the ship into a twirling corkscrew. Elio struggled to stabilize it.

"Has the navicomputer found a path through, yet?" Despite the frantic situation, Elio's voice remained characteristically calm. "This is starting to get hard, here!"

"I told you it would take at least thirty seconds," Ridley screamed as he frantically pressed buttons on the computer to get it to work faster. "The damn thing is still collating. We're at thirty percent now."

Outside, the monster noticed its scurrying prey and roared terribly. It immediately pursued the ship, even though it was constantly pummeled with debris. It was numb to every feeling except hunger.

Driving a straight line through the churning storm, the monster quickly gained ground with the corvette. It bit off the rear wings of the ship, its teeth starting many fires on the tattered, severed hull.

Inside the cockpit, a litany of alarms blared for attention, alerting the passengers of the missing sections of the ship. But all anyone could focus on was making it out alive.

Ridley was only paying attention to the loading navi-computer, which had surpassed 50% collation but had still not found a path to the planet clearing. He banged at the keyboard and the screen, desperately wishing the fucking thing would hurry up and work.

"Breaking it won't help us out at all, Ridley," Silas offered as he placed his hands on the boy's shoulders. "Patience is what's useful now."

More shudders erupted from the rear of the ship as the beast continued eating it away. Elio tried to swerve out of the creature's path, but the constantly changing landscape made that impossible. There was no way for the ship to speed up either, for it was already going as fast as it could.

"Look! The storm is lightening up!" Mycroft excitedly pointed out the viewport at the swirling clouds. "Or is it just some fucking optical illusion?"

"I see it too," Silas replied calmly.

"You are correct, Mycroft," Elio said. "The storm is lightening up. We must be near the planet clearing, or at least *some* type of clearing. But we still have quite a ways to go, yet."

The ship suddenly veered down as the beast took a large bite out of it. The sub-light engines were completely ripped off the ship and went down the beast's gullet. With every stroke of its fin, the beast came closer to the kill.

Inside the cockpit, everyone was completely silent, with the same thing on their minds; they weren't going to make it. Sparks erupted from the ceiling and small fires erupted from various areas of the control board. The navi-computer was still collating an escape path at 60%, while the walls slowly buckled in on themselves. Fires erupted from where the engines used to be, and ironically helped propel the broken corvette.

Desperately, the broken ship flew towards the storm veil, with its speed decreasing with each passing linear foot. The monster was enjoying the chase, but growing angry and impatient to make the kill.

The beast reeled its terrible head to take the killing bite, when a piece of wreckage slammed into its eye and ruined the shot. The beast howled in pain as it suddenly stopped swimming and was swept up in the strong currents of the storm.

The heroes inside the ship knew nothing of this, as once they heard that devastating roar they braced themselves for the killing blow that never came.

CHAPTER 22

The blaring sirens inside the cockpit masked the notification from the navi-computer that a path had finally been found. Elio was the first one to notice that the ship had not been destroyed by the creature and commanded it to take the newfound course. He then proceeded to awaken the others who had fainted from fright.

Within five minutes the ship carved through the storm veil and broke free from the cosmic tempest, and calmly floated in the quiet void of the planet clearing.

"We made it?" Ridley said, more of a question than a statement. He was still groggy from his panic induced cat nap.

"See!" Silas smiled warmly. "I told you we would. All we needed was to trust ourselves." Every trace of his panic had completely vanished.

Mycroft remained silent and just rolled his eyes at his master's old corny sayings, and sighed deeply with relief.

The clearing was only large enough to contain the three small planetoids within it, surrounded on all sides by the thick green wall of the cosmic storm. None of the worlds looked habitable, let alone inviting. All three planets had harsh and deserted climates with barely any color besides red, brown, or orange. The smallest one had a large chunk of it blown away, exposing a frozen and crumbling core. What was left of the surface was pockmarked with large, continental areas of snow.

The second planet was surrounded by numerous satellites and war wreckage. One hemisphere was veiled in an atmospheric minefield, preventing anything from entering or leaving. This planet was covered in a brown and red sea, undulating and cresting with strong currents. There was no large land mass in sight.

On the opposite side of the planet clearing was another minefield, similar to the one above the sea world. This area appeared to have known only war and strife, as it was engulfed in a tragic atmosphere of heartache, and bloodshed.

"No doubt we should first try the planet with the orbiting ship," Ridley said. "Is that an Axis carrier?"

"No, they don't look like that at all," Mycroft replied. "It looks similar to the illustrations in the history books. That's the Hyde's ship." A sense of dread covered the Specter, and the feeling that he wasn't going to survive the day returned to the forefront of his consciousness.

Silas looked at him, and the two Specters exchanged another silent conversation. After several seconds of staring at each other, both men just nodded their heads.

"Lovely. Just fucking great!" Ridley jumped out of his seat and ran to the lavatory. The sounds of the boy heaving filled the wrecked ship.

"Well, it seems like we have a couple options here, fellas." Silas clapped his hands lightly. "Shall we board the ship, or try planetfall first?"

"I'm afraid we'll board the ship only to learn that they're down on the surface," Mycroft replied. He stared at the frigate, trying to study as much as he could. "Which will waste what little advantage we have."

"That has already been wasted as the battlecruiser is scanning us," Elio said. He was in the electrical closet trying to get the ship some propulsion. "No doubt they will bring us in with a tractor beam." His voice lightened a bit, "At least we do not have to worry about repairing the missing engines."

"They won't pick up anything wrong with our registration tags," Ridley said as he reentered the room, his face looking less green. "All they'll see is a piece of shit used 'vette. We don't belong to anyone officially, except maybe JeffCo. We should be fine, right?"

"Oh no, they will still shoot us, regardless. In fact, being unaffiliated is worse because that means we really have no reason to be out here," Silas was fairly calm about that grim fact. "Why else would we be here, if not to look for them?"

Ridley's brows furrowed but the boy didn't skip a beat. "We could have gotten caught up in that mess and just happened to end up here, and now we need to repair the engines."

Mycroft was quite impressed with Ridley's quick thinking. He would have said the same thing.

"We've waited here long enough," Mycroft said. "We're already arousing suspicion. Let's try to land before they realize they're not shooting at us. And kinda make it rough on our way down, like we're losing power."

"We do not have to act, it is actually happening," was Elio's response. He finished some connections in the electrical closet and returned to the pilot's seat. Elio managed to get some of the gas leaks to propel the ship. The pitiful corvette was barely moving, but at least it *was* moving.

"So much for a 'quality, used vehicle.'" Ridley mocked the dealer's greeting, which got a laugh out of everyone and lightened the mood a little.

The ship lumbered into the planet's gravitational pull and barely survived the fall onto the mountainous surface. Elio's superhuman piloting skills got the ship into a valley with a heavy canopy of shade that hid it mostly from view. They wouldn't stand a chance against radar, but this was as good as they were going to get.

Everyone gathered in the small mess hall, assembling what weapons and supplies they could muster in preparation for only who-knew-what. While a Specter's standard weapons cache was full of multiple knives and blasters and grenades, the group had to make due with only two small blasters for Elio and Ridley and two ethellite swords for Mycroft and Silas. The group was able to procure a few grenades, explosive charges, and a bunker-blaster with only one shot.

Silas was helping the two kids pack their gear while Mycroft was raking his mind for the right words to say to inspire the group. This was probably the last time all four would be in the same room together and he felt obligated to not waste the moment. As usual, nothing adequate came to mind.

"Nothing I can say can prepare you for anything that is about to happen. All I can promise you is that nothing you've experienced up until now will be like what you'll see here. The best thing you can do is listen to us and follow our lead. If we tell you to run, you run. If we tell you to hide, you hide. Obeying everything we say is truly the only chance you have of staying alive here."

"And if we tell you to leave us and save yourselves, you'll obey," Silas said solemnly. "No questions asked. Someone needs to be able to return to the headquarters and tell them what has happened here. *Your* survival, above all else, is paramount. Understand?"

"Duly noted." Elio said. "Our primary objective is self-preservation."

"I thought our mission was to find Ulysses?" Ridley asked. He was visibly shocked by the Specters' warning. "It can't be so dangerous that we all can't make it back alive right? At least to the ship?"

The older Specter held up a hand calmly. "You and Elio's mission is to rescue the senator's son, while Mycroft's and I will do our best to capture the duelist, alive."

Mycroft looked at Silas. "We never agreed to that." Betrayal was laced in his voice.

"If you kill him, you will not be able to mine his brain for information," Elio interjected. "After all, that was the real reason you came here. Killing him will render that objective moot."

"The chiefs would want to interrogate him," Silas added, talking to Mycroft rather than the rest of the group. "Remember, we answer to them—I answer to them. And as your superior, I *order* you to not kill him."

Mycroft started to protest but respected Silas' silencing hand.

"Mycroft and I will hunt for the duelist," Silas repeated. "You two will look for Ulysses. We'll stay together as much as we can, but when we find something of interest regarding either of our objectives, we'll split up."

"Rendezvous back here at sundown, and if we don't make it, leave without us," Mycroft said.

Ridley started to protest, but was cut off. "What did we say?"

"Self-preservation is our first objective," Elio said, and Ridley reluctantly repeated.

"If that means you leave us here, leave us here," Mycroft said. "We'll make our own way home."

"We always do," Silas said with a wink.

The team ventured out, traversing the mountainous terrain. The high and narrow valley provided ample shade, making the trek in the sweltering heat somewhat bearable. Soon, they found a set of rail tracks that ran parallel to a road. The team flipped a coin as to which direction to take.

After two hours of hiking, and not leaving the valley or making any other sort of meaningful progress, Ridley's fury boiled over. "How do we know we're not walking away from our destination? How long are we going to keep going before we realize we're going the wrong way?"

"What do you suggest we do," Silas calmly asked. "Start walking the back way we came? That will only show us what we've already seen."

"From the depth of the most recent tread marks, we are going the most traveled way." Elios said, examining the ground with his high-powered eyes. "It is only a matter of time before we run into something."

"But we could be wasting what little time we have just to *find* this place," Ridley retorted. The boy resisted the urge to stomp his feet.

"Do you have a better idea," Mycroft asked calmly. He simply crossed his arms and waited for the young man to respond. Admittedly, he shared the same thoughts, but was also able to see that they were on the right path.

"Yes, actually." Ridley raised his chin and blinked quickly a few times. He clearly was not prepared to have to provide an explanation. "We go back to the ship and run more scans to see what the hell is even here. For all we know, we landed on the complete opposite region of the planet."

"And how shall we remain undetected? The frigate up there can absolutely track our instruments. Just hiding under the brush is not going to conceal us," Mycroft said dryly. "They probably have landed at our ship already and are searching it right now."

"Not to mention that whatever we're looking for won't be scannable," Silas added. "The technology the Hyde possesses is too outdated for any of our equipment to read. That's to say if there's even a readable signal."

"And our ship's scanners cannot scan the entire planetary surface," Elio added. "Not to mention, they do not even work at the moment."

The team simply stared at Ridley, who stared back in defiance. After a few seconds, Ridley walked away from the group, off into the thick brush lining the valley floor.

"Where are you going?" Elio asked.

"We're supposed to stick together," Silas yelled out.

"I'm preserving myself," Ridley shouted back. "You go your way and I'll go on my own."

"That is not a great idea," Elio said, only to Mycroft and Silas.

"You'll get lost," Silas shouted.

"Or captured," Mycroft said.

"How can they find me when they can't see me? I've survived the Gambit, I can—"

Ridley's voice cut out and the sound of cascading gravel came from his direction.

The three immediately rushed to the rescue, and right as they approached Ridley's disappearance sight, the floor dropped out from underneath them. as well

For ten seconds, everyone was in complete darkness. Then both Mycroft and Silas ignited their swords, revealing a long tunnel. No light came from either end, but a faint mechanical sound echoed through the long corridor.

"What worm is this big?" Ridley remarked. The tunnel was easily tall enough to fit five of him stacked on top of each other.

"None. This is a mining access tunnel," Elio said. "Look at the repetitive patterns along the wall. This was cut by a machine."

"Your eyes are better than all of us, Elio. So we'll trust you," Silas said.

"This bisects the road," Mycroft said, "running perpendicular to it. But where is that sound coming from?"

"That way," Elio pointed down a particular direction. "Maybe another half-mile or so."

The Specters looked at each other, nodded, and headed in that direction.

"See?" Ridley said, vindicated. "My idea to leave the road paid off. Now we have a lead to follow!"

"Don't celebrate yet," Mycroft said. "We could be killed by a machine at any moment."

Ridley fell silent as a large lump of reality swelled in his throat. The team continued walking in silence.

The corridor continued in a monotonous straight line, with the faint noise growing louder in the distance ahead of them. The air grew damp and cooler, meaning they were walking down a gradual descent.

After an eternity of walking, the team came to a large chamber. Unlit torches lined the walls, which were ornately carved with multiple scenes. Alcoves with statues dotted all sides of the room. In the center was a large stone slab, with an ornate pedestal. The carving on the pedestal was in a language none of them—even Elio—could understand. Dust covered the thing, and there was a clear mark on the slab where something used to rest.

"What is this place?" Ridley asked. "Some type of exhibition hall?"

"No, a library," Silas replied. "This is one of the original locations for one of the scriptures. No doubt the carvings are prayers and quotations from the text."

"None of the symbols match what is located in the Specter's archives," Elio announced. "There are not even any remote similarities that I can recognize."

"That's because each planet had their own languages when these texts were written. Clearly, this temple is at least five thousand years old. Just keep a sharp eye, Elio, and try to soak in and remember as much as you can." Silas smiled and patted the boy's shoulder. "It's okay, son, we're learning as we go too."

Mycroft walked around, finding excavation tools that had recently been discarded. "Someone has been in here recently."

"If we're lucky, we just missed them," Ridley said worriedly.

"If we're lucky, we'll catch up *soon*," Mycroft winked and gave Ridley a friendly slap on the cheek.

Elio discovered another passage and led the team through. The team found a second library with significantly different inscriptions in the same language, most likely indicating it was for another scripture.

"So how do these work? Aren't you supposed to closely read the manuscripts to get their power?" Ridley asked, trying to pronounce an incantation.

"One Hyde shaman would master each text and impart his wisdom to their disciples. One's scripture was chosen for them, and most only ever attained one power," Silas said. "Only a special chosen one was allowed to study all the scriptures, for they would in turn be given the control of the Hyde as a whole."

"Were all of them duelists that tried to kill onsite?" Mycroft asked sarcastically. "Enough looking back at the old ways and wanting to study them, and let's view each one of them as they truly are, dangerous."

The clanking noise grew louder as they passed through three more chambers, descending further into the depths of the planet. The journey abruptly ended in the largest chamber, surrounded by an enormous seating gallery. It was like an ancient stadium, covered by an enormous dome with an oculus in the center. Giant carvings covered every visible surface.

In the center of the room was another altar table, but this was human-sized and caked in dark stains.

Ridley was immediately disgusted at the sight. "Good grief, is this the sacrificial chamber?"

"It appears to be something of the sort," Silas replied. He was genuinely intrigued and confused. "But why would it be surrounded by those libraries?" He stood in the center of the chamber and looked around, puzzled.

"The Hyde was always clear about their priorities," Mycroft said. "It makes sense. Kill first, study later."

"But look at the murals," Ridley said. "They seem to tell a story."

The faded paintings and carvings illustrated some ceremony, with spectators and shamans and multiple bloody victims. The oculus channeled the cosmic energies. The victims were mutilated by a jagged knife, slicing just above the waistline from hip to hip. The remainder of the mural had faded into oblivion, yet the ceremony was completed with a shaman bathed in the oculus' energy.

"Such an elaborate process just to light someone one fire," Mycroft quipped.

"No doubt the missing pieces contain the mystery's conclusion, and were probably taken down on purpose." Silas said. "Look at the precision of the break in the stone. This was not an accident."

"This doesn't look like a sacrifice," Elio said, looking back between the mural and the table. "The table forces the victim to sit with their legs splayed, not lying down."

"Perhaps that's how they killed," Ridley proffered.

"No, because look at where the majority of the blood is," Elio said. "This is a *birthing* chair, I am sure of it."

Everyone looked at the chair and murals again, trying to catch up to Elio's fast-paced thinking.

"The final picture, it's not a body—it's a *baby*," Mycroft said, taking a closer look. "And that energy is from the scriptures. See that glowing stack of blocks. That's where the light comes from."

A silence engulfed the room as the group gradually connected the dots. The clanking in the distance grew louder, as though it was coming closer.

"Good Gods, this is a breeding chamber for the next masters," Silas said. "There are twelve blocks in that stack."

"But then why did we only find five libraries?" Ridley asked. "Where are the other seven?"

"These were the only scriptures the Hyde ever possessed," Silas elucidated. "Most of the others were in the hands of the Specters. So this mural must be the whole process, and the Hyde was trying to replicate it."

"Still, the Hyde masters would have had a general knowledge of what the other scriptures contained," Mycroft added. "So it wasn't totally outside the realm to be able to at least partially replicate the full procedure." Mycroft studied the mural once again, entranced.

Ridley only grew frustrated. Everyone was assuming he knew what the hell they were all talking about. "The process for what?"

"Breeding the *next* Hyde master," Silas and Mycroft answered simultaneously.

Suddenly the young Ridley connected all the dots, and was shocked. "So that is what Ulysses' purpose is," Ridley asked. "To breed the next Hyde master?"

"He is a member of the Myx genus," Elio said. "And unlike his birth parents, Ulysses possesses the recessive genome twenty-eight."

"What does that mean?" Ridley was once again confused. All the progress he made catching up was completely obliterated.

"He's one of the few human breeds that can give birth," Mycroft proffered. "His kind is especially coveted by the Hyde. Even in the Syndicate that is still an elusive talent to have."

The young Ridley was taken aback, and not by what he imagined. He struggled to keep his mind focused. "Wow. That's...hot," was all he could muster.

Mycroft rolled his eyes at the boy's immaturity.

"And more dangerous than we could imagine," Silas said solemnly.

"We have twelve months before the fetus comes to term," Elio replied.

"Wait," Ridley bounced out of his funk. "Ulysses *is* pregnant?"

"We don't know that, which is why we have to move fast!" Mycroft led the group out of the chamber.

CHAPTER 23

The small shuttle came out of interspace and orbited the mountainous planet Tartarus Prime. Count Lucilous hated coming here, for even with his ship's special deflectors he always just barely made it out of the cosmic storm alive every time. But he also recognized that that was the test; only those who can survive will make it anywhere in this life.

But all it did was add to his frustrations. Lucilous fumed as the shuttle auto-piloted to the surface, his rage blinding him to the fact his master's ship was already orbiting the planet. Count Lucilous had only one thought on his mind, revenge.

When his shuttle touched down on the mine's landing pad, Lucilous stormed down the ramp, pushing past the platform guards and charging directly for the traffic control booth.

Around him, the planet's acolytes, the Hyde's most loyal servants, mined the hard-packed soil, searching for any valuable artifacts scattered throughout the earth. The job was painstakingly done by hand, so as not to damage the precious artifacts. These acolytes devoted their entire existence to the Hyde—keeping the vestiges of the dying religion alive for its imminent return.

As Lucilous marched along the narrow path, the nearby acolytes stopped working and sneered at the count. They were not afraid to show their contempt for him, and frankly did not care for him at all.

The count entered the booth, located in the center of a star of intersecting corridors. He approached the overseer and violently turned to look at the foul man

"Why are you here?" the overseer spat at Lucilous' feet. While he was not an acolyte, the contempt for the count was shared.

Lucilous bared his teeth in anger. It took all his strength not to growl. "I'm conducting a surprise inspection."

The man was not intimidated in the slightest, and took another bite from his sandwich. Food flew out of the man's big mouth where teeth once stood, right onto the count's face. "Where's the Master? Or the Disciple?"

Lucilous threw the man back into his chair, causing him to choke for a few seconds. "They gave me authority to conduct these inspections on my own. You know that you stupid wretch. Now tell me where–"

"No they didn't!" The man was not about to let the count finish his sentences, either. "They would never allow you to come here yourself." A crooked smile carved onto his face. "And *you* know that, stupid."

"How dare you accuse me of lying! I'll inform my master of this insubordination. I demand you tell me where the asset is located." Lucilous grasped the hilt of his sword and held it, unignited, at the overseer's throat. "Or shall I ignite this into your thick neck?"

The overseer eyed the sword wearily, then looked into Lucilous' eyes with a hardened resolve. "We only show you courtesy because the master ordered us. Only because you are in his presence do you remain alive."

The nearby acolytes quit working and entered the control room, slowly and threateningly surrounding the count.

Lucilous looked around, and saw they all carried their tools as weapons, ready to strike. He swallowed the lump in his throat and held back the urge to kill the overseer. He wanted to fight, but knew he would lose.

"Just what are you implying?" he asked the overseer, whose expression had remained unchanged. "That I'm not welcome here?"

"Not only that, but that your, supposed, authority means less than nothing." The overseer's voice was deadly cold. "You're only breathing and still talking to me because I have not given the order to dispatch you. So if you still want to remain as such, you had best lower your toy, and return to your ship." The man smiled, and his surrounding cronies hungered for violence.

Lucilous lowered his sword, but ignited it. "Is that a threat?"

The overseer smiled more. "It's a promise, mate."

The crowd came closer. Lucilous' brow soaked with sweat. His options were quickly diminishing

"Just tell me what I need to know. None of this is necessary nor productive."

The overseer's smile disappeared. "Oh, we have already told ya, mate. We have."

Lucilous swung his sword with a flourish as the crowd rushed him.

* * *

The distant clanking noise was the loudest it's ever been, and the path grew lighter as the team continued down the corridor. The walls of rock grew rougher and the path narrowed, meaning this section of the tunnel was rather fresh.

After making the final twist, the team emerged in the middle of a maintenance hallway. Tools were scattered everywhere, and the occasional cart full of dirt zoomed by on magnatracks.

The Specters continued ahead alone and found a swath of acolytes sorting through the mined dirt, emptying the full carts, and sifting for artifacts. The Specters eventually discovered an exit, and beyond that a landing pad with a ship.

"Ulysses is not here, so he must be on the ship," Elio concluded when the Specters returned to report. "But how do we get there without getting ambushed?"

"That's ok, we'll just clear our path!" Ridley brandished his small rifle, eager to see it in action.

"There's too many and they're too strong," Mycroft said. "The four of us would be wiped out in thirty seconds."

"Not to mention they have friends and reinforcements," Silas added. "We're all we've got."

"So then what do we do?" Ridley was obviously disappointed.

"We cannot hide for very long," Elio offered. "The path is a clear shot with no hiding opportunities."

"Surely we can dress up in their uniform and sneak past them," Ridley said. "They can't be that smart."

"Those acolytes have a hive mind, and can telepathically communicate with each other," Silas said. "They don't have to talk to know when something is happening."

"What one feels, they all feel. By no stretch of the imagination are those things human, kiddo," Mycroft said.

"So then we're fucked?" Ridley asked.

"In essence," Elio confirmed.

Suddenly a loud screaming carved through the passage followed by the sounds of fighting, and an ethellite sword.

"Quick, you two hide and stay out of sight," Mycroft ordered, as the two Specters rushed to the commotion.

Silas and Mycroft found an ongoing skirmish just around the corner. The acolytes were clearly holding their own against the lone sword wielder, who was lost in the thick of the fighting crowd.

Mycroft rushed to join the fight, but was held back by Silas. "Do you want to kill yourself now, or let them weaken him and take him on later?"

The younger Specter relented and allowed the fight to continue unabated. The two eventually got a clear view of the swordsman—Count Lucilous.

Both men audibly gasped.

"Why would he be here instead of on the front lines?" Mycroft wondered.

"My suspicions were true, the Axis is under the Hyde's influence. How can we have been blind to this for so long?" Silas was visibly distraught.

But the scene didn't add up, and Mycroft was confused. "But if he's one of them, why are the acolyte's fighting him?"

All Silas could do was shake his head. "I don't know, but I have the feeling he will lead us to the boy's location, and to our duelist."

The two continued watching the fight unfold. After several seconds, Mycroft finally asked, "Should we stay, just to make sure he survives?"

Silas looked on at the fight. "No, he'll be scratched up good but he'll make it. If they wanted him dead they wouldn't have taken this long."

They returned to Elio and Ridley to share the latest updates.

"Count Lucilous?" Ridley was completely ignorant. "Who is that?"

Elio started reciting facts about the count, but was quickly silenced by the Specters.

"We don't have time for a history lesson," Mycroft screamed. "We have to go now!"

The heroes ran to the ship, surprisingly unnoticed. Once they made it inside, they encountered five acolytes dismantling the shuttle's interior.

The fight ensued, and it was intense. Ridley and Elio were no match for their opponents and were quickly overcome by them. Mycroft and Silas had a difficult time as well, for their opponents' brawn was the perfect counter to the Specters' abilities.

All the attackers were quickly dispatched just before they could summon reinforcements. The travelers just barely had enough time to settle into their cramped hiding spaces before Lucilous rushed into the cockpit.

Lucilous was furious and bleeding profusely. He muttered under his breath, cursing every few words. The only audible comment he made had to do with beheading the overseer.

Suddenly the rockets came to life and the ship jolted into movement, and soon all five were en route to the orbiting battle cruiser.

CHAPTER 24

Across the stars, on board the *Imperatrix*, the Specter Chiefs gathered around the battle map in the war room, intensely studying it. Thousands of yellow dots of varying sizes, representing the position of the Syndicate fleet, amassed around a cluster of red star pieces representing the planets of the Sargasso Cluster.

One of the chiefs zoomed in on a particular collection of six planets, possessing an area large enough to hide an entire Axis garrison. This was the area of particular interest to the chiefs, because all of the recon they could gather labeled this the prime spot for their enemy's location. They marked it the strike site.

This was, after all, a guess. The chiefs frankly had no idea where the Axis was located, and could not adequately help the Syndicate's admirals in properly preparing for an ambush. That is why they ordered Mycroft to the area to gather the necessary intelligence.

The air was heavy with a pregnant silence, with everyone solely focused on winning the upcoming battle and putting an immediate end to the civil war. Various radio frequencies from across the galaxy competed with each other for the limited ears that were able to listen and respond to their cries for help. The hundreds of hologram projectors and computing terminals scattered around the room all hummed quietly with efficient action, their first time ever having been put to the test.

Chief Latiolais checked his pocket watch for the fourth time in 30 seconds, anxiously awaiting any communication from Mycroft. He, like his companions, was growing increasingly worried at the lack of any form of communication in the two days since the experienced Specter departed.

The other chiefs were growing increasingly restless as well, for they could only order the admirals to postpone the battle for a little while longer. The only one to visibly hold out any type of hope was Albus, but even he was growing increasingly weary.

Latiolais looked at his watch one last time. The second hand was furiously marching along, counting the seconds the galaxy no longer could afford to wait. He closed it with a defining snap and cleared his throat. He surprisingly found this difficult to say.

"It's been seventy-six hours since last contact. We've already waited too long."

Most of the gathered chiefs merely hummed and slowly nodded their heads, acknowledging the unfortunate truth.

Albus, on the other hand, grew animated and raised his voice. "He still has twelve more hours! He was ordered to give us an answer within *ninety* hours of departure, and for all we know he is still looking. We can at least wait *that* long before declaring Mycroft dead."

"Can we?" Latiolais pointed to the battle map. "Any second now we are going to get ambushed on that battlefield, and then we'll know everything that we ordered him to find out for us! We are supposed to be coming up with a plan to deliver to the admirals, not constantly wait for the fucking telephone to ring. We have to get to work and make some decisions."

Latiolais turned to walk away but Albus pounded his fist on the hologram table. "Fighting blind and shooting randomly in space at the first ship that moves will lose us this war quicker than we can ever win it. Impatience is just as strong an enemy as the Axis, and we cannot allow it to become their ally."

Chief Burgess was moved by the statement. "And if we lose our humanity, we are no better than our enemy. The least we can do is hold out for twelve more hours, at least to get confirmation of...mission failure." He couldn't bring himself to say "Mycroft's death," for that would make it too real.

Latiolais' jaw dropped, and he was in pure awe. "Gentlemen, listen to yourselves. Do you not realize that we no longer have any *time* to hold out hope? With each passing minute that we don't fire the first shot, the chance of them striking us increases tenfold. Shit, by the end of this fucking conversation we might not even have the Fourth Fleet anymore!

"I know you all understand that I would, of course, wait for Mycroft, but frankly we are far past the time for even he to be of any help to us! We have to deliver a solid attack plan for the admirals, otherwise there will be more than just Mycroft's blood on our hands."

"Don't mock my intelligence," Albus protested. "I've always understood that the mission is always bigger than just one individual. But listen to what I'm telling you; Mycroft is not dead yet."

It was Latiolais' turn to slam his fist on the table. "Sonofabitch, do you think that I don't think that? Do you think I want the bastard to be dead just so we can move on to watch thousands of young, innocent people lose their lives over some fucking Senate squabble? Of course I believe Mycroft is still alive. Of course I believe he hasn't failed, but if we keep holding out hope for the best solution, we definitely will fail."

The two tempers gradually subsided. The pressure of the situation was becoming too much even for the most experienced Specters to handle. It was easy to forget, even for them, that they too were only human beings that could only do the best they could with what they had.

Albus remained silent, brooding at the unfortunate reality of the situation. He was so angry, a tear of fury slowly descended his cheek.

Chief Burgess understood his colleague's pain and gently patted him on the shoulder. He looked at Latiolais and gently asked, "What if he updates us *after* we deliver the plans?"

Latiolais' eyes were red with regret, yet dry as a bone. "Then all we can do is pray he can get to the admirals before the first shot."

The Specter Chiefs returned to formulating their battle plan, keeping a close look at the clock, desperately hoping that the elusive Mycroft would contact them before the admirals would arrive for the completed plan.

After three hours, the chiefs were compelled to submit their proposal and resorted to praying for the best for their missing colleague.

* * *

The Primarch stood before the assembled soldiers in the *Imperatrix's* main military hangar. Large screens on either side of the wide stage enlarged the Primarch to multiple times his height, and transmitted his words to the hundreds of thousands of soldiers scattered across the stars.

"This is the beginning of a new era. The beginning of an unfortunate era. One where we have to prove to ourselves how much we value each other. How much we value our home. Our freedom. Our democracy. Our way of life.

"Unfortunately you brave few have to be the ones to set the example. The ones we must look up to and admire, forever. But know that everywhere, all across the Cosmic Syndicate, we are cheering you on. We are supporting you one hundred percent, and we'll do whatever it takes.

"As we know you will."

CHAPTER 24

Across the stars, the Archon's message was being transmitted to every corner of the Axis of Independent Systems.

"Those defiant, obstinate beings on the wrong side of history do not pose as great a threat as they wish they could. While they posture and flex their weak, useless muscles, we know their threats are empty. Nothing can match the power of our faith in victory.

"However, this does not mean the road will be easy. This will be a long, tough, battle. And not everyone will make it to the victory parade. But know your sacrifice won't be in vain."

The Primarch and the Archon both paused for effect. The soldiers in both crowds were riled up and furiously applauded.

Both of their voices blasted through their soldiers' ears. "Our victory will be earned, and our victory will teach those cowardly fuckers who are the real holders of power!"

Everyone broke out into the applause heard around the galaxy.

CHAPTER 25

Lucilous' shuttle lumbered into the orbiting frigate's hangar. Inside, the pilot was angrier than before he left the mining facility on Tarturus Prime. His mind could only focus on how those pitiful acolytes could dare defy his rightful authority and attempt to kill him. The part that really pissed him off was how formidable of a fight they offered. His wounds, which were numerous, were just now starting to hurt, and that increased his anger even more.

The count furiously depressed the necessary controls to finalize the landing sequence. There was only one person who was remotely responsible for this, his thoughts kept repeating. His anger had boiled to the point where he muttered under his breath, often incoherently.

"I'll give that bastard the same fucking treatment I just had. Teach that fucker to underestimate me. Motherfucking piece of shit."

The ramp was not fully lowered when the count furiously stomped onto the landing pad. His anger only increased because the blasted technology wasn't fast enough. He completely ignored the salutes and salutations offered by the attendants and officers on deck. Count Lucilous' attention could not be bothered with such things. He had only one focus—finding the Archon.

Lucilous' feet seemed to know exactly where to take him, because in the blink of an eye the count was standing face to face with his master in the frigate's war room.

CHAPTER 25

The hooded figure's displeasure could not be overstated, and immediately overshadowed the creature's surprise at seeing Lucilous. The red eyes squinted in a curious anger. "Why aren't you addressing your troops on the battlefield? Why are you here instead of staring the men you are about to send to their deaths once more in the eye?"

The count's anger-fueled strength wilted under the sheer power of the Archon's stare, yet not fully. While Lucilous was always quick to talk a big game, he could never put his money where his mouth was.

He took a few seconds to clear his throat, trying to get his mind back on track. "You know why I'm here. You think I'm just a stupid stooge, who you can lead on with a carrot and keep ordering around. Well, fucker, I've finally caught on to you!"

The hooded creature tilted his head in curiosity. "Oh?" Doubt flooded every droplet of his voice.

Lucilous was slowly gaining back his resolve. "And you can no longer hide anything from me, because I always find out. You're not as smart as you think you are."

The figure was unmoved. "Do tell."

"You didn't kidnap that little brat for the Axis, you're using him to advance your hocus pocus agenda. Which you promised that I would learn as your apprentice. You plan on taking that shit as your new pupil and killing me off. Eventually, you're going to install that bastard as head of the Axis, and then you'll finally have the willing puppet that you've always wanted.

"All I am to you is a bank! Yet without me and my resources you wouldn't have your vast military or your high tech weapons! Without my workers and money, the largest armada the galaxy has ever seen would never have been built. Without my supervision your vast military infrastructure would not have been constructed, let alone ahead of schedule!

"You are nothing without me! You have nothing without me, and you have done nothing. *Everything* that has happened to this point is all because of me."

Lucilous was talking so fast that he forgot to breathe, and had to pause for a few moments. The Archon remained completely still, watching the count's tirade unfold.

"And then" Lucilous screamed and pointed an accusing finger at the Archon, "you have the nerve to order those putrid sentries down there to only show me respect when I'm in your presence? And yet I'm the selfish one? They nearly killed me, down there! "

* * *

Tucked behind some storage boxes stacked in a corner of the war room, Mycroft and Silas listened intently to this exchange. They could barely hear the count's words, and worried that their recorders, which transmitted directly to the *Imperatrix*, couldn't pick up the conversation either. The Specters also worried that the surrounding storms would prevent the transmission from getting to the space station in time.

Mycroft's sword was in his hand, just aching to be ignited. He wanted a fight to ensue so he could join in on the action. Silas remained more relaxed and at ease, as if he was watching a stage play.

The younger Specter shifted and knocked over a can on top of the crate. The can's noise seemingly went unnoticed.

"Don't blow our cover," Silas signed to Mycroft in the Specter's sign language. "Fighting won't get us anywhere. We'll learn more if we just let this play out."

"Don't you want to be prepared when this shit ends and we're detected?" Mycroft was always annoyed at Silas' wait-and-see approach. "Be prepared. You taught me that. The whole reason we came here was to fight."

CHAPTER 25

Silas calmly rolled his eyes, and signed, "And I also told you to wait for the right time. Patience, boy. Patience!"

Mycroft shook his head, and jumped at the sudden ignition of a sword. Silas laid down a calming hand on the Specter's shoulder.

* * *

"Your life should be protected only when you're in *my* presence." Lucilous screamed at the top of his lungs, his sword ready to strike. "From now on you call me, 'Master!'" His eyes showed the lunacy that fueled him.

The Archon slowly moved his head, at first looking down and then staring directly into the count's eyes. He didn't seem to be threatened, or even angered at all. He almost sounded bored.

"My greatest regret," the creature spoke slowly and deliberatively, "is that I didn't kill you sooner. Those poor, pitiful acolytes wouldn't have had to bother with you, and I wouldn't be disappointed in them for not finishing you."

In one fluid motion the Archon lunged, wrapping his hands around the count's neck. Lucilous dropped his sword, which extinguished as it bounced on the ground. Suddenly, the man that was strengthened with intense hatred was now struggling desperately for his life.

The Archon laughed, a slow, guttural, terrifying laugh. "Yes, everything is because of you, Count. Yes, without you I would already have amassed the Hyde forces that will take over this measly galaxy. Due to you, I have to fight a pathetic army tooth and nail just to get what is rightfully mine!"

The hooded creature's grip strengthened, and Lucilous struggled for breath. He tried to pry off the Archon's hands but it was impossible.

"Nothing has succeeded because of you, dear Count. Nothing has emerged victorious, and no one is grateful because of you. Your heart continues to beat only because you have money, but even that is because of me."

Lucilous' face turned a deeper shade of red as the Archon's grip only tightened. The count's neck popped a few times, and the dying man tried to scream out for mercy.

The Archon continued unnoticed. "Without me, you would have lived the way you will die—a nobody. Without me your planet's revolution would have been successful, and all those souls you leached off of your entire life would have killed you along with the rest of your mooching class."

Red lightning erupted from Lucilous body. He released a powerful scream, which was nigh impossible thanks to the Archon's continued squeezing of his neck. The torture was non-stop and continued for a full minute. Lucilous' screams increased with the intensity of the painful lightning, with both reaching a blood-curdling crescendo.

The Archon spoke loud enough to be heard without shouting. "You are not a leader, and will never be one. No one feels anything more than contempt for you. Your essence brings irritation to everyone that's heard of you."

Lucilous could only scream painfully. The lighting continued to intensify mercilessly.

The red eyes beneath the hood stretched into evil slits. Every word the Archon spoke dripped with unbridled fury. "You think you deserve to call yourself my apprentice? I've never met a more unqualified individual."

The lightning suddenly extinguished and the Archon threw Lucilous to the floor. "You're not even worth my energy."

Mycroft's grip on his sword tightened. The time he awaited, and dreaded, had finally arrived. He hated being right.

The Specter looked over and saw Silas un-belt his sword and whisper a silent prayer. Mycroft raised his eyebrows, he thought he was the only one that prayed before dueling. He then recited his own.

The Archon walked back to studying the battle map, leaving the whimpering count to wallow in his own failure. A few moments passed before the count lunged to his feet, ignited his sword, and ran for the kill.

Another sword met the count's as he struck his torturer. The Archon slowly turned to stare the count in the eye. "Only *you* would try to stab me in the back."

* * *

Elio and Ridley stealthily sneaked through the bustling corridor. They had no idea where they were going or which direction to take, so they picked a corridor at random and followed it. All they really knew was where they needed to be. Technicians, guards, and random crew went about their duties, while the duo hid in the shadows and waited for the right moment to move to the next hiding spot.

It was a painstakingly slow process.

As the heroes slipped into their latest hiding spot, they once again just barely missed a close call. Ridley had finally had it. "In twenty minutes we've moved a whole twelve feet," he whispered to his companion.

"Actually we have only moved two-and-a-half yards," Elio replied.

Ridley only pounded the wall, frustrated. "See! That only supports my argument. We need a faster way to search this place."

"We do not know where to look or which section of the ship we are even headed to. Yet we need to move faster?" Elio's blue eyes roved around his head at rapid speed. The poor fellow was genuinely confused. "How are we supposed to do that?"

Ridley was unsure of that as well. "I don't know Elio. At this rate the war will be lost by the time we find Ulysses. Hiding and waiting for the coast to be clear isn't working. And all we're doing is running the risk of getting caught."

Elio had been simultaneously paying attention to the corridor traffic, timing their next move. Staying in any one place for too long was just as dangerous as traveling.

"Now!" Elio prompted Ridley and the duo moved spaces, but had to go back to where they were because a crewmember was approaching

This exacerbated Ridley's frustration. "See, we're not gonna make it."

"We could dress up like one of them," Elio pointed to the people walking past.

Ridley looked unbelievably at his companion. "And then get interrogated for why we're not where we're supposed to be. And that's only after we can catch two people near our size. Why not?" he mocked. "We're not dealing with enough issues as it is."

Elio missed the sarcasm and took his friend's words as approval. He walked behind the last passing guard and was about to strike when Ridley quickly pulled him back into hiding.

"The fuck? Are you crazy?" Ridley slapped Elio lightly on the face. "What are we supposed to do with the body? Also, what about me? You get a uniform and what, I'm your prisoner? Fuck that!"

Elio's eyes roved around again for a few moments. "Why do you say this is a bad idea when you are coming up with improvements? This could actually–"

"Improvements?" Ridley just shook his head in frustration. Now he understood what Mycroft went through.

Elio gave the signal to move again, and the duo was able to travel the farthest distance yet. The team's new hiding spot was at the foot of a small entrance corridor, concluding in a sealed door marked "maintenance."

Ridley heard approaching footsteps and panicked, thinking they

CHAPTER 25

would get caught. On a whim he opened the door to see if it would work, and to his surprise it was unlocked. Without thinking twice, the duo quickly entered the room.

It was a small cramped closet, containing two large server towers reaching into the ceiling. Each tower contained a small readout screen with hundreds of adjustable knobs. Miles of tubes, wires, cords, and other ducts reached from the towers into the walls, floor, and ceiling, resembling an electronic tree. Both machines hummed with life, their readout screens displayed constantly changing data.

"What are these?" Ridley asked as he brushed his fingers on one of the knobs. The screen suddenly changed to a specific menu displaying a dial with increasing numbers. Ridley jumped back in fear and placed his hands behind his back. "Shit!"

"These are the ship's atmospheric control modules. All the gravity, air, and life support systems are all controlled from right here. We can map out the entire ship and see where we need to go." Elio approached one of the screens and started pressing buttons, digesting the massive information with superhuman abilities.

Ridley just watched his friend work his magic. He was awed and slightly terrified. "Do you think it can tell us where Ulysses is?"

"It will not necessarily give us his exact location, but we can pinpoint the general area." Elio expertly manned the computer, executing his requests as if he's always used it.

The moments passed by, and Ridley grew increasingly worried that someone was going to come in and catch them. He stood with his ear against the door, trying to listen to the outer corridor.

"Are you about done there?"

"I do not know how long this will take," Elio reported. The data on the screen flashed by at a million miles an hour.

"Well hurry the fuck up! We don't have time to look for everything!" Ridley only grew increasingly nervous.

Elio turned to his companion, with one of his blue eyes still on the rolling screen. "While I am still looking, you can disrupt the air purifiers and switch off the condensers. That will give us some cover to rove the corridors, and provide a distraction for the crew."

Ridley looked at the other tower and raised his eyebrows. "Right. I'll get right on it."

The vast number of blinking knobs was intimidating, and then there was a separate keyboard that controlled who-knew-what.

He looked at Elio's fingers dance expertly over all the buttons. A lump grew in his throat. Ridley didn't want to be the one who single-handedly failed the mission because he choked under the pressure.

"C'mon Ridley," he coached himself. "You survived the fucking Gambit, you can change the settings on the bloody computer." He pinched his hand and started adjusting knobs and pressing random buttons and keys.

The server tower started humming louder and an alarm from somewhere started blaring. The readout screen started blinking in various colors, alerting them that something was wrong. The more actions Ridley took, the louder and angrier the machine grew.

When sparks erupted from the machine, Ridley took a few steps back. "Um, Elio? Is this supposed to do that?"

Elio was focused intently on his screen, completely ignoring Ridley.

Smoke started to come from the machine now, and the tubes and piping glowed red. The heat emanating from the thing was unbearable. "Danger, overloaded," messages flashed on the screen. Suddenly a huge billow of smoke erupted from the machine. All the lights shut off and the whole closet was engulfed in a silent darkness.

The only light in the room came from Elio's glowing irises. "I told you just to power down the condensers and purifiers, not the whole maintenance mainframe." He tried to key in commands on Ridley's terminal, but the screen remained black and unresponsive.

CHAPTER 25

Ridley punched Elio in the shoulder. "Well pardon me, I guess I hit the wrong button. I'm not as mechanically inclined as you, sir."

Elio didn't even flinch. "That is obvious. Well, you shut down my search. I was just about to discover Ulysses' location."

"Maybe we can restart this thing so you can finish," Ridley started pressing more buttons, but the server tower remained unchanged.

Suddenly there was a loud banging on the door, followed by furious attempts to open it. Someone was trying to enter, but thanks to the rod Ridley shoved into the door handle, they were at least temporarily delayed.

"Shit," Ridley screamed. "We have to get out of here."

Elio's blue irises roved around the room, searching for an escape. Ridley stumbled around the cramped space, shoving anything that moved in front of the door. The least he could do was attempt to keep out the intruders.

The rod within the door handle failed and the door opened a few inches, saved only by Ridley's makeshift barricade. A rush of cool air entered the small closet, followed by a thick cloud of fog.

Elio pointed at something unseen. "There! Quick, go!" He immediately grabbed Ridley's ankles and pulled him to the floor. He then started dragging the boy towards the far corner, near the steaming hot ducts emerging from the server towers.

When the air came back into Ridley's lungs, he was not happy. "The fuck, Elio? What are you doing?"

All the response he got were the sounds of metal getting unscrewed and slamming to the floor.

"A vent," Ridley said. "Genius!"

The closet door was fully shoved open at the exact moment the duo resealed their escape vent. The three intruders immediately attended to the broken machines, and didn't bother searching for the two boys.

CHAPTER 26

Deep in the bowels of the ship, Ulysses was restrained to a medical bed, awaiting his next round of excruciating torture. His restraints were so tight that his limbs were completely numb. His mouth was bone dry and his body was pockmarked with burns and cuts of varying size.

Two guards surrounded Ulysses and never took their eyes off him, their trigger fingers itching to fire.

Suddenly the lights extinguished, veiling the room in darkness. The only lights came from small medical devices running on the emergency generator.

"The fuck is going on?" the taller guard asked.

The smaller one shrugged her shoulders. "Maybe it's another drill."

The taller guard poked Ulysses in the rib with his rifle. The restrained man screamed dramatically, though it didn't really hurt. "Ouch! Well I didn't fucking do it!"

The smaller guard jabbed him in the stomach with the butt of her rifle. "Shut up, you! No one needs to hear your bitching."

The two guards started discussing who was going to check on what was happening, and an argument began over who got to remain with the prisoner.

After a few moments the argument only worsened, and Ulysses had had enough. "Why don't both of you go and see what the fuck is going on? I won't move and stay right here. I promise." A wide smile cracked on the boy's scarred face. No amount of torture would remove the wise-ass twinkle in Ulysses' spirit.

The guards glanced at each other for a few moments and then nodded. They each jabbed their rifles into Ulysses once more before leaving the room.

* * *

Count Lucilous' and the Archon's duel continued unabated even as the ship fell into pitch darkness. The brilliantly illuminated ethellite swords danced and parried in the black void. Every so often they illuminated the determined faces of the duelists, each fighting to the death and refusing to let the other reach victory.

When the lights suddenly extinguished, both Mycroft and Silas nearly jumped into the ongoing fight, for surely they wouldn't be able to hide for much longer. But this time Mycroft was the one to hold Silas back.

"If we go now, we'll both be killed," he whispered into his old mentor's ear. "Let them weaken a bit more."

The Archon's loose clothing shrouded his movements and expanded his mass, offering quite the challenge. Lucilous could barely move out of the monster's way, for even though he was an accomplished swordsman, the hooded creature's speed and intensity were unmatched.

The count's anger grew with every swing of his ethellite sword. No matter which direction he used, Lucilous' sword would not strike the Archon. It was as if the murderous monk had a deflective shield surrounding him. Lucilous was not used to having to work *this hard* to kill something.

The more fury the count channeled into his attack, the sloppier it became. The Archon never took more than a knick from the count's blade, while his blade constantly kissed Lucilous, drawing many streams of blood. For every one strike Lucilous took, the Archon took two, and both connected with their target.

Within five moves, Lucilous was almost overtaken. It was only because of his hard-to-reach position that he was able to escape the Archon's latest onslaught. The Count dashed on top of the map table a split second before the Archon's blade would have sliced him in half.

The Archon's attack was getting sloppier as well, the Count noticed. No doubt because the creature was as frustrated as he was.

Lucilous threw his sword at his opponent and leaped into the air. The sword bee lined for the Archon, while Lucilous somersaulted over and behind him. The Archon deflected the sword and Lucilous caught it just in time as he touched the ground.

The two continued dueling each other. The Archon's relentless attack was only growing stronger, while quickly deteriorating Lucilous' energy. The count tried to use some of the furniture and terminals to hide behind or to throw at the hooded creature, but the Archon's sword sliced through everything in its path like butter.

The Archon left a brief opening in his defense, and Lucilous took advantage by shoving a small storage tank at him. The Archon stumbled and the count was able to strike the creature in the side, just below the kidney.

For the first time, Lucilous heard Archon scream with pain, an intense, terrifying howl that reached every corner of the frigate. The red eyes beneath the hood illuminated with an intense fury that was, previously, never present. The Archon was beyond infuriated and increased his already assiduous attacks.

The Archon's pain gave Lucilous a second wind as well, for he finally had evidence that he was getting *his* point across. This was the first time that he felt that the Archon was truly hearing what he was saying.

The room grew muggy and filled with a thick fog, with only the bright ethellite blades visible. The two white blades danced the violent tango of death, embracing and deflecting each other loudly.

Gradually, the two duelists destroyed nearly everything in the room. Count Lucilous was losing his energy and places to hide. As he searched for one, he tripped over a rolling storage crate. The Archon struck the count as he laid on the floor, cutting down the last bit of resolve left in the pathetic man.

Suddenly, in a flurry of movement, the Archon sliced off Lucilous' sword arm with a graceful single swing. The smell of burnt skin and blood filled the air, accompanying Lucilous' blood curdling scream.

The Archon moved to strike again, but the count quickly scurried into a corner. The murderous monk slowly followed, his breathing labored yet controlled. The glowing red eyes were still illuminated with the assiduous anger that only grew more furious.

"What is this?" The Archon's voice was light, almost humorous. "Is the leader, the architect, and mastermind of everything, *unsettled*? Have you been taken off guard? How, pray tell, is that even possible?"

The count cowered into the corner, nursing his missing arm and crying pitifully. All he could do was shake his head.

The Archon taunted the count with his sword, twirling it right in front of the poor man's face. "True, without your contributions we would not have made as much progress as soon as we did, but all that you've ever bought us is time. Our preparations were well underway long before you even existed. You are nothing, Lucilous, not even worthy of a footnote in history.

"All you have done since the beginning is be in the way. You killed our first vessel and allowed the second one to kill itself. Then you almost allowed this one to get captured. You have failed in exterminating our pursuers, and all you can do is demand *more*?"

The count loudly whimpered while the Archon's sword kissed his cheek, leaving a large burn. Tears reflected the brilliant light of the blade, and the screaming only intensified.

A hearty laugh came from the Archon. "Not even your money is needed anymore, now that I got the Corporate Conglomerates to see our way." His red eyes turned to angry slits. "I could end all of our troubles right...now."

Lucilous leapt to his feet and held out his hand, begging. "Please, master. I beg of you. Have mercy! Accept my apology! *Everything* I am is because of you. Please. I've learned that now. Accept my apologies. I know I am nothing. Take my arm as payment but please, I beg you, let me live!"

The Archon was silent for a few moments, his sword remained unnaturally still. "Why do we need to keep you? We now have everything we need to launch the full-scale, multi-year campaign. At this rate we'll win the war by the end of the solar cycle. You'll only be a liability we need to look out for, and a threat to our victory."

"Please, master. I beg you! Don't kill me! I still have much to offer the Hyde. Please, I am at your mercy. I will only do as you wish. Your will is my command. Let me continue to serve you. Please!"

An evil laugh emanated from the hooded figure, shaking every cell in every living thing within hearing range. "Just to ensure, you've truly learned your lesson." The figure jabbed his sword and burned out one of Lucilous' eyes. The count's screams were voluminous.

After several painful seconds the Archon removed his sword. "Now, get out of my sight, and join the other pathetic grunts on the battlefield. Consider this your final opportunity to prove your worth."

The count groveled for a few moments until he was shooed away. As he was leaving, he asked in the most pitiful voice he could muster. "Am I still the Prime Minister of the Axis? You will still allow me to participate—*assist*— you in the Syndicate's destruction?"

Furious once again, the Archon threw his sword, just barely missing the count. The sword decimated a stack of storage crates and revealed the two hiding Specters. Without any further word, the count quickly exited the room.

Mycroft and Silas leapt out from the storage crates just before they exploded. The two fighters ignited their swords and immediately jumped to battle.

* * *

The air in the vent was stuffy. Ridley could barely see Elio's feet which were only a few inches in front of him. Surrounding him were the veins of tubes, cords, and ducts that brought the various parts of the frigate to life, and it was a completely tangled mess. Every few moments Ridley's feet would get caught in a knot of cords, and his anxiety would only worsen every second until he detangled himself. The vent shaft was so narrow he couldn't turn around; his shoulders barely fit. Only the glow from Elio's illuminated blue irises could even break through the thick fog, and offered Ridley a modicum of comfort.

After crawling for what felt like an eternity, and finally feeling that they traveled a safe distance, Ridley asked Elio, "Do you know where we are? Were you able to see at least this part of the ship on that readout screen?"

It took a few seconds for Elio to respond, and it wasn't heartening. "No, I do not know where we are. Probably not next to a corridor, otherwise there would be vents every few feet. And since I do not know where we are, I cannot answer your question as to whether or not I saw this section of the ship."

Well that's just fucking great, Ridley thought to himself. "Well you do at least know if we're going in the right general direction?"

"Yes," Elio answered lightly, "towards the medical bay. And that is where I think we need to go. Before you disrupted the power flow I was able to look through the ship's medical manifests and noticed there was one non-soldier. It is at least worth taking a look. The ship's diagrams indicated that this shaft heads straight through that wing."

Ridley's attitude brightened slightly. "Great! But if there aren't any vents to exit through, then how do we get out of here? And when?"

Elio stopped crawling for a few moments. Ridley imagined his eyes were roving around furiously in his head.

"I predict we have quite the distance to go," Elio announced after a few moments.

All of Ridley's positive thoughts immediately disappeared. Now he was downright grumpy "Great. Just what I need. Oh and by the way, you piece of shit, your feet stink."

"What was that?" Elio turned to look at him.

"My foot's caught in another kink." Ridley grumbled to himself as the two continued crawling inside the vent shaft.

* * *

In the silent darkness of the empty medical room, Ulysses was able to wiggle one of his wrists from the restraints. He audibly groaned with relief as he finally straightened his arm, but luckily that did not attract any attention. Instead of trying to free the rest of his limbs, he spent the rest of his time filing one of the restraint buckles into a sharp shiv.

He counted that he had been alone for 20 minutes, and in that time he was able to hone the buckle to as much of a point as he could. Ulysses then started to slice his wrist with it.

He had been molested by his hooded captor a dozen times since his initial capture just a few short days ago, and he did not want to live long enough to see if anything would come from all of those forced inseminations. He also did not want to have to be forced to decide what to do with a life that didn't deserve to live in the first place. Life was sacred and he, Ulysses, could not be the creator, or destroyer of it.

Looking back, Ulysses admitted to having made many mistakes throughout his life, and he felt that this moment was the final culmination of all of their consequences. He felt that this was the time to pay his penance, and for the first time in his life was going to go out of his way to do the right thing, irrespective of how difficult it was.

The dull piece of plastic didn't hurt as it barely scratched his skin, but he was determined to get it to work. Ulysses pressed with all of his might, and started to feel the now-familiar tinge of pain. Soon, he smelled the sour odor of his blood. He pressed down harder.

A loud clatter erupted in the ceiling above him, shaking the loose dust to fall like rain. Ulysses assumed it was one of the ship's crew repairing the electricity. He blocked it out of his mind and continued cutting his wrist.

Suddenly a heavy mass fell on him, followed by a second loud and heavy thud. The mass started writhing and wriggling above Ulysses, and the captive used his shiv to stab it. The mass struck back at Ulysses, and then another punch from the side of the medical table struck him as well.

Did the guards return, Ulysses wondered. If so, then who the fuck was wriggling on top of him?

Soon a fight broke out amongst all three opponents, with each hitting each other as hard as they could, blindly aiming in the dark. Eventually the mass on top of Ulysses tumbled to the floor. A brilliant pair of illuminated blue irises carved through the pitch darkness, followed by a monotonous and oddly mechanical voice.

"Stop, stop, stop! Look, we found him!" The blue-eyed voice tried to sooth the other mass that was still writhing. The sound of limbs moving through the air filled Ulysses' ears.

"The fuck we did!" the other one spoke, in a younger and much more passionate voice. It finally calmed enough to stop writhing. "Then why is he fighting us, dammit, we're trying to save him."

"You'd be fucking fighting too if two goons just all of a sudden fall from the fucking ceiling right on top of you. Doesn't matter who they fucking are," Ulysses was angrier than scared, and not just because they interrupted his suicide attempt. "Who the fuck are you guys?"

The blue eyes remained solidly focused on the restrained Ulysses. "I am Elio and this is Ridley. We are here to save you."

Ulysses snorted, for this was the first time in a long while that he'd been genuinely surprised. "Save me? Well as you can see it's a bit late for that! Sorry you had to waste your grand entrance fellas."

The younger voice somehow grew angrier. "The fuck you mean we're too late. You're not dead, yet. But that could change quickly if you keep up with your bullshit attitude!"

Elio looked over at his companion. "Ridley, why do you wish to harm the one we just rescued?"

"Because the bastard stabbed me!"

Elio's eyes illuminated the sharp plastic piece sticking out of Ridley's shoulder, then turned to Ulysses.

All the man could do was shrug his shoulders and smile smugly. "Again, when two men fall from the sky..." Ulysses let the sentence hang, for they could complete it.

Elio carefully pulled the shiv from Ridley's shoulder, whose spirit didn't really improve afterwards. The two men then untied Ulysses, who despite the emaciated appearance, was quite energetic and inquisitive.

"Who are you fellas with?" he asked as he sat up and watched them untie his ankles.

"The Specters. Two of them are here looking for that hooded man that took you," Ridley said. He had lightened up a little bit. "The two of us split up once we got here and haven't seen or heard them since."

CHAPTER 26

Ulysses was moved to tears, for he thought no one was looking for him. "How did you get here? Wouldn't your ship be shot down on sight?"

"We stowed away on the count's ship," Elio replied.

"He's here too? Wow, is that a group of low-grade celebrities or what? So what's the plan, now that you've found me?"

Ridley struggled for a few moments with the ankle strap. "We're supposed to rendezvous at the ship with you, and hopefully them as well, and go back to the *Imperatrix*."

"*Hopefully*, them?" Ulysses raised his eyebrows inquisitively.

"They ordered us not to wait for them. Our main priority after finding you is self-preservation," Elio said. "We are to wait no more than ten minutes before leaving by ourselves."

That didn't sit well with Ulysses. "But what if they don't defeat the hood and the count? Are we just supposed to leave them here for dead?"

Elio and Ridley were silent for a few moments. "That was not included in their orders," was all Elio could eventually say.

"Well that's not cool! If they helped us then the least we can do is see if we can help them," Ulysses picked up his plastic shiv and jumped off the bed. He stretched for a few moments and his gaze landed on Elio. "Since your eyes are glowing, Can you navigate through this ship through all this muck?"

"Yes. Though, I have seen only eighty percent of the ship's schematics and know the rough location of the ship's major wings." Elio continued giving a dense explanation replete with statistics, percentages, and probabilities.

Ridley put his hand to his mouth. "Needless to say, he's a bit eccentric, but useful once you get used to him. Yes, is the short answer to your question?" He smiled, slightly embarrassed.

Ulysses returned the smile, displaying many empty spaces and once brilliant white teeth that were splotched with blood.

"Hey, just like my father's friends. Well, let's get the fuck out of here."

Ulysses followed Elio out of the room, while Ridley hung behind for a few moments. His stomach was all aflutter, and for the first time in a long time he felt excited. Ridley figured it was because he had found Ulysses, and successfully helped Mycroft and Silas—so far. But this feeling felt deeper than that, somehow. No doubt it was the adrenaline, but he couldn't quite put his finger on it.

The only thing Ridley did know was that he liked it.

CHAPTER 27

Even without a blade, the hooded duelist was a force to reckon with. The Specters' two ethellite swords were no match for the Archon, who gracefully fended off the attack with only his wrist bracers. The warrior monk danced around the destroyed room, kicking and punching at the attacking Specters with a supernatural strength.

The Specters attempted to keep up the offensive, but struggled to simply stay on their feet. They assumed a man who had been fighting for already as long as the Archon had would be tremendously more exhausted. Oh how wrong they were.

Blinded by their arrogance, the Specters let their guard down just long enough to get shoved to the floor. The Archon took the opportunity to retrieve his thrown sword, and within mere seconds was back on the attack.

Flabbergasted and enraged, Mycroft screamed, "Who are you?"

A tremulous laugh emerged from the hooded cloak. It was menacing and full of evil. "You still don't know? Surely your petty Specter teachings haven't blinded you to the obvious."

The three swords danced for a few moments more, with each strike a death blow.

"Give up the act, Hyde," Silas ordered.

Another laugh erupted from the hooded creature, its effortless and lackadaisical tone was a stark contrast to the constant state of dynamic fighting. "Pitiful. But at least you figured out that much. Let's just say that without me, the galaxy would be in far more turmoil if left alone with the Syndicate."

"All those soldiers and civilians you killed would disagree," Mycroft fumed. "And trying to kill me on Ampheres doesn't support that at all."

The Specter swung his ethellite sword, hoping to carve the hooded creature in two. But the Archon leapt over Mycroft's head and attempted to strike his back, but Silas was able to deflect the blow and counter attack.

The Archon was impressed at his opponents' resolve. "That is why the Hyde will forever be superior. Hyde thinking is the clearest in the galaxy, and it's unfortunate that the magic of its logic is lost on the majority. Without their deaths, the inevitable change would not come as easily as it has."

Mycroft rushed the Archon, who easily deflected the attack. The three duelists circled the destroyed room attempting to end the battle once and for all. Sparks flew everywhere as the ethellite blades sliced through walls and broken machines, cutting pipes and severing cords. One particular unit expelled a cloud of thick fog, forcing the fighters to temporarily separate.

Only the lights from the swords cut through the thick veil, as well as the Archon's voice. "For too long the Hyde have lived in the shadows. Withering and suffering while you Specters and your precious Syndicate continue to lay waste to the galaxy. You consolidate power into the hands of the elite few while you compel the plebeians to slave their lives away to provide everything. And you have the nerve to label it as for the common good."

The fog had filled the entire room, and while it had thinned slightly, only the bright swords were visible. The three duelists circled each other, waiting and begging for the other to make the first move.

"The Hyde Empire would execute those for being weak," Silas added. "Doesn't sound any better to me."

"At least we never pretended to look after anyone besides the capable," the Archon added. "The Syndicate claims to care about everyone, yet consistently demonstrates they actually do not.

"But that only points to the larger issue of the Specter's ineptitude, which has been ingrained since the very beginning. Take the Sacred Scriptures. You bumbling idiots only see them as advice books, and are blind to the true power they possess."

"Power that you intend to abuse," Mycroft said. "Just who the fuck are you?"

"Power that isn't used is the most abused, and doing nothing with it is the greatest sin."

Silas and Mycroft both screamed, *"Who are you?"*

The Archon's voice grew to encompass every corner of the room. "I am the one who will usher in the renaissance of truth and success. I am the composer of the symphony of prosperity and the conductor of the choir of death. I am the master of the Hyde's scriptures, and the Archon of Destiny."

The Archon lunged into the air and violently swung his sword at his two opponents. The Specters were caught off guard for just a second, but managed to quickly reach the pace of this movement of the duel.

Despite being on different sides, all three fighters had the same thought: at least one of them was not going to make it out alive.

***

Across the stars, a small Syndicate convoy was returning from the strike site, containing intelligence regarding the current location of the Axis fleet. In short, there was still nothing to report as no evidence the fleet was even there could not be found.

A tense and fragile peace hung over the area. Each second that passed was another second closer to all-out war. Time was an ally for no one.

Suddenly, an asteroid struck the convoy as it was preparing to dock into the command frigate, the S.M.S *Ethel*, destroying three out of the four vessels. A multitude of the surrounding asteroids split open, releasing hundreds of Axis ships into the battle space. Then, a half-dozen Axis command ships emerged from the dark sides of the largest asteroids, releasing even more spit fighters into the fray.

The first battle of the civil war had begun.

Across the battlefield thousands of fighters engaged in hundreds of dogfights. Bright flashes erupted all across the black canvas of space, signifying both Syndicate victories and defeats. Many of the fighters, on either side of the conflict, were firing on ships for the first time outside of a simulator, let alone with live rounds. The average age of the soldiers was 20.

Most of the Axis vessels were repurposed from the Syndicate military, with some so new that they still bore the Syndicate's markings. Likewise, most of the Syndicate's ships were so fresh from the factory that they were only bare metal and not painted at all. This naturally caused confusion amongst the rookie soldiers and most ended up shooting their own squad mates.

The Syndicate's five battle carriers, the *Ethel*, the *Lucille*, the *Lorraine*, the *Coreen*, and the *Hadley*, circled around their spit fighters in a bid to protect them from the ongoing barrage of Axis fighters. In turn, the Axis cruisers advanced, attempting to break the barrier, launching a fusillade of materiel. A large wall of explosions incinerated thousands of soldiers from both sides.

Within 20 minutes, 10% of the Syndicate's fleet was destroyed.

Across the stars, in the command center aboard the *Imperatrix*, the Primarch silently watched the chaos unfold on the view screens before him, grimacing every few moments. Fed up, he slowly turned towards the Specter Chiefs, menacingly glaring at them. They all slowly bowed their heads in shame.

*　*　*

Elio's illuminated eyes gave off just barely enough light to navigate the dark maze of corridors in the Archon's ship. The halls were mostly empty and there was no indication that anything had gone awry. Every so often, Elio, Ridley, and Ulysses would encounter a small gathering of people, but luckily there was always a hiding place just near enough for them to use.

The ship's inhabitants wore jumpsuits that had illuminated strips sewn within it, giving the wearer an aura of light just bright enough to see what was right in front of them. Ridley surmised blackouts like these were fairly common.

The game of dark hide and seek continued until the travelers reached the main engineering bay, which was illuminated in the blood red hue of emergency lighting. The entrance catwalk encircled the large room, with multiple levels of engineering terminals underneath it. This area was tremendously busier than the corridors, with techs bustling about the various levels of consoles. Something was indeed wrong with the ship.

After vigorously searching for several moments, the trio hid in a repair hole behind a large and pulsing trans-mogrifier. The machine made enough noise to mask their whispers, and this area of the engineering bay had remained relatively unoccupied.

"Now what are we going to do?" Ridley asked. He was no longer scared, but excited. His heart was nearly beating out of his chest. He had never felt an adrenaline rush like this, and he was becoming addicted.

"Good question," was the entirety of Ulysses' answer.

Ridley's excitement dimmed significantly. "The fuck you mean 'good question?' Wasn't this a part of your plan?"

Ulysses gave Ridley a death glare, almost identical to Ridley's grandmother's. "There isn't any plan! I just know that all of the ship's critical controls are located here. Surely we can find something that will blow up the ship."

"Blow up the ship?" Ridley repeated. All of the color had drained from his face and the enthusiasm completely left his body. "I thought you said you didn't *have* a plan?"

"How are we supposed to make it back to the shuttle, and fulfill our second mission, before the ship explodes?" Elio asked. "We have only retrieved you, and still need to bring you back to the *Imperatrix*."

Ulysses shrugged, his face completely unconcerned. "Run really fast?"

"Run really fast? Do you even know how to get to the hangar from here?" Ridley was scared, and manifested it by growing more agitated. He grabbed Ulysses' shoulders and shook him.

Ulysses easily removed Ridley's arms and slapped him strongly across the cheek. The boy calmed almost immediately. "Of course not, stupid. I've been strapped to a bed ever since I got here. Certainly you all cased the place?"

A silence hung between them for a few moments, causing the moment to grow increasingly awkward. Elio remained silent because he was struggling to determine what the phrase "case the place" meant.

Finally not able to take it anymore, Ridley finally confessed. "No, stupid, we didn't get to case the place. We were too busy looking for *you* to really pay attention. We just turned when we were forced to and kept going until we found a locked door."

"Ugh, do I have to do everything?" Ulysses growled loudly enough to make Ridley jump and look out for any approaching crew members. Ulysses then yanked off a piece of the transmogrifier and quickly crept out of the hiding place.

It wasn't a few steps before Ulysses found a busy technician and bashed him on the head. Blood pooled on the floor as the poor man convulsed and died slowly. Ulysses gave him another blow on the head, and the tech remained silent. The senator's son then pulled the tech's identicard from his chest, as well as a few tools from the man's tool belt before returning to Elio and Ridley at the hiding place.

"That was efficient," Elio said, as impressed as he could be. "But what are we going to do with the body? It will attract attention lying right there."

Ridley was going to chime in before Ulysses cut him off. "Details, details. Someone else will deal with him, and they'll discover him long after we've escaped."

He winked at Elio and beckoned Ridley to follow with his fingers. In a flash he was gone, once again skulking up the corridor.

Ridley was silent, still struck by seeing Ulysses murder someone right in front of his eyes with such clean, heartless precision. The young boy was amazed at how Ulysses moved with such cool confidence in everything that he'd done.

A warm feeling erupted inside Ridley, filling every cell of his being.

"Fuck, he's hot," Ridley said, just barely loud enough for himself to hear.

"Your attraction to him has been obvious since you first saw him," Elio said. Of course nothing but complete silence could escape his superhuman hearing.

Ridley elbowed his companion lightly and left without saying a word. It was clear Ulysses was not going to return to that hiding place.

As Ridley left, he missed Elio mutter, "And according to Ulysses' actions and voice tone, the feeling is mutual."

Elio and Ridley eventually met up with Ulysses, who found another hiding place in another maintenance console. The man was ripping off panels and clipping wires with a pair of shears he found.

"Now what the fuck are you doing?" Ridley's amazement with this man was growing by the moment, but now he was also increasingly nervous. What was this crazy kook up to?

A sinister smile carved itself on Ulysses' face, which only added to Ridley's arousing consternation. "Sabotage! Just find something and rip the shit out of it." He proceeded to sever every wire he could see.

Elio remained still, watching for a few moments. "I think this is the entirety of his plan."

"To kill us all?" Ridley asked exasperated. "Just why the fuck do we have to sabotage the ship?"

Ulysses stopped what he was doing and glared at Elio. "Good grief, are you that thick? Why did you come here if not because this is the center of the whole fucking war? Certainly the fucking Specters couldn't be bothered to save a spoiled politician's son unless it was central to the war effort?"

The silence between the two was tense. Ridley didn't want to admit that he had not even thought of that; he was simply too caught up in the adventure of it all. He had never bothered to ask "why" about anything. He really wanted to not be attracted by Ulysses calling him out, but he couldn't help it.

Elio interrupted the pregnant pause. "This is the most logical course of action. I suggest we follow suit." He then proceeded to a panel and ripped the exposed wires to shreds.

Ridley remained still, locked in a staring contest with Ulysses. He then blinked and slowly nodded his head. "Okay," he mumbled. "Okay."

The trio tore their way through all the machinery they could easily destroy with their limited tools, inching their way down that level

CHAPTER 27

of the corridor. Surprisingly, they didn't encounter any of the ship technicians, and were left virtually unattended.

Eventually Ulysses, Ridley, and Elio reached the entrance to the main engine bay, but it was sealed. Ulysses used the stolen identicard, and the door effortlessly opened, revealing a gigantic artificial cave, with catwalks connecting the three levels of engine controls to a central terminal hub. Three technicians were stationed on each level, casually monitoring the various readout screens under their charge.

Carefully, the trio snuck their way to the door of the central terminal hub, where another three technicians were conversing about the latest land speeder models.

Ulysses looked at Ridley, and nodded at him to go in, but he vigorously shook his head no. Ulysses rolled his eyes and moved in himself, followed closely by Elio. Together the two silently dispatched their unwelcome company.

When Ridley entered, they all stared at a collection of complicated and intricate control panels, with symbols and words written in an unrecognizable language.

"I take it we just destroy this too?" Ridley asked rhetorically before rushing to work, but Elio held him back.

Elio studied the control panels intently. "If we want to die *right now*, destroying everything is the best thing to do."

"But if we want time to get off?" Ulysses asked. Sweat poured down his face and for the first time sounding scared.

"I need a few moments to study this," Elio replied.

"We don't really have that," Ridley and Ulysses both quipped.

"Nor do we have a choice," was Elio's response. He kneeled to get a better look at the levers and buttons, and remained completely still.

CHAPTER 28

Despite their early losses, the Syndicate managed to make up for their lost fighters with sheer firepower and decimated 10% of the Axis fleet, even managing to destroy a heavy battle cruiser. While it still looked like a long shot, the Syndicate was beginning to grow optimistic.

A small group of Syndicate spit fighters managed to infiltrate a weakness in one of the Axis battle carrier's shields and flew extremely close to the hull. The surrounding Axis battleships attempted to fire on the fighters, but ended up doing more damage to their own carrier.

In turn the carrier launched its own attack, but mostly damaged its allies in the surrounding cruisers and left the Syndicate fighters unscathed. The fighters bombed the surface of the carrier, not destroying it completely but critically damaging it.

A fleet of Axis fighters launched from the carrier and immediately surrounded the Syndicate fighters like a fly to honey. Despite the onslaught, the Syndicate managed to make another bombing run.

The battle seemed to continue for an eternity, with one Axis fighter dying for each Syndicate fighter. The fight was a draw.

Suddenly a wave of reinforcements arrived from the *Ethel*, successfully dispatching the continuing stream of Axis fighters erupting from the damaged carrier.

The damaged carrier was stranded, surrounded by defenders that could either watch helplessly or destroy one of their own. The carrier was completely empty of any of its own fighters to deploy, while the Syndicate squad coalesced and completely blew the carrier out of space. The shockwave was strong enough to critically wound the surrounding battle cruisers, turning them into sitting ducks.

The victory was felt in every Syndicate hangar and cockpit and by each soldier and pilot. Everyone on the battlefield, in a fighter or cruiser or carrier, all cheered in triumph. Suddenly the battle seemed like it wouldn't be a total defeat after all.

The warm sentiment, however, was not felt in the *Imperatrix* command center. Everyone was tense and on edge, with straining white knuckles and deeply furrowed brows.

Specter Chief Latiolais chewed on a cigar, his voice full of disdain. "At this rate all our boys will be wiped out in four hours."

Chief Albus was scrolling through pages of ship manifests. "That's nothing. Our battle cruisers are running out of arms. We didn't anticipate a battle lasting this long."

All the Primarch could do was pace around the room and get upset, barking orders just to be able to tell people he was doing something. "Summon reinforcements."

Chief Latiolais rolled his eyes as he looked at the leader of the Syndicate, thoroughly unimpressed. "We *did*, hours ago. They're still on their way."

All anyone could do at this point anymore was desperately wish for the arrival of a glimmer of hope.

***

The three dueling men continued their dance of death with no end in sight, each fighter wanting to kill their opponent. The fight transitioned from the ship's war room to a nearby staging area, surrounded by cages of weapons and armor. Small explosions erupted with every sword deflection or every stray strike, filling the air with a thick, acrid gas.

The mugginess was only interrupted by the light of the ethellite blades, dancing about the air so fast they carved streaks in the cloudy gas. The blades took on the personality of their wielders, and appeared as though they wanted to kill each other as well.

The Archon's strength was immensely powerful, and he seemed to grow stronger with each passing sword strike. He could move just as fast now as when the fight first began and appeared to have not tired at all. He was always able to meet every counterstrike and deflect every attack. This was a fight he was looking forward to finishing, and was willing to work for as long as it took.

After battling for so long the Specters were beginning to weaken. Each deflection and counter blow ate at their increasingly depleting energy supply. Mycroft's shoulders screamed with pain and his arms contributed to it with their own chorus.

Silas was really struggling to hold his own. It wasn't so much the lack of energy but his advanced age. His body just wasn't able to move as fast as he needed it to, and that was growing more obvious with each passing second.

The Archon jumped over a toppled machine gun turret and swiped it with his sword. It erupted into an enormous ball of flame that threw the Specters off guard. The Archon then threw his blade at them, but Mycroft deflected it just in time and bounded over the flames to relaunch the attack. Silas struggled to return to his feet, and was even slower to return to the fight. In the time it took Silas to get his bearings, the Archon maneuvered closer to him, and the poor Specter was again caught off guard from the attack from a new angle.

The trio continued the battle, but by this time the Archon could sense he had a major advantage. He bounded into the air again and pulled

CHAPTER 28

a tube of flash bang dispensers from one of the wall cages. Dozens of metal balls covered the floor, causing the Specters to slip and lose their balance. In the struggle Silas dropped his sword, which ignited a few of the dispersers and created a grand explosive display.

Mycroft was blinded by the conflagration and tumbled to the floor. Silas was still standing, but struggling to save his balance. The Archon seized his sword and threw it straight at Mycroft. Silas jumped into the sword's path, taking it right in the chest and tumbling to the floor.

The first image Mycroft saw when his eyes finally adjusted was Silas' lifeless body staring back at him.

A tear streamed down his face as he lunged at the Archon. With his bare hands Mycroft grasped the figure's wrist and kicked its sword out of its hand. The Archon managed to get Mycroft to drop his sword and the two fell into a fist fight on the floor, punching everything they made contact with.

Somehow, amidst the fray, a stray sword made contact with one of the stored weapons in the cage, creating an explosion that rocked the room. This triggered a chain reaction of weapon explosions within the rest of the cage, comprising the wall's structural integrity.

The explosions, however, did not phase the fighters at all. Mycroft grasped the Archon's throat and shook violently. He then slammed the creature's head repeatedly against the floor. The hooded figure could only laugh, its red eyes boring into Mycroft's soul.

"You lose your friend and suddenly get a second wind? Just like a Specter." The voice didn't betray an ounce of exhaustion.

This only pissed Mycroft off even more, and the Specter's attack intensified. Blue blood, spurted through the monk's clothing.

The Archon just continued laughing. "Yet your strength and furious passion speak of the essence of the Hyde. Interesting."

An anger like never before burned within Mycroft. He saw nothing but red, and wanted nothing more than to hold this creature's dying heart in his hands.

* * *

Elio hadn't moved a muscle for almost four whole minutes. Both Ulysses and Ridley were afraid he might have died. After the two argued for a few moments over who should touch him, Ridley flicked him on the shoulder.

Their companion remained intensely still. "I am still studying this layout. It is grossly inefficient."

Ridley's shoulders lowered with relief, and he let out a great sigh. Then he rolled his eyes with annoyance. "Well buddy. I know we've been through a lot, and I should know better and trust you, but I'm afraid we'll just have to wing this one. I mean, that's how I won the Gambit, so how much worse could it get?"

"The Gambit?" Ulysses asked, intensely thinking. His eyes suddenly widened and his voice rose to a scream. "You came here because you won a *game show*?"

Elio ignored the little spat the two were having. Despite the intensity of the situation, his voice remained as stoic as ever. "I have already said, one wrong calculation and we will all die with the ship."

Now it was Ulysses' turn to get irritated with Elio. "Well we haven't got anything more to lose kiddo. So just fucking pick something!"

Ridley glanced out the window, and immediately grabbed the others' attention. "Quick, I think I see someone coming.'

Suddenly Elio started keying in commands, his fingers moving as gracefully as a pianist's. Within a few seconds alarms blared in the distance, then were suddenly silenced. Then the ship lurched and vibrated steadily, the pipes along the hull and within the engine module pulsated, growing brighter with each passing second. The air in the large chamber grew musty, and the boys struggled to breathe.

CHAPTER 28

"What's going on?" Both Ulysses and Ridley asked in unison.

Suddenly the ship lurched violently forward, and one of the engine modules burst into flame. Green flames spread from floor to ceiling in less than a second, creating a fiery pillar.

Elio's fingers stopped gracing the keyboard and he looked at his companions. "We have three minutes to leave the ship. I calculate it will take at least three minutes and thirty-three seconds to reach the hangar. Another two minutes to –"

Ulysses clapped his hands and said, "Shut your mouth, let's move!"

The trio headed out of the control bunker and were immediately run over by the stampede of evacuating technicians, who didn't notice them at all. The flames from the destroyed module grew an even deeper shade of green and expanded to engulf a whole section of the catwalk.

As the three ran, the walkway swayed beneath them, causing them to trip and lose their balance. Just beneath their feet, the ship's reactor pulsated and vomited spears of nuclear flame.

The ship violently lurched again as another engine module exploded. Ulysses tumbled off the edge of the catwalk and nearly fell into the reactor. Ridley was able to grab his hand just in time.

"I'll pull you up, hold on!" Ridley struggled to get his other hand to grab Ulysses. Beads of sweat poured down his face and his knuckles cracked.

For the first time since his rescue, Ulysses panicked, and not at the thought of dying. "No, let go! Save yourselves. Let me die!"

Ridley's grip was gradually slipping. "No! You're the whole damn reason we came here! You're going to make it dammit, and I'm going to help you! Hold on!"

Ulysses let go, and slid a few inches before Ridley caught him again. "No! You don't know what you're doing. Killing me now will end the war and stop the Archon. Let me die, save yourselves."

By now Elio had come to assist. Together they pulled Ulysses up a little, but the hanging man tried to let go and fall again. Elio and Ridley barely caught him in time.

Ulysses protested profusely. Tears streamed down his face, and he could barely let out the words. "No! Let me die! Save yourself!"

"Self-preservation is our second mission," Elio said didactically." Our primary objective is to get you safely out of this ship—alive!"

Elio effortlessly pulled Ulysses up, despite the man's constant struggles. Once Ulysses was on the catwalk, he started punching at the two and tried to jump back down the reactor.

Ridley was getting angry at these antics, but also scared. "Hey, hey! Just what the hell are you doing? We're trying to fucking save you here! Why do you want to kill yourself?"

Ulysses tried to continue struggling but finally ceased. "You bumbling idiot don't you understand? That hooded fuck wants only one thing from me, to breed more of him. More people—*things*—that make lightning erupt from your body."

Tears ran down Ulysses' face. "That piece of shit raped me thirteen times. Thirteen! I thought I was going to die, and wanted to after the first time, Let alone thir-fucking-teen! So now I probably have an egg, a *rotten* egg, fertilized with his tainted shit swimming through my body. I will not have it develop to term, but I don't have the courage to take a life I create, no matter how evil."

"Yet you mercilessly beat people to death," Elio murmured. Ulysses slapped him across the face, but he was unfazed and remained silent.

Ulysses could barely be understood through his tears. "The only way I can kill it is by killing myself. There's no other choice."

Ridley was tearing up too. "Oh, but there is! Think of all the medications and procedures that painlessly get the job done. You won't be doing anything immoral, the medics will. You have an obligation to destroy it, but not yourself. Think about your father, and all your loved ones. Your career, your followers, your boyfriend."

That line wrenched Ulysses' heart, and he sobbed more. The only thing he and his husband ever really wanted was to start a family, yet his love was killed before that could be accomplished. The first man to impregnate him was supposed to be his lover, not that hooded fucker who kidnapped him!

The ship violently shuddered again. This time the command module exploded into a ball of sparks and flame. Ulysses surrendered his argument and decided to go with his rescuers. The trio struggled to not fall into the reactor themselves as they continued along the catwalk.

Another explosion shuddered the ship just as the trio exited the maintenance wing. Technicians ran about wildly, not noticing the three very out of place characters. Small explosions erupted from everywhere, leaving no nook or outlet left unaffected. It was every man for himself.

The heroes rounded a corner and encountered a small personnel convoy. Five guards escorted Count Lucilous, with a newly installed mechanical arm and a thick, metal eyepatch. Ulysses, Ridley, and Elio tried to hide but were half a second too late.

"You," the count screamed loudly when he recognized Ulysses.

Ulysses stopped trying to hide and smiled at him. "Hey you! I'd shake your hand, but we gotta run."

The trio ran down the corridor just as the guards opened fire. Lucilous clumsily attempted to draw his sword, but his new mechanical arm was not fully calibrated with his central nervous system and fine movement was virtually impossible. The healing process would be long, and painful. This lack of ability only angered Count Lucilous more.

He threw his sword in the trio's direction. "Seize them! Get Ulysses alive!"

The guards hastily made chase, while Lucilous stayed behind and continued fumbling with his new arm.

The trio attempted to get away from their pursuers, but the ship lurched each time they gained any considerable distance. The guards fired stun shots, not only in order to take the captive alive, but also because the stun shot had a wider range.

One of the guards fired a shot as the trio turned the corner, connecting with Ridley's foot. His leg went limp immediately, and he fell further behind his comrades.

The guards gained ground, and were mere inches from reaching Ridley when Elio effortlessly lifted his companion and ran away. The guards soon became a distant dot.

Another violent explosion rocked the ship, creating another wall of flame that cut off the trio from the pursuing guards, giving the trio a slight buffer.

"How much time do we have?" Ridley asked his savior.

"We are cutting it close."

CHAPTER 29

The frigate's gradual destruction didn't deter the dancing duelists, who used their training to gracefully adapt to the changing fighting landscape. All they focused on was killing each other and staying alive.

Mycroft attacked with all the fury and strength he had, still fueled by the recent death of his mentor, Silas. While he could feel his opponent weakening, it was only just. However, the more tired Mycroft grew, the stronger his attack grew because he was getting increasingly desperate. He was dying, but he wasn't going to let this fucker walk away alive.

The ship's latest shudder was the first true indication that the Archon was weakening, for Mycroft was able to exploit a weakness in his defenses and lay a volley of punches onto the creature's face. The Archon kneed Mycroft in the stomach to end the attack.

"Do you think defeating me will end the war?" The Archon slowly rose to his feet. "This fight is bigger than both of us, and nothing other than *total annihilation* will end this."

Mycroft rolled and pulled the Archon's leg out from under him, tumbling the warrior monk once again to the ground. More laughter erupted from the evil creature. "Killing me certainly won't bring him back," He gestured towards Silas' dead body. "His efforts were wasted, but won't go unnoticed. You still bear his memories. But once you die—he'll be forgotten."

Mycroft screamed and lunged at the Archon, his sword once again in hand for his final offensive. Even with his sword, the Archon struggled to keep up with the Specter's attacks, and the ship's now constant shuddering was no help at all.

At one point the Archon almost sliced off Mycroft's head, but a well-timed leap saved the Specter just in time.

"Timing won't always be on your side," the Archon sneered, each syllable dripping with evil.

Just as the Archon leaped into the air to deliver the killing strike, the ship lurched forward, throwing off the warrior's trajectory. Mycroft twisted his body and swiped his sword at the moving mass in the air.

The smell of burnt flesh and blood filled his nostrils as the mass tumbled to the floor. Mycroft slowly strolled over to the screaming, legless body of the Archon. Burnt blue blood covered the void beneath its belly button.

Mycroft smirked, "It won't always be on your side either."

* * *

The trio ran through the maze of corridors, expecting at any moment to be intercepted by one of the ship's guards. Both Mycroft and Ulysses were completely lost, but Elio knew exactly where to go.

The boys turned a final corner and came face to face once again with Count Lucilous, this time wielding a giant anti-tank rifle.

"Time to die!" Lucilous screamed as he pulled the trigger. A large projectile pierced the air and destroyed the wall the trio was standing in front of just moments prior. The tremendous explosion that followed knocked everyone, including the count, to the ground.

The blast was so powerful it pierced the outer hull, creating a fierce vacuum leak that sucked everything untethered towards the exposed hull. The void of space wasn't visible yet, but another projectile or few moments would do the trick.

Ulysses grabbed a stray gun that flew through the air and started firing at the count.

A volley of shots returned like a boomerang. Count Lucilous was no longer alone, and joined by several guards.

One of the guards rushed towards the group, but Elio knocked the weapon from his hand and engaged in a fierce fist fight.

Lucilous fired another round in the direction of where he thought the trio hid. A small storage closet was destroyed, revealing the trio's position down the corridor around the hall.

Ridley steeled his nerves and ran down the corridor, tackling Lucilous. The sudden fall made the count fire another shot through the ceiling.

Ridley and the count tumbled and rolled, with both men vying to scratch off the other's face. Lucilous punched Ridley with his robotic arm, knocking out a few teeth. Ridley pressed Lucilous' freshly patched eye with his thumb causing the count to scream in pain.

Elio finally dispatched his opponent by breaking his neck, and rushed to help Ridley with the count. In a blink of an eye Elio was on top of Lucilous, pummeling his fists into his face. Elio ripped open Lucilous' face stitches, garnering another fierce scream from the count. Lucilous repeatedly punched Elio in the head with his robotic arm. While the young man was mostly unaffected, his blue irises would not stop flickering.

Ridley returned to the scuffle, adding in his own volley of punches, but it didn't help much.

After several moments Lucilous managed to get everyone off of him and jumped to his feet. He brandished the tank rifle once again and pointed it at Elio and Ridley. Ulysses suddenly jumped in the fray and aimed his pistol at the count, but he was comically out-gunned.

"Shoot me and they die," Lucilous yelled at Ulysses. "Drop it."

Ulysses complied and was seized by a guard and held at gunpoint.

Lucilous expelled a nervous laugh. He screamed every word he spoke, and sounded terribly frightened. "Now, the roles are as they should be. Come quietly with me and no one will die, *painfully*."

"You're a nothing! Why should we go with you?" Ulysses spat. He was not intimidated at all.

"Oh? Because the way I see it, one more shot in the hull and we're all dead. See," Lucilous chuckled nervously, "now I'm sharing with you all the pain and torment that I go through. No decision is easy and each choice is far from perfect.

"All he wanted was you!" The count pointed at Ulysses as a stream of tears cascaded down his face. "The bastard never gave half a shit about me or my abilities. All he wanted was someone to expand his dynasty!

"I gave him an armada of soldiers! But all he wanted was your taint!" Lucilous shakily pointed the rifle at his greatest enemy. "He looked passed my intellect and resources and only wanted to *fuck* you!"

The count was increasingly losing control. His eyes had that gleam of a person about to fall off the edge. "But now I have the power! I'm in possession of the master's favorite token! And I now have all the control."

The ship shuddered as the outer hull gradually peeled away, increasing the strength of the vacuum pull, and making it harder for everyone in the hall to remain standing.

"Just what are you going to do with us?" Ridley asked, indicating himself and Elio.

Lucilous dismissed him with a flick of his chin. "No one cares about you two. I might not even waste a shot on you."

Ridley briefly raised his eyebrows. "Gee, thanks a lot."

Count Lucilous returned his attention to Lucilous. "But you, the vessel of all I despise, will be coming with me. No doubt the Archon has already successfully consecrated you. Well we'll see just how much he really cares for you and his legacy." He moved towards his prey, his mouth nearly watering with hunger.

"Hasn't he already warned you not to cross him again?" Ulysses asked, struggling against the guard holding him. "You'll only get injured even more."

The count stomped his feet on the floor, demanding attention. "Silence! No one will tell me what I should and can't do!"

He pointed the rifle at Elio and Ridley and held it there for a few seconds. A creepy smile carved into his face. "In fact, I've changed my mind. All of you will die, including you, precious Ulysses. This will cement my place as heir to the Hyde."

Lucilous raised his weapon to fire. There was no escaping now.

CHAPTER 30

Mycroft stood over the Archon's body, brandishing both swords at the monk's neck. The creature still smoldered at the amputation point.

The red eyes glaring at Mycroft from under the hood were brilliantly illuminated, and showed no ounce of fear or weakness. "What are you waiting for? This is the moment you've dreamt of. You have me right where you need me to be."

Mycroft readied his swords and steeled his nerve, but still hesitated.

"C'mon! Be more than your Specter companions and make the kill! Do it now and end the war! Unite the galaxy and all will be right again."

Moments went by and Mycroft still didn't move.

The Archon snickered. "Just like a Specter! All grandstanding and pompous morality, but when it comes down to it, you're just another weakling." The snickering expanded into full maniacal laughter.

Mycroft was finally taken out of his trance, and could now see the hideous creature in front of him for what it was. "Says the one cowering on the ground."

The warrior monk's laughter suddenly ceased. "Taking my legs is nothing. Even Lucilous could have done that. But you two are just alike. You don't have the balls to kill me, and you know that that won't solve your problems. Like it or not, this moment has only just begun the journey of your troubles."

CHAPTER 30

The ship shuddered and lurched to the side, compelling everything untethered to once again tumble to one side. Mycroft lost his footing and dropped his swords. The Archon grabbed and ignited his sword and swung at Mycroft, who barely had time to block the hit with his wrist bracers.

The duel continued until the ship righted again. Even nearly dead, the Archon fought with such fury, and Mycroft barely had room to dodge.

The ship pitched again, this time in the other direction. The Archon managed to crawl to a crate and jump off it, landing on Mycroft's shoulders. The Specter struggled intensely to get the fighting stump off him. The heat of Archon's blade scorched his skin, but thankfully the awkward angle made it impossible for the hooded monk to make a killing blow.

Another loud explosion rocked the ship, and the bow started separating from the stern and falling into the planet's atmosphere. After several seconds the entire frigate was ripped into two pieces.

The room where Mycroft and the Archon fought split apart in the center. A large force pulled everything into the room through the floor and out into space. The Specter was pulled from his feet, and barely had enough time to grab a storage rung in the wall. While the Archon hung onto Mycroft's shoulders for dear life.

"Let go, brother!" the Archon enticed. "Let's end our suffering and leave the galaxy for those to destroy it."

Looking down into the void, Mycroft could see the open half of the bow slowly tumbling towards the planet's surface. The Specter looked at the creature on his shoulders, and thought of Silas.

"No" was all he said and he let go, sending both of them into the cosmic abyss. The Archon lost his grip on Mycroft's shoulders and disappeared into void.

Mycroft managed to grab onto a protruding piece of the ship and save his fall. He quickly climbed back into the damaged stern and headed for the hangar.

On his way, he found Silas' body and carried it home.

* * *

Ridley stared down the barrel of the anti-tank rifle and closed his eyes. 1,000 different thoughts raced through his head, all so enticing he didn't know which one he wanted to remember before dying. All he knew was that he looked forward to seeing Grandma Oz again. He grasped Elio's cold hand and squeezed it as hard as he could. At least he was with a friend and wouldn't be dying alone.

Right as Lucilous pulled the trigger, the ship proceeded to lurch to either side for several seconds, throwing everyone to either side of the corridor before finally splitting in half.

The count's half tumbled toward the planet's surface, his screams echoed all the way down.

Ulysses and Elio quickly jolted Ridley out of his trance and continued their escape to the hangar.

"We won't make it," Ridley kept repeating.

"Not with that attitude, we won't," Ulysses kept countering

Elio led the team along a beeline to the nearest hangar, their path littered with fires, small explosions, and constantly flying pieces of debris. On a couple occasions the floor paneling fell out from beneath their feet, nearly sending them into the bowels of the deteriorating ship.

When the trio finally arrived at the remains of the hanger, there were no functional ships they could use to escape.

"Fuck!" They all exclaimed, even Elio.

"All that trouble for nothing," Ridley lamented. He kicked a stray box across the floor.

CHAPTER 30

"I guess this is the end of the road," Ulysses looked into Ridley's eyes. There was an instant connection, and the two held each other's gaze for several unbroken moments.

Ridley offered a cute, crooked smile. "Sorry we failed and didn't get you home to your father."

"Screw it. I never wanted to see him anyway. But hey," Ulysses warmly embraced Ridley. "Thanks for coming to my rescue. There aren't many people in this galaxy that would risk their life to save me. And I just want you to know how much I appreciate you. Really!"

The men continued looking in each other's eyes, and slowly moved in for a kiss. They were just about to make contact when Elio stole their attention.

"Look!"

A small shuttle hovered in the entrance to the hangar and lowered its ramp. Mycroft's head emerged from the entrance bay.

"Quick, let's get out of here!"

"Where's Silas?" Ridley asked, once the trio boarded the ship. He anxiously wanted to share everything that happened with him. He was the closest Ridley had to a father figure.

Mycroft stayed silent, just barely nodding towards the sleeper cabin. His eyes said it all.

All of the enthusiasm in Ridley's face evaporated, and he looked just like he did right after his grandmother passed.

Mycroft placed a heavy hand on the boy's shoulder. "Don't get all emotional, kid. Loss is a part of life."

Moments later, the shuttle made it safely out of range at the exact moment the frigate's orbiting half burst into the flame. The only evidence of the frigate were the remnants of the bow tumbling towards the planet's surface.

* * *

The Syndicate carrier *Hadley* put up a valiant effort throughout the battle, but was eventually destroyed by the Axis, marking the finale to the battle. Across the battlefield, skeletons of Syndicate fighters and frigates floated throughout space, accompanied by the frozen bodies of their pilots. The death toll was catastrophic, and the materiel loss was even more pronounced. The battlefield was the galaxy's newest cemetery and war memorial.

While the four remaining Syndicate carriers limped home to undergo extensive repairs, the Axis generals celebrated their resolute triumph on the bridge of their command ship, the *Prentice*. Champagne bottles were opened and the victory party was underway on every deck of the ship. This was only going to be the first of many.

Across the stars, on board the Syndicate capital, the *Imperatrix*, the generals and Chief Specters were consumed with assessing the magnitude of their defeat. Over one-third of the Syndicate's fleet was destroyed, and the reinforcements had only just arrived within the last few hours.

The military generals were honest in their criticism, assessing blame on all parties involved for their lack of preparation. But the Primarch could only be convinced of one fact, and one fact only;

"The Specters lost us this battle, and single handedly plunged the galaxy into war."

CHAPTER 31

Five days after the Syndicate's disastrous defeat, the casualties from the battlefield had finally returned to the *Imperatrix*, and were now making their way to the repair facilities, hospitals, and morgues. Technicians muddled through the twisted bodies of damaged spacecraft in the hopes of salvaging useful parts. Doctors and nurses raced against the clock to salvage lives and limbs, and often had to make the hardest call at a moment's notice. Loved ones were either reuniting with relatives long-thought deceased, or finally having to deal with the somber truth.

The Chamber of the High Senate, usually locked in a constant state of chaos and disorder, was unusually quiet and sedate. All of the day's business had concluded earlier that afternoon, and the chamber was sealed for a private, invitation-only event. All of the attendees, a motley group of politicians, military personnel, and Specters, wore black formal suits.

In place of the Primarch's dais, a black, nondescript casket draped with the Seal of the Syndicate commanded the room's attention.

Everyone that was still present on the station and knew Silas was in the chamber—less than 100 people. Ridley and Elio were the only civilians to officially know of this particular Specter's existence.

As this was an official state funeral, the Primarch officiated the proceedings. Ever the skilled politician, he was able to hide his personal feelings about the matter and craft a beautifully emotive and heartfelt eulogy. His booming words painted the picture of a man who devoted his entire life to service and retired the only way he wanted.

"Silas' dedication to his duty was unmatched, as well as his work ethic, and he will forever serve as the prime example for us all to live by.

"There is a tremendous amount we can learn from Silas. Indeed, there was a lesson to learn from every action he took. One; to never give in to an idea that you do not support with all of your being. Another; to always do the right thing, even if that means disobeying your superiors." The Primarch remained silent for a few moments, finding the lump in his throat hard to swallow.

"But the most important lesson Silas taught us was the true meaning of devotion. No one could ever question whether or not he supported the Syndicate, nor could anyone ever doubt his integrity.

"Silas' life was the prime example of giving back to those who brought you into the present, and ensuring that those who will take the hand of tomorrow have a solid and firm foundation. Silas was never put out to offer some of his infinite wisdom, and was always ready to offer aid in any form required. He embodied the core value of the Cosmic Syndicate; to always be there and ready to perform.

"Ladies and gentlemen, no one represented the Cosmic Syndicate more than Chief Specter Silas. He was an elite member of the most elite group in our organization. The Specters, in particular, have never cowered in the face of adversity, nor have failed," the Primarch paused again, struggling to finish his sentence, "to complete their mission. Despite the increasingly negative sentiment felt by the public of the Specter organization, I want you all in this room to know that I stand by and support you all one hundred percent. We are all on the same team, ladies and gentlemen, and we are all in this together until the

CHAPTER 31

conclusion of this horrid war. Only by combining all of our skills and efforts can we quickly pass through this shadow of darkness."

The Primarch concluded his speech, gave a final bow to Silas's casket, and exited the chamber. The rest of the guests followed suit, and within 15 minutes only Mycroft remained, silently paying respects to the Syndicate's greatest man in the Syndicate's most abysmal location.

The Specter remained perfectly still, only his eyelids indicated he was alive. Silently, Mycroft profusely apologized to his former instructor and mentor for never meeting expectations. All the young Specter ever wanted to do was impress Silas, only his approval counted. Often, Mycroft would retell what he thought was his greatest escapade and only ever receive a pensive nod from his old master. No words, no smile, no frown, just a nod.

Standing there, despite carrying an immense level of sorrow, Mycroft did not shed a single tear. He was just too sad and numb to react.

Mycroft's countenance only worsened when he reported to his disciplinary hearing with the Specter Chiefs half an hour later.

"Two hundred and ten thousand soldiers, fifty thousand fighters, twelve battle cruisers, one spacecraft carrier, and a veteran Chief Specter were lost because you deliberately disobeyed a war directive. Insubordination, as you are well aware, is never taken lightly, especially when it results in such a massive loss of life."

The Specter Chiefs stared stone-faced at Mycroft, who assumed a perfect parade rest position like the consummate agent that he is. Was? He honestly didn't really care what his punishment was, or about anything else really. All the Specter could do was listen while he got ripped a new asshole.

Specter Chief Albus continued his tirade. "Perhaps we failed to impress upon you the importance of your objective, which was to gather the necessary intelligence to avoid the very losses we sustained those five short days ago?"

The room fell silent, growing increasingly awkward with each passing second. Mycroft took that as a cue that he was supposed to respond.

"On the contrary, sirs, I never misunderstood my directive. In fact, my interpretation of said directive led me to take my course of action, ultimately fulfilling both my current and previous objectives."

The faces staring at Mycroft only grew more agitated. Chief Latiolais was especially displeased, replete with a vein of temper throbbing on his forehead. "Please explain," he growled.

Mycroft went into detail about the Archon, with a thorough explanation of everything he had learned and theorized about the creature, from its origins with the Hyde to its behind-the-scenes control of the war.

"So you see," the Specter concluded, "if I followed your orders to the letter, we'd probably be in a far worse spot than we are now."

Chief Latiolais grew increasingly unimpressed that he nearly jumped over his desk. "You are going to stand there and defend the killing of innocent lives by stating it is better that we now know —admittedly not a whole-fucking lot—about a defunct magical cult. Never mind the fact that our enemies on the other side of the galaxy are growing more powerful and knowledgeable, from a military perspective, with each passing moment."

Another period of silence followed this latest tirade, and Mycroft was admittedly at his own wit's end. He shrugged his shoulders and raised his arms, "That's all I can do, sir."

"Let me just conclude by saying that you, Mycroft, have single-handedly made time an ally of the Axis," Latiolais sneered, every word dripping with contempt. "I hope you can live with yourself."

"If I may," one of the other Chiefs, Dantam, said. "Discounting Mycroft's and Silas' opponent as a mere magician is, I think, a grossly inaccurate description. And being that this Archon single-handedly killed one of our own, an experienced veteran no less, is not a matter to be dismissed. This creature, whomever or whatever he is, is a force not to be taken lightly. We should view him no differently than any other enemy of this war."

"True," Latiolais jumped in, "but according to Mycroft here, this Archon has been *exterminated*, rendering that issue moot. Am I incorrect?"

Chief Dantam continued calmly. "That does not remove or belittle the threat from where he comes from. He cannot be the only one of his kind."

"This should be investigated further, as Silas would want," was all Mycroft added. He had never seen this level of disagreement amongst the Chiefs before, and found it quite amusing. It was almost a vindication for his deceased mentor, and himself.

Latiolais remained steadfast in his condemnation and was not going to budge. "While Silas would have endorsed such radical actions, currently we do not have the resources to devote to such hogwash." He turned to Mycroft, "Shit, we can't even punish you to the fullest extent of the canon because we need every hand we can spare for the war effort." A shroud of disappointment hovered over the angry Specter Chief.

"And we have to search to fill Silas' vacancy," Chief Albus interjected. "Not to add to the to-do list."

The Chiefs on the bench grumbled for several minutes while they contemplated the appropriate punishment for Mycroft. These were increasingly strange times, and while the edicts of the Specter canon needed to be respected, more practical matters needed to be taken into account.

Finally, Chief Latiolais issued the ruling. "Circumstances being what they are, yet still accounting for the severity of your crime, Specter

Mycroft, you are hereby suspended for thirty cycles. You're ordered to not leave the *Imperatrix* for any reason unless otherwise ordered. Do note, however, that the terms of your sentence may change due to the needs of the war."

Mycroft remained silent and bowed his head. The sentence was less severe than he expected.

"This seems to be the only way we can get you to take some leave time," Albus said, in a warm and familial tone. "And please allow yourself to work through *at least some* of your unresolved issues."

Several hours after the hearing, Mycroft sat on a bench in the necropolis wing of the space station, staring at the pristine white marble walls. Hundreds of plaques with varying degrees of information dotted the wall, some accompanied by beautiful bouquets of brightly colored flowers.

The spot on the wall commanding Mycroft's attention, however, bore none of these things. It was only marked by a single, black star.

A Specter's existence is a lonely one.

For the first time since his husband died, Mycroft allowed himself to cry. The tears cascaded down his face and he couldn't remain upright. The Specter, who stared death in the face countless times, finally collapsed under the weight of his own grief.

He cried for every life he had ever taken, and for every life he couldn't save. He cried for everything that he could not experience, and for every experience that he had.

After 45 minutes, Mycroft wanted nothing more than to fade away and disappear.

CHAPTER 32

The mood aboard the *Imperatrix* had significantly shifted, especially within the Chamber of the High Senate. Hundreds of political and business celebrities gathered for a commemoration ceremony honoring Ridley and Elio. They were receiving the Syndicate's highest civilian award, the Senate's Seal of Merit.

Presiding over the celebration was Senator Pircilla, who could only praise the two men and shower them with compliments at rescuing his son, Ulysses, from behind enemy lines.

"It is with great pleasure that I present these two fine heroes with our Syndicate's highest honor. Both of these true gentlemen have demonstrated such courage and allegiance to the Syndicate that we are honored to have them amongst us."

The chamber thundered with applause as Senator Pircilla placed the medal on Elio and Ulysses placed Ridley's.

Ulysses punctuated this with a kiss on Ridley's cheek. "Thank you Ridley, truly."

Ridley beamed, and his face turned a deep shade of red. "Even though you're back with the people you hate?" he coyly asked.

Ulysses fluttered his eyebrows and slowly smiled. "There's one person here that's not too bad."

The two moved in for a kiss when they were interrupted by the Primarch.

"Gentlemen, before you all start celebrating, there's another surprise I'd like to share with you. Due to your courage and spirit, you and your companion Elio have been assigned to the Specter Corps, and we hope you will continue to serve the Cosmic Syndicate well! Congratulations!"

The Primarch vigorously shook Ridley's hand and announced the news to the rest of the room. Applause once again erupted in the chamber.

Ridley didn't know how to handle it. Not two weeks before he was just another slave working for JeffCo, and then he all of a sudden traveled across the galaxy, saved a politician's son, and is now a Specter with the Cosmic Syndicate. He was so nervous and filled with anxiety that he suddenly had the urge to vomit.

Immediately, Ridley rushed to the nearest hiding spot he could find, and all of the contents of his stomach spilled onto the floor. He looked around afterwards to see if anyone saw him, and his gaze landed on the piercing eyes of Mycroft.

The veteran Specter was sulking in the background, straining not to be noticed. But once he realized Mycroft saw him, a large crooked smile carved onto his face, immensely proud.

A rush of pride welled within Ridley, and he immediately felt a little bit at ease. While his grandmother Oz would no longer be with him, Ridley knew that he wasn't going to be alone, he had Elio and Mycroft to look after him, and likewise to look out for. For the first time since Oz passed, Ridley realized that everything was going to be alright.

Ridley composed himself and moved towards Mycroft when he was interrupted once again, this time by Ulysses, who wore that same beaming smile.

"Well, Specter Ridley, I guess we have three things to celebrate now."

The young man furrowed his brow. A lot happened today, but he thought he was keeping track pretty well. "Three?"

"Mmm, hmm. Your new medal, your new title, and the fact that only *two* people are standing in this very spot."

Ridley's brows furrowed further. "I'm sorry?"

Ulysses embraced Ridley in the strongest hug he'd ever given. He then gracefully whispered into his lover's ear. "I'm *not* pregnant! The Archon failed!"

Intense excitement welled within Ridley, and his entire body grew warm with fiery passion. "Oh! Well...then, we have four things to celebrate!"

The two men embraced in the deepest kiss affirming their love for each other.

Afterword

Across the stars, deep within the cosmic storm of the Tartarus system, a large group of Hyde acolytes scrambled to salvage the wreckage of the Archon's frigate that tumbled to the planet's surface. The landscape was so desolate, and the area so remote, that everything of any remote value would be repurposed.

Additionally, the acolytes searched for any salvageable religious relics, for they believed that they contained a magical essence that could be repurposed as well.

Hours passed with very little to show for their search. The scavengers began searching through the most mangled section of the wreckage and discovered the Archon's mutilated remains. Immediately the salvage effort was ceased and funeral rites were prepared.

On the third day of the funeral, the Archon's eyes suddenly opened and he took a deep breath...

(The conductor sweeps his arms gracefully through the air, leading the symphony through the final notes of the coda. He swims his palms upwards, sending the music off into the heavens. He slowly lowers his arms, his palms folding in on themselves like a flower in the moonlight, and the music comes to a close. The conductor bows his head.)

END OF MOVEMENT I

About the Author

Cullen T. Madrid is a native of Denver, Colorado. He spends his days creating, playing his piano, and listening to Stevie Nicks.

Also by Cullen T. Madrid

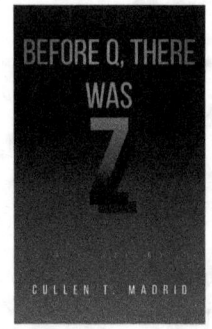

Before Q, There Was Z

By Design, Life Was Miserable. Zebulon was the epitome of a Nobody, whose only purpose was to maintain Society's status quo. He had no input in any facet of his life, and because he didn't know any better he was happy about it. After the inauguration of the Nation's new Leader, Zebulon is personally chosen to uncover the truth behind the Great Question, the catastrophic event that many blame for the present state of affairs. The public's distrust of the government is at record levels, and the Leader believes solving the matter will finally bring the Nation to the fabled Prosperity. If The Design Is Discovered, the Misery Will End. The young man immediately makes progress, which irritates the true holders of power, the High Court of the Seven. They created the Society and are sustained by the design of the present. To preserve their legacy, they battle against Zebulon's crusade. The Misery Serves a Purpose. Surrounded by enemies, Zebulon must straddle the tight rope between life and death to uncover the hidden truth and deliver it to a desperate Nation. Before Q, There Was Z.

Space

The crew of the starship *Atreon* is awakened out of cryosleep to attend to a catastrophic event with the hull. After making repairs, the stress of awakening years before their intended time affects the crew, with the science officer proclaiming they are not in space but in fact aboard a submarine, and declaring there is a serial killer aboard the ship. He is dismissed as crazy, until the ship's engineering technician suddenly disappears, and the *Atreon's* artificial intelligence corroborates his story...

...In a time when Artificial Intelligence can do no wrong, can you still trust your gut?

The Branagh Disaster: The True and Accurate Account

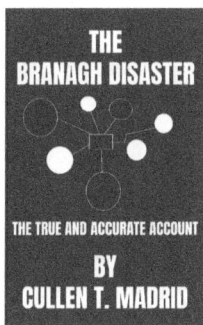

Ten thousand feet below the surface of the Earth, an elite team of workers are inaugurating their company's latest and greatest piece of machinery, the Branagh Drill. Suddenly, a catastrophic event traps the team and the brand-new drill at the bottom of the mine shaft. In order to reach the surface, the ten survivors must *continue their descent*—which sounds counterproductive, yet is the only accessible way. But the perilous journey proves even more harrowing when the survivors realize they are not the only ones trapsing amongst the ruins and searching for a way out.

www.ingramcontent.com/pod-product-compliance
Lightning Source LLC
LaVergne TN
LVHW021650060526
838200LV00050B/2292